Shane Briant wa[illegible] w at
[illegible] er in
t[illegible] over
t[illegible] ions
i[illegible] *bber*
A[illegible] Wendy and
their wonderdog, Coco.

Also by Shane Briant

The Webber Agenda

THE CHASEN CATALYST

SHANE BRIANT

HarperCollinsPublishers

HarperCollins*Publishers*

First published in Australia in 1995

HarperCollins*Publishers*
25 Ryde Road, Pymble, Sydney, NSW 2073, Australia
31 View Road, Glenfield, Auckland 10, New Zealand
77–85 Fulham Palace Road, London W6 8JB, United Kingdom
Hazelton Lanes, 55 Avenue Road, Suite 2900, Toronto, Ontario M5R 3L2
and 1995 Markham Road, Scarborough, Ontario M1B 5M8, Canada
10 East 53rd Street, New York NY 10032, USA

National Library of Australia Cataloguing-in-Publication data:

Briant, Shane.
The Chasen catalyst.

ISBN 0 7322 5194 X.
I. Title.
A823.3

Cover illustration by Spike Wademan
Cover design by Darian Causby
Printed in Australia by Griffin Paperbacks, Adelaide

9 8 7 6 5 4 3 2 1
99 98 97 96 95

For Wendy

And in memory of my brother Dermot

The Chasen Catalyst is entirely a work of fiction. There has been no intention on my part to impute the existence of corruption to any organisation or diplomatic mission. The flies in the ointment are the target in my flights of fancy – and these are fictional.

ONE

It was suddenly raining like hell. Chasen flicked a switch and the strong wipers went into overdrive, fighting the lashing torrent. In any lesser car he would have been forced to stop.

He glanced again to his left. She was like a magnet – he couldn't help himself. The bare olive legs seemed to stretch for yards, the flawless skin, the warm firm curves and undulations of the strong thigh muscles.

He swerved to avoid a falling branch, trying to focus completely on the narrow road ahead, a blur of flashing cat's eyes and country hedges, as the Porsche's powerful headlights cut a swathe through the lashing rain.

The seconds passed – ten, twenty, thirty. In his peripheral vision Chasen saw her again caressing the bare flesh of her right thigh, gliding the long fingers with an easy grace halfway to the knee then back up to her hips, where they made a deft and languid detour over the thigh, and on towards the buttons that ran down the front of what scarcely passed for a minimalist black evening dress.

Jesus, there's only one hook and eye left holding it together, he thought, a bead of sweat racing down the centre of his spine.

There was a swift movement somewhere down to his left. Her hand hung in the air inches from his leg then moved forward, a long finger pressing a button on the stereo console. The music ceased mid-bar as the woman's delicate fingers returned to the soft contours of her olive thigh.

The road veered abruptly to the right. Chasen spun the wheel hard, the left front tyre gouging mud and earth from the side of the road, sending a wall of water crashing into the hedge. His heart was pounding – he'd almost lost it. She didn't seem to care; he could hear her gently humming some soft Brazilian samba.

'Why don't we stop for a while?' Her voice was a silken whisper – a first thing in the morning, just after awakening voice. It was sexy as hell and she knew it. 'We wouldn't want an accident, Sir Ivor, would we?' she continued in her softly accented murmur, then paused, letting her hand rest briefly on the telephone sitting on the console dividing the seats. That accent. Chasen couldn't pick it. Colombia? Costa Rica?

Pull yourself together, Chasen told himself. Concentrate on the road, for heaven's sake! She'll be out of the car and gone in less than fifteen minutes.

'The rain's not really so bad,' he lied. 'Besides, it's late and I have a bag full of papers to attend to when I get home.' His voice had developed a thick and febrile quality.

A signpost flashed by, a blur in the rain as the car sped across a minor intersection.

'Where was it again?' he asked.

'I'm sorry?' she said, sinking even lower in the leather seat.

'Heston Langley, did you say? You said it was just past the Chalgrove turn-off. Should be only a couple more miles.' There was no reply. Instead she eased the last hook and eye open, drew up one leg and rested the knee against the passenger door as her fingers slid up her inner thigh.

'Jesus Christ,' he murmured, barely audibly.

A split second elapsed as he stared, then his eyes flicked upwards to meet hers. Those eyes. Those cold black eyes. Black as a coal seam – the pupil appeared to melt into the iris, as if one.

Chasen swallowed hard – he was out of his depth with this one.

She laughed softly, enjoying his discomfiture.

He cleared his throat again. Christ, it was like some weird dream. 'I asked you whether it's in Heston Langley that you live? Are we close?'

'That's absolutely right. But don't hurry. Slow down so we can talk – I love to talk.'

Chasen gripped the wheel like a vice as he weaved the car through a succession of snaking bends. Too fast, he thought, I'm going too fast!

He grimly strained to focus on the road ahead, but the image of the girl was still there on the windscreen, burnt into his mind like a brand, as if he'd stared too long at the sun.

A loud clap of thunder burst overhead with the force of a grenade, a sheet of lightning turning night into day.

'Christ Almighty!' he screamed. The figure of a man had appeared for a split second, a negative silhouette in the lightning.

Chasen wrenched frantically at the wheel, sending the Porsche skidding sideways across the road. The man threw up his arms to protect his face, there was a dull thud and then he catapulted over the bonnet and disappeared into the darkness on the other side of the road.

'My God, I've hit someone!' Chasen yelled, standing hard on the brakes. The Porsche evened out of its drift and came to an abrupt halt, the thunder crashing once more with ear-splitting intensity directly overhead, followed instantaneously by another blinding sheet of lightning.

For a moment Chasen was frozen in shock, then he snapped his head round anxiously to his passenger. She lay in the seat, a look of serene control on her face.

Snap out of it, man – now! Get moving! Do something, for fuck's sake! The thoughts flashed quickly through Chasen's mind.

Panic-stricken, he threw open the door and ran back down the narrow country road, the rain pounding down on his head with the force of a fire-hose.

'Where the hell are you! Are you alright? Can you hear me?' he screamed as he ran blindly through the downpour into the blackness.

Suddenly Chasen was bathed in the powerful headlights of the Porsche as it swung round, throwing a giant shadow down what now had more the appearance of a river than a road. Thank God! The woman had turned the car round to give him light.

Now that he could see, Chasen looked left, then right – still nothing. Dear God, he thought, the man's dead. Must be lying in the hedgerow somewhere. He couldn't have been any further down – it wasn't possible.

The Porsche inched up the road towards Chasen as he stood in the centre of the road in his shirtsleeves, the rain lashing at his body. The sound of the horn blared just as another clap of thunder ripped through the night. Chasen fell to a squatting position in shock, his nerves in shreds. As he whipped his head round to face the car, he could just make out the figure of a man leaning on the bonnet. The girl was cradling his head in her arms, his face on her chest. Chasen almost shouted with relief as he ran back down the road to the Porsche.

'Are you alright?' Chasen gasped as he reached the car.

The man raised his head and looked at Chasen, the rain flooding down his face. 'I'm fine,' he managed with the faintest of smiles. The woman was inspecting a bruise on his left temple.

Relieved that the man was not badly injured, Chasen studied him more closely. He couldn't be much more than thirty, well-heeled and surprisingly composed considering what had just occurred. 'What on earth –' Chasen began, but the man interrupted him.

'Thought I'd lost a rear wheel spat. Car's a classic, you know. Hate to lose it. Stopped to find it.' His speech came in short bursts as he fought to catch his breath, yet he appeared totally oblivious to the elements.

As Chasen stared at him, the man abruptly stopped speaking and, with a great exhalation of breath, his legs crumpled beneath him and he sank to the bitumen. Instantly Chasen dropped to the ground, lifting the man's head gently off the road. The eyes were closed and saliva was beginning to dribble from one corner of his mouth. My God, he thought with desperation, the man's going to die! Chasen could hardly breathe. As he pressed his fingers to the man's carotid artery, frantically searching for a pulse, they were lit by another flash of dazzling white light, and the man's eyes fluttered open.

'For God's sake, let's get him up and into the car! Don't just stand there!' Chasen yelled to the woman as the thunder crashed again. But the man was already struggling to his feet and moving round to the passenger door.

The woman squeezed into the back and the young man sank into the seat in front of her, holding a handkerchief to his temple.

'Let me see your head,' Chasen said as he took hold of the young man's hand and lifted it away from his head. There was a livid bruise and a few smudges of blood.

'Look, my car's just up ahead. Just give me a lift there and I'll be fine.'

'But I can't just let you drive on like this,' Chasen argued. 'You may be in shock. You should see a doctor. We need to get you to a hospital. Let me –' Chasen continued, but he was cut short by the woman.

'I will drive him home.' It was a statement of fact, not a request for confirmation. There was a new-found hard edge to her tone. She leant forward and began to massage the muscles of the injured man's neck while she stared strangely at Chasen, as if in a trance.

A wash of relief flooded Chasen's very being. He would be rid of them both, away from this surreal drive – it was too wonderful to contemplate.

'Well, only if you're absolutely sure –'

'I am,' the man replied.

'You're quite certain – ?'

'I am,' came the instant reply.

Chasen thrust the gear lever into first and swung the car round in a sharp semicircle. The wheels dug deep into the mud at the road's edge.

The young man pointed as the Porsche accelerated down the silver-washed road. 'It's no more than a couple of hundred yards.'

The car came into sight as they rounded a bend. It was a beauty – a British racing green two-seater Jaguar XK120. Chasen stopped directly behind it and the man turned to face him.

'Sorry for all the bother. But don't worry, I'm fine,' he said as he opened the passenger door. Then he paused. 'Look, I don't even know your name. Mine's Erskine.'

Chasen held out a hand towards him, deliberately evasive. 'I hope you feel better very soon. Go on, get out of the rain!'

Erskine smiled, shook Chasen's hand, then shuffled through the driving rain to the Jaguar.

As he disappeared, the woman pushed the passenger seat forward and leant over Chasen, her cheek barely an inch from his. Chasen was again struck by her smell. It seemed almost animal in its sexual intensity. She paused again briefly at the door.

'I will look after him, Sir Ivor,' she said softly with a smile. '*Ciao.*' Slowly and deliberately she blew him a kiss, then turned and disappeared towards the sports car.

Chasen tilted his head back, closed his eyes and took several deep breaths. The veins in his temple throbbed violently. The roar of the Jaguar rang through the night and Chasen watched it snake down the road and out of sight. He closed his eyes again. He was free at last.

TWO

She made a sharp left turn then pulled the Jaguar over to the side of the road and killed the engine. They sat in silence, the stillness broken only by the rain pounding on the roof and the occasional metallic tick as the engine block cooled. He turned to look at her. She was staring back through the rear window at the main road, impassive. The rain continued to drum on the roof.

'Was I good?' the man who had called himself Erskine said softly, trying to break the tension. She ignored him and he immediately wished he'd kept his mouth shut. There was something genuinely disturbing about this woman – she inspired fear, no question about it. He was scared. Shit! He was actually *scared* of her.

The woman continued looking back intently over her shoulder at the intersection with the main road.

'Do you mind if I change?' he asked tentatively. Still no reaction. He waited about a half-minute then rolled up his left trouser leg and pulled down a heavy knee pad, easing it over his shoes. He rolled up the other trouser leg, did likewise, then leant forward to remove his jacket.

The look of concentration on the woman's face intensified. Then, with a flash of light, Chasen's Porsche sped down the road past where they had turned off. The woman finally relaxed and turned to face Erskine, who was now unstrapping pads attached to his back and sides.

'Yes, you were good. Do you have any injuries?'

'Nothing serious – few bruises, maybe.'

'Remove everything,' she said sharply.

He looked at her. She was serious. She meant business. He wasn't going to fuck around with this one. He peeled off his top, his eyes avoiding her gaze.

'Come closer,' she said matter-of-factly. He did as he was told at once. She studied his chest with the greatest care, running fingers across a couple of small contusions, her lips moving slightly as if committing them to memory. Satisfied, she spoke again.

'Now the back.' The words had the clinical interest of a physician. He could feel her hands running over his back with a feathery touch.

'Now the legs.'

'The legs are fine. I checked.'

Slowly she leant forward until her face was practically touching his and spoke with an easy deliberation. 'Now *I* check.' There was a beat, then she opened her mouth and sucked in the young man's upper lip, closing her teeth on it with a steady pressure. She bit hard.

Erskine yelped with shock.

'If you once more question what I say you will be very sorry you did so. I will cause you more pain than you ever imagined possible. Pull down your trousers.'

She studied every inch of his lower torso and thighs, then indicated she was finished. As he pulled his jockey shorts back on she dipped her long fingers into the inside of her short black jacket and removed an envelope.

'This is for you. Now get out of the car.'

He stared at her in shock, trying to make sense of her bald statement. What? Get out? Here?

'Take the money and get out of the car. Do it now!'

'In the middle of nowhere? Give us a break – it's pissing with rain.'

'Now!' It was almost a shout. A gun appeared as if by magic. She pressed it to his temple.

'Okay! I'm leaving! Please . . . take it easy . . .' he stammered, searching frantically for the door lever, at the same time trying to maintain eye contact. Grabbing the handle, he pressed downwards and the heavy door swung open behind him. A shaft of icy air hit him and he gave an involuntary shudder.

'Could you pass me the knee and body pads?' he said, holding out his hand.

'The pads stay with me.'

He straightened, adjusted his clothes and moved back to slam the door.

In one fluid movement a dark shadow emerged noiselessly from a nearby copse, took three strides towards the car and administered a carefully judged blow to the man's head. The thickset assailant caught the man as he collapsed.

'How's the bruising?' he asked the woman as he levered the young man up over his shoulder. He was in his mid-forties, with short-cropped salt and pepper hair, grey executive suit protected by a transparent raincoat, and tight, well-muscled body.

'Perfect,' the woman replied evenly, exiting the Jaguar. 'More than enough.' She slid a hand into the young man's jacket pocket and retrieved the envelope.

'You want me to do it here?' he asked, with the sang-froid of a cleaner asking permission to steam a carpet. Animation was alien to his face – humour a concept he had never been able to grasp.

'No, better take him back. Let's move.'

They bundled the unconscious man into the car, drove up the narrow laneway back to the main road and sped down it for about a kilometre. Drawing to a halt, the woman emerged from the car with a small pencil torch that she directed downwards a few feet in front of her. After a quick search she went back and indicated to the thickset man to follow her. They stopped and she pointed to a spot five feet ahead of her on the left-hand side.

'Do it there.'

The man swung the limp body from his shoulder and laid him down flat on his back. The woman walked a few paces further and peered round the curve to check for oncoming traffic. Satisfied, she signalled to her companion to go ahead. The heavy man put a hand in his inside pocket and withdrew a length of shining chrome pipe. Though it had the outward appearance of a cut-down section of a car's bumper, the metal was the thinnest veneer that masked three inches in diameter of solid lead.

Holding the young man's shoulder at arm's length so as to avoid any possible spatter, he brought the gleaming metal bar crashing down on the back of the young man's head. There was a muffled crunching sound as a spray of blood and tissue flew in an arc away from the thickset man. He knew his job, his angles. Deftly, he slid the body towards the hedge.

'Let's go,' the woman said flatly.

'The position okay?'

The woman looked down and thought for a second. The body was three-quarters in the mud near the hedge, the head and shoulders protruding into the left-hand lane.

'More to the side of the road. Don't want his head run over.'

The thickset man made some adjustments to the cadaver. 'Right?'

'Right. Give me the camera,' she replied, holding out a hand.

He pulled a small titanium Nikon 35TI from his inside pocket and passed it to her. She took two steps towards the body, chose her angle and took a couple of shots, the flash reflecting off the glistening roadway. Then she set off back to the Jaguar. The man followed, wiping some blood and matted hair from his chrome cudgel.

THREE

Edward winced, screwed up his face and flung down his baton.

'Right – let's have a break. When we begin again, do try and concentrate.'

Gosia put down her violin, opened a battered leather satchel and pulled out a bag of peppermints, offering them around. Only Nigel, the cellist, continued to play. Gosia maintained Nigel was slightly deaf and could only hear his own instrument, Edward that he was a renegade, though both agreed he was a natural soloist.

'Care for a peppermint, Edward?' Gosia asked mischievously, playing to the gallery. They'd been practising for hours and needed a laugh.

'No, thank you. I'd prefer to get through the last movement so that we're prepared for tomorrow.' He rapped his baton on the music stand then pointed it threateningly at Nigel, who was still in a personal oblivion of deep resonant chords. 'For pity's sake, Nigel, be quiet! This isn't your personal cadenza, it's an ensemble piece, and I just happen to be conducting it!'

Nigel's bow came to an abrupt halt and he raised his head. 'Sorry, Edward. Got carried away.'

'I hope you don't get carried away tomorrow,' Edward snapped in frustration.

They'd been rehearsing Mozart's string quartet *The Dissonance* and Beethoven's *The Harp* for the best part of the Trinity term.

The Holywell Music Room, where they practised, was the oldest purpose-built concert hall in Europe and had played host to many great musicians and composers, including Handel, Hayden and Mozart. Aware of its history, and fearing the ghost of Mozart might appear and strike him dead should he not do justice to *The Dissonance*, Edward was determined the concert should be a tour de force. It irked him that they weren't taking the rehearsal seriously.

'Perhaps we could continue from the fourth bar after Hamish's entry. And Nigel, if I may be so bold as to offer a suggestion, this passage quite patently requires much more of a martelé stroke, yet you seem intent on the staccato. Is this a personal choice to differ with the intention of the composer or merely an error of technique?'

This was Edward at his pompous best. Gosia started laughing and was soon joined by Hamish, the violist, and Linda, the second violin. Nigel stared coldly at Edward. As far as he was concerned Edward should conduct, leaving the real artistry to the players.

'Edward,' he began with studied dignity. 'Why don't you help yourself to a peppermint and stick it up your arse. Might sweeten your demeanour, not to mention the interpretation.'

'Right, that's it!' Edward snapped, folding the music. 'Find yourself another conductor.'

Gosia skipped over to Edward, throwing her slender arms round him. She was actually very fond of him, they all were – he just had a tendency to take himself too seriously at times.

'I'm really sorry, Edward. *Really* sorry. We don't mean to give you a hard time. Please don't get cranky and leave. You're our leader and we'll all buckle down and make you proud.' She pressed her face close to Edward's cheek and made a face at her companions as she spoke.

Edward felt the warmth of Gosia's body pressed against his from the waist up, and the smell of her young skin was overwhelming.

He'd fallen headlong for her the first time he'd seen her on the other side of Hertford Hall at formal dinner the first Sunday of Hilary term. She'd looked simply divine in the type of crumpled black gown everyone was obliged to wear at dinner on Sundays, and he'd been instantly drawn to her.

They'd been thrown together two weeks later through a fellow classicist friend of Edward's who'd given a drinks party in his top-floor room overlooking the quad in the old building, the part of Hertford that dated back to the thirteenth century. The room had been filled with young girls, but there'd been no doubt in Edward's mind that Gosia was the jewel. They discovered common interests, not the least a love of classical music. Gosia had confessed to playing the violin more than passably well and Edward had admitted to fancying himself as a composer, explaining it had been a hard choice between classics and music.

Gosia was soon aware that Edward was madly in love with her and she found it amusing, though Edward was far from being her type. She found Englishmen hard to fathom. In fact everything in England was so different from the student life in Kraków.

It had been Edward's idea to form the string quartet and Gosia's to name it after a nearby village; and so the Ducklinton String Ensemble had been born.

Gosia gave Edward one last squeeze then returned to her seat and picked up her violin. The rest of the ensemble looked down at their music, avoiding each other's glances, then up at Edward.

'Alright. One more chance.' Edward lifted the baton and looked deep into the eyes of each member of the quartet. All appeared serious and had their bows ready. With a bold sweeping motion he brought it down and they continued with the final passage.

As the last chord resonated through the magnificent building, Edward smiled broadly. 'Excellent. See what you're capable of! Alright, that's it. Relax tomorrow – maybe see if you've got time for a spot of practice in the morning. Don't overdo it though, the fresher the better. Let's go and have an ale at the King's Head.'

Two hours later, Gosia and Edward were seated in a corner table at Browns in Woodstock Road, a familiar student haunt. Edward was in an expansive mood – it was the first time Gosia had agreed to let him take her to dinner. Everything was going wonderfully. Finals were a few short weeks away and he felt enormously confident, as did his tutor. A first was a matter of course. The concert tomorrow would be as good as he'd envisaged, and Gosia was at his table for dinner.

The conversation drifted from music, through politics, to the advent of the college balls. Edward was determined to take Gosia to the Magdalen Ball, one of the big three at Oxford each year.

'Seems an awful lot of money,' Gosia said.

'Yes, but it includes dinner. Well worth it. Only an extra twenty quid for a dining ticket. Four courses, excellent wine. Besides, it'll be my treat. Think of it as a cultural exchange between England and Poland,' Edward joked, trying to slip by the implication that she'd already agreed to be his partner.

'Absolutely not! Out of the question. I shall pay for myself,' she replied, adding as she raised her eyebrows, 'that is, if I decide to go at all.'

'Come on, you've absolutely got to go to at least one grand ball while you're up at Oxford, and this'll be your last chance.'

'True,' she replied, 'but whoever suggested that you were the only one to have invited me to partner them?'

The twinkle in the eye was back. 'Hey, why don't we gatecrash! Saves money and it's much more fun anyway. We could leg it over the wall!'

Edward looked at her, horrified. The thought of mixing with the Rottweilers head to head inside the walls of Magdalen filled him with horror.

'Out of the question! You've been listening to my father's hoary old stories.' In Edward's father's day one only had to contend with the 'Bulldogs' – the university policemen. 'Nowadays they have professional security firms hired specially for the occasion. And they have *real* dogs. Besides, if you don't have a programme you won't get any champagne or nibbles and you can't get on any of the rides.' There was usually an element of the fun fair at the Oxford balls.

Gosia mulled this all over. The thrill of outwitting a professional security team had to be counterbalanced with the lack of food and drink, and she knew which was paramount. She decided to change the subject before Edward could tie her down to accepting his invitation.

'Talking of your papa –'

'Which we weren't,' Edward interrupted, determined to stay on the subject of the Magdalen Ball.

'We were. You said I'd been listening to too many of his old Oxford stories,' she insisted.

'True,' he grudgingly had to admit. 'What about him, anyway?'

'It's just you never talk about him.'

'You hardly even *mention* yours,' Edward countered quickly. Whenever he'd brought up the subject of Gosia's parents, she invariably clammed up. He looked across at her. She averted her eyes.

'Anyway, why should I talk all the time about my father? We're a pretty ordinary family, really. You've been to our house countless times and you get on famously with my mother and father,' he continued.

'That's true. But it's always so formal – maybe it doesn't strike you as such. Family life's so different in Poland. We hug each other a lot, yet here you're all so frightfully English.'

Edward studied her. She was the most exquisite woman he'd ever laid eyes on – deep blue eyes, high Slavic cheekbones, straight chiselled nose, soft full lips and shortish curly blonde hair fringing her face. The thought of next year without her was too terrible to contemplate.

'Come on, Gosia, my father gives you hugs all the time,' Edward said defensively.

'Are you suggesting your papa's a dirty old man?' she teased.

'God forbid. He's the least likely man on the planet to let his fingers do the walking. But seriously, I suppose it's fair to say that we're quite an old-fashioned family. Goes with father's job, I expect. Always in some country other than England. Always a nanny to look after me – one of the perks of being a diplomat. I have to say I felt a good deal closer and more at ease with the nannies than I did with my mother, primarily because I spent more time with them than with her. I remember my father always being very demanding. Mother had to be the perfect diplomat's wife, I the perfect child. I think the greatest concern he's ever had is that I might possibly be an under-achiever – that probably gave him many a sleepless night.'

'Well, he can sleep easy now. If ever there was a student with double first stamped on his forehead, it's you.'

Edward took a sip of claret and looked down at the table for a few seconds. After finals she'd be gone and he'd be alone.

As if sensing his thoughts, Gosia said, 'I'm going to miss you next year. Mind you, it must be a relief to be nearly finished. And your father must be terribly proud of you.' Gosia sighed. Edward was so earnest – he took life so seriously. She loved life with such a passion, and he was so restrained. He was in serious danger of becoming as stuffy as his father. He'd asked her to dinner so many times she just couldn't think of any other reasons not to go. In her book, lunch was one thing, dinner very much another. She had no boyfriends, preferring to remain unattached – there were just too many things going on to waste time on a predictable Oxford relationship. But this evening was special – it was a time to relax and look forward to the concert.

'You're right. In many ways I'll be relieved when I graduate. It's been a monkey on my back for years, living up to his expectations. You see, he believes we Chasens to be an island to ourselves. Suits him, not my mother. She never wanted to live on an island as small as that. People tell me she was quite gregarious when she met him, but my father crushed it out of her as the years rolled by. He hated company and seldom socialised unless it was part of his duties. Because I was an only child I never had children my own age to play with.'

'Edward Chasen,' Gosia interrupted, reaching out and taking his right hand in both of hers and squeezing it tightly, 'stop – you're breaking my heart!'

He looked at her earnest face, the eyebrows furrowed with concern, then down at his hand, sandwiched between hers. Then she began to laugh.

'You've got to enjoy yourself a bit more Edward – got to have a bit more fun. Life's too short.'

Edward was very aware of his hand in hers.

'You're right,' he said. 'I do take myself too seriously. Maybe America will change all that.'

'When do your parents leave?'

'Next Friday. Actually I've been thinking of taking a PhD at Harvard.'

'Odd place for a classics scholar?'

'Not really – I've looked into it. Besides, I'll be working on my own most of the time anyway, so I might as well follow the family.'

He caught the attention of a passing waiter and gestured for the bill.

'Have you heard from your mother recently?' he asked. 'She's still in Paris?'

'Yes, still in Paris.'

He looked at her and she looked away – as usual, she didn't want to discuss her family. 'So, you'll come with me to Magdalen? Come on, say you will,' Edward pleaded.

Gosia leant forward. 'We'll see. Give a lady some time.'

'Agreed. Okay, let's settle the bill on the way out and take a walk. Come and have a nightcap back at Home Farm. If we get a move-on we'll miss the storm.'

FOUR

Chasen turned up the car heater, directing the flow of air onto his face. He was wet through and his body was still shaking – he'd had a really bad scare. Thank God it was over. The man was alive – a few bruises, but that was all. Unbelievable that he'd been silly enough to be walking on such a dangerous road and during that bad storm.

He continued taking deep breaths and the knot in his stomach began to unravel. His heart was still hammering away, and he could feel the adrenalin pumping through his body. Christ, what if it had been different? A foot further across the road and he, Sir Ivor Chasen, Her Majesty's Permanent Representative designate to the United Nations, might have been standing by the side of the road being questioned by the Oxford Constabulary, while a covered body was lifted into an ambulance. And that woman would have been standing by his side. His passenger, for Christ's sake! That would have looked just fine. End of his career – no question. And he on the brink of taking up the position that would be the pinnacle of thirty-seven years of dedication and service!

He felt like killing Aubrey. *Don't be so stuffy Ivor old boy, give the poor girl a lift home – it's practically on your doorstep,* the fool had said as he walked down the steps to his car. To fall for bloody peer pressure at his age! Peer pressure – how apt, he thought bitterly. The likes of Lord Bruton's coterie had changed little in hundreds of years. Their kind. A world of inherited privilege they considered their natural birthright. An attitude of innate superiority that made Chasen feel quite ill. Selfish, self-interested, self-satisfied, arrogant men who walked the corridors of power, still the backbone of the ruling class, the ruling party, the unseen driving force of the civil service, achieving little for their country, and so often up to deviance of one kind or another that brought down either themselves, their friends, or the Conservative Party. He thought of the fix Geoffrey Dalton, the leader of the opposition, now found himself in. Wait till the tabloids got wind of that one!

But to saddle him with that woman – Aubrey really was the limit! The muscles at the side of his mouth tensed with anger.

He tried to clear his thoughts as he searched for the Chalgrove turn-off. Wasn't it just round this corner? No, a bit further on. He pressed the play button on his CD player. Perhaps some Vivaldi would soothe his nerves. But no, his brain was instantly in overdrive once more. To hell with them all! As long as he had Lily and Edward. They were his life. Lily, Edward and the diplomatic corps – in that order. He loved all three. A woman of substance he'd worshipped all his life, a son of whom he was intensely proud, a career filled with achievement and a name that commanded the respect of his colleagues in the diplomatic corps.

He gripped the steering wheel again as the events of the evening assaulted his mind. How was it possible that a man of his age and training had made such an elementary mistake? A momentary lack of judgment and he'd been driving home someone who, his intuition told him, had every intention of compromising him given half a chance. Or was she just playing with him – toying with him?

He eased his foot off the accelerator as he approached the Chalgrove turn-off. Soon he'd be home, the entire incident forgotten. Perhaps he was seeing phantoms where none existed. Could she just possibly have thought he'd pay for sex the way Aubrey did? If so, she'd been mistaken. He was the future Permanent Representative to the UN, not to mention the Security Council Rep. He wasn't about to be compromised now.

He slowed as he approached the outskirts of Oxford, turning left onto the ring road, then accelerated again.

Did the girl think he was the same as all the others? If so, she had miscalculated. Of course he'd been aware of her at the dinner party. Who hadn't? She must have stood close to six foot in her stockinged feet. And those legs – they seemed to go on for ever. Olive skin, full but firm breasts, and dark – no, practically black – luxuriant hair falling like a single ebony wave to her shoulders. They'd all been sniffing around her tonight. She'd behaved as though she'd expected such attention, yet it meant nothing to her. He in turn had successfully avoided her all evening, until Aubrey had appeared with her beside the Porsche. He swore again. Had he suspected it was to be one of Bruton's notorious 'gentlemen's evenings' he would never have accepted.

As he turned off the dual carriageway towards Wytham he could see the lights of Home Farm on the other side of the paddocks between the trees. He took another deep breath as he listened to the last few bars of the Vivaldi. So he'd made a mistake, let that be a lesson. Even Homer nods, his tutor had been fond of telling him at Magdalen. He smiled as he turned into his driveway.

The lights in the downstairs drawing room were blazing as he drove into the twin garage and parked next to Lily's Range Rover. Mrs Brown must have inadvertently left them on. Lily would not have been expecting him for dinner, and on these occasions usually ate upstairs in her bedroom annexe. He sincerely hoped that Edward hadn't brought any of his chums home for drinks. He glanced at his watch; it was almost one o'clock.

He composed himself then got out, locked the car, and was about to pull down the roller door when a thought struck him and he walked back to the car. He crouched down, looking for any damage to the front of the Porsche. He glided a hand over the paintwork. A few scratches were evident on the left-hand wing, and the centre of the bonnet where the man had rolled had a wide concave indentation. As he turned to leave, he noticed the chrome wing mirror was buckled backwards and the left indicator housing was broken. He swore.

He made his way down the gravel path that led to the kitchen entrance. If Edward was entertaining, it was wiser to nip up the back stairs.

He searched for the kitchen latch key, feeling worse-tempered by the second – he was wet to the skin and bloody cold. The events of the night, now coupled with the fact that he had to skulk in the back door, annoyed him.

Finally he found the right key, opened the back door and stepped into the large kitchen, still warm from the Aga cooker which burned day and night. He walked swiftly across the dark room and opened the door that led into the hall. As he walked down the corridor to the foot of the back stairs, he glanced at the small Henry Moore bronze on the long refectory table in the corridor. Any intra-family messages, together with the mail, were usually placed there by Mrs Brown. There was nothing.

As he reached the third step of the back stairs there was a sharp call from the direction of the drawing room. Chasen glanced back.

'Father? Is that you? Father?'

'Oh shit!' he muttered to himself, continuing up the stairs. 'Yes, it's me, Edward. Who the hell did you expect, the Moors Murderer? Now you've probably woken your mother.'

The hall light was suddenly switched on and Edward walked towards him, his friend Gosia a few steps behind.

'Won't you join us for a nightcap, father?' Edward began, before stopping and staring at him in surprise. 'Good Lord. Whatever happened? Did you have a puncture or something?'

Chasen just looked back at his son, trying hard to mask his fury and frustration.

'Good evening, Sir Ivor,' Gosia said politely. 'Would you like us to get you a whisky while you put down your things?' She could see that Edward had considerably embarrassed his father, who was clearly anxious about something.

Chasen's features assumed a more controlled look. 'Good evening, Gosia. A whisky would be wonderful. I'll just go up and dump these bags and be down soon.'

Ten minutes later, a showered and changed Ivor Chasen reappeared downstairs, determined to be genial. 'I expect you two have been out to dinner somewhere in town?'

'Edward very kindly took me to dinner at Browns,' Gosia replied, smiling.

'Oh good,' said Chasen, a distracted air still clinging to him.

There was a protracted silence, as Edward and Gosia searched for conversation.

'As you may have noticed,' Chasen eventually volunteered, 'I was as wet as the proverbial shag on a rock. I'm afraid I hit a dog on the main road. At least I think it was a dog; the rain was bucketting down so hard I'm not exactly sure. It could have been a fox, I suppose.

Dashed out of the hedge. Gave me a terrific shock, I can tell you. I thought it might have been lying by the side of the road in pain so I got out and searched – got soaked to the skin.'

'Did you find it? Was it a fox?' Gosia asked as she poured the drinks.

'I've no idea, I'm afraid. Not a bloody sign of it. Must have got the shock of its life, though – plus a pretty bad headache.'

'Whisky and water, Sir Ivor,' Gosia said, handing him a glass.

'A girl after my own heart. Thanks.'

Edward prodded at the embers of the fire, encouraging a few flickers of life. 'Rotten luck, father. Any damage to the car?'

'I didn't look. Would you? In the sort of weather that would have set Noah checking the oars?' Chasen chuckled as he vainly tried to make light of the incident.

'I'll go and have a look, father.'

'Don't bother, Edward. Actually, I did have a quick look in the garage when I got in. Just a broken indicator housing. I'll have a better look in the morning,' said Chasen, but Edward was already on his feet and walking to the door.

'It's no trouble, father. Really.'

'Why don't you just do as your father asks, for once? Would that be too much trouble?' Chasen spat out the words with such vehemence that Gosia didn't know where to look. Edward stopped dead in his tracks. There was another silence before Chasen spoke again.

'I'm sorry, Edward. I didn't mean to fly off the handle. I apologise to you too, Gosia. I'm just a bit on edge tonight, that's all. Thought I'd killed a dog, damaged the car, then got soaked . . .' His voice trailed off. 'By the way, where's Heston Langley?'

'I'm sorry? Where's what?' Edward replied.

'Heston Langley. It's a small village, I'm told. Pretty close to here I'd imagine. A colleague at the department mentioned it the other day. Said he was thinking of buying a house there.'

'Never heard of the place.'

'Well, that doesn't necessarily preclude its existence, does it?' The edge was back in Chasen's voice.

'No, it doesn't. You're absolutely correct, father,' Edward replied quietly. 'I can look it up right here,' he said, standing and pulling a local Oxford road map from a shelf above him. He flipped through the pages at the back, then snapped it shut.

'No such place.'

'Are you absolutely sure?' Chasen asked slowly.

'Well, it's not listed in the road book, so it can't exist. Your friend must have been mistaken.'

Chasen held out a hand and Edward gave him the book. 'Maybe there's a place that sounds just like it.'

He looked down at the book and turned a few pages. After a thorough search he closed it slowly, finished his drink and stood up.

'Well, I'm off to bed. Sorry about my evil mood this evening,' Chasen said, then left the room, closing the door behind him.

FIVE

Nigel was the first to arrive. He struggled in through the door with his cello, looking around for Edward, who invariably turned up before them. He unzipped his case, took out his cello, arranged his seat and began the cadenza from the Shostakovich Cello Concerto by way of a private joke with Edward – he wanted a cadenza and he was going to get one, wherever he was.

Linda was hot on his heels, wearing an organza summer dress. She hummed along with Nigel as she unpacked – she knew it drove him mad.

He stopped mid-bar. 'It's a joke! Remember what Teddy said at rehearsals?'

'As far as I can see it was all true. You'd much sooner be playing a solo, albeit with the Boston Symphony!'

Nigel laughed.

'Where is he, anyway? He's always first,' Linda asked, looking around.

'No idea,' Nigel replied, then waved at Gosia as she flew up the steps of the Holywell towards them.

'Where's Edward?' she panted.

'No idea,' they chorused.

'What time is it?' She looked at her watch. 'Christ, it's five past eleven. He's late for God's sake, he's actually late!'

At twenty past, their initial humour had turned to concern, and then panic.

With only ten minutes to spare, Gosia decided she'd have to dash across to Hertford, to Edward's rooms. But there was no sign of him. She raced back down the stairs and across to the public telephone. Another quick glance at her watch told her there was no time to call his home.

As she re-entered the Holywell Music Room, Gosia was sure he'd be there looking sheepish, but she could see at once from the looks of the other three that there was still no sign of him. There was nothing for it – they'd have to muddle through without him.

The concert was a great success despite Edward's absence, but within seconds of their final bow Gosia had packed her violin away and was out of the building, running back to the Porter's Lodge. Had there been an accident? Was he in hospital? There had to be some serious explanation for him not to have turned up – she knew he wouldn't have missed it for the world.

She rounded the corner of Holywell Road and ducked into Hertford again. She raced up the six winding wooden stairs on her right to the Porter's Lodge. Mrs Etheridge was on duty, a woman renowned for her sternness and lack of humour.

'Good afternoon Miss Dobra. What can I do for you today?'

'I wonder if you've seen Mr Chasen recently?'

'Let me see . . .' She thought for a few seconds. 'Don't think I've seen him since Thursday.'

Gosia thanked her politely then hurried out to the quadrangle towards the telephone, searching as she did so for some change. To her relief there wasn't the usual queue of students waiting to use it. She inserted her coins and dialled. A few moments later the phone was answered.

'Hello. Is that Lady Chasen? It's Gosia Dobra speaking. I was wondering if Edward was with you? He's not? I see. Well, he was supposed to have been conducting with us this morning at the Holywell and he didn't turn up. That's right, it's most unlike him. I was afraid he'd had an accident or was ill at home.' She listened for a few moments, scrunching the handles of her satchel unconsciously.

'Well, I'm sure there's no need to worry. He'll show up for his tutorial, I'm certain of that. I hope I haven't worried you. Certainly – I'll tell him to call home as soon as he appears. Bye.'

She replaced the receiver. She hoped she'd been convincing – she didn't like to worry Lady Chasen, but in her own mind she was certain that something serious must have happened.

She reached deep into her satchel, withdrawing paper and a biro, and scribbled a message for Edward to call her as soon as he arrived. She pinned it to the notice-board and on her way back through the Porter's Lodge pinned another to the board there. What else could she do?

SIX

Chasen chuckled as he sipped his morning coffee and read the political leader in the *Guardian*. The leader of the opposition was getting a roasting for being foolish enough to trust the denials of a shadow minister embroiled in a seedy paternity case with a coloured prostitute from Durham. Colour still seemed to make a difference, he thought with disgust. But he'd never liked either man, so it was doubly delicious.

The telephone rang – his personal phone. He lifted the receiver.

'Lily?'

'Have you read this morning's paper, Sir Ivor?'

For a split second Chasen felt his stomach turn over.

'Who am I talking to?' he replied evenly. He knew damn well, but he was buggered if he'd give the woman the satisfaction of knowing it. That silky voice, the accent – they were unmistakable.

'I'll repeat the question. Have you read –'

Chasen cut her short. 'I have no intention of conducting a conversation with anyone who will not identify themself,' he snapped and slammed the phone down.

A few seconds passed, then the phone rang again.

'Hello?'

'You may call me "Midnight" if it makes you happy.'

'Don't waste my time –' Chasen began.

'So now that I have "identified" myself,' she interrupted, deliberately stressing the word, 'perhaps you could answer my question.'

'You're that friend of Lord Bruton, aren't you?'

'If you like.'

'Who gave you my number? Aubrey?'

'Your number is a matter of public record, Sir Ivor.'

'It is nothing of the kind, madam.'

'I am short of time. I have things to do as, I imagine, do you, so please let us get to the point – my question.'

'Yes, I have read the morning papers!' Chasen spat the words out.

'Please turn to page five of the *Oxford Mail*, Sir Ivor.'

'The *Oxford Mail* is not amongst my "must read" items.'

'Is that so?' Her voice had a mocking tone. 'Well, it should be. It really should be. I suggest you make a point of reading it as soon as possible. It could change your whole outlook on life. I will call back in an hour.'

'I have no intention whatsoever –' he began, but she hung up in mid-sentence.

Chasen replaced the phone, picked up his coffee and took a sip. It was cold and tasted bitter. What on earth had she meant? Had he read the *Oxford Mail*?

He stood, walked to the door and opened it, then abruptly turned and slammed the door shut. What on earth can I be thinking of, he fumed. This woman rings, tells me to read a local newspaper and here I am bowing to her orders! To hell with her! He had a good mind to call security in London and ask someone to have a word with whoever she was.

He walked back to his desk and opened his briefcase. He'd finish off a little work and take the dog for a walk to calm himself down. Then a thought occurred to him and he picked up the phone.

'This is Sir Ivor Chasen. Is Lord Bruton available? Thank you.' Chasen drummed his fingers on the desk – he'd get to the bottom of this, one way or another.

A voice came on the line. 'Ivor? Good morning. What can I do for you?' Lord Bruton's tone was smooth.

'For a start you can tell me who that woman was you unloaded on me on Saturday night. I didn't appreciate it at the time; perhaps it was your idea of a joke. I can only presume it was you who gave her my private number, because she's been making a thorough nuisance of herself all morning.'

'I've no idea what you're talking about, Ivor,' Aubrey replied calmly.

'The woman you asked me to take home, for heaven's sake!' Chasen's temper was beginning to deteriorate.

'I have no recollection of having done anything of the kind. And I'd appreciate it if you didn't shout. If you've somehow got yourself entangled with a "young lady", I do not wish to be involved,' Aubrey replied crisply.

Chasen was speechless with rage.

'I suggest you think very carefully before you include my name in any unpleasantness,' Bruton continued in a threatening tone. 'I suggest you consider your position.' Then the phone went dead.

Chasen slowly replaced the receiver, his brain a turmoil of conflicting thoughts. No sooner had he done so when the telephone rang again; his private line. He stared at it for several rings, then snatched up the receiver.

'Yes? Chasen!'

'Shall I read you the headline, Sir Ivor?' the silky voice intoned. 'Otherwise you might be tempted to ignore my advice to read the article in question.'

Chasen sat in silence, the knuckles of the hand grasping the receiver white with the pressure.

The woman broke the silence. 'The article concerns an accident. Apparently it took place two nights ago during that terrible storm. Hit and run. A man was *killed* . . .' She let the last word hang in the air. 'As yet they have not identified the body, or so it says here.'

Chasen's heart momentarily stopped beating and his mouth tasted like ash.

'Sir Ivor? Are you still there? You see, I have to drive right past your house on my way home to Heston Langley at around nine tonight. Would it be convenient to call in? I promise I won't take up too much of your time.'

'There's no such place,' Chasen's voice was a hoarse whisper.

'Is that so?' There was a moment's silence.

'I cannot see how any of this is relevant,' Chasen finally managed. 'You say someone was knocked down and killed? Well, in that case –' Chasen would have continued but was interrupted yet again.

'I shall be with you at nine this evening, Sir Ivor,' she said, and this time her tone had changed; it had a definite edge and demanded attention.

Chasen stared down at the article, re-reading it for the fiftieth time. He tried to calm himself – he had to think quickly and clearly. It was becoming quite plain that he had been set up, and the nasty stench of blackmail hung in the air. The conversation with Bruton had shocked him deeply. It was quite incomprehensible. Why had the man lied? Why were his words unquestionably imbued with menace? It was unthinkable that Bruton could be personally involved, and yet logic dictated very differently. Chasen ran his fingers over the newspaper.

A 32-year-old man, so the short article in the *Mail* stated, had been the victim of a hit and run accident on the road just past Cuxham two nights before, and the police had yet to identify the body. But the man, Erskine, had sped off in his Jaguar, so what was the woman threatening him for?

He put his head in his hands. He desperately wanted a drink, but he needed to keep his wits about him. The whole day had been pure torture, filled with supposition, denial, incredulity, fear. Now, finally, it was five to nine. Lily wasn't due back from her bridge party till after ten and Edward, to the best of his knowledge, was dining in college. Thank God for small mercies.

Perhaps he should call security, he thought for the umpteenth time. That was the advice he'd give to anyone else. It was plain logic, and hell, that was what they were there for. But something held him back.

Chasen looked again at his watch – it was a few minutes past nine. Where was she? Goddamn it, he had to have a Scotch. Just one. He needed it. He felt angry. He had done nothing wrong. He had not run from the scene of any accident. His conscience was clear. What was he worrying about?

As he poured the straight malt into a tumbler, the headlights of a car swung across the front of the house. Through the French windows Chasen identified the outline of a sports car coming up the drive. It was the Jaguar! He drained his glass and helped himself quickly to another, then walked to the side of the window. The car came to a halt and the lights were extinguished. The driver's door opened and the woman stepped from the car. He couldn't make out whether she had travelled alone – the car was swathed in darkness.

The doorbell rang as he left the study and crossed the hall to the front door. As he reached for the doorhandle, he already regretted the two large malts.

Chasen was momentarily taken by surprise when he opened the door. The woman who stood before him now was a far cry indeed from the siren who had sat beside him in the Porsche during the storm. The sensuality was absent. Her clothes were conservative, and her black hair was tied back in a bun. But the black eyes were unmistakable – though there was no evidence of a smile, they seemed to reach into his very soul to mock him.

Chasen stood at the door, frozen, until she finally spoke. 'Shall we go inside?' Not waiting for an answer, she brushed past him into the hall.

Chasen closed the front door. She'd done it again: taken the mental advantage, put him on the defensive. He pointed her towards his study. 'We shall discuss whatever we have to discuss in my office.' He followed her, closing the study door behind him.

She walked to the desk, withdrew a medium-sized manila envelope from inside her jacket and placed it on the leather writing pad. As Chasen approached, she held up a four-inch square card in front of his face, at the same time placing a finger to her lips as a gesture of silence. He looked at it – there was writing. *If there is a tape recorder running, tell me now.* Chasen was momentarily taken aback. He shook his head and spread his hands, indicating this was not so.

She walked to the telephone, lifted the receiver, then replaced it. She quickly removed the baseplate and checked the input condenser. Replacing the base, she unscrewed both ends of the receiver. As Chasen watched her, fascinated, she walked slowly round the room, checking the walls, the ceiling and the skirting boards. She then held another card out to him. *Are you aware of any bugging devices in your study? If so, for your own security, tell me now. You may not wish others to hear what I shall shortly tell you.*

Chasen was unnerved. Though he knew he had nothing to fear, he felt a deep and abiding apprehension. Christ, what was happening to him?

The girl snapped the card again with her fingers, only inches from his face. She was obviously in a hurry.

Chasen shook his head. No bugs he was aware of. Hell, he'd never thought of the possibility.

'Is there anyone in the house?' she asked, in a pleasant tone that didn't reflect her expression.

'No. No one,' Chasen replied.

She motioned to him to sit in the chair. As he did so, she pulled a black plastic case measuring less than six inches by three from inside her jacket and flicked a switch on the lower right-hand side of the face, glancing down at the lead crystal read-out at the top as she walked slowly round the room holding the Vascon TTD–1A RF bug detector close to each electrical fitting in the room. Satisfied, she pointed to the manila envelope she'd placed on the leather deskpad. Chasen gazed at it.

'Open it,' the girl snapped coldly.

His fingers fumbled with the flap of the envelope. It was stuck down. The girl slid the metal letter-opener across to him irritably. Chasen slit the top and withdrew the contents. Inside were four colour photos. As his eyes focused on the top-most photograph he was convulsed with fear and panic. The photos fell to the desk as he pushed his chair backwards and staggered to the window, breathless.

The girl gathered up the four photos and fanned them out on the desk, then said calmly, 'That is the face of the man you killed with your car. It is you the police seek.'

'I killed no one,' Chasen said weakly, 'we both know that.'

'Indeed we do, but it is only *we* who know. These photographs show otherwise.'

Chasen lurched back to the desk and sat down. He lowered his head to his knees and took some more deep breaths. What on earth was going on here? He had to think quickly. Raising his head, he pulled the photos across towards him. Looking closely, the top-most resembled a police incident shot. The man he had last seen climbing into his Jaguar was lying face down by the side of the road. The base of his skull was crushed and resembled the shell of the soft-boiled egg Chasen had eaten for breakfast. The road was awash with blood.

The second photo showed the man lying unconscious by the side of the road. He, Chasen, was on his knees by the man's side staring at him. This one appeared to have been taken by flash while the others had an infra-red quality.

The third was a less detailed shot – one of the Porsche, Chasen and the young man. The final picture was a full-length shot of the body lying half in the hedge, half in the road.

'The mere existence of these photographs reveals their purpose of blackmail. Someone had to have taken these photographs. What the hell was he doing in the bushes? Answer me that!'

'That was never their purpose. I show them to you to signify our resolve. We can be anywhere and everywhere. We never had any intention of publication. As you correctly state, they would make no sense. However, the blood and tissue traces on your car will be difficult to explain, and we will make certain they are brought to the attention of the authorities.'

'There are no such traces.'

'They exist now.'

There was a brief pause, then she continued. 'Now this need never happen.'

Chasen held the close-up of the man's crushed head and stared at it incredulously. 'I presume he is the unidentified body in the *Mail*. Did you murder this man just to get to me?' He leant back in his chair and covered his face with his hands. 'Jesus Christ, what do you expect from me that's worth the life of this man? Don't you realise I will do nothing for you?'

'I rather think you will,' she replied mockingly.

The muffled sound of a door closing somewhere down the hall made her swing her head. 'You told me we were alone,' she whispered with venom.

'As far as I know, we are,' Chasen replied defensively.

She moved without a sound across the room to the door, opening it a fraction. There was no sound from the hall. Satisfied, she closed the door once more and returned to Chasen.

Chasen watched her, then made up his mind. 'I shall not be blackmailed, and that is an end to the matter. Do what you like. Publish and be damned, as they say. Their purpose will be immediately apparent.'

The girl leant across the desk and focused her black eyes on Chasen's. 'We anticipated this reaction, Chasen. However, you will do as we say or it will be the end of you – your career of thirty-odd years' hard struggle, and your happiness. You also have the happiness of others to consider. This would kill poor Lily. She deserves better, don't you think?'

Chasen looked into her eyes. His heart felt as though it was fibrillating; the sweat was pouring down his back.

'And you have your son to consider,' she continued. 'We are looking after Edward until you leave. He will follow, should you be cooperative.'

Chasen was flooded with this new horror. Edward . . . What had Lily said before she'd left? That Edward had missed the concert. So unlike him. His limbs felt suddenly chilled. 'What are you saying? Edward? You have kidnapped my son?' His voice gave out.

'As I said, we are currently looking after your son. He is perfectly safe for the time being. What we require is not great. You will do this thing for us. It is not so terrible.' She bent and her lips brushed the side of Chasen's head. 'Should you decide otherwise, our retribution will be swift. Call security and our retribution will be immediate – on you, your wife and your son. Do I make my position very clear?'

Chasen could not move. His muscles had ceased functioning. 'Who do you represent?' he breathed, his voice barely audible in the small study.

The woman laughed. 'The CIA? KGB? Is this what you mean? Perhaps the NIS? MI6? Mossad? You make me smile Chasen, you live in fantasyland. We are who we are, and it does not concern you. Must we wear badges?'

She picked up the photographs and slipped them back into their envelope. Then she pulled a slim cellular phone from an inside pocket and offered it to Chasen.

'This is for you. I will call you at exactly five minutes past one o'clock every morning until you leave for New York. Please make sure you are alone when you take the calls. You will receive instructions as to what you must do. You will take the phone with you to New York. It will be collected there. It is digital, so the line is secure. We will regard any outgoing calls as a breach of faith by you, so guard it well. What you will be asked is not so great and you will be happy to oblige. In a matter of days your son will be released and you will have a choice – whether to bring this matter to the attention of the police or not. I assure you the latter alternative will be more to your taste. You will know nothing of what we do and it will not reflect on you personally. You will be safe – as will your family. The alternative is too dreadful to contemplate.' She walked to the study door, then turned. 'Think smart, eh?'

The study door closed softly behind her. Chasen sat still as a granite boulder on a sandy beach, the blood pounding in his temples. A few seconds passed, and he heard the sound of her car in the drive as she turned on the ignition. Then the sound faded and the house was enshrouded once more in silence.

Chasen put the phone down and leant his head forward to the level of the desk, resting his forehead on the edge.

Chasen's hand shook as he poured the Glenlivet into his tumbler. He had to pull himself together. If anything was to be done it should be done at once. Time to throw his career and the happiness of his family to the wind or lie down with dogs and join all the other moral bankrupts of the world. But what real choice did he have? They had Edward. Or so they said. Should he put his son's life on the line – in the hands of the Special Protection Squad? It was government policy not to deal with terrorists, and he was Her Majesty's Government's representative – but how one's opinions changed when the life of one's flesh was endangered.

Who were the people that the woman represented anyway, and what did they want from him? The thought of ever being involved in any kind of espionage had never occurred to Chasen – it was the stuff of novels. The woman had not asked him for information of any kind or suggested he should spy for them. When it came to decision-making and lobbying at the UN it wouldn't be long before people were reporting back to headquarters saying he wasn't toeing the line. His area of discretion was strictly limited – policy was paramount. Perhaps they were terrorists, he thought with horror – it was unthinkable to make deals of any kind with terrorists.

After a while Chasen became aware of a soft knocking. He hastily tried to marshal his thoughts. Turning from his desk, he saw that the study door was slightly ajar.

'Yes? Is there someone there?'

The door inched further open and Gosia's head appeared round the doorframe.

'I'm really sorry to disturb you, Sir Ivor,' she said hesitantly. 'It's just that I'm so terribly worried about Edward. Have you seen him? He didn't turn up at a concert we gave, and he hasn't appeared now for two days. We had a date tonight.'

Chasen's head spun. 'Edward? I believe he's . . . I believe he's dining in college.'

'That's just it – he's not. He hasn't been seen in college since Saturday.'

'Really?' Chasen managed. 'Well, he must be somewhere else. I'm sure you needn't worry unduly.'

'Forgive me, Sir Ivor, for pursuing the matter, and I don't think I'm being unduly apprehensive, but he's just vanished without a word to his friends or his tutor, and I can only now presume without having informed either of his parents.'

'He may have told his mother. I suppose he has.'

'I spoke to Lady Chasen on Sunday – she had no idea where he was.'

'Gosia,' Chasen cut in shortly, 'Edward's a grown man. I cannot be expected to know his whereabouts twenty-four hours a day.'

Gosia studied Chasen's back. His shoulders were hunched forward and his right arm was visibly shaking. There was no point in pursuing the matter. 'Of course you can't. I'm sure there's some logical explanation. I'm so sorry to have troubled you.'

'Not at all.'

She stared at Chasen in silence. 'Sir Ivor? I hope you don't mind my asking, but . . . are you alright?'

Chasen turned awkwardly to face her. 'What do you mean – am I alright?'

'I'm sorry . . . you don't look very well.'

Chasen didn't smile. 'It's good of you to be so solicitous, but I'm fine. Just had a bit of bad news on the telephone – a personal matter. I lost a dear friend. If you don't mind, I'd rather not talk about it.'

Determined to see for herself whether Edward was at his parents', Gosia had bicycled over from Oxford. It hadn't been far, no more than a couple of miles, but with her headlight on the blink it had been an obstacle course.

When she'd arrived, the lights had been on in the study, and the kitchen door was ajar – Mrs Brown didn't usually lock up till ten. She'd knocked lightly to alert the housekeeper, but no one was around, so she'd entered the house. As she'd reached the study door she'd been surprised to hear the unfamiliar voice of a woman – not Lady Chasen, a younger woman.

The words were indistinct and she'd turned to leave as Chasen raised his voice. He'd sounded very distressed.

She could only make out snatches of the conversation. Chasen was saying something to the effect that he would do nothing for the woman.

Gosia had been rooted to the spot, when she'd heard the back door slam shut. Abruptly the voices in the study had ceased. She pressed herself against the wall of the hallway, holding her breath. A few seconds later the outline of a woman appeared and peered down the hall. Satisfied that no one was around, the woman closed the door and the conversation continued, Chasen sounding more distraught than ever. 'I shall not be blackmailed,' she distinctly heard him say. 'Publish and be damned.'

Shocked, Gosia pressed her ear to the door, but it was still very difficult to make out the woman's words. '. . .

would kill Lily,' she heard the woman say, or something like it. What would kill Lily? What could Chasen conceivably have done that would kill Lily?

She strained to hear Chasen's reply but was unable to pick it up; she could only make out the odd broken phrase. 'You will do . . . retribution . . . terrible . . . Edward . . .' Then suddenly the woman had laughed. There was a cruel edge to it. Gosia stood in the darkness debating what to do.

Before she could do anything, the study door opened and the woman stepped once more into the hall. She looked no more than thirty – tall, long legs, well dressed in a subdued way, with her hair tied in a bun. She had an unforgettable face. Quite beautiful. But in the shadowed light cast by the hall lamp she appeared to have no eyes at all. There were just pockets of darkness. Gosia was reminded of a line from Macbeth – a face 'filled top full of direst cruelty'. The woman strode to the front door, disappeared through it, and in a matter of moments Gosia heard a car leave.

Gosia stood where she was for a while – her mind racing. She knew she could not just walk away. Maybe she could help? So she'd knocked on the study door.

'I'm afraid I happened to be outside the door when your other guest was here,' Gosia said finally.

Chasen stared at Gosia in disbelief. 'What guest? I don't know what you mean. I had no guests.'

'I was about to enter and I overheard the greater part of your conversation. I didn't intend to spy on you. However, I really want to help you in any way I can, and if you'll allow me –'

Chasen sprang to his feet in fury. 'How dare you come into my house and casually inform me you've been listening at keyholes, then offer me advice as to how to conduct my affairs! You have not the slightest idea what the conversation concerned. Suffice it to say it is absolutely none of your business!'

'Sir Ivor,' Gosia pleaded, 'I'm trying to help. I can be a witness if this woman threatens to compromise your position.'

'Gosia!' Chasen shouted, 'as it happens it was a personal thing, quite unconnected with any affairs of state. I am quite up to dealing with the matter myself and I would be most grateful if you would let me do so. I fear you've been watching too many films – I am not about to become a Burgess, a Maclean or a Blunt.'

Gosia could see further conversation was useless. 'As you wish, Sir Ivor. However, if there is anything I might do to help, you have only to let me know.'

'Very kind of you, Gosia,' he said, holding out a hand. 'I appreciate your concern. Please don't mention any of this to Lily. Just keep it to yourself – let me sort it out my own way. As I say, it's personal, if you understand me. Very personal. Would you do that for me? Please?'

'Of course, Sir Ivor,' said Gosia, turning to leave. As she reached the door she stopped abruptly. 'You have no idea where Edward is?'

'You've not seen him today?' Chasen asked rhetorically, sinking into a chair.

'No I haven't,' she replied. 'I'm sorry to labour the point at a time like this, but he was to have conducted us at the Holywell Music Room yesterday and he never showed up. I've left messages everywhere, but he's simply vanished. Then today he skipped his tutorial – I know that because I had a word with his tutor, who was as surprised as I was that Edward should miss it. As I'm sure you know, he hasn't missed one in three years. With his finals only weeks away I'd say that was the strangest part of it all. Wouldn't you?' She looked at him searchingly.

Avoiding her eyes, Chasen rose from the chair and walked to the door.

'Oh my God! I remember!' he said, as if the scales had suddenly fallen from his eyes. 'Look, I'm sorry he should have worried you. Very careless of him. He decided to go to Scotland to cram for a few days up in Sutherland. He's staying with the Dillons. How could I have forgotten? Do you know them?'

'No,' she replied. She didn't believe him for one second.

'Haven't even had time to tell Lily yet. Maybe he has, I don't know. Anyway, not to worry. I'm sure he'll be in touch very soon. He's very fond of you and will be most unhappy that he's caused you concern.'

They stared at each other for several seconds, Chasen's expression not altering.

'So, if there's nothing more . . .'

The tone of the remark suggested dismissal, so Gosia turned to the door. 'Thank you, Sir Ivor. I'm sorry to have troubled you at such a testing time.' Her words had a hard edge.

SEVEN

Guy Cooper stopped as he reached the doors of St Thomas's Anglican Church and looked back down the length of the aisle. For the first time in many months he felt alone. For weeks he'd had so many things to occupy his thoughts, so many details to attend to and so many people to support emotionally that he'd had little time to imagine the reality of a life without Coco – she'd always been there.

Only a matter of weeks ago she had lain in bed and held his hand, her whole body wasted by the ravages of multiple sclerosis. 'When all the details of my death have been attended to,' she had said, 'when everyone has cried on your shoulder, that's when you'll think of me – and that's going to be hard for you. But I want you to feel me there with you.' He'd held her as tightly as her wasted limbs would allow, and kissed her.

'Guy?' Cooper turned, snapped out of his reverie. The image of Coco had been so real he could almost have reached out and touched her.

'I'm sorry, I didn't mean to startle you.' It was Christian, Coco's sister. 'Do you want me to take the flowers, or would you like to deal with them yourself?'

Flowers? The funeral had been held ten days earlier. He hadn't expected any more flowers at the memorial service.

'What flowers? Where are they?'

'Some roses. Over there,' she pointed. 'There's an envelope attached. I haven't opened it.'

He put an arm round Christian. She was showing great strength. Over her shoulder he saw Andrew, her husband, waiting at the bottom of the steps by the car.

'I'll handle it, thanks Christian,' he said. 'You're going home now?'

She nodded.

'I'll pop in on my way back.'

She gave him a hug and walked down the steps towards her husband.

As he followed her out, Cooper picked up the cellophane-wrapped roses – all yellow apart from two red roses at the front. He knew at once. Marysia. Yellow for remembrance.

'You must buy me roses,' she'd said in Kraków. 'It's traditional. This one is for Sam.' And she'd plucked a single red rose from the bucket.

Memories of Poland flooded back. He sat down in the alcove, and opened the envelope pinned to the flowers. *In memory of Coco and Sam – may they now look after each other. Take care, tough guy. M.*

The emotions that had been building for months suddenly demanded release. Guy sat on the wooden seat, held his head in his hands and wept.

Late that night Guy sat on the verandah, looking out at Whale Beach, the sound of the crashing surf loud in his ears. It was past midnight. The full moon was so bright you could have read the *Sydney Morning Herald* by it.

He'd thought he had his emotions under control – that he'd adjusted and adequately prepared himself for Coco's death. Now he realised how wrong he'd been. The flowers from Marysia had been the catalyst that had sent him haywire.

He pictured her waving goodbye as she walked down the Pijarska wearing her man's crumpled burgundy raincoat. He'd helped Marysia through the grieving process when Sam had died. He wished he could talk to her now. She'd understand.

He recalled the shock of Sam's murder and the truth of his closest friend's past. Sam, a sleeper for the East Germans and keeper of the Stasi bankroll. And Marysia, the elfin innocent who'd joined him in their relentless struggle to bring Sam's murderers to justice, an agent for Mossad. Those terrifying days had changed him for ever.

He heard a possum making its clumsy way towards the plate of fruit on the corner of the verandah. A few years ago, it would have been a difficult operation. When Clamp, their Australian cattle dog–bull terrier cross, was alive, he'd lie in wait ready to surge forward and bark his head off. Now the verandah was a popular rendezvous for the possum population of Pittwater. As far as Guy was concerned, they'd earned the respite.

His mind drifted back to the year Sam was murdered in Palma. The Berlin Wall had still been standing and no one would have believed the entire political structure of Europe would be transformed in a few short months.

Where was she? Where was Marysia? Why did she send postcards yet never tell him where she was? The cards were always postmarked from Paris – of course that didn't necessarily mean she lived there. She'd always been on the run, always one step ahead of the bullet. Was he being too theatrical? He didn't think so. In '89 he'd returned to the humdrum world of films – she'd most probably gone back to a world of espionage and terrorism.

The possum finished the banana and toyed with the passionfruit, holding it with both small hands and dipping its nose into the purple seeds.

'It's all I got, kid. Sorry,' he said softly. Guy knew they preferred the soft fruit, but he hadn't had time to replenish stocks. How Coco had loved the possums. There was always a good feed to be had on the verandah, despite Clamp – she had made sure of it.

She'd entice Clamp into the kitchen with barbecued chicken; he'd bolt it down as quickly as possible, his strong jaws snapping, the bones cracking, before rushing back to take up his usual position by the window to watch his quarries feed.

Guy looked at his watch. A quarter to one. Tomorrow he was flying to Paris to persuade his old friend André Picheot to continue editing the script of a film he was now dreading beginning work on. Perhaps it was too close to Coco's death to be wheeling and dealing – he could practically read the articles in the magazines already. 'Frailty thy name is Cooper.' He didn't care. Coco would understand, and who else mattered?

The sound of the phone ringing broke the spell. He felt like ignoring it. Then he changed his mind – it could be a change of plan from either Paris or London.

EIGHT

Gosia had hardly slept and she felt filthy. Too many cigarettes and too much cheap South American red wine – she always resorted to them if she couldn't sleep. It was just after seven in the morning as she brushed her teeth, going over and over again the events of the previous two days. She knew she had to do something – the question was what? Her first reaction had been to call the police, but what on earth would she say – that she felt sure Edward had been kidnapped? His father would simply assure them that he was safe and well, staying with friends in Scotland. Who would accept her word over that of a prominent diplomat? Yet something was very seriously amiss. She could hardly approach her tutor – what could he do to help? Then the idea began to form. Guy Cooper. Her mother had talked about him so many times. 'The last of the good guys,' she was fond of saying. Gosia knew enough of the events of '89 to realise he'd be able to help. And she'd read in a recent article that after the long illness and death of his wife, he was coming to England to work for a few months. Her mother had always told Gosia that should she ever need assistance and couldn't reach her she should contact Guy Cooper. Well, now was the time. He'd probably think her insensitive to bother him so close to his wife's death, but Edward's safety was paramount. Perhaps he'd arrived already, and if so, where was he staying? She knew he was the silent trustee of the foundation that had granted her her scholarship, but a call to its headquarters in Poland at midnight wouldn't do much good.

She opened a drawer and riffled through a mass of papers till she found the envelope her mother had given her. There was a number in Sydney, and a note to call the ICM agency in Los Angeles if he wasn't contactable in Australia. Initially a call to Sydney seemed worth a shot. She paused, thinking about the time differences. It would be late at night in Sydney, but not too bad.

She emptied her satchel on the bed and sorted out the coins. Four pounds and eighty pence. Enough for a couple of quick international calls.

Grabbing her change she ducked out of her room, ran down the stone staircase to the pay phone, put in a pound and dialled. After two rings she heard the coins clunk, but her excitement dampened at the sound of a recorded message informing her he was unavailable. She pressed the follow on button, took a deep breath and dialled again. The phone was picked up almost immediately.

'ICM. Good afternoon.'

'May I speak to Guy Cooper's agent. I'm calling from London. It's an urgent matter.'

'May I tell him the party's name and the matter this concerns?'

'My name is Gosia Dobra and it's an urgent personal matter. I'm calling from England.'

'Thank you. Would you please hold.'

A full minute passed while Gosia put in the rest of the coins and eyed the digital read-out of her remaining money. She'd have to be quick.

'Sol Westerman. May I help you?'

'I only have one minute to tell you this. I desperately need to reach Mr Cooper. Can you contact him and tell him that a friend of Marysia Knoll needs to speak to him urgently. He can reach me in Oxford at –' she paused. 'Do you have a pencil?'

Westerman's voice smiled down the line at her. 'Sure, I have a pencil – any good agent worth his salt has a pencil.'

'Good,' she replied. 'The number is Oxford 2453765. If he could call between eight and nine tomorrow morning London time that'd be great. If he doesn't I'll call you back at ten. Please take this call seriously, it's a matter of life and death. Remember the name: Marysia.'

'I'll let Mr Cooper know you called.'

Gosia was about to thank him when she was interrupted by the pips. As she struggled with her coins the phone went dead. She replaced the receiver. She'd made a start. But maybe agents got a lot of crank calls from desperate people who sounded very much as she had done. She hoped not.

She stuffed her remaining coins in her pocket. She'd spend the day searching every street in Oxford. She'd ask everyone she could think of who might have seen Edward. There was little else she could do while she waited for Guy Cooper to return her call.

At fifteen minutes to eight the following morning Gosia stood by the telephone, shifting from foot to foot. She was, if anything, more tense than the day before. She'd walked the streets of Oxford till ten the previous night, but no one had seen Edward for days, nor could anyone provide a single logical reason for his sudden disappearance. It looked more and more as though her worst fears were going to be confirmed. Now she had to convince Guy Cooper to help her. But it was confronting enough to talk to a celebrated film actor she'd only seen on the covers of magazines, let alone to have to discuss the matters she had in mind.

As she checked her watch again, a Chinese student brushed past her and reached for the phone. Gosia sprang forward, wrenching the phone from his grasp.

'Please!' she shouted. 'I'm waiting for a call – it's very urgent. Do you mind? Please?'

As she replaced the receiver, she looked pleadingly at the young man. 'From the hospital,' she added, hoping she was convincing.

The young man smiled at her reassuringly. 'Don't worry. I'll wait till later,' he said sympathetically as he walked into the quad. 'Good luck!'

She breathed a sigh of relief. Just to be on the safe side, she lifted the receiver and placed her finger surreptitiously on the rest, nodding her head occasionally, as though in the middle of a conversation.

For the next twenty minutes she stood almost wrapped around the phone, chatting away into the mouthpiece each time she saw someone even hint that they were waiting to use it.

By half-past eight she was beginning to feel despondent. Perhaps the agent hadn't been able to reach Guy. Perhaps neither of them had taken her seriously. But she refused to budge from the phone till ten. Just then the phone rang. She snatched it up.

'This is Guy Cooper speaking. Is that Marysia's friend?'

'Yes it is,' she replied.

'I've just got in from a 24-hour flight from Sydney to receive a message from the States informing me I should call you about a matter of life and death.' He paused for some reaction. 'So here I am,' he coaxed after a few seconds.

'My mother . . .' Gosia broke off. This wasn't going to be easy. 'My mother grew up in Kraków with someone I believe you know very well – Marysia Knoll.' She paused. It was so silent the other end, she thought she'd been disconnected.

'Mr Cooper? Are you still there?'

'Yes, Gosia, I am still here. Forgive me but I haven't heard her name mentioned for some years. But you're right, I knew Marysia very well.' There was a beat, then he continued. 'So you are in some kind of trouble? Tell me how you think I can help.'

'I'll try to be as brief as possible. A friend of mine has disappeared. I am quite close to this friend, not in an emotional way, just platonic, you understand. Now, I have substantial reason to believe he is being held against his will so as to make sure that his father performs some task for those holding him.' She was about to continue when Guy butted in.

'Okay. Hold it right there. Forgive me interrupting, but let's get this absolutely clear. Are you saying that you think a friend of yours has been kidnapped and is being held as ransom and that his father is being blackmailed?'

'In so many words . . . yes,' she replied.

'Okay, if this is the case, have the police been approached, either by you or the father?'

'Please, Mr Cooper. Forgive me – but the reason I am putting things in my own way is because what I have to tell you is something I would prefer not to discuss over an open telephone line. I don't think I am being sensational when I say this. As I'm sure you are aware, eavesdropping on phone conversations has become a common fact of life. Also there is the question of the sensitivity of what I would like to tell you.'

'Sensitivity of what kind?' Guy asked.

'Political sensitivity,' she replied.

'I see.'

'However, I can tell you that as far as I know, the father in question has decided not to share this matter with the police or security services and that he is a prominent member of the public service – very prominent indeed, Mr Cooper.'

'Gosia, I'm sorry if I appeared patronising – I didn't mean to. Who else have you told about this?'

'No one. I didn't see how my tutor could help, and apart from him I had no idea who to turn to. That's why I called you.'

'What does your mother say about all this? She suggested you call me?'

'I've tried to reach her without success. She's in Kraków, and telephoning Poland's always painfully difficult. As this is so urgent, I felt I couldn't wait any longer.'

'I see,' Guy replied thoughtfully. 'I just don't see what help I personally could be.'

'You have contacts. My mother said that Marysia had told her once that if ever I needed a friend I could call you – for Marysia's sake. You owed her one – that's how she put it.'

The seconds ticked by until Guy finally spoke. 'Do you have enough money to get on the first plane to Paris?'

'Paris?' Gosia hadn't expected this. 'To be perfectly frank, no I haven't . . . but I'm sure I could borrow it. You think I should fly over to see you?'

'I think we have to have a more serious talk. And as you correctly say, it would best be done in private. It's just not possible over the phone, is it? However, I've flown in here today from Australia for a vital meeting that I just can't break. So what I suggest is this. You go to the British Airways ticket collection counter at Heathrow. Have you got enough cash to get to the airport?'

'Yes,' she lied. She'd borrow it.

'Good,' Guy replied. 'I'll arrange for a ticket to be waiting. Jump on the first plane. I'll be here at the Meurice Hotel all day. Call me from the airport and I'll collect you. How does that sound, Gosia?'

'Sounds perfect.'

'Your mother was right. I do owe Marysia that much.'

'I can't thank you enough, Mr Cooper. It's such a relief to know I have someone to help me – I really felt so alone.'

'Don't get your hopes up too high. I may not be such a great help. But we'll see.'

'Look, I'll get to London as soon as possible. I really am very worried about Edward. I think he could be in real danger.'

'Well, shift yourself into gear,' he said, adding as an afterthought, 'and just one other thing. When you get to Paris you'll call me Guy. Mr Cooper makes me feel old. Deal?'

'Deal,' she replied, smiling for the first time in days.

NINE

Chasen sat at his desk in a state of desolation, utterly unaware of his surroundings, his mind consumed with vivid images of his son – Edward as a baby, Edward taking his first steps, Edward splashing in his plastic swimming pool, Edward running towards him in the garden with a wildflower. Chasen felt as though his chest would explode, suffocated by a nightmare of guilt, self-doubt, indecision and despair. Edward, Edward, Edward. His son! His head spun with the appalling thought of a life without him – an empty wasteland.

He pounded his fist down on the desk, then froze as the sound resonated loudly through the house. Lily would be back from lunch any minute now. He had to pull himself together. His body tensed further, as he strained to listen for sounds in the empty house. Thank God – there was silence.

At all costs he had to remain calm. He had to retain some small semblance of composure or all was lost. He had to make the right decisions.

He opened his clenched fist slowly, the blood racing back into his fingers. Which was worse, he thought despairingly, the waiting, or the knowledge that his son's life rested in the balance – at the whim of that woman? He had no choice, for God's sake! He either did as he was told or let her destroy his family, his life.

He abruptly stood, unable to remain still for another second, and began to pace the study. The logic was clear as day. There should be no question of dealing with this woman. She was a criminal. One did not deal with criminals. He ground his teeth. Oh yes, the logic was clear – clear when it was an objective determination.

How easy it was to pass judgment on others! Send in the SAS – the special forces! He could always assess the mayhem later, with regret for those who'd died. That had been his life till now – one of detached judgments, made in the quiet of an embassy; decisions upon which rested the lives of thousands. 'It is the position of Her Majesty's Government . . .' 'We cannot allow the will of the criminal minority . . .' 'The policy of the United Kingdom is quite clear . . .' Sanctimonious humbug! Political refugees had been turned away, redirected back to their executioners; innocent hostages had died in hijacked planes; thousands had perished in 'ethnic cleansing' because he had made the politically correct decisions that had spelt disaster. Yet Her Majesty's position had been 'clear', and he had calmly made these decisions. They had been so easy. Life had always been a matter of cold logic. And it had all been for the best – his conscience had been clear. But now . . .

Oh, God Almighty, help me! he pleaded silently.

The ticking of the small ormolu clock on his desk sounded loud as a metronome in the silence of the room. He felt profoundly alone, with no one in the world to share his anguish and desperation. To tell Lily was out of the question; he doubted she could handle the crisis emotionally. He had never had a close male friend – he was utterly isolated on a private island of his own making. Ironically, his closest friend was Ambrose Leston, but involving the Service was out of the question – he knew how MI5 would react, and their priority would be the interests of Her Majesty's Government rather than Edward's safety. No, he could trust no one, a fact amply demonstrated by Bruton's cold, uncaring attitude. It wasn't even fanciful to think his supposed friend of ten or so years was implicated in some way with the blackmail, and this only reinforced his view that to tell anyone of the events of the past few days would merely put Edward at more risk than he already was. He wrapped his arms round himself in an attempt to stop the pounding in his chest, the torment in his head.

Edward. He had to safeguard Edward. There was no longer a question of doing otherwise. It was rank weakness – he knew it, but there was no alternative. Edward must live. Perhaps, as the woman had said, the stakes were not that terrible. He had to think optimistically. Was he grasping at straws? No, he was not! He would wait and see. A wave of hope now flooded through his brain. He would wait and see.

Edward lay in the shadows, a single blanket wrapped round his waist. He was cold, and still numb with fear. The tape over his mouth had made breathing increasingly difficult. Twenty feet or so in front of him, across the bare concrete floor, he could see his captor leaning against a steel girder reading a paperback by the light of a pencil torch.

The blinding pain in his head had diminished slightly, but he still felt constant waves of nausea. His only recollection of the abduction was regaining consciousness in the back of a van as it sped through the streets. He remembered the desperate mental struggle to avoid vomiting – he knew this might choke him to death. Then after what had seemed like a two-hour drive, he'd been led to the deserted building, dragged up the stairwell, and chained to a steel ring in the wall. He'd known he was in London when he'd looked through the unclad walls of the building and seen the Thames. Then he'd lost consciousness again.

It was only after he'd awoken the following morning and gazed at his surroundings that he'd realised with a sudden sharp lance of terror that he'd not been blindfolded. The significance was clear. The man didn't care if he could be identified – it would never come to that!

A gust of air blew through the open floor of the building and Edward shuddered involuntarily – it was the fear, not the chill. It had been four days now and the initial terror had turned to a constant dull pain of apprehension. Four days. Four days of the same relentless routine – shackled by his foot to the wall day and night, freed only to relieve himself on the bare concrete a few feet from where he lay. And each evening his captor would leave to bring back some fast-food, leaving him alone, hog-tied and gagged. Then they'd eat and the man would chat in a disquietingly removed way. He always talked about himself. Since these were the single few minutes the tape was removed from his mouth, Edward always did his best to draw the man out – to establish a relationship. Wasn't that the key to hostage situations?

Soon someone would come for him, that was a certainty. He knew his father's views on hostage situations. There would be no bargaining. Rescue was the single option. So now he'd have to ready himself for the inevitable, and this put his life on the line. Who'd be sent in? Special police? The SAS? He studied the burly man, the light of the pencil torch spilling onto his face as he turned a page. If they sent in a team, the odds were very much in their favour.

He was a hostage, that was fundamentally clear. His father was the target – that much was a safe bet. Could there have been some connection between the abduction and his father's strange behaviour the night of the storm, the last time he saw his father? Though a reasonably strict father, it was quite uncharacteristic of him to have spoken to Edward so rudely in front of

Gosia. He'd looked really badly shaken. At the time he'd accepted his father's explanation of the shock at the collision with the dog; now he was thinking along different lines. Yet if he'd had the slightest suspicion of impending violence, his father would have instantly taken steps to safeguard the family, so it didn't make sense.

And Gosia? Christ, what might she be thinking now? She'd know he would never have disappeared without a word. Would his father have shared the facts of the situation with her? Or would he have thought it best not to do so? Either way, she'd be frantic with worry.

He shifted his weight from his left side to his right to bring some feeling back into his left-hand side. Who were they? And what was their purpose? It didn't matter; he respected the moral strength of his father. He'd make sure the right team was sent in – he'd take care of his son.

Edward again shot a look at the figure opposite. He'd stopped reading and was studying him. Then the man shone the torch up into his eyes, winked, put down his paperback and snapped off the light.

TEN

Harry Costra sat in the back of the stretch metallic silver Cadillac Fleetwood as it sped down the Pacific Coast Highway, and stared at the ocean. He was tired. Tired of his job. Tired of the pressure. Tired of having to keep looking over his shoulder, keeping the young turks like Brooks at bay. At sixty-two he felt the pile he'd amassed was sufficient even for Christina, his second wife of half his age, and his two daughters, both of whom were now at Pepperdine University. They all enjoyed spending his money at a prodigious rate. How much could they get through, he wondered. Last year they'd dented his current account by close to two million, and that was just for what was, in their book, 'a few necessities'. Hell, what did it matter, Christina could have what she liked – she was the best thing that had ever happened to him. She was young, intelligent, a sexual athlete who enjoyed the training, and she never questioned his judgment. So what was the money? The money had always been a breeze.

He'd lived in the Malibu Colony for fifteen years and he liked it. It was sufficiently far from the dirt and grime of Los Angeles, and afforded him the peace and tranquillity he needed at the end of a day at the Wilshire office. Most evenings he'd walk down his private path to the beach with a glass of champagne, sit on his favourite rock and stare out to sea. He needed his own space to think.

He looked at his watch. It was twenty to seven. He'd be at Howard's at exactly seven. Howard Mamasian didn't like to be kept waiting and Costra was a precise man – it was the key to his success. Nothing was left to chance, each detail carefully considered and assessed so that the business ran ever smoothly. That was the way Harry liked it.

Howard and he had been a team for fifteen years. Mamasian was the man of ideas with the lateral vision, while Costra was the logistical brain who kept things functioning with the precision of a Swiss watch. And now there was Brooks, the third partner. In the unspoken company hierarchy Mamasian was the CEO, the man who made the final decisions – primarily because it had been his massive seed money that had started them off; Costra was the – marginally – junior partner; and Brooks came a distant third.

In the early years Mamasian and Costra had concentrated mostly on narcotics trafficking. Initially, business had been brisk and relatively trouble-free, but towards the end of the eighties the going had become tough. They were losing too many consignments. Couriers were being picked up with sickening frequency. Airport security was fast becoming a nightmare, the Coast Guard had beefed up their efficiency beyond measure and the governmental crack-down on drugs was a reality that was driving them to the wall. They had to broaden their field of vision. The question had been how?

It had been Mamasian's brainchild to target the international diplomatic corps for their particular purposes. The diplomatic bag was still inviolate – that was the key. The idea had appeared so obvious they'd been surprised no one had developed such a systematic worldwide organisation before. Financial incentives usually sufficed in third-world countries to bring a diplomat 'onside', and where it didn't, pressure in the form of blackmail or threats of a more physical nature usually paid dividends. Once in, the diplomat was theirs for life. It was soon to become their particular and unique courier network. What Federal Express was to the honest Joe, the worldwide team of corrupt diplomats was to Mamasian and Costra. The consignments entered the US on average every five weeks, mostly through Europe, sometimes directly from Asia, very occasionally from South America. The size and nature of the shipment was dependent on the nature of the goods and, in the case of narcotics, on supply from South America and Asia. Only very occasionally did the need arise to break in a new courier, and with the inconveniently early death of Adrian Bouvier a new man had been targetted to take over. Now was the time to closely monitor and assess the man before the green light was given.

The beauty of the system was that providing the goods were of a reasonable size and weight, they could be anything – a nuclear weapons component, a flask of plutonium, a sealed container of bacillus, narcotics, fine art – the options were limitless. But the success of their operations had meant that delegation of responsibility became inevitable and imperative. Costra had never liked it. He'd been a hands-on man since his twenties. Delegation invited betrayal, especially when the stakes were as high as they were in their business. Too many people had the means to sink their ship. Too many could point the finger. And now there was young Brooks – the man with the figures, the man with the computers. How life had changed. Maybe it was time to retire, to live off the fat of the land in Europe before someone put his head on the block.

Costra reached forward and turned the airconditioning control to cold – it was always unbearably hot at Howard's, even at this time of the morning, so he'd better freeze himself in advance.

The car made a left into Sunset. He'd be there in ten minutes.

Howard Mamasian pulled up the plastic trapdoor on the lid and lowered his hand slowly towards the mygalomorph. Sensing his presence, it tensed its body, lifting up its abdomen and vibrating the thick hairs on its bright orange hind legs. Mamasian made a soft cooing noise as his bony fingers made a slow circular motion round the baboon tarantula. Gently he lowered his head so his face was at the side of the plate-glass cage and he could look into the largest of its eight black eyes. He was less than an inch from the spider – their eyes now locked on each other. As the seconds passed, the tarantula appeared to relax as Mamasian's fingers continued to circle, his cooing increasing in volume. It lowered its abdomen and the legs stilled.

'You want to come play?' he called softly. The tarantula stared back at him through the glass.

Mamasian carefully opened the palm of his hand and lay the back of it on the sand in front of the spider's head. Then he gently encouraged it forward with a slow beckoning gesture with his middle finger. The two palps at the side of its head waved back and forth, then the arachnid slowly edged forward, lifting the front two pairs of legs and crawling onto Mamasian's hand.

Mamasian's face creased with pleasure as he gently lifted the tarantula from its glass prison. Though his bony fingers were long and spread wide, the spider's legs had a width that took its tarsal claws to the extremities of his palm. A seven-inch span would have been a rough estimate – it was a splendid creature and Mamasian's pride and joy.

He lifted the spider close to his face, allowing it to feel his thin lips with its palps. He loved the feeling, it gave his whole being a kind of frisson he found better than sex. Then he rested the giant mygalomorph on his shoulder and closed his eyes as it walked slowly behind his neck.

Costra's Cadillac turned left off Sunset and into Bellagio Road, slowing momentarily as it passed under the proscenium arch of the West Gate entrance, proclaiming 'Bel Air' in wrought iron above. An empty booth stood where guards had once attended to the security of the estate. Now the rich and famous took care of their own individual security needs.

A mile down the road the limo turned into Mamasian's cypress-tree-lined driveway, the black steel gates swinging open as they approached. As it halted in front of the house, the lean fit figure of Kaspar emerged from the massive oak front doors.

Security was something Mamasian had always considered a top priority. In his business it was both logical and prudent to have the best, and the best was Kaspar – a man of fierce intelligence and loyalty who could smell deceit across a room with the accuracy of a bloodhound. Ex-KGB and once a member of Brezhnev's security detail, Kaspar had seen the writing on the wall as Gorbachev rose to prominence, and decided to move to the United States.

Pete, Costra's chauffeur, opened the rear door of the Cadillac and Costra stepped out.

'Good morning, Mr Costra. Mr Mamasian is down by the pool in the glass-house. He's expecting you,' the tall Russian informed Costra.

Hell, thought Costra, it'd be stifling in that fucking insect house, even more so than in the library. Howard loved the heat, he thrived on it nearly as much as those damned insects of his.

'I'll tell him you're on your way down,' Kaspar said, as he reached for his mobile phone.

Harry Costra nodded absent-mindedly as he walked down the oleander-lined path that led to the pool. Perhaps he could get the meeting over within half an hour or so and be back home by half-past eight. He had a big day ahead. Both his daughters were visiting for lunch, and one of them was bringing a new boyfriend. He was supposedly a big wheel in the movies, but Harry doubted it – more often than not Athena's men were all show and no substance, trying to schmooze him out of cash for some project. It was no accident that this guy was taking out the plainer of his two daughters. He'd check him out thoroughly later.

He walked down the last flight of steps that led to the pool. The glass vivarium was to the right of the pool. Forty feet by thirty, it looked like a state of the art greenhouse, always reminding Costra of the Biosphere. The tall skinny frame of Mamasian was clearly visible through the glass front door. There was no way he was going into that madhouse, Costra thought with distaste, as he tapped on the pane. Mamasian looked round, smiling, and beckoned him inside. Shit, he'd have to go in.

The humidity hit him like the backdraft of a jetliner as he opened the door. Inside, the vivarium had two central aisles and two trancepts. Running the length of the house were three levels of glass cages. These were home to the three major sub-orders of spiders: the Mesothelae on the top, the Orthognatha on the bottom and the Labidognatha sandwiched in between. Glass cages also ran laterally, housing snakes and scorpions. Hanging from the domed roof every ten feet were lights and heating units that controlled conditions.

'Good to see you, Harry. Isn't she something else?' Mamasian whispered, as he gestured with his eyes to the baboon tarantula inching its way round his shoulder blades.

'Now, you know how I feel about your spiders, Howard,' Costra said without malice. 'They're ugly as sin.'

Mamasian studied Costra briefly as he closed the door. A short man with a big gut, Harry Costra stood just over five feet. His face was undeniably plain, as though some major plastic surgery had only been marginally successful. His eyes were round and small, his nose splayed very wide and his lips fat, bulbous and forever wet. He was also a terminal sweater. The beautiful tarantula ugly? It was a startling case of the pot calling the kettle black, but Mamasian let it pass – when it came to strategy, Costra had few equals. He seemed to have an instinct for when people would jump, long before the idea ever entered their heads.

Mamasian reached round with his right hand and lifted the fat spider from his shoulder. It shook its hind legs, briefly startled, then curled up slightly as he opened the trapdoor of its cage and placed it inside.

'We have a great deal to learn from spiders, Harry. Their defence strategies are wondrous.'

Costra feigned a modicum of interest – he knew how much they fascinated Mamasian. 'Yeah?' he replied, relieved that the hairy creature was back behind glass, out of harm's way.

Mamasian studied the tarantula through the glass. 'Takes a lot to make this one mad. She's really very placid. But take a look at those legs. See the hairs? If you startle her she vibrates them so fast she can send a cloud of tiny hairs shooting at you, each with a minute little barb. They can penetrate to a couple of millimetres into human skin and they sting like hell. Gives them time to get away if they feel like it.'

'Give me a gun any day,' Costra observed flatly, unimpressed.

'Not much good against one of these mothers, though.'

'Don't find I'm often attacked by bugs, Howard,' Costra replied, running a finger round the inside neck of his shirt.

'It's a fact that there can be up to two million spiders in an undisturbed acre of grassland, Harry. Think of that when you enjoy your next picnic.' Mamasian chuckled as he watched Costra's reaction.

'Never know how you can think when it's so darned hot.' Costra found it hard to stomach heat in excess of sixty-five degrees and each visit to Mamasian's home caused him angst. This greenhouse was a nightmare.

'You find it hot – I call it luscious,' Mamasian replied softly.

Christ, Costra thought, it's so fuckin' hot I may just burst into flames!

'You want to hear about Chasen, Howard? How about we step outside?'

'Sure, Harry. First, have a look at my new arrival. She's quite spectacular.'

'As long as you're not going to take it out and play with the sonofabitch, eh?' Costra joked.

'Oh no. Not this one. Definitely not. We've hardly had time to get aquainted. She'll take some time,' Mamasian murmured as he moved down a few feet and lifted a small glass cage to show to Costra.

'*Atrax robustus*. Arrived from Sydney last week. The funnel-web. A female. As you'd expect, the females are the most beautiful, and naturally the most deadly.'

Costra peered through the thick glass. All he could see were a few twigs and some torn scraps of paper and sand.

'Under the wood. Just there,' Mamasian said, pointing to the side of the glass.

He tapped sharply on the cage and there was an immediate flurry of movement as the jet black spider ran in the direction of the noise. It reared on its hind legs, baring its chelicerae, the twin jaws from which hung a glistening liquid.

'That's the poison hanging from the tip,' Mamasian observed with fascination. 'The female *Atrax robustus* are the most aggressive of all the mygalomorphs. They'll actually run after you if disturbed. A bite from her and you could well be history. Severe pain, numbness, nausea, vomiting, blockage of the lungs, breathing difficulties, frothing at the mouth, then coma. Without the antivenene – end of story.' He looked adoringly through the glass. 'Black as night,' he murmured to himself as he replaced the cage.

'Let's have a drink, Harry,' said Mamasian, finally opening the door of the glass-house. They both stepped out, Mamasian carefully closing the door behind him.

Costra loosened his tie and unbuttoned the top of his shirt as he walked over to the cabana. His shirt was so wet it clung to his sides and stomach like a limpet.

Mamasian stood behind the wet bar and pulled two champagne flutes from the shelf.

'Champagne, Harry?' Mamasian knew Costra's taste – vintage Krug.

'Sure,' Costra replied, relieved to be out of the furnace.

'So how are things progressing? Is our friend buttoned down?'

'I'd say it's all going pretty nicely. He's at a stage where he could jump either way – they're always a bit unpredictable early on while they have their private struggles with their consciences. Doesn't usually last too long when they realise how little our alliance will affect their lives. They soon hardly even know we're there.' He gulped down the ice-cold Krug and poured another, pulling his shirt away from his hairy body.

'That's what Heinrich told me in Bonn last week. Now he's a happy man. His personal struggle lasted about three and a half minutes, I'd say.'

Costra chuckled noisily.

'Let's hope he doesn't jump the wrong way.'

'I doubt that will be the case, Howard. He's got too much to lose.'

'So have we, Harry.'

'Painfully aware of that fact, Howard. I won't put anything at risk until we know he's onside – one hundred per cent. That's why we've worked so hard at the preparation this time, and why we'll hold off with the next stage until we're certain.'

'Was his initial reaction promising?'

Costra toyed with his champagne, lifting the cotton shirt from his fat torso, allowing the beginnings of a cool breeze to circulate round his hairy back.

'Not as much as we could have wished for, no,' he admitted, careful that his tone should not hint at alarm.

'What's that supposed to mean?' Mamasian snapped, sensing Costra's reticence. 'Come on, Harry, you can speak plainly with me. Don't pussyfoot. I've got to know now.'

'What I mean is that initially he was antagonistic. It was bluster, of course – he knew we had him by the balls. Then he folded. It was his son that was the clincher. Garcia said he looked a mess by the time the woman had spelt it out to him.'

Mamasian nodded slowly, making a humming sound as he mulled this over.

'What's your man's assessment, as of now?'

'He's happy. At least for now. He says we'll soon know if he's going to jump the other way. So I've told him we're still on green.'

Mamasian looked out towards the Bel Air Country Club golf course. After a few seconds' silence he spoke again.

'Let's not wait around for a man in his condition to come to any nasty decisions that might upset us. Ask your man to send in someone to firm up his bowels – might be a trifle watery at present. Any feedback when they go in – we're out. Then we'll have to think again.'

'Good as done,' Costra said as he drained his glass.

'Anything else I need to know?'

'Not a thing. Brooks has the detailed figures ready in Wilshire, but that can wait.'

'Then I expect you'd like to get back home. How's the lovely Christina?'

'Lovely as ever.'

'I'm sure she is,' Mamasian grinned and Costra laughed.

ELEVEN

Garcia exited Earls Court Station and paused at the traffic lights. Across the road he caught sight of Luiza leaving a small tobacconist's shop. She was dressed in a baggy jogging suit that did the exact opposite of enhancing her figure, her hair was roughly dragged back, her face untouched by make-up and her eyes masked by cheap sunglasses. Glamorous she wasn't.

Garcia caught her eye, but her face registered nothing. She walked on, turning right into Hogarth Road. Outside their apartment they were strangers.

The lights changed and Garcia crossed busy Earls Court Road, the air thick with the scent of curries and Thai spices. It was a great place to get lost among the crowds of tourists, drifters, grifters, backpackers and criminals who used the place as their jumping-off point when arriving in the UK. Fifteen or so years ago the Pakistanis had moved in in a big way and now controlled the cheap air travel business – 'bucket shops' as they were known. This was another positive advantage to Earls Court as far as Garcia was concerned. He could walk into almost any upstairs travel agency and come out with a ticket to wherever he wanted, without ever having to show his passport. What did they care? It was his problem if push came to shove at the check-in. And providing he chose a third-world airline, dressed well, and bought a first-class ticket, it seldom did.

It began to spot with rain as he turned into Knaresborough Court. He didn't care, his plans were panning out well. The Chasen kid was secure with Van Rouen. Luiza had performed with characteristic professionalism. They'd be out and away in three days.

His mind filled with images of Luiza's strong olive thighs braced either side of his midriff, riding him to orgasm the night before, and he quickened his pace.

Luiza. She'd been part of the team many times – maybe this time would have to be the last. He'd committed the cardinal sin of sleeping with the staff – he'd never done that before. He'd wanted to many times with a multitude of women he'd worked with, but he was a thorough professional and it just wasn't the way to go about things. But with Luiza it had been an entirely different matter. He'd used her in Germany. They'd both been aware of the chemistry but had pretended it hadn't existed. Then in Barcelona it had become more difficult. He'd known he had to fuck her – simple as that. Given the opportunity, who wouldn't? So he had. Now it was fast turning into an addiction, and she knew it.

As he turned the corner he saw her up ahead in the doorway of the apartment block, searching in her bag for the door key. A second later she was inside.

She was a habit he'd find difficult to break. Maybe even more so than heroin. But he'd gone cold turkey after a bad five-year smack habit as a kid, so anything was possible. As he reached the doorway he pulled out his own key.

He entered the building, walked past the elevator and made for the stairs – elevators were cages where people died. He thought back to a killing he'd done in Rio years ago. He'd still been a kid, doing the wet work for someone else. He'd been shown a photo of his target and given a zip-gun. A very crude weapon, it was fortunately designed to carry a large calibre dumdum bullet so the inaccuracy was amply made up for by the devastation it caused on contact. He'd done his home-work, deciding to kill the target in the elevator of his luxury apartment block. He still remembered the look of surprise on the crime boss's face as he'd aimed the barrel through the bars of the elevator, pausing momentarily – curious to see how the man would react knowing he was just seconds from certain death – before blowing the top of the man's head off.

He missed the actual killings now. There was little adrenalin in ordering someone else to kill.

As he slid the key into the lock he could just make out the soft lilt of Luiz Bonfa's samba music. Jesus, how he hated that bossa nova shit! Whatever taste she had in other things, music wasn't one of them. He opened the door and stepped inside.

She was standing three feet in front of him, stark naked, her legs apart, gently shaking her long arms by her side, as if relaxing them after a work-out session. Her flesh gleamed as she stood rolling her head slowly round on her neck, her eyes fixed steadily on his.

As he reached her she raised her hands to his face, outlining his features gently with her fingers, gliding the tips over the skin of his cheeks, his nose, his eyelids, and finally pushing her index finger between his lips, running it over the tip of his tongue. It felt like a succession of small electric shocks. As she did so, she lazily lifted her right leg like a ballet dancer and coiled it round his waist, pressing her sex hard against his growing erection.

Garcia felt the heat of her belly as she pushed him back against the door for several seconds. She was on fire. She drew back and her quick hands grasped at his belt. In a matter of seconds, his boxer shorts were at his ankles and her naked loins were against his.

Grasping the hair at the back of her head with both hands, he pulled away the combs that held it in place. Suddenly there was soft black hair everywhere. God, how he loved the smell of it. Running his hands over the deliciously warm contours of her firm buttocks, he lifted her onto him. She was like a warm bath.

She held either side of Garcia's head with her hands as he thrust into her. She liked to watch him as he quickened the pace until he finally climaxed. The thrill was knowing he was losing control while she was gaining it. For that moment in time he was hers – entirely, every shred of him.

He threw his head back and shouted loudly as he accelerated the back and forward momentum of his hips. She locked her ankles together behind his back, deftly manipulating her inner muscles to give him the greatest pleasure as their bellies pounded together.

With a great cry of exultation it was all over. Garcia held her firmly with both his strong hands as he gasped for air. Their bodies were awash with sweat, her black hair clinging to the muscles of his shoulders.

Luiza draped her arms round his neck, happy to stay suspended where she was, with his hardness still embedded deep within her. Sometimes they'd stay locked together for fifteen minutes while the blood drained from his penis. She liked that – that he was still with her mentally afterwards, and she with him. It had never been like that with other men.

'Is Mr Mamasian quite happy,' she asked in the softest of whispers, her head resting on his shoulder.

'Quite happy,' he replied. Then the nagging concern he'd had all morning returned and he cursed himself silently. He should never have got so involved with her. Stupid. He'd broken too many rules – not only sleeping with her, but also letting slip the name of his employer. It was a fundamental rule that the only direct link between the employer and the action should be himself. That was why people used him and that was why he had become known as the man who could deliver with no fear of blow-backs. If a job went bad and anyone was picked up, it never reached further than Garcia – that was the deal. If it did, then they knew where to direct retribution.

His mouth felt suddenly dry. He shuffled through to the kitchen, Luiza riding up and down on his erection, which was beginning to harden again.

'Fix us a drink, *Corazon*,' he said. It was a facetious nickname he'd given her on their first job together – she was pitiless in her work.

She reached behind his head, picking a bottle of tequila and two shot glasses from a shelf. Then Garcia walked the two of them back through the hall and into the small bedroom where he sat on the edge of the bed. She continued to grip him firmly round the waist with her long legs, the ankles still locked together, holding his erection strongly with her muscles. It wasn't going to escape yet – not till she'd finished. Now it was her turn and this could take some time.

As she poured the tequila, Garcia lay back on the bed and took a deep breath.

'That was good. Hell, that was good.' His eyes closed, he gently stroked her luxuriant jet black pubic hair with the fingers of his right hand as he accepted the drink she offered with the other.

'It always is,' she replied and, noticing his distraction, added, 'Don't worry, he's ours. I can guarantee Chasen won't fuck us around.'

Garcia lay back naked on the sofa, the shower sounding like Niagara in the adjacent bathroom. He thought of Van Rouen. The South African could be one mean bastard if left to his own devices, but in this instance he'd decided to give the big man some reign. There didn't seem much point in dividing his time between the kid and the pick-up – there were the fine logistics of the transfer to think about.

He reached across the floor and pulled his jacket towards him, taking the Apple Newton from the inside pocket and turning it over in the palm of one hand. He punched a few keys and the five-inch screen shone brightly. Another key and a row of computerised ascii figures appeared. He walked over to the phone and flipped open the A–Z directory to where a sheet of foolscap lay, then picked up his cellular phone, glanced at the Newton and punched in some numbers. The ascii figures gave way to telephone numbers. He then dialled, bringing the phone up to his face. The smell of her sex was still strong on his fingers. He inhaled deeply as he waited. A few seconds later a voice came on the line.

'Yes?'

'It's me.'

'Any problems?'

'None. Are we still on green?'

'Still green. But now we need to confirm compliance. Send in the woman. Call tomorrow.'

The line went dead. Garcia flipped the phone shut and returned to his drink looking thoughtful. The shower was still thundering like a torrent in the bathroom. Why did they want Luiza to confirm compliance? Had something gone wrong? Was there something they were not sharing with him? He frowned. He'd always had misgivings about Chasen. It was the first time they'd marked a man of his calibre. They'd generally used junior ministers or a *chargé d'affaires* in the past, but their immunity from airport searches was no longer guaranteed. He'd always felt that with a man of Chasen's prominence, personal blackmail might be insufficient. For the very first time, he'd questioned their judgment. That was why he'd recommended the snatching of the son, and they'd given him the go-ahead. It made sense. Insurance in this case was a must. Initially his paymasters had appeared assured of Chasen's compliance. But now they wanted confirmation. Why the change of heart? As far as he was concerned, everything was going ahead smoothly. They had the kid, Luiza seemed confident – now it was the bosses who were getting edgy. 'Send in the woman,' Costra had said. This needed careful thought.

He returned to the sofa, slipping the computer back into his jacket which lay by his feet. There was only one reason. They figured that if Chasen had decided to call for help, the police would arrest her when she made contact and go from there. Either that or put a tail on her.

The waterfall in the bathroom abruptly ceased and a few seconds later Luiza walked through into the living room wrapped in a long white towel, her wet black hair clinging to her shoulders.

'Change of plan. You go in again.'

She looked casual and unfazed. 'Why?'

'They need confirmation of compliance. You're it.'

'When?'

'Get dressed.'

She sat on the edge of the sofa, running her fingers through her hair, then shaking it languidly. 'It's to see if he's still ours, isn't it?'

'I'm afraid so,' he answered.

'I'm the sacrificial lamb,' she said bluntly.

She had balls, this girl – there was no doubting it. 'They've got nothing on you if they take you now. Just his word, no proof. Nothing they can hold you for.'

'And if they do take me in?'

'The usual. It's off. We quit. You'll be paid in the normal way, but you're on your own.'

She began to hum Desafinado softly, opened her eyes and mouth wide in a silent scream, then said casually, 'He's ours, I guarantee it.'

'Get dressed and do it now. I'll call Van Rouen and tell him to stand by to leave if you make the wrong contact.'

As she disappeared Garcia picked up the phone again and dialled Van Rouen. She was confident, and she was one of the best, but it was as well to make contingency plans. If it all fell down, they'd be out of the country in two hours. Luiza would have to look after herself. She knew that – it was part of the deal.

TWELVE

As the plane began its approach to Charles de Gaulle Airport, Gosia tried to envisage what Cooper might look like in person. How old was he now? Just over fifty, she judged.

She saw him immediately she passed through the customs hall. He was unmistakable. The craggy, attractive lean features, the trademark rebellious dark hair she'd seen in magazines, now touched with quite a few silver streaks above the ears. The denim eyes. He actually looked better than he did in the movies – more relaxed, more real.

She was about twenty feet from him, when his face creased with the broadest of smiles. 'You must be Gosia!' he called as they approached each other. 'I'm an expert on Polish women, especially the beautiful ones.'

He shook her hand, taking her small holdall from her. 'This it?'

'That's it.'

'A woman who travels light – a rare commodity. Okay, let's get out of here. I hate airports.'

He led the way through the sliding doors on the ground floor of the building, then turned left towards the carpark.

'You can start to fill me in on some of the basics on our way into Paris. You've been to Paris before?' It was a rhetorical question.

'Never.'

'Never! Pity this isn't the best time for your introduction to the most beautiful and romantic capital city in the world. I take it you speak French – you're studying languages?'

'Far Eastern. Japanese, Mandarin and Cantonese. But I do speak French, and German. It's costing your foundation a lot of money so I'd better be good.' Her eyes seemed to sparkle.

That twinkle in the eye – it reminded Guy of Marysia.

'This is it.' Guy stopped and indicated an old Peugeot, a parking fine stuck under the wiper. It had definitely seen better days.

'This is it?'

'Something wrong with it?' he asked with amusement as he held open the door.

'Not at all,' she replied quickly. Subconsciously she'd expected a fancier car.

'Sorry if I've disappointed you, Gosia. I happen to like old cars. Jump in!'

As they drove through the rather bleak and barren outskirts of Paris, Gosia told Guy what had transpired the night she'd come searching for Edward. She told him of the woman with no eyes she'd seen leaving Chasen's study, describing her as best she could. She went over the conversation she'd overheard, the one she'd had with Sir Ivor, and what he'd told her. Guy listened closely to both her tone and what she was saying – he could see she was deeply worried.

'What convinces you he hasn't already put the whole thing in the hands of the Special Protection Squad?'

'I don't know for a fact that he hasn't. But he lied to me. Firstly he told me that the woman didn't exist. Then he told me she did, but that it was a "personal matter". Then he told me that Edward was in Scotland.'

'But he may very well have thought at the time that it was better to keep you out of it. Remember, if you read the situation correctly, he'd have been in a state of emotional turmoil. How would you have reacted? Think of that.' Guy gave her a quick glance.

'I appreciate that. But I effectively told him I'd overheard the whole thing – that I was a witness. If he was going to inform the police, surely he'd have wanted me to corroborate his story. Also remember that I saw the woman too, and could identify her.'

'Did she see you?'

'No. I'm pretty certain of that. There was a noise, and she came out of the study – she looked as though she was checking the hall – but I was well hidden, and she went back to the study soon after that.'

Guy thought for a while. All of what she said made sense. Yet it was still possible that Chasen had been confused – thoroughly shaken by what the woman had said and wanting to get rid of Gosia so he could think clearly and plan his course of action.

'Look at it another way,' Gosia continued. 'If he'd telephoned the police immediately after I left, wouldn't he have told them as a matter of course that I'd been there?'

'You'd think so, yes,' Guy replied.

'Well, why didn't they contact me that night? Or even early the next morning?'

'It's possible they agreed with Chasen that you were best kept out of the whole thing. He'd be treated with a great degree of respect and you would only have been able to corroborate his account. If he told them he'd been threatened, and that his son had been kidnapped, he'd hardly need anyone to back up his story, would he? They'd take it as read that the facts were as he stated.'

'True . . . I just *know* he hasn't told them anything. Sorry, but that's my feeling. You only had to see the state he was in that night. He'd been drinking, he was sweating, he was a complete emotional mess.'

'As would anyone be who'd been told his son's life was at risk. It's not all that surprising.'

'Okay, point taken, but let's get back to the basics. Point one. From what I heard in Chasen's study, it's clear that Edward has been threatened. The woman mentioned his name – and in the same breath as "retribution", "terrible" and finally "you will do this thing". You don't need to be Einstein to consider the possibility she was telling him she was holding his son as hostage. Then I come in and refer to his visitor, and he denies he's had one. In my book that indicates that at that stage he was leaning towards the idea of going along with them, rather than telling the police or whoever. Then he changes his tune and we get to point two – Chasen lies when he tells me Edward's in Scotland.'

'Do you know that for a fact – that he's not there?'

'He'd never leave Oxford for Scotland without telling me. He'd certainly not just cut the concert and leave us all in the lurch without at least contacting us.' She looked at Guy in silence, then began drumming her fingers on the dash of the car. 'Look, he's got his finals in a few weeks. Do you really think he'd swan off to Scotland?'

'Maybe he needed the time to himself. Peace and quiet. Could be he wanted to work for a few days in isolation.'

'Absolutely not. Edward doesn't work that way. Never has. He works with cans on. Listens to Schoenberg as he translates Plato. And another thing, he'd never miss a tutorial, he's a real spod.'

'I beg your pardon?'

'Spod. You know, hard worker. Anyway, as I said, Edward would never have just left without telling me – I'm his closest friend at Oxford. Absolutely not – no way. Chasen was lying. He's told no one!'

'And you're quite sure that Edward hasn't "swanned off" to make a point – you know, a personal one between you two?'

'Absolutely not. There was never anything like that between us – we were just really close friends. How can I make you believe me?'

'Okay, relax. I believe you, but I had to be sure.'

He thought for another moment. 'Why not telephone their place in Scotland – see if he's there?'

'No phone. It's a shooting lodge – he mentioned it once. I don't even have the first idea where it is!'

'When does Chasen leave to take up his post in New York?'

'Not sure. Soon. I think Edward said it was a matter of days. The worst part is they probably have Edward locked up somewhere.'

Guy could see how worked up she was. Somehow he'd have to calm her down.

'Steady, Gosia, you've got to relax and think clearly. It's still possible that Edward is away somewhere – but safe.' He held up a hand – Gosia was already opening her mouth to argue. 'Hold it! I know you don't think so, that goes without saying, but it's a possibility.' He could see she was about to interrupt again, so he ran on swiftly.

'Now, it seems clear to me that something has to be done – the question is what. We have to decide what will have the maximum effect. Also we always have to bear in mind that Chasen may very well be what they call in the courtroom a "hostile witness". As far as Edward's safety is concerned I'd be pretty certain that he won't be harmed. What we need to ask ourselves is why his father is being blackmailed.'

'But who's doing this? Who are they?' she interjected as Guy paused, his attention diverted to a student on a bicycle who'd crossed dangerously in front of them, a tiny grey vervet monkey anchored to the handlebars. 'I just can't work it out. You know, there was a moment on Monday when I told myself that perhaps I shouldn't butt in – that it was up to his father to decide whether it was too dangerous for Edward not to take their threats seriously. But then I asked myself this question. Suppose they were terrorists? What if they were some kind of fundamentalist religious group or the IRA, and they wanted access to some UN building to explode a bomb? What if they wanted Chasen to lobby for them at Security Council meetings, or even carry parts of a sophisticated nuclear device into New York via the diplomatic bag? Whether or not Chasen might wish to deal with them would be irrelevant. It would be my duty to do something.'

'Well, your imagination has run the full gamut of possibilities,' Guy said, trying to introduce a little humour to calm her down. 'All we have to do now is find out what they want from Chasen, who they are, and where they're hiding Edward. Shouldn't be too hard.'

'I'm sorry if I seem so serious – I'm just so worried. Imagine what Edward must be going through right this second. He might have been injured in the struggle and is lying bound and gagged in some basement, bleeding!'

'Hey, hold on! I know you're worried – I can see that. But you've got to retain a sense of humour somewhere or you're lost, take it from me. Now, can I ask you for the very last time whether you are absolutely certain of all your facts. Are you certain of what you heard and prepared to stand by it if I take this further up the line?'

'I am.'

'Good,' Guy said with a tone of finality. He'd made up his mind on a course of action. 'We're almost there. Dead ahead is the Louvre. The Tuileries gardens are further down. The Meurice is right here.'

The doorman walked forward as the Peugeot stopped.

'Come on in. I think it's one of the loveliest hotels anywhere. But firstly let's decide on a few things. I'm going to cancel a few meetings so I can get to London tomorrow. From what you've told me, I think it's vital I get onto this right away.'

'That's terrific,' said Gosia, brightening. 'Sorry to screw up your work, though.'

'Look, I had to be in London in three days anyway. Just a bit of rearranging. You presumably have to get back to Oxford.'

'As soon as possible.'

'Right, you can fly with me tomorrow first thing, if that's soon enough for you. I'll book you in for the night, make a few calls. There's not much we can do until those calls have borne fruit, so this afternoon we take a break from solving the problems of the world and I take you on my favourite walk. How does that sound to you?'

'Not sure I'll be a very jolly companion the way I feel at the moment.'

'Well, you'll just have to trust me and do your best – worrying won't get us where we want to go any quicker. Deal?'

'Deal,' she replied.

Twenty minutes later they were back in the old Peugeot, speeding down the Quai des Tuileries towards Notre Dame.

As they passed over the Pont au Change connecting the Ile de la Cité to the Boulevard de Sébastapol, Guy fished some wraparound sunglasses from the dash of the car and took a right turn into the entrance to the Conciergérie Palais de Justice. A gendarme held up his arm. Guy leant his head out of the window, at the same time pulling a plastic card from his top pocket. The policeman took the card, smiled, then handed it back to Guy, saluting as he did so. 'Merci, Monsieur Lefèvre.'

As the barrier was raised and the old Peugeot moved through, Guy sneaked a conspiratorial look at Gosia. 'Lefèvre's a friend of mine, a judge. He lets me park here.'

Guy locked the car and lead the way along the Quai de la Corse.

'I always start here and then walk along the footpath so I can see Notre Dame across the water. Then when I get to the end of the Ile St Louis I cross over the Pont de Sully and mooch around the little back alleys and laneways. We used to do it every time we were in Paris – Coco and I. Then we'd go to Le Montebello on the quai and eat air-cured beef and pickles.'

Guy reached down the jar for a particular pickle. 'Have I met your mother?'

'I don't believe so. She and Marysia were very close as children. When Marysia left for Israel they lost touch for a long time. But she came back and visited us quite a lot from about '83. The last time we saw her was in '90. She told us what a wonderful man you were, how you'd saved her life. When I told her I wanted to study languages at the Jagiellonian University in Kraków she suggested to my mother that I apply for a Webber Scholarship.'

Guy was silent, thoughtful, sad.

'When did you last see her?' Gosia asked softly, sensing his mood.

'I haven't seen her since she waved goodbye and walked down the Pijarska in Kraków in May '89.'

A waiter refilled their glasses but Guy didn't seem to notice. Gosia waited patiently for him to continue.

'I didn't know where I could reach her so I had to

wait for her to contact me. I thought she'd write and let me know where she was.'

'She never wrote?'

'Yes, she wrote. She sent me postcards every couple of months or so. Always from Paris. I thought she'd decided to live here. But she never wrote her address so I couldn't reply. I think she meant it to be that way. I was married to Coco and very much in love with her – I was to the day she died. But the moment Marysia disappeared that day round the corner of the Church of the Transfiguration in Kraków, I knew I could have fallen deeply in love with her if things had been different. I'd never considered the possibility before of feeling love for two women at the same time. I missed her terribly when she left.'

A small bird landed on thc table next to them, disturbing Guy's concentration. He smiled across at Gosia, suddenly embarrassed that he'd been sharing such intimate details of his life with her.

'I'm sorry. I'm boring you with all this nostalgia.'

'Not at all,' Gosia replied.

'Did she ever marry – Marysia?'

'Not as far as I know.'

'Do you have an address for her?'

'No, but I can try and get it if you like.'

'I would like. I would like very much.' Guy signalled a waiter and his tone became lighter. 'Enough of the past. Here we are in Paris, the sun's out, the roses are in bloom and it's your first time here. Take your mind off things for a few hours – until the phonecalls I've made pay off.'

She smiled. 'I'll do what I can.'

'Can't say fairer than that,' he replied, paying the bill.

'Just one thing. Do you think we should take this matter directly to the police right now?'

'I've thought about it, Gosia, and the more I do the more I think not. Point is, if Chasen hasn't told them anything they would be more inclined to believe his version of events than yours. So you'd end up stirring everyone up, including the woman you saw and her friends, without having achieved anything.'

'Whatever you think. You're the master spy, Mr Bond.'

'You'd better believe it, blue eyes,' he said, laughing.

She turned her head towards Notre Dame and her brow furrowed slightly. She was making a brave fist of things but obviously she couldn't shake her worry for Edward.

'Let's get back to the Meurice and see if any of my calls came good.'

'Yes, let's,' she said, quickly rising from the chair. Her air-cured beef lay untouched.

Gosia sat on the enormous sofa in Guy's suite and looked through the double doors to where Guy sat by the bed, the phone in one hand, a writing pad in the other. He was listening intently while making notes with a silver pen. She was too far away to be able to make out the conversation – it was just a gentle burble. A few moments later Guy put down the receiver and walked through into the living room.

'I've made contact with a couple of useful people. Now I've got to follow up. An old pal of mine in London will do a spot of digging and we can share notes tomorrow. Meantime, I've got to get myself over to Ireland.'

'Ireland? Aren't we travelling together tomorrow?' Gosia looked crestfallen.

'Of course. We'll fly to London. You go on to Oxford – keep looking for Edward. I fly to Dublin. I've made an appointment with an old adversary of Marysia's. He's retired now, so he's no longer based in London. However, if there's one man who can help us, it's him and he seems anxious to do me a good turn.'

Gosia was about to probe when Guy held up a hand. 'It's a long story and I won't bore you with it now but he owes me one. Providing he hasn't become completely senile he'll be able to point us in the right direction. Now, I have my meeting to go to. Script stuff. I'd ask you along but it's not going to be much fun. While I'm away I want you to try to relax. Remember, there's nothing you can do right now and worrying won't help. If I help you, you have to agree not to worry unnecessarily.'

'Okay,' Gosia replied glumly.

Guy stood up to go. 'See you in a couple of hours. Then if we haven't had any more encouraging calls we can both worry ourselves to death together – preferably at *Roger la Grenouille,* they serve the best *canard à l'orange* in town.'

He kissed her on the forehead then walked back into the bedroom, closing the double doors behind him.

THIRTEEN

Chasen sat at the head of the table, Lily to his left. She'd prepared an early supper. It concerned her that her husband looked so very tired, and she'd decided to do her best to get him to bed early, away from all the paperwork.

It had rained all morning, haunting Chasen with nightmare images of his first encounter with the woman on the Cuxham Road. He was glad to be back in London.

They ate in silence, the atmosphere thick with the unspoken. Chasen ate sparingly, forking the cold salmon round his plate, occasionally lifting a small morsel to his lips to please his wife. The silence between them was becoming unbearable.

'I don't care what you say,' Lily said softly, 'I think it's very thoughtless of Edward to take off like that. Not a word to either of us. And when are we likely to see him again? When we're in New York after his finals? That's weeks away.'

Chasen attempted a reassuring smile at his beautiful wife. He would have done anything for her. She and Edward were his life. But there was no way in the world he could tell her the truth about what was happening. No way in the world. It would kill her. He'd shoulder the burden, the responsibility for making the correct choices. Somehow he had to continue presenting this mask of calmness.

'It was a bit thoughtless, I agree. But he needs the time to himself. Sounds as if everything was beginning to get on top of him and he needed the peace and quiet.'

'Can't we get the Dillons to pop over and ask him to give us a call? At least I could say goodbye. What if he doesn't phone us from the village before we leave?'

She looked down at her plate, then put down her knife and fork. 'I'm not hungry either,' she said, pouring some Sancerre into her glass.

'Look, I'm sure he'll call before we leave. He knows we're off Friday.'

She sipped her wine and stared accusingly at her husband. It was too much for Chasen.

'Please don't look at me like that,' he said. 'It's not of my doing and it's out of my hands. He's old enough to shoulder the blame for his own actions. If you feel angry with the boy, wait till he calls and get cross with him, not me.'

She thought about this, then rose from the table and walked round behind Chasen, placing her fingers on his temples and rubbing with a steady pressure.

'I'm sorry, darling. I know you've got a lot on your plate at the moment.'

Chasen closed his eyes; the soft therapy of her fingers was heaven. He tried to clear his mind and relax the taut muscles of his face and neck.

'Let's go to bed. What do you say?' she whispered into his ear.

Before he could reply, the doorbell rang. It took all his willpower not to leap from the chair. His nerves were in shreds.

'Who can that be?' Lily muttered.

'I don't know. Let Anna get it,' Chasen replied.

A few moments later there was a soft knock on the dining room door.

'Come in,' Chasen called from his chair.

The door opened and their cook stepped into the room, closing the door behind her.

'There's a lady to see you, Sir Ivor. She says she knows you. She's a friend of Lord Bruton. Would you like me to ask her to wait in the living room?'

'If you would,' Chasen replied with a restraint he thought he'd lost.

Anna left, closing the door softly behind her.

'A friend of Aubrey's? Do I know her?' Lily asked with curiosity.

'Not if she's the woman I think she is. I was pressed into giving her a lift home on Saturday – she lives quite close to us in Oxford. I presume it's the same woman. One of Aubrey's floosies, I'd venture to say, and that's being charitable. What she wants I can't imagine. I'll go and see.'

'I think I'll join you. I'd be interested in seeing what you'd classify a "floosie",' she said with amusement. 'You know, you're gloriously old-fashioned.'

'If you like. Please do. Give me a bit of moral support.'

There was nothing for it. Besides, the woman must have known that his wife might be home at such an hour. How the hell he was going to introduce her to Lily he didn't know. He could hardly call her Miss Midnight.

As Chasen opened the living room door he saw the woman sitting on the chesterfield, her legs elegantly crossed. She was dressed classically with the minimum of jewellery.

'Good evening, Sir Ivor,' she said, then smiled at Lily who had walked past Chasen holding out a hand.

'How do you do, Lady Chasen. Carole Dawson. I do hope I haven't interrupted your dinner. I'd hoped to catch you before you sat down. I'm off to the theatre with my husband. I have a letter I promised Aubrey I'd drop in for him.'

She handed Chasen a plain white envelope. It was sealed.

'Thank you very much, Carole. It was good of you to go out of your way,' he said, putting the envelope in his inside jacket pocket.

'Have you time for a drink, Mrs Dawson? Is your husband outside?'

The woman glanced at her watch. 'It's very kind of you but I'm afraid I might be late unless I hurry. I'm meeting him there. Nothing worse than missing the beginning. We might miss an essential clue.'

'Is it a thriller you're off to?'

'Yes, at the Criterion. "A Question of Priorities", I think it's called,' she said, directing her eyes at Chasen.

She looked back charmingly at Lady Chasen. 'So, if you'll excuse me, I'd better be off.'

'Let me see you out,' Chasen managed, opening the living room door.

'Goodbye, Lady Chasen,' the woman said politely.

Lily waited in the living room as her husband followed their visitor into the hall.

As he opened the front door, Chasen fully expected the woman to whisper some violence into his ear, but instead she merely held out a hand which he was obliged by etiquette to take. She held it softly for a second, then squeezed hard as her eyes bore into his. Then she turned, stepped through the door and was gone. Chasen closed the door.

Lily was standing at the foot of the stairs as he turned.

'Floosie indeed,' she said, laughing lightly. 'A very charming young woman. I'm going to bed to read. Will you be up shortly?'

'Yes darling, very shortly,' he replied.

He re-entered the living room, closing the door behind him. Then he pulled out the envelope and ripped it open. Inside there was a folded sheet of blank writing paper.

FOURTEEN

As he turned a tight right-hand corner, Guy was confronted with a horse and cart taking up all the narrow road. It was a toss-up which looked older, the vehicle or the driver. The cart was piled high with what could have passed for the debris of the central core of post-meltdown Chernobyl – twisted metal of every conceivable configuration piled precariously high, and threatening at any second to tumble onto the road. The driver looked unconcerned. He smiled through his few remaining broken teeth, touched his cap with an expansive gesture as he burst into song, then coaxed the nag into an opening to a field. Guy waved and drove past.

'You're at the Shelbourne so you're right in the centre of Dublin. Get yourself to Rathfarnham,' Critchley had said. 'Then go down the Ballyboden Road, past Rockbrook, where you'll pick up the signs to Glenncullen. When you reach Johnny Fox's you'll be almost there. Straight on at the crossroads – it's the first house on the left.'

Guy continued up the steep narrow road, zig-zagging the car to avoid the myriad deep pot-holes, till the road planed out and he was atop the Wicklow Hills, Sugarloaf Mountain visible fifteen miles away in the distance. On either side for a mile or so was a wide expanse of heath and heather – not a house nor a sign of humanity to the horizon. It was scarcely credible that he was twenty minutes from the centre of Dublin.

Ten minutes later he caught sight of Fox's Pub on his right. Established in 1795, it was possibly the oldest and certainly the highest pub in Ireland. The whitewashed façade of the building looked to be held together with a jigsaw of old enamel and metal signs advertising Will's Gold Flake. Sitting on the roof was a motley collection of old beer barrels, cartwheels and a rusting harrow.

Guy paused briefly at the crossroads then drove across, looking to his left for Critchley's house. A hundred yards down the road he saw it. It was quite substantial, four or so bedrooms, Guy fancied. A small neglected garden stood in front, the lawn consumed by weeds and the trees the victims of slow strangulation by ivy. The remains of what had obviously been a splendid display of sweet peas hung limply either side of the dark green front door.

There was no driveway so Guy drew up behind a Ford Fiesta – presumably Critchley's runabout – that had its left-side wheels up on the verge just past the house.

The front door was opened by a shy but friendly woman of around sixty. She stood only about five feet something and her legs were so bandy you could easily have run a bulldog through them without fear of brushing her thighs.

'Sure you'd be Mr Cooper,' she said. 'If you'd care to come in and take a seat in the parlour, I'll tell Mr Critchley you've arrived.' She stood in the hallway, an arm outstretched, indicating the room to her right.

'I'm Mrs Dooley,' she said as an afterthought. 'I'm the home help.' She brushed some crumbs from her pinny and smiled shyly.

'Thank you,' Guy replied, entering the room indicated. The door was closed behind him.

Guy glanced round the living room. Mrs Dooley was obviously a real treasure – the room was spotless. A large Victorian roll-top desk stood in front of double windows which commanded a spectacular view out over the Wicklow Hills. A comfortable sofa and armchairs surrounded an open hearth where a cheery blaze warmed the room. Beside what appeared to be the best-used armchair was a magazine rack filled with copies of the *New Scientist*, the *Spectator*, the *Listener* and such-like. There was no sign of a television – Guy was not surprised.

On the mantel above the fireplace stood an assortment of silver-framed photographs. Most seemed to be of loved ones – relatives, Guy presumed. Judging by the dress and hairstyles, all were long since dead. Only one photo appeared to have been taken within the last twenty years. It was a black and white of Critchley in a very Whitehall suit with Baroness Thatcher. She was shaking his hand warmly and looked as pleased with herself as ever. Critchley, by contrast, looked suitably phlegmatic. In the background was the ubiquitous Dennis Thatcher. He appeared to be picking his nose.

Cooper heard the click of the door as it opened behind him.

'I see you've spotted my favourite snap. Most people think I display it for reasons of vanity. Not so. It makes me smile each time I look at it. You see, one cannot look at it without focusing immediately on poor Dennis's gesture. Actually, on closer examination it becomes apparent his finger's nowhere near his nostril – but first impressions are always the ones that endure, aren't they? They published it in *Private Eye*, you know. It was supposed to be an in-house snap, but my colleagues couldn't resist leaking it to the press. The only time my cover was blown in the British press in forty years.' He took a pipe from his jacket pocket and examined the bowl for an instant.

'I'm sorry to have kept you waiting dear boy. Plumbing problems, you see.'

'I'm sorry to hear that,' Guy replied. 'I do hope I haven't dragged you from your sickbed?'

Critchley's eyes sparkled with amusement. 'Not *my* plumbing, Mr Cooper, the house's.' He opened the blade of a small penknife and began roughly scraping the pipe's bowl.

'The drains in County Wicklow are somewhat primitive to say the least – probably haven't seen the light of day for half a century. Mind you, I can see why you should think that it were my pipes on the blink rather than the sewer's – as I remember, when we last met I was suffering from what felt like a terminal attack of piles.'

Critchley looked older than Guy had anticipated, his shoulders were rounded and he walked with a pronounced stoop.

'It's good to see you, Guy. Is that alright? Calling you Guy? Can't go on calling you Mr Cooper, can I?' He smiled warmly as he carried a few peat briquettes to the hearth, setting them down with difficulty and proffering a hand to Guy.

'Of course not,' Guy replied.

'In return I'll afford you the particular pleasure of calling me by my Christian name – Eugene. Wouldn't let anyone in the Service call me that for close to forty years, but it's a funny thing, as dotage falls like an invisible cloak of feeble-mindedness round one's shoulders, the strangest things happen. You see, I rather like the name now. Of course, there's no one to call me by it any more – only Mrs Dooley, and I can't prevail on her to refer to me as anything but Mr Critchley or "Sir".'

Satisfied that his pipe was ready, he withdrew a round tin of tobacco and unscrewed the lid, at the same time gesturing to Guy, who was standing by the fire, to sit down and make himself comfortable.

'Please take a seat. I've no doubt the old dear will be in shortly with a plate of some Irish something-or-other. Any excuse and in they come – and you definitely qualify. You are a famous *film* star,' he said with obvious amusement, pronouncing the word with a heavy emphasis on the 'l' of film to mimic Mrs Dooley's accent. 'Says I don't eat enough. Probably right on that score.'

He paused for a second as he eased himself into the comfortable armchair that was obviously his habitual nest. 'Also says I talk too much – she's probably right there too.'

'It's good of you to see me so promptly,' Guy faltered slightly, 'Eugene.' The name didn't fit the old man somehow. He seemed more of a Walter or a Miles. As far as Guy was concerned, he'd always be just 'Critchley'.

'Not at all, my boy. Bugger all else to do these days. Men like me are subtly discouraged from writing their memoirs for all the obvious reasons. The subtlety comes in the sledge-hammer form of the Official Secrets Act rather than the financial inducements offered to everyone else in the business community. Of course some go right ahead regardless – Peter Wright for instance – but these people usually do it because they feel they have a score to settle and they scribble away regardless of the risk. Mind you, the Service usually reacts in such an hysterical, incompetent fashion they finish up focusing even more attention on the issue – sells more books in the end. I think Wright did very nicely out of the whole affair and made the establishment look very foolish. Poor old chap's dead now though.'

He waved a hand at the roll-top desk as he packed the bowl with Balkan Riff. 'Do you think you could do me a favour and pass me that folder sitting on the top of my desk?'

'Of course,' Guy replied, fetching the manila binder and holding it out to Critchley.

'I felt I owed you one after the debacle in Kraków, so I made a few calls for you.' He fumbled for a match, pulled one out and lit his pipe.

'How long has it been, Guy? Dear me, must be ten years or so. I must say, I never expected you'd get in touch.' He chuckled as he sucked strongly on the stem, clouds of thick smoke practically engulfing his head. 'I hope you no longer bear the Service or myself a grudge?'

'I've put Sam's death behind me,' Guy replied softly. 'If anyone on our side was to blame it was the system, not yourself.'

'You still have a suspicion that it was our people who had him killed?'

Guy was about to speak when Critchley held up a hand. 'I'm sorry, I shouldn't have raised the subject. I apologise. But I would like to repeat just once more what I told you in Poland, that it was not the doing of our people. Now, to Sir Ivor Chasen.'

He flipped quickly through the four or so pages of foolscap he'd plucked from the folder. 'Now that I've been put out to grass, so to speak, it's harder to get people to talk. They just think I'm an interfering old fart who should be enjoying his retirement. Added to which is the problem that most of the people I knew during my time with Intelligence have been elbowed out by a new generation.' He tapped the top of the bowl of his pipe with his forefinger as he continued.

'Well, grudgingly, for old times' sake, an old pal at GI – that's the General Intelligence Group – asked his friend in the Protective Security Branch to do a spot of checking for me in the Registry – just to see what they had on Chasen. You see, the comment your young friend overheard – "publish and be damned" – it intrigued me. Publish what? Compromising letters, photos? The answer from the Registry was that they had diddly squat.

'You see, it's government policy now that each of its departments is responsible for its own security, and the role of the Service is to advise and assist in that. The Protective Security Branch recommends what they think are measures that would reduce staff vulnerability. Chasen would fall within the ambit of the Foreign and Commonwealth Office. When it comes to vetting of employees, the Service gives advice and info on anyone who might have access in the future to classified material. It's coordinated within the Protective Security Branch – any of the Service's intelligence records stuff that might be relevant. Then it's all sent on to the relevant department – in our case the Foreign and Commonwealth Office. Officially the Security Service doesn't investigate what they refer to as "aspects of character and behaviour". That kind of background would be the responsibility of the departments themselves and would doubtless be done at a very early stage in the career of a diplomat. However, it was always my experience that we kept pretty up to date on the personal stuff – that is, if it was significant enough to become an issue.' He paused for a moment and Guy moved his chair closer.

'Well, my old friend works for the director of one of the five Intelligence Branches of the Operations arm of the Service – the other arm is Admin. Chasen's records were at the Foreign Office not Thames House. In my day, before the Security Service Act of '89, you could more or less do as you please: open a file, create one, cross-reference them – generally have a lot of fun. That was before MI5 moved to Millbank, with all its modern systems and facilities. "Spook house" in Davis Street was my home away from home for most of my working life – the Service was split up all over London before '94. Now it's Millbank for the Service and Vauxhall Cross for the SIS.

'Anyway, the Act makes the Director-General responsible for ensuring the control of information has strict parameters. Now there are detailed Security Service manuals governing the creation and maintenance of records, which didn't exist in my day. They have pretty strict and detailed guidelines. I'll give you an example. A file generally starts as temporary, with a maximum life of three years. If the criteria for opening a permanent file are satisfied – things that involve the Service's functions and require a very high standard of accuracy – you move on to a permanent one. I'm telling you this because it relates very much to your other enquiry, the one about Miss Knoll, but more of that later.

'When a file's opened it's colour-coded "green", during which time enquiries are made. It could stay "green" for a long time – depends on whether more information comes your way and is being added to the file. At the end of this period it becomes "amber". Actual enquiries are prohibited, but info that may come from other sources can be added. At the end of the "amber" period, the file becomes "red" – no more enquiries, no more adding. Finally, after a while at code "red", it's microfilmed, the hard copy is destroyed and it goes into the Research part of the Service's central index – as opposed to the Live Index. It's pretty rare that a file in the Research Index is accessed, unless an old file becomes relevant to an ongoing new file. The odd thing is that they're not consulted in vetting checks, which is to my mind a mistake.' He glanced at the pipe briefly, then drew quite forcibly. 'But where was I when I drifted off into all this new procedure?'

'You were saying that your friend at the Protective Security Branch took a look-see at Chasen's old file?'

'That's right. He knew I wanted the info quickly, so he used an old trick of mine to get some fast answers. You see, everyone is supposed to clear their desks at the end of each day – an obvious security measure. Everything on it goes into your small personal safe. So if you want a quick response you write a short note of your requirements, then attach it to a really bulky file that has absolutely no relevance to the note in question, then send it to the person who might be able to help you. He or she takes one look at the wad of papers, says to himself, 'Jesus, I can do without that heap of shit in my safe overnight,' quickly reads the note rather than the file, answers your question ASAP and shuttles the monster file together with your info back to you before five o'clock. Works every time.' He chuckled.

'Anyway, where was I? Oh yes – Chasen's file. Well, there was a small research file, dating back thirty-odd years, and another one at the Foreign and Commonwealth Office that he took a gander at. Chasen was positively vetted as a young man and unofficially the general climate of opinion at the Foreign Office was that the man was so proper, dull and boring that, as my friend told me himself, he'd trust Chasen in bed with his daughter on a hot night in Tunis – felt sure he'd do the right thing. Mind you, to be called dull by MI5 may not be such a bad thing – merely means they don't think you're likely to jump into bed with Christine Keeler, or be caught at the rear of Hampstead Heath public toilets.' Critchley snorted at his own joke.

'Anyway, he told me he'd had a word with another friend at SIS – that's MI6 – and they had little more, just an agenda of his foreign comings and goings over the years. Said he'd never gone anywhere more interesting than Torremolinos, let alone Russia or China – apart from his postings, naturally. Fiercely ambitious though, quite single-minded in that respect. Ambrose –' Critchley stopped abruptly. Guy looked at him enquiringly. Slightly flustered, he continued.

'Well, I've told you now, so the damage is done. Doesn't really matter – you'll doubtless meet him sooner or later. Ambrose told me it came as no surprise to him that Chasen'd been chosen as Permanent Rep to the UN.' Critchley paused, looking into the fire. 'Actually, that's the kind of thing that always set my alarm bells ringing – naked ambition.'

Guy leant forward in his chair to gain Critchley's attention. 'Being dull, boring, predictable and squeaky clean doesn't necessarily mean he couldn't be bought or suborned by some other means.'

'Of course not. And he may very well be acting for some foreign intelligence service out of a genuine belief in some ideal.'

'Exactly! That's my whole point. The one I alluded to on the phone. He's being pressured – well, that's what we think. That's the reason Edward was kidnapped – unless he was taken as insurance and they already have some other major hold on him, which is where "publish and be damned" comes in. But if the man's so bloody dull and incorruptible, what on earth can they have on him?' Guy stopped speaking for a second as a thought struck him. 'By the way, I suppose it's alright to discuss these matters openly like this. I mean . . .' Critchley cut him short with a lazy wave of his hand.

'No one has the slightest interest in me, or how I feel, or how I think. Believe me, the only sweeping that's taken place in this house in the last nine years has been with a broom, and the only bugs are in my bed. They might still listen to the odd call from time to time – I'm sure the Irish Security Service would accommodate them there. But that would just be routine – a once a year thing, you know.' The matches were in his hands again and the pipe was once more a small furnace.

'Besides, you were so circumspect on the phone yesterday I didn't really know whether you thought old Chasen was planning to assassinate the Queen or you were about to ask him to join your board of governors.'

There was a soft knock at the door.

'Do come on in, Doody. I'm sure young Cooper here is as hungry as a Mayo pony.'

Mrs Dooley entered carrying the anticipated tray of assorted goodies. But a bottle of Paddy had been substituted for a pot of tea – and no cups, just tumblers. Guy smiled – there was something so very likeable about Critchley. He had a sense of humour and some style.

'Set the tray down here, Doody. By the fire. Then we can add the inner warmth to the outer, eh? I hope you thought to make sure the bottle wasn't poisoned before you brought it in, and had a small nip?' He winked conspiratorily at Doody.

She laughed. 'You're a bad man, Mr Critchley. Indeed I have not.'

Critchley looked down at his notes.

'I'm afraid I tease old Doody quite mercilessly,' Critchley said as the door closed behind her, 'but she's a wonderful woman – she has a great sense of fun. You wouldn't think it, looking at her now, but she was one of the original Gaiety girls – something made even more remarkable by her bowed legs. "Sex appeal in brackets" they used to call her.' He put down the pipe and pointed to the tray. 'Why don't you pour us a snifter of Paddy, eh?'

Guy did so, handing a tumbler across to Critchley, who took it without looking up from his notes and quaffed marginally less than half the contents.

'Here we are. Chasen. Ivor. Born '36, Epping. Father career army. Solid upper-middle-class family upbringing. Educated Oundle. Scholarship to Oxford – Classics first. First posting as Third Secretary Vienna, one year then moved on. Cairo, still as a Third Sec. for two and a half years. Promoted and returned to London. Sent to Brussels pre-EEC as part of the UK delegation. Part of the negotiating team for five years.' He looked up briefly from his notes and helped himself to a finger sandwich. 'Reads like a classic boring career diplomat – nothing really unusual.' Then he adjusted his spectacles and continued reading in a monotone. 'Promoted councillor . . . Chef de Cabinet for Sir Adrian Poulter . . . head of Far Eastern Department at the FO . . . then went to head the Middle Eastern Department . . . promoted Undersecretary of State in '87 . . . couple of years in Washington, then back to Brussels as Permanent Rep to the EEC. Never put a foot wrong in his career, seemingly bloody good at his job. Private man, so I'm reliably informed. Dotes on his wife, blessed with the surprisingly lively name of Lily, and worships his son who's up at Oxford. No scandals, no fancy women, fancy boys, nichts, niente, nada, nothing.'

'Was your chum surprised that you should have any interest in the Chasen file?'

'Well, come to think of it, he was. But then so would I, had I been him. I mean if someone had asked me to look through the files of someone with the obvious charisma and latent naughtiness of Profumo in the sixties, I would have thought it quite normal . . . but Chasen?'

'Easy to say with a bit of hindsight perhaps?'

'That's what everyone always tells me. But I'm on record at the Registry as having had serious reservations about using Ward. It was sheer madness, the man was out of his depth – thought the whole thing was a big game.'

'You're referring to the Profumo–Ivanov affair?'

'Correct. The idea was to use Stephen Ward – osteopath to the gliterati – to lure Ivanov, who we knew to be spying, into the usual compromising position.'

'And Christine Keeler was the "honeypot"?'

'One and the same – sweetness herself. But to engineer the scheme down at Cliveden was quite absurd. We knew full well that Ward was a close buddy of Astor's at the time, spending his weekends down at Cliveden. And who were Astor's house guests? The likes of Mountbatten, the President of Pakistan, and Jack Profumo – but no one at the Service gave that a second's thought. We should have seen it coming that there was every likelihood that the honeypot would attract the wrong bee. And of course that's exactly what happened. Before we knew what was happening, Keeler was skinny-dipping in the Cliveden pool, Profumo was completely infatuated, and Ivanov was standing idly by conjuring up ways of manipulating the turn of events to his own advantage. I'm sure he couldn't believe his luck – I mean Jack Profumo was Secretary of State for War, for Christ's sake, and here he was sharing the same call-girl with him!'

Critchley paused for a few seconds as his mind returned from the sixties. He glanced across at Guy.

'Christ, you haven't taken a drop of your Paddy yet. Fill me up, will yer. I've a fierce thirst, and that's a fact.'

'Your Irish accent's atrocious. Stick to the tales of old Whitehall,' Guy said as he leant across and poured Critchley another generous measure. 'A sandwich, Eugene?'

'Thank you, no,' Critchley replied, relighting his pipe. 'What's all this to you? I mean, personally? The well-being of Queen and Country?'

'Not exactly. I'm concerned for a friend of mine. She's involved personally.'

'Not with Chasen I trust?'

'No. The son.'

'And she's the one who overheard this conversation?'

'Yes.'

'And you've no cause to disbelieve her?'

'None. Why should she concoct a story like this. She's fond of Edward – Chasen's son. She's been a good friend of the family for over a year. It's not in her interest.'

'Problem is, you have precious little to go on. Just her impressions and her recollection of what transpired. Snatches of conversation,' Critchley said. 'I mean, has the man behaved normally for the past few days? That might be a clue.' Critchley finished his Paddy, then quite suddenly stood and turned to Cooper. 'Wait a moment! Wait a moment. Profumo . . . The key may be there.'

'Stretching it a bit, aren't we? That was more than thirty years ago, for Christ's sake,' Guy said.

'No, dear boy. Not him personally. But the link. His friends. It was Profumo's friends who were ultimately his undoing. We should have kept a weather eye there. Of course, none of my superiors at the time thought my advice was worth a damn.' He stared levelly at Cooper. 'Would you like me to follow that line of thought through?'

'Are you sure it wouldn't put you to too much trouble? Or get you into any bother in the corridors of power?'

'Absolutely not,' Critchley replied jovially. 'I don't feel ready to lie down and die quite yet and quite frankly once I've read the papers in the morning I've got sweet

FA to occupy myself with, barring my thoughts and a walk down to Johnny Fox's. No family, you see.'

He looked down at the tray of sandwiches and helped himself to a neat finger filled with what looked to be salmon. 'I don't mean to sound pathetic – I certainly don't feel it. I rather like my privacy – my life of quietude. It's just that sometimes I feel an uncontrollable urge to talk to someone with whom I might concievably be on the same wavelength. Once in a blue moon some young turk from Thames House telephones me, then appears on the doorstep to winkle details from my fading memory of some "op" that took place years before he was born. Then he scoots back to London. Sometimes I wonder if they go through the rigmarole just to see if I'm still *compos mentis* enough to remember anything at all, and whether I'm worth considering a security risk any more.' He paused to reach for another salmon finger.

'Now to the other matter you asked me about, Cooper. Here I came across something very odd indeed.'

'Marysia's whereabouts?' Guy interposed.

'Exactly.'

'What did you find out?'

'Well, as far both the Security Service and SIS are concerned – she never existed.' Critchley paused for effect, looking across at Guy.

'What do you mean – never existed?'

'Just that. No records. None. Not a file. Nothing on microfilm in the Research Index. Not a word. Of course, *we* both *know* she existed. She was a major player in the Microsat conspiracy affair. But as far as the agencies are concerned – that's another matter.'

'Could this be a simple Registry mistake? Someone misfiled?'

'Absolutely not. No way. Rules are ultra strict when it comes to records. You know what the British are like about bureaucracy – a place for everything, rules and regulations. Well, the Intelligence rule of thumb is that a file is inviolable. If you want to change so much as a word you have to add your personal code, initial the addition so everyone knows the authorship, and add the date of alteration. If you wish to delete something – and every now and then an error may come to light and therefore require correction – you draw a thin line through the word or line to be altered so that the words underneath are still clearly legible. Then you initial and date, etc. But to *remove* a file is anathema – always was. Hollis tried it once during the Profumo debacle – and bear in mind he was Director-General at the time. Even he got a lot of flack from Ian Carroll who then ran the Registry. Carroll maintained that if it was alright for Hollis to try to cover his arse, it was on for one and all.'

'But what's the relevance of all this?' Guy wished Critchley would get on with it – charming as the old buffer was, he did like the sound of his own voice.

'Well, my point is it's next to impossible to draw a complete blank in records for someone we *know* existed. It just doesn't make practical sense. There must have been dozens of people who knew of her existence. I can name at least five colleagues who I know for a fact were cognisant of her activity. Her Mossad codename was Nomad but she was always referred to by us as Curly because of the poem – you know the one?'

'Yes I do,' Guy replied.

'Well it was true – she *was* "very, very good" at her work, and could be an adversary to be reckoned with if things turned bad. But you'd know that yourself, eh? Anyway, to pretend she never existed seems to me to be utterly pointless. Unless . . .'

'Unless what?'

'It's just an idea I have. I've got to get back to Ambrose anyway. I think I gave him a dose of the jitters – wanted to know why I was asking all these questions suddenly about Chasen. Point is, he'll be our Security Council Rep when he takes up his post in New York with the UN. Now Ambrose thinks it's possible he might have missed something and he's getting twitchy. I fobbed him off with some plausible piece of pap about why I wanted to have a gander at his file, but Ambrose knows me too well. After all, it's been years since I asked him anything of a professional nature.' He paused for a couple of seconds and looked at Guy.

'How much of this girl's story – her secret fears – can I share with him? Really feel I ought to. Could be a matter of national security and, if so, I'd have to let Ambrose be the first to know – I owe him that. Plus the fact that the boy could be in real danger if her scenario's anywhere near the truth. Personally I doubt it, but there's no harm in making absolutely sure.'

'I'll leave what you tell Ambrose up to you. But bear in mind we don't have any concrete evidence and I would hate to ruin a career like Chasen's on the basis of hearsay.'

'Absolutely. But there's no need to worry there – he knows the form. Rimmington – she's the new DG – is actually very keen now for members of the public to approach the Service directly with any useful information, part of the new "spirit of openness" she espouses. In my day neither MI5 nor 6 existed officially and no one knew where to find us. Now it's a matter of record and we even have a PO box number! If there's nothing to what your young friend says, they'll find out soon enough, and old Chasen'll never know he's been researched. I'll also get Ambrose to track down Edward.

I've an old buddy at Special Squad, he can help there – don't want to involve the Diplomatic Protection Squad officially yet since we don't have any hard evidence, and they'd be duty bound to talk directly to Chasen about what your friend says she overheard and that might tip everything in the wrong direction. They'll probably find the boy in a couple of hours and the whole thing can be put to sleep. I'll also have a chat – very unofficially, that is – with another old chum who's with the Diplomatic Protection Squad. I mentioned them just now; they're part of the Special Operations branch of the Metropolitan Police. If Chasen's actually told anyone what's going down but wants to keep the matter close to his chest, he'll have told them. If that's the case, we'd better back off quick-smart.'

Critchley held out his glass again and Guy did the honours.

'And what about Marysia?' Guy asked anxiously. 'You seemed to indicate just a moment ago there was some funny business going on at MI6 – a cover-up or something. How can we get to the bottom of that one?'

'Yes, well, as to Marysia, I'll look at a few angles. Do it with a little of the finesse I was known for. I assure you that's the best approach. Matters of this nature are seldom solved by going in gangbusters and confronting a lot of people.' He studied the plate of sandwiches – there were now only two fingers remaining. 'My God, I've practically eaten the lot. Quite the piggy, eh? Aren't you going to have a sambo?'

'A what?'

'Sandwich. They refer to them as "sambos" here. Quaint, isn't it?'

'Thank you, but I won't.'

'Well you can pass me one. Salmon please. You've given me quite an appetite. I feel as though I'm alive again and back in business, not some geriatric waiting to kark it in front of a peat fire.' He looked completely animated. 'You know what? I think I might take a break from my somewhat premature retirement. Maybe a short holiday in Whitehall might chivvy up the grey matter. I could go back to London this morning with you – got nothing planned. What you're after is the fruit of cosy chats in gentlemen's clubs – secrets are seldom divulged on the phone. Besides, you said I owed you one. How am I doing?'

'You're doing just fine, Eugene,' Cooper replied. You just couldn't help liking the old fellow – he definitely had style.

FIFTEEN

The offices of Mamasian, Costra & Brooks occupied two floors of a modest-looking building in the Wilshire business district midway between Beverly Hills and downtown Los Angeles. There was no fancy sign at street level, just the company name listed, along with the other occupants, in the foyer by the lifts: Mamasian, Costra & Brooks, Financial Consultants. The company operated as a legitimate financial consultancy on the lower level, far from legitimately on the upper floor where the partners had their offices.

On the eleventh floor, Howard Mamasian stood by the floor-length window looking out across the city. Sitting at the boardroom table were Harry Costra and Alan Brooks. Brooks was the financial wizard. A good-looking man of twenty-eight, he made financial reality out of Mamasian and Costra's schemes – he conjured the figures.

Costra leant back in his chair and eyed Brooks. He was one of a new generation that Costra despised, the self-assured yuppie generation. They knew no fear and were relentless in their tunnel vision of ambition. Costra knew Brooks meant to elbow him out of his position as Mamasian's right hand, but he no longer had the will to involve himself in a power struggle.

'Our guy in Whitehall says back out now,' Costra said firmly. It was seldom he found himself in what he would have described as an 'adverse' situation, and it irked him to have to admit it in front of Brooks. But the logistics of operations were his baby and that's where the buck stopped. He wouldn't put the company at any risk. No, he'd already made a decision about Chasen – their man in London had merely reinforced it.

'He advises we pull back completely and sever links,' Costra continued. 'But I figure that's just caution speaking.'

'How sure is he that Chasen's talked?' Mamasian asked.

'He's not. That's my point. And Garcia's woman maintains she's sure he hasn't – he's too scared for his son. Here our guy tends to agree with her.'

'I'm not sure that I want to hear any of this, Harry. The whole point of using Garcia was that we would keep some distance. I don't want to involve myself in details – that's your area. I just want to know I've got Chasen's balls in the palm of my hand. I'd rather we didn't go hands-on ourselves in London unless it becomes absolutely necessary. Let Garcia's people take the risks. We don't pay the big bucks for nothing. If we have to move our people in to clean up, then we have to. That's your decision.'

'My bet is it won't come to that,' Costra replied with a studied easy smile, assessing Mamasian's need for reassurance. 'Hey, come on, we don't know for a fact Garcia's screwed up. He's still antsy to move. He says things are still tight. It's Whitehall who's ringing our bells.'

'Okay. Let's take this one step at a time. Why is Whitehall giving us this advice?'

'He's careful. That's what I like about him. He's got instincts like mine. He can smell trouble. Anyway, the point is that someone up the line put the Watchers on Chasen – round the clock, and he doesn't know why.'

'Couldn't that be just routine?'

'No way. He says someone's been stirring up a heap of shit. Someone outside the department. He doesn't know who, and that's what's bothering him. Then Chasen's file is accessed from records. In itself that's not a problem, there's nothing there to compromise the operation or involve either Garcia or us – Garcia didn't make a move till Saturday. Then a photo turns up at the office for filing down in the Registry and it's Garcia's woman. Surprised the hell out of our guy, I can tell you.'

'You mean they know who she is?' Mamasian was incredulous.

'No. They don't know. And they don't know what she's up to either. They just know that she was one of maybe a dozen people he saw yesterday in London. The Watchers take pictures of everybody. Then Analysis runs them through the photo file. But they came up empty-handed with her. That's why Garcia uses her – she's fuckin' good.'

Brooks took notes as he listened.

'The Watchers could be a precautionary measure. Simple as that. That's the way I see it,' Costra continued quickly. Mamasian hadn't moved a muscle in several minutes and Costra was beginning to find it off-putting. 'The worst possible scenario would be that they're there because Chasen decided not to take up our offer and has alerted the Diplomatic Protection Squad. If that's the case we close down immediately. Won't leave any smell on our fingers. But I'd bet he's still with us. After all, that's why we sent Garcia's woman in to confirm his position, and there was no reaction from anyone.'

Mamasian ignored the last remark. It had been his idea to send in the woman. It had been a gut feeling. Things were getting very complicated. They'd have to tread carefully.

'What do Whitehall's superiors think's going down? Do we know?' he said at length.

'Not yet. He's doing all he can to get into their heads, but they're not giving anything away. All he knows is that the top man's tail's twitching and he doesn't know why. Someone's made him very nervous. Whitehall thinks someone knows or thinks he knows what's going down and has passed it on up the line.'

'Jesus Christ, Harry! Knows *what*, for fuck's sake? That we got a hold on Chasen – or why?' Mamasian shouted, the veins in his forehead standing out.

'Just that we got a hold. No one knows what we've got for him, and that's the way it'll stay. Garcia knows, but not his people,' Costra continued softly.

'I'm glad to hear that, Harry. Very glad! I don't want Chasen's fingers anywhere near the stuff until we're sure as shit he's going to do the right thing. There's a major fuckin' investment at stake here.'

'Aware of that, Howard,' Costra replied, maintaining a calm tone.

'Could I just ask one question, Howard?' It was Brooks. He usually bided his time then cut to the heart of the matter. 'Doesn't it come down to whether Chasen's decided to join us or not? If not, then there's nothing we can do short of Garcia making good his threats. If he's still with us, we have to decide whether to continue and be even more careful, or pull out right now and leave Chasen.'

'If Chasen's to be believed, he's told no one,' Costra said quietly.

'What do you mean?' Mamasian looked shocked. 'Someone's actually asked him?'

'Sure, the woman calls him every day on a secure line and went to see him a few hours ago. His wife was present. The way she figured it, he was still our man, no question. I'd say that was when the photos were taken, but whether it was because he'd spilled to the police or it was just the Service sniffing around is debatable.'

'Well, that's the fuckin' issue of the hour!' Mamasian snapped. 'So when did she ask him straight out if he'd talked?'

'Well, she was madder than shit when she found out they had her picture on file at the office, so she let him have it when she rang him this time. Gave him hell.'

'On the freakin' phone? Jesus H. Christ!' Mamasian exploded. 'You're telling me she's discussing –' he roared, but was cut short.

'Howard!' Costra shouted back, 'Take it easy! Give me a fuckin' break – the line was secure!'

Mamasian was breathing hard as he stared at his partner. Then he waved a hand. 'You tell me how that's possible,' he said in a more controlled tone. 'You're the technical genius.'

'Garcia's using digital not analog for communication – there's a big difference. The girl gave it to Chasen with the first contact. Garcia calls him every morning at just after one a.m. No need to worry about drop-ins, etc. If someone tried deliberately to tap in on the line all he'd hear is encryption algorithms.'

'What the fuck's that?' Mamasian cut in.

'Doesn't matter – a bunch of noise. It's the base station that turns it back to speech with their code. Even if Special Branch wanted to tap in, they'd have to get a warrant and then have it done at the exchange of the digital carrier. But the real fun is they'd have to know the service number and account name first – and they don't 'cos it's Garcia's, not Chasen's. Take it from me, the new GSM digital systems can't be broken into. So basically the Watchers can watch all they fuckin' want.'

This seemed to calm Mamasian. 'What did Chasen tell the girl?' he said as he sat.

'Well, he promised he hadn't breathed a word to a soul and pleaded with her not to hurt his son. She told Garcia that Chasen sounded scared as hell.'

'Does he know yet what he's got to do?' Mamasian asked quietly.

'Not yet. Same as ever – they never know till they leave. We transfer the goods as arranged. No need to tell him the contents, but stupid he's not. On the plus side, every hour Chasen vacillates puts him deeper in our pockets.'

There was a long pause. Mamasian wrapped his arms round himself as he thought. 'Is the consignment in place with Quddus?'

'Yes. It's in Lowndes Square right now. Came in with him from Karachi last night. It's secure. Garcia will monitor the transfer when we give him the go-ahead. Muhammad checked the seals.'

'Then my decision is we stay on it. If Chasen had talked, Garcia's woman would've felt the heat by now. But we have to know the reason those pictures were taken, and we have to find out who the outsider is who's fuckin' us up, stickin' his nose in where it doesn't belong. We're only three days from our deadline. It's too near to close it off right now unless it's absolutely necessary – we've got too much invested.' He looked at Costra for agreement.

'Okay, Howard.'

'Right, let's see how things shape up over the next twenty-four hours. Any sniff Chasen's not behaving, the case never leaves the Embassy. Then you clean up.' Mamasian pressed a button on the desk console and spoke into the machine. 'Turn off the fucking aircon – you'll freeze us all to death!'

A voice crackled at the other end. 'Mr Mamasian, the air's linked up for the whole building. We don't have the controls up here.'

'Then turn off the whole Goddamn building! Got that?' Mamasian snapped his finger off the console without waiting for a response and walked back to the window.

'The woman. Are you sure she doesn't know it's us?'
'The only link's Garcia,' Costra replied.
'That's something we better keep in mind over the next few days.'

SIXTEEN

Cooper walked up Lancaster Terrace and entered the Elizabeth Hotel, where he'd arranged to meet Critchley. Inside the Nash façade, the reception area was a festival of chintz. In the far corner a pair of brogues at the bottom of brown corduroy trousers were all that gave away the presence of a human being behind a spreadeagled copy of the *Independent*. It had to be Critchley, thought Guy, as a plume of smoke rose from behind the newspaper and the unmistakable smell of Balkan Riff hit him.

'Ah, Guy,' Critchley called out, lowering the paper as he heard Guy approach. 'Good to see you. Before I ask you if you'd like a drink, could I suggest we take a brief walk? I don't think I've been out of leather armchairs for the last couple of hours. Besides, it's such a lovely day – and they occur so infrequently in England I always feel we should make the most of them.'

'Why not?'

'Good. Hyde Park alright with you?'

'Perfect.'

They walked in silence to the corner of Bayswater Road and waited for the lights to change. On the other side of the road a hamburger vendor the image of Idi Amin stood next to a steaming aluminium trolley. They crossed into Hyde Park through the Marlborough Gate. It was a gloriously warm day with just a few spots of cloud and there was a new-found spring in Critchley's step. He seemed to be enjoying his London holiday. As they took the path past the Italian Gardens, Guy broke the silence.

'So, what's the news? How did Ambrose react?'

'He wants to meet. ASAP. You and the girl. Do you think that's possible?'

'Absolutely. When?'

'I'll tell you in a minute. Right now I'd better fill you in about the other matter – the one concerning your friend Marysia. You see, I've arranged a meeting with someone who might be able to help you there. Israeli Intelligence. Mossad. Never actually met him face to face but we shared a lot of notes while I was in the Service. You really need to know a few things before you speak to him.'

'I see. Alright, fire ahead.'

'Well, I've made quite a bit of progress with her mystery disappearance, and now have some idea what's been happening and why the records appear to have been sanitised.'

'Yes?'

'They're protecting her.'

'Who are?' Guy asked.

'Her people. And then our people at the request of her people, presumably. Doesn't really matter who exactly, but I'd say a directive came through to bury her identity so she could disappear.'

'Why would erasing everything be necessary, rather than just her current address?'

'It's quite easy for an old hander to track down an agent based on a file of information – places, contacts, old haunts, etc. Most people are creatures of habit – they tend to return to their favourite spots time and time again. That's where they're likely to seek sanctuary.'

'So you're suggesting she was being hunted and someone requested her file be removed before the hunters could take a look?'

'Well, that's what my contact in Registry said. He was there when the microfilm was requested. Not destroyed, mind you, just taken elsewhere. Limited eyes only – that kind of thing. No one destroys any information in Registry. Not any more, anyway. He told me it was a directive of Cunningham's, facilitated at the request of Mossad. Presumably okayed by Ambrose – Cunningham wouldn't have had the clout back then.'

'Who's Cunningham?' Guy asked.

'Works under Ambrose in Counter-terrorism International.'

'Our people would oblige such a request from a foreign agency?' Guy interrupted.

'Why not? They're supposed to be our friends – it's the Arabs we have to watch. I always found the Israelis helpful and willing to share information when asked. Mind you, of all the foreign agencies, Mossad would be one of the last to ask a favour. Their policy is self-sufficiency. Anyway, it appears in this case they did ask for a bit of cooperation and we agreed. They were retiring her for her own safety.'

Critchley stopped at the intersection of two paths and looked around. Then he lifted a hand and waved at a man standing by a small lake, feeding the ducks.

'Is that the Israeli?' Cooper asked, as the man walked towards them.

'Yes – if that's who I think he is. As I said, I've never met the man in person – just had to mentally recall the file snaps.' Critchley suddenly laughed as he turned to Cooper. 'This must seem ridiculously cloak and dagger. It's just he was a bit reluctant to meet you at the hotel, insisting we meet in the open somewhere. Maybe he doesn't have the clearance to discuss this with us and is doing me a favour. Anyway, I think he can tell you what you need to know.'

As Critchley finished, the man approached and held out a hand which Critchley shook warmly.

'Mr Critchley,' the man said smiling. 'You don't look a day older than your file photo.'

'Didn't know you had one of me, my friend,' Critchley replied in a teasing tone. 'However, I'm delighted to see you face to face after so many years. Guy, may I introduce Ehud Shapiro. Ehud, this is my friend Guy Cooper, the man I mentioned – he was a close friend of Marysia.'

Shapiro was serious-faced, curly-haired and around forty. Dressed in an anorak and jeans, he was a great bear of a man, towering over them both. He shook Cooper's hand for several seconds, then let it fall.

'Shall we continue to walk?' he asked.

'Of course,' Critchley replied, pulling a small knife from his pocket and stabbing at his pipe. Guy flexed his hand to bring back some of the blood Shapiro had squeezed almost to his shoulder. They walked on down towards the ponds, Critchley between them.

'Mr Critchley . . . ' Shapiro began, addressing Guy, 'Eugene, I should say, tells me you wish to contact Marysia Knoll, as she called herself then. That is correct, yes?'

'That is correct.' Guy looked up sharply at Shapiro. It had never occured to him that her name was anything but Marysia. 'We became close friends a few years ago,' he managed after a beat.

'Yes, I am familiar with the background,' Shapiro said. 'She was retired two years ago for her own safety. There are people who have sworn she will not live. When she left Poland in '89 she returned to Israel and was reassigned to a deep penetration operation in Lebanon. Her instructions were to infiltrate a cell of the Hizballah in Lebanon. Are you at all familiar with the name, Mr Cooper?'

'They're an Islamic Shiite group?'

'That's correct. They call themselves the Party of God, sometimes the Followers of God. They are a very strong political force with a powerbase in southern Lebanon and are supported by Iran. They conduct raids into the security zone that separates Israel from Lebanon, and sometimes deep into Israel. You see, in '82 when we invaded Lebanon for the second time, we advanced right up to Beirut, but withdrew in '85, under world political pressure, to a point eleven kilometres from the Israeli border. Those kilometres became the security zone. Anyway, her task was to identify a rogue splinter group headed by Mahmud Abdul Wassim. Our intelligence was that they intended to instigate lightning civilian bombing raids across the security zone into northern Israel. They were an extreme group with extreme ideas – operating without the authority of the Hizballah or Iran.

'It took her eight months. When she had identified all the cell members and their support groups we moved in with a strategic unit. All their top people, including Wassim, were killed. The operation was a major coup. Marysia deserved all the credit – she had lived as a Hizballah member for over a year and they had accepted her as a friend. However, intelligence reports soon made it clear that she'd been placed on a death list.

'She was sent to Paris for a cooling-off period and was about to return to Israel when there was an attempt on her life in France. Five innocent people died – the occupants of a car which was passing as the explosion occurred, shielding Knoll from the blast.'

'So she left Paris?'

'Yes, she left Paris. With the help of friends we sent her into deep cover for security. But these people will not rest until she is dead.'

'Can you tell me where she is?'

Shapiro studied Cooper's face in silence for a few moments.

'Since she kept her whereabouts a secret from you all these years I have to conclude that she never meant you to have it. Besides, I don't have clearance to give it to you. However, I will tell you this much. She is not in Paris. She is in South Africa – I cannot be more precise.'

'South Africa?' Guy said, surprised.

'The country was her choice. Our friends at NIS gave her a fresh identity. You would be more familiar with the acronym BOSS – that was their name pre-'78, the Bureau of State Security.'

A football flew over a small wooden fence surrounding a nearby children's playground and bounced on the path in front of Shapiro. A little boy rushed to the fence waving his arms. Shapiro trapped the ball expertly with his foot, flicked it to knee level and punched it back lightly to the child.

Critchley snatched the moment, holding up both arms. 'Excuse me, gentlemen, but could I suggest we sit down for a moment, I'm sure we've been twice round this park already. I'm exhausted.'

After they'd seated themselves on a park bench, Shapiro turned and smiled at Guy. 'I would be more than happy to forward a letter to a colleague in Pretoria. I am sure he would send it on to her,' he said.

'That's good of you, Ehud,' Guy replied, grateful.

Shapiro pulled a card from his wallet and handed it to Guy. 'You can reach me at this number during the day and on the lower number after working hours.' He tucked his wallet away in his jeans pocket as he continued. 'Now, if you will excuse me I must leave you. It has been a pleasure.'

'I'll be in touch very shortly, Ehud. Thanks again,' Guy said as Shapiro stood.

They shook hands and the Israeli jogged off along the path back to the ponds, covering at least five yards with every bound.

'Shall we get back to the hotel? Must be close to lunch now – you can buy me an Irish whiskey,' Critchley said.

'I'd be delighted to, Eugene,' Guy replied as they strolled back to Lancaster Gate.

'Nice man, Shapiro. Father was a conductor. Ever heard of Menachem Shapiro?'

'The Hallé?'

'That's him. Retired a long time ago. Passed some of his genius on to young Ehud. You wouldn't think it, looking at the man, but he's reputed to be a first-rate violinist. Played with the Tel Aviv Symphony for a few years before he joined the diplomatic corps.'

'Not the man I'd lend my Strad to if I had one – probably reduce it to matchwood if he was startled by the timpanist,' laughed Guy.

'Yes, he's a big lad. Beneath the seriousness lies a wicked sense of the absurd. Told me a delightful anecdote a couple of years ago. Next time you pass the Israeli Tourist Office in Great Marlborough Street take a look up at the third-floor windows. You'll see a scruffy teddy bear with its head torn off dangling from a piece of string. Now why do you think it's there?'

'I can't imagine,' Guy replied. 'Leftover Jubilee decoration?'

Critchley shook his head and smiled. 'Security device. No teddy – no entry. The moment there's a security alert the small bear is pulled in. Rather quaint, isn't it? Simple but effective.' He chuckled, then his tone became more serious. 'Anyway, to the more pressing matter. As I said earlier, Ambrose wants to see you – and Gosia.'

'How did he react to what you told him? Is he going to do anything? Time's of the essence if Gosia's got her facts straight.'

'Well, that's the point really. And I'm afraid I have to tell you that Ambrose thinks she's barking up entirely the wrong tree. He's known Chasen personally for years, you see.'

'Sounds as if he's going to do diddly squat,' Guy said angrily.

'Hold on, Guy. That's not being fair. He set the Watchers on Chasen as a purely precautionary measure within minutes of my first phonecall, then he apparently gave Chasen a call, but didn't find anything in Chasen's tone to indicate there was cause for concern. Now he's delegating the job to a chap called Cunningham – the one I mentioned before. Young buck. Counter-terrorism is his forte and from all reports he's good – very good. I think Ambrose would prefer not to involve himself officially at this stage – obvious conflict of interest. But if there's anything to turn up, Cunningham'll do it. Ambrose has the utmost faith in him.'

'Fair enough. When do we meet?'

'This afternoon. Three o'clock at the Ministry of Defence. I presume Gosia will be available?'

'She will. Why the MOD? Thought MI5 were at Thames House?'

'They are. The location's Ambrose's idea. Thames House is strictly private. They have a fortress mentality. Rows of neat little vacuum space capsules you can scarcely struggle into. Of course that's the whole point of them – no room for briefcases and the like. Then once you're in, the bloody toughened plasto-glass slides round behind you and you're trapped. Security could keep you in there for good if they cared to. As it's the only way in and out of the place, it works pretty well. I wouldn't like to have to fight my way out of there, and that's a fact.' He bent down, picked a wild rose from the beds and placed it in his buttonhole, winking at Guy as he did so.

'Where was I?' Critchley looked suddenly old, as if the walk had taken it out of him. 'Ah yes, Thames House. No, we don't conduct interviews there.' He grasped Cooper's arm and guided him to the right. 'Over there!' he said, pointing to a plain-looking pub the other side of the road. 'Can't wait till we get back to the bloody hotel, I'm parched. Let's have a snifter in the snug at the Raj. It's an old haunt. Not the prettiest of pubs, but a familiar one. If the fundamentalists were after *me* they'd have a chap staked out at the Raj for sure.'

They found a quiet corner and settled with their drinks. Critchley had a self-satisfied look as he raised a large whiskey to his lips. When the level had fallen to less than half, he spoke.

'I don't know if you recall I alluded to the Profumo affair when we met in Glenncullen?' he said, relishing the discovery of a significant new piece of the puzzle.

'I do, yes. But you didn't feel like expanding on your thoughts at the time.'

'No I didn't. I wanted to do a bit of digging first. I thought it might be pertinent to find out the kind of company that Chasen kept. So, I asked around. Initially it led nowhere. Chasen's not a social animal, keeps himself very much to himself. Then it came to light that he numbers Lord Bruton and Mark Armstrong amongst his buddies.'

'Never heard of either. Are they dubious?'

'Not exactly. Armstrong's alright. Likeable. Big spender, but he can afford to spend – family's worth many millions. But Bruton's quite the opposite. Arrogant snake. Spent all his money and now sponges off people like Armstrong. No one knows how he manages to keep his estate running. A real rogue. Likes the ladies, and his proclivities tend towards the deviant – you know, S & M.'

'Bondage?'

'Yes. At least that's the word around the traps.' He lifted the glass and drained the remaining contents.

'So I asked myself what Chasen would have in common with him.'

'And you found?'

'Not much, really. They're not close. But I did discover that Bruton had a very jolly party a few days ago. Lots of ladies bought and paid for. He knew Armstrong would expect it, and the man's got the best shoot in Cambridgeshire, so Bruton made bloody sure that he had a good selection of lovelies. But here's the point. Guess who left with the loveliest?'

'Chasen.'

'Spot on, my boy. Mr Clean himself.' He stared in triumph at Guy.

'The same woman who visited Chasen the night Gosia overheard the conversation? Is that your line of thought?'

'It's worth thinking about, wouldn't you say, Guy?'

'It certainly is, Eugene.'

SEVENTEEN

As Guy and Gosia pinned their security tags to their lapels, the elderly uniformed security officer stared at a point a foot above their heads and droned on.

'Please keep these attached to the front of your clothing at all times while you are in this building. Visitors are permitted to leave only via this door. When you do so, please hand in the badge and sign your name, adding the time of your departure. You'll find Sir Ambrose Leston if you walk to the end of this corridor, then turn left. Halfway down the next corridor you'll see a lift. Please take it to the third floor. The room will be the corner room on the right. Thank you for your attention.' The elderly commissionaire stopped and pulled a medihaler from his trouser pocket. Then he sat down.

'Thank you,' Guy said politely as they moved away. Then, as he led Gosia down the hall, he whispered, 'That man needs a new needle for the record as well as a fresh set of lungs for the speakers.'

The lack of carpet made their footsteps ring out loudly in the corridor.

'This is not what I expected at all. It's like a rather dreary provincial bank,' said Gosia as they walked on.

'Somewhat larger building, wouldn't you say?'

Gosia nodded. Yes, she had to admit the Ministry of Defence was a considerable building, though more impressive outside than in.

'Will they sit me in a small uncomfortable chair, draw the curtains and shine a harsh light in my eyes?' she said, hoping an attempt at humour might relieve her tension.

'Absolutely. As a matter of course. Just remember, if there's anything you don't want to tell Sir Ambrose

Leston, don't. Unless of course he brings out the pliers,' Guy replied.

Gosia threaded an arm through Guy's. She didn't know quite what to expect of this interview nor what kind of worms might crawl out of the can she was about to open. She was becoming increasingly worried about Edward's welfare – it had been five days since his disappearance.

They arrived at the lift. Guy pulled back the gates and they stepped inside. 'My friend – the one I told you I visited in Ireland – he says Ambrose Leston is really very easy to get on with, so just relax and take it as it comes.'

They left the lift at the third floor and turned right. The corner door had no name or number on it. Guy knocked lightly. Gosia adjusted her jacket lapel as she waited, then looked at Guy, who smiled back reassuringly. The door was opened by a middle-aged man who more closely resembled a pheasant than a human being.

'Miss Dobra and Mr Cooper? Ambrose Leston. Please come in.'

The room was plain but comfortable in a gentlemen's club sort of way. A large '30s desk, several leather chairs without arms and a winged sofa in the corner. All the lights were on. Gosia could see why – the one window in the room was high in the wall and small.

'Do take a seat. Good of you to come.' Leston indicated two seats in front of the desk. He then sat down behind it, unbuttoning his elegant pinstriped suit as he did so. Guy and Gosia seated themselves.

'I hope you'll forgive me, I've asked a colleague of mine to sit in. I have to attend a meeting in Brussels tomorrow and may be away for a few days. I want someone here today so we can have some continuity of events over the next few days – if we decide that there's anything we need to attend to in this matter.'

Just then the door opened and a strikingly attractive young man entered. He looked to be in his late twenties, with short dark wavy hair and a double-breasted suit similar in style to Leston's, the stripes a touch slimmer. As he stepped forward between Gosia and Guy, Leston introduced him.

'Gosia Dobra and Guy Cooper, this is Neville Cunningham, who will be assisting me in this matter.'

'How do you do,' Cunningham said lightly, drawing up a third chair and sitting down behind Guy.

'Perhaps I should start the ball rolling,' said Leston, as he cathedralled his fingers. 'I had a long talk to Eugene Critchley yesterday afternoon and that's why I asked you to come in to see me today. In the meantime I thought I might just give vent to my instinct, so I rang Sir Ivor, who you may or may not know has been a friend for some years, and asked him if he was free to join me for lunch today.' He looked up from the desk where he'd been staring. 'Fortunately he was, and I've just returned from a very pleasant couple of hours with him at Whites. I have to say that he seemed in the very best of spirits – quite relaxed, very jovial and his appetite didn't seem in question.'

Gosia leant forward in her chair, alarmed. 'I'm sorry to interrupt, Sir Ambrose, but you didn't –'

Leston smiled patronisingly. 'Naturally I didn't voice any of your fears to him. It would have been very rude to do so, quite inappropriate. No, I just wanted to sample his general demeanour. From what you have been suggesting to Eugene Critchley, I would have expected to find a man close to the edge. But I have to say I did not find this to be the case. Unless he was masking his feelings with the professionalism of a master spy . . .' He paused for effect. 'And that I find hard to believe.'

Cooper noticed Leston's eyes flick behind him towards where Cunningham was seated. 'Was there something you wanted to say, Neville? Please feel free to do so.' That was Leston's style. He'd get the meeting off to a pleasant start, then toss the ball to his junior who would continue, giving him the opportunity to analyse faces, body language and any signs of duplicity.

'If you don't mind, yes I would,' Cunningham replied. His voice was very BBC. It had that soothing quality.

'Miss Dobra, I gather from what you told Mr Critchley, and he then passed on to Sir Ambrose, that you only overheard a small part of the alleged conversation between Sir Ivor and the woman. Would that be accurate?'

Gosia turned slightly in her chair to face Cunningham. 'Yes, that's correct. But the tenor of the conversation was quite clear. He was manifestly upset and seemed to me to be afraid – of her, the woman.'

'In your opinion,' Cunningham said, adding quickly, 'from the other side of a closed door.'

'That's right.'

Cunningham smiled very charmingly. 'Please don't misunderstand me, I am not trying to poo poo what you are alleging you heard. Far from it. We are very grateful that you should have been so public-spirited as to come forward to voice your fears to us. But you must realise that we need to tread very carefully here. Sir Ivor Chasen is one of this country's very top civil servants – shortly to take up the post of Permanent Representative to the United Nations. In conversations that Sir Ambrose has had with him, he assures us that he knows the current whereabouts of his son, that he feels relaxed and is looking forward to taking up his position in New

York. Naturally we did not confront him with your allegations – all of this came forth in casual conversation.'

Good-looking he might very well be, thought Gosia, but she felt an instant dislike for his easy manner. Regardless of how he couched his words, Gosia knew he'd made up his mind that she was some silly young girl.

'Mr Cunningham, I would like to assure you that those parts of the conversation I passed on to Mr Cooper, and he to you via Mr Critchley, were not figments of my imagination. I heard Sir Ivor Chasen say quite distinctly, "I shall not be blackmailed", then "publish and be damned", and a few minutes later I heard the woman say the words, "retribution", "terrible" and "Edward".'

'Were the last three words linked, though?'

'I beg your pardon? What exactly do you mean?' Gosia snapped, annoyed.

'Well, quite clearly if the words were linked then they would have a much stronger import than if they were not. You follow me?'

'Of course I do, Mr Cunningham,' she replied in a saccharine tone. 'However, if you were protecting the President at the inaugural dinner and you heard someone close by mention the three words, "bomb", "martini" and "President" – though strictly speaking it's possible that the second word would interrupt the logical link to the third, you hopefully would still draw your weapon.'

Both Cunningham and Leston laughed.

Suddenly Gosia stood, her face flushed with anger. 'I don't believe you people!' she shouted. 'Lives hang in the balance, and you just sit there having a good laugh, dismissing it all and doing absolutely nothing!'

There was a shocked silence.

'This hasn't been an easy time for Miss Dobra, as you can imagine,' Guy began, attempting to smooth Leston's feathers. 'I'm sure she didn't mean to be rude.' There was no doubt they needed him onside.

'Please don't apologise for me, Guy,' Gosia continued with renewed vehemence, never taking her eyes off Leston. 'What I'm saying is true! This man has absolutely no sense of urgency, regardless of the fact that Edward's fate rests in his hands!'

Leston cleared his throat and adjusted his shirt cuffs – the only tell-tale sign of annoyance a twitch in a muscle at one corner of his mouth.

Guy put a hand on Gosia's arm and tugged slightly. She sat.

'Please believe me, Miss Dobra,' Leston continued after a few moments, as if her outburst had never occurred, 'when I say I find the entire episode very puzzling indeed, and we have taken on board every single thing you have told us. It will now be up to us to make sense of what you have said, bearing in mind the conversation I had with Sir Ivor Chasen over lunch. Naturally I cannot tell you the thrust of it – that would be breaching a confidence. And it's possibly because of this that you may not at this moment appreciate the position we are taking, and may take in the future. All the same, we are most grateful to you.'

'Don't mention it,' Gosia replied with control. 'I did what I thought best, both for Edward and the good of the country as a whole. I fully appreciate that you must be circumspect in these matters – you have to decide whose version of events you find more plausible. The rest is up to you.'

Gosia turned to Cooper and raised her eyebrows as if to leave. Leston spotted the gesture and reached into a drawer by his desk.

'Before you leave, Miss Dobra. Would you be kind enough to look at some photographs and tell me whether any of the faces are familiar to you?'

'Of course,' replied Gosia, as Leston slid a sheaf of eight by tens across the desk. She leafed through them then stopped abruptly at the tenth photo.

'This is the woman Sir Ivor Chasen talked to that night.'

'You are absolutely sure, Miss Dobra?' It was Cunningham again. 'Please remember, it was dark and I believe you told Mr Critchley that you only caught a brief glimpse of the woman by the door, that she was lit only by a small wall lamp and that you could not see her eyes clearly at all.'

Gosia stared at Cunningham coldly. 'Yes, I am certain that the woman in this photograph and the woman I saw at Chasen's house that night are one and the same.'

'I like a woman who knows her mind,' said Leston, trying to diffuse the tension. 'Thank you for coming in and being such a help with the photograph.'

Gosia rose and the men in the room followed suit. 'I'm glad you have faith in us to look after the country's wellbeing. I trust it is well-founded. Rest assured we will look at each and every possibility.' He looked across at Cunningham.

Cunningham opened the door as Leston walked round from behind his desk and held out his hand to Guy and Gosia.

'My thanks again. Oh, by the way, you know you have to leave the way you came.'

'We do indeed,' said Guy.

'Fat lot of good that's done!' Gosia snapped as they stepped into the street. 'Patronising bastards. What do they think I have to gain by inventing all this?'

'Calm down, Gosia. I'm sure they don't think anything of the kind. But you must see it from their point of view too. Their terms of reference are limited strictly to countering activities that can be assessed as threatening national security, or safeguarding the economic wellbeing of the UK from overseas threats.'

'That's exactly what this may involve! They must see that, surely?'

'I'm sure they can see the possibilities, but then again this may look to them like either a personal matter or one that should be the province of the Metropolitan Police – the Special Protection Squad. They can't just take it upon themselves to institute a search and rescue operation based on what must amount in their eyes to hearsay.'

'Hearsay?' she exploded. She stopped walking and turned to face Guy.

He put a calming hand on her shoulder. 'Yes, I'm afraid at this stage it is still unsubstantiated hearsay.'

'You don't believe me?'

'Yes, Gosia, I personally believe everything you've told me. How you interpreted what you heard is another matter, and I hope for Edward's sake you got it wrong. But you must bear in mind that Chasen has effectively denied that anything happened. Leston told you that at lunch Chasen seemed relaxed and said he'd been in touch with Edward. What's Leston supposed to say? "Really? Are you quite sure, Ivor? Word has it your son's been kidnapped. No truth in that rumour, is there? You wouldn't be keeping that back, would you?"'

'There's no need to be fatuous,' she snapped, then was instantly contrite. 'God, I'm so sorry, Guy. I didn't mean to be rude. You've been so good to help me but I'm really wound up about this and it seems no one's going to do anything, certainly not *that* lot.'

'Don't you believe it. They'll nose around, smell out any bad news. It's not in their interest to ignore it. They'd look pretty silly if something happened to Chasen and it came to light you'd already warned them about it.'

'I suppose so,' Gosia said, unconvinced.

'Also, remember they're hardly likely to tell you what they've got planned.'

'I suppose not,' she agreed.

'And my friend Critchley will enjoy his bit of personal digging, as will I – something will be done, the cogs will turn.'

'But will they turn swiftly enough to save Edward's life? That's what bothers me most, Guy. What the hell can I do? I can't just go back to Oxford and sit on my hands.'

Guy flagged down a passing cab and they climbed inside and sped off towards Trafalgar Square. 'I suggest you go back to Oxford and make absolutely sure that Edward isn't around somewhere. Try and establish when he was last seen and where. This might help the police if and when Cunningham or Critchley decide it's time to call them in.'

'But I've done all that. What do you think I've been up to since I last saw you! He hasn't been in his room for days and no one's seen him. I've been into every pub, shop, hotel, bus station in Oxford!'

'Just keep asking. There's not much else you can do at present. I know it's frustrating, but we have to put ourselves in the hands of people like Leston. They know the form and they can do a lot more than we or the Oxford Constabulary can. We have to remember it's quite possible that they're all lying to us – that Chasen alerted them the moment he became aware of what was going on, and they're negotiating as we speak.'

'Then why wouldn't they tell us, for God's sake? At least we'd know that something was being done. We wouldn't feel so helpless.'

'In their book we probably don't need to know anything, so they won't tell us.'

Gosia sat back in the cab mulling this over for a moment, then her face was animated once more. 'What are you going to do?' she asked, as the cab made its way up Park Lane towards Marble Arch.

'I've got meetings with American producers and suchlike. I'll keep in touch with Critchley, and hopefully he'll be able to tell me what line Leston and his people have decided to take.'

'Do you think there's any point in going to see Chasen again?'

'Not really. He lied to you the first time and it looks like he lied to Leston. He's not about to change his tune at this stage. Going to see him would only exacerbate the situation. Just make it your priority to ask as many people as possible around Oxford if they saw Edward, whether he was alone – you know, that sort of thing.'

'Shit, it's all so frustrating,' she said as the cab turned into the entrance to Paddington and drew to a halt.

'I'll try to clear up my business this afternoon and be in Oxford tomorrow night. That'll give me time to meet with Critchley tomorrow morning. You never know, he might have turned up something. Okay with you?'

'That'd be great,' said Gosia.

'Okay, you call the shots. Where will I meet you? What time?'

'Let's say at the King's Head at eight. It's in Holywell Street, near Hertford. Think you can find it?'

'I'll try,' Guy replied with a grin. 'Eight. It's a date.'

Gosia stepped out of the taxi and slammed the door shut. Guy leant forward. 'Wardour Street please, driver.'

He looked back at Gosia, who was standing at the entrance to the railway station smiling and waving as the cab drove away.

Twenty minutes later a man in a pinstriped suit walked slowly along the Thames embankment, then sat on the stone wall and pulled a phone from his pocket. The tone rang in his ear for a few seconds, then there was a voice on the line. 'Yes?'

'Whitehall calling,' said Pinstripe. 'I have that name for you. Gosia Dobra. She's a hostile element. Student at Oxford. Shouldn't be too hard to find. Polish, five-eight, attractive, blonde curly hair, Slavic appearance, eight stone or thereabouts.'

'What the hell's that in pounds?'

'Wouldn't have the first idea,' Pinstripe replied calmly.

He flipped the phone shut. It was such a nice day, he thought he'd take the rest of it off.

In Earls Court, Garcia's cellular phone rang shrilly. He flipped it open.

'Yes?'

'I have a name for you. Gosia Dobra. Oxford University student. Polish. She's the one who ID'd your friend. She's your only witness.' He gave Garcia the description.

'What's that in pounds?'

'How the hell should I know. Look it up.' Costra hung up.

Garcia flipped the phone shut. He smiled. He'd deal with this problem himself.

EIGHTEEN

'There's nothing our man in London can do about the photo. It's as good as published. Not that he could have just extracted it from the Registry anyway – it's the one thing that sets bells ringing. Much better to leave a damning piece of evidence on someone's desk for a week. The moment you take it away you're playing your cards, aren't you?'

'So they all know who she is? Jesus!' Mamasian exploded.

'Hold it a second, Howard. For a start, she's got no record in London, and by the time they liaise with Interpol, it'll all be over. But more importantly, they're not sure that she's done anything anyway. They figure maybe the Polish girl's got in a snit about nothing at all. They had a long chat with Chasen and seemed to be happy with the outcome. Have to hand it to the man – weak as chicken shit when it comes to a little personal violence, but a fucking good diplomat if he can pull the wool over the eyes of the whole bunch.'

'What about the Polish girl – Gosia? How do you figure we move there?'

'I've passed it on to Garcia. Should be no problem.'

'But the fact remains that Garcia's woman has been positively ID'd by the girl,' Mamasian continued. 'So it would be safe to presume they'll make an attempt to pick her up – see what she says. Right?'

'True, but that may take time and Chasen leaves tomorrow.'

'I don't like any of this, Harry. The way this has been shaping since its inception. We've never had this kind of aggravation before.'

'We've never gone for someone high profile like Chasen before.'

'I know that,' Mamasian snapped harshly, annoyed that Costra was pointing the finger. 'It was just so damned convenient – the timing was perfect. How the fuck else could we have moved the stuff, for Christ's sake?'

'Could have waited.'

'Could have waited?' Mamasian slammed down his fork and the table shook. 'Harry, we got eighteen kilos of ninety-four per cent pure sitting in an office in London. Eight hundred dollars a fuckin' gram – maybe more when it's cut to hell and on the street. We're talking close to fifteen million US dollars, not chopped liver! Wait? No way! We had to move the shit fast! And with Bouvier dying on us in Paris what choice did we have?'

'Easy, Howard. Sure we had to choose. I just think we chose wrong 'cos we were rushed. We got the wrong psychological profile – Chasen turned out too clean. And I never liked using his son. Too much of the stick necessary because the man didn't bite the carrot.'

Mamasian's face was puce with rage. 'If we hadn't used the boy we'd be in the deepest shit right now – he'd have screamed all the way to the Special Branch; we'd be left without a courier; and fifteen million dollars worth of shit'd be hangin' around in that Paki's hands!'

Mamasian forked a slice of smoked salmon onto his plate then squeezed a lemon wedge, trying to regain control of his temper. 'We have to accept the fact that we made a big mistake. No way is he suitable in the long view. So I'd like you to close the whole of it all down when he reaches New York. Is that a logistical problem? Means setting up a housekeeping team at short notice?'

'It does, but that's no problem,' Costra said as the lobster claw he was gripping suddenly shattered, squirting juice across the table. 'Sorry, Howard,' Costra apologised matter-of-factly, taking the limb in his fingers and dipping it in the hot butter. He was inured to Howard's violent mood swings. They came and went with the abruptness of twisters. A few seconds passed.

'Butter still hot?' Mamasian asked amiably.

'Yeah.'

They ate in silence for a couple of minutes, Costra sucking at the ends of the shell. 'Garcia's worked with us for a long time, Howard.'

'I know that, Harry. You suggesting I buy him a gold watch *then* whack him?' Mamasian chuckled gently.

Costra laughed loudly, small pieces of shellfish flying from the corners of his mouth. 'Very good, Howard. Very good.' He lifted a napkin to his fat buttered lips, wiping them clean.

Mamasian pushed his chair back and placed his napkin on the table, speaking almost as if to himself. 'Let's see. There's Chasen, his son and Garcia. Well, Garcia can handle the boy . . . Edward, is it?'

'That's right,' Costra answered, helping himself to a toothpick.

'We handle Chasen in New York and then you send a housekeeper to visit Garcia. That the way you see it too?'

'That's about it.'

'What about the identification of the woman?'

'We don't have to concern ourselves with her. She can't point the finger up the chain to us because she doesn't know. That's always been the deal. By the time they pick her up, Garcia's got to be dead.'

'I'll arrange for Garcia to be taken out as soon as the transfer is complete.'

'What about the son?'

'Better take him out too. Hostage situations can lead to complications.' Mamasian sipped at his Perrier. 'That can be done at the same time. Tell Garcia to do it – he may as well have some last use to us before he disappears. Better tell him to do it after the transfer. Keep his mind clean for the business – the essentials.'

'Leave it with me, Howard,' Costra said, getting up.

NINETEEN

Luiza sat in a small Fiat Uno parked on the side of Lowndes Square that was furthest from the Embassy, facing towards Chesham Place. She wore a blonde curly wig and a jacket, the padding of which took her from a size ten to fourteen. Her make-up was a flat pale beige, the outer third of her lips painted in with the same colour to reduce their contours.

Lowndes Square was a rectangle, with a small gated park in the centre for the residents. The Embassy stood in the far right-hand corner, the Consulate on its right. The street was clear of traffic and had been so for more than five minutes. Luiza checked all the cars in the square, pulled her digital phone from the pocket of her raincoat and dialled.

Garcia was in a third-floor room of the Lowndes Hotel in Lowndes Street, directly facing the Embassy. From his vantage point he could look straight across the corner of the square to the Embassy buildings – the main diplomatic entrance dead ahead, the consular entrance to the left. He'd been there since the afternoon of the previous day, checking for any untoward activity in the square. It was always possible that the drug squad had the place under observation – so much of the heroin that found its way onto the streets of London nowadays had its origin in Pakistan.

The transfer here would be the only time the goods were vulnerable. At present they were in the building, covered by diplomatic immunity, and they'd been inviolate since they'd begun their journey from northern Pakistan two days before. Now they had to be passed over to Chasen. And though the journey was a short one, it was fraught with possible complications and dangers. There was no room for error.

Garcia's mobile rang.

'Garcia? Has the call come through?' Luiza asked.

He spoke slowly and deliberately. 'It's through. Quddus is expecting the pick-up at five to five. The two Pakis by the door are staffers having a smoke – they're on the list. Any activity your end?'

'Nothing I can see. We're clear and no traffic.'

Garcia glanced at his watch, then out the window. He could see the two Pakistanis smoking and chatting on the steps of the Embassy. To his right down the street was the grey Fiat.

'Call Van Rouen. We go now.' He flipped the phone shut and put it in his inside pocket. As Garcia entered the elevator of the Lowndes Hotel, Luiza pressed the end button on her mobile and checked the time. Fifteen seconds from six minutes to five. She dialled again.

Van Rouen sat by the window in the breakfast room on the second floor of the Sheraton Park Tower Hotel. He could see directly down the side of Lowndes Square to Luiza, and also had a clear view of the two Pakistanis joking with each other at the far end on the steps of the Embassy. The door of the consular entrance on the right-hand side was open and a few students were entering and leaving. When his mobile rang, an American sitting at a table two down from Van Rouen looked up from his newspaper with an expression of annoyance. Van Rouen looked coldly at him till the American averted his eyes – Van Rouen was not a man to stare at. Van Rouen placed the phone to his ear and listened.

'Go pick it up. You're expected.'

Luiza turned the ignition key as she saw Van Rouen exit the Sheraton and walk down the far side of the square towards the Embassy. He was dressed in a conservative grey suit and carried a copy of the *Times*. No briefcase. When he was fifteen feet from the Embassy entrance, she released the handbrake. She gave the engine a few revs as Van Rouen walked up the four steps to the front door and rang the bell of the building. The two Pakistanis paid no attention, and Van Rouen looked back towards the square – he never left his back vulnerable.

Luiza glanced again at her watch. It was exactly five to. She was excited – she loved the hands-on work. She revved the engine again, checking forwards and behind her for movement. There was none. As Van Rouen reached for the bell a second time the door was opened by a staff member. Her adrenalin was flowing now. Her hand slid down to the Browning automatic wedged between her thigh and the car door.

The Pakistani staffer stood by the open door. He was young and well dressed in a crisp dark suit. The faintest flicker of a smile crossed his face.

'Good morning, Sir. Can I help you?'

'My name is Connors. I have an appointment with Mr Muhammad Quddus.'

'Please come in, Mr Connors. Mr Quddus is expecting you.'

Van Rouen walked past him through the door and into the house. The door was closed behind him. The staffer gestured with a lazy arm. 'Please, straight ahead down the hallway. The last door on the right.'

Van Rouen halted by the door as the staffer knocked then opened it without waiting for a response.

'Mr Connors, Mr Quddus,' he said, holding the door wide open.

Quddus stood by a bay window that looked out over the houses in Montpelier Walk, at his feet a black leather case. As Van Rouen entered, he held out a hand and smiled.

'Good morning, Mr Connors. You have come for the case,' Quddus stated simply as he lifted it from the carpet and carried it to the desk. Van Rouen nodded. He had no time for niceties. The sooner he was out and had covered the half-mile to Chasen's without incident the better.

'The seals are to the right of the locks and at the base. As you will see, they are untouched.'

Van Rouen drew a small magnifying eyeglass from his pocket. Two small holes had been drilled into the top of the case near the locks and a thin wire had been threaded through the leather, effectively securing the top to the bottom. A gram or so of red sealing wax secured the ends. At the base of the case there were two further wires, threaded through the sides and the bottom. He cradled the top left wax seal and examined it closely for any fractures or signs of tampering. There were none. He checked the other three. All were in place and untouched.

'May I see your wrist, Mr Connors?'

Van Rouen pulled back his right shirt cuff. Quddus look a brief look at the scar. Satisfied, he smiled and gestured towards the door.

'I will not delay you any further, Mr Connors,' said Quddus.

Van Rouen picked up the case. It was heavy, around eighteen to twenty kilos, he guessed. On the side, embossed in gold, were the initials 'I.C.'.

Van Rouen had been inside just over a minute when Luiza flicked off the safety on her Browning, placed her right hand at the top of the driving wheel and pushed the gear lever into first. She looked briefly one more time round the square. A young woman was walking an alligator of kindergarten children down towards Pont Street. One last look at the roof tops, then she fixed her eyes on the Embassy door.

Seconds later Van Rouen stepped out into the street carrying the black case. He paused for an instant, looking towards Luiza's car, then walked to a point fifty yards ahead. Luiza pulled out sharply from the side of the road and accelerated down the street towards him. The precise moment he reached the other side of the square, the Fiat was at his side, braking abruptly, the passenger door thrown open. In a split second Van Rouen was inside, the door closed and the Fiat was racing down Lowndes Street towards Chesham Square. Van Rouen sat with the case on his lap looking ahead, behind and to the sides in quick succession.

A hundred yards down the street the car passed Motcomb Street. As it did so, a big Mercedes screamed out of the intersection, missing the rear of the Fiat by inches. It then tailed them at speed, only centimetres from their bumper till they reached Chesham Place, then braked heavily and slewed across the road, effectively blocking the street behind them. Luiza looked in the rear-view mirror with satisfaction as they flew on across Chesham Place and dived down Lyall Street. The manoeuvre had worked like a dream – Garcia had cut off any possible pursuit.

Less than thirty seconds later, Luiza braked hard, and Van Rouen was out and striding quickly through the cream arch of Lyall Mews towards Chasen's house. The Fiat stood right across the entrance, blocking anyone from entering the mews. Luiza watched as Van Rouen knocked at the door of Chasen's house, her hand closed on the Browning. The door opened and Van Rouen was inside. Lifting her foot from the clutch, Luiza pressed hard on the accelerator and shot off down Lyall Street towards Eaton Square.

'What the fuck's their game? It's not the Monte Carlo, for Christ's sake,' Pender remarked as he pressed the motor-drive continuous servo focus button on his camera.

'Fucked if I know,' Addison replied, sitting well back from the window opposite Chasen's house.

The camera was fitted with an AF-I 600 mm Nikkor telephoto IFED lens on an F4 aperture; it could identify a humming-bird at a hundred feet. Pender never used anything else – it was a must in his surveillance work, perfect for fast focusing in low-light conditions.

He concentrated the camera on the man walking down the mews, only realising his error as the Fiat pulled out and shot away. He managed a quick burst of shots on the driver's window, then returned to the figure of the man as the car disappeared.

'Whoever was driving was giving it the business,' Pender observed under his breath.

'Did you clock the rally driver?'

'Short burst, I was on the bloke.'

'Shit. Where's the big guy off to?' Pender's companion thought out loud as he gazed through his powerful binoculars. 'Shit! He's stopping at our man. Can you get a good angle?'

'He's facing away from us. His head's down anyway,' Pender replied, snapping off another burst just in case.

'Get him on the way out, for fuck's sake, or the boss man's going to piss all over us!'

'Mr Connors will deliver the case at precisely two minutes to five. Make sure you take delivery personally. Take care of the case. You will be shown the seals. Do not under any circumstances tamper with them or allow others to do so. The case will travel with you on the plane inside the cabin. I suggest you carry it at all times – do not let others carry it for you. After all, it is your son's insurance policy. To lose it would mean your son loses his life. *Ciao*.' That's what she'd said in her 1.05 a.m. call.

Chasen stood with his back to the open door of the living room. It was two minutes to five and they would be delivering the case any second. It was imperative he answer the door himself – the last thing he needed was for Lily to start asking questions.

A car braked violently at the top of the mews and moments later there was a sharp knock at the front door. 'I'll get it, darling!' he shouted.

'Sir Ivor Chasen?' asked the burly man at the door.

'That's correct.'

'This case is for you from the Ministry. Could I step inside for a moment?'

Chasen couldn't take his eyes off the case. He gestured towards the hallway. 'Of course, please come in. My study is first on the left.'

The man walked past him and entered the small study. Chasen followed, closing the door behind him.

The man placed the case on the desk, then turned to face Chasen. He pointed to the seals one by one in silence, raising his eyebrows for confirmation. Chasen nodded.

'Thank you, sir. Please have a pleasant trip. A Mr Turnbull will relieve you of the case in New York. There's no need to see me out.'

The man was already halfway to the study door when it opened and Lady Chasen entered. 'I'm sorry,' she said, 'I didn't realise you were in a meeting, Ivor.'

'Not at all, darling. Mr . . . er . . .' He searched desperately for the name the woman had given him. 'Mr

Connors was just leaving. He's brought some important papers I have to take with me tomorrow.'

'How do you do, Mr Connors,' Lily smiled sweetly.

'I'm afraid I must leave you and get back to the office, Sir Ivor,' the man said pleasantly as he made his way into the hall.

As the front door closed, Lily walked over to her husband and took his hand. 'Some tea?' she asked softly.

'Thank you, no,' he replied unsteadily. 'Maybe in a few minutes. I have a few things to do. Take a tray into the living room, I'll join you in twenty minutes or so.'

Lily looked into his eyes. There was something there that disturbed her. He looked so tired, yet he should be so happy. All they'd aspired to for so many years was about to come true. 'Are you feeling alright, Ivor darling?' she asked. 'You look pale.'

'I'm perfectly fine, Lily. A little tired, perhaps – there have been so many loose ends to tie up before tomorrow. Oh, by the way, the phonecall last night, late. I didn't want to disturb you. But it was Edward. He sent his love. He's still in Scotland with the Dillons. Said he'd try and call before we left for the airport tomorrow.' He loathed having to lie, but what choice did he have? He would have to shoulder the burden of worry for another two days, then he could tell her.

She kissed him on the cheek, smiled up at him, then left the room. As the door closed behind her, he walked over to his desk and sat. The case stood on the desk as if accusing him of some dreadful crime. How had it come to this, he wondered? What terrible thing had he done to deserve all this? In a few short days he'd plunged from unsurpassed happiness to total despair.

He breathed in deeply, trying to calm his nerves, and the strong smell of expensive leather invaded his senses like a canker. He knew what lay inside. They'd told him and he believed them. To some extent it made his choices easier. They were criminals, greedy men who were prepared to kill for a few pieces of silver. Prepared to kill his son. But they weren't terrorists – he would never have countenanced putting the lives of innocents at risk. And yet wasn't he doing exactly that? What was the difference between placing a bomb in a jet and couriering heroin to millions of children around America? Did Edward's life, put in the balance, weigh more heavily than a million unknowns?

He cast his mind back to his lunch with Ambrose. All those years of diplomacy and soft lies had stood him in good stead. Had Ambrose been fishing? Had it been purely fortuitous that after more than a year his old friend had rung him out of the blue to invite him to lunch, asking all those solicitous questions? There was no reason to suppose otherwise. There'd been something in Ambrose's eyes. A look that seemed to say, 'If you need a friend I am here. Trust me.' Yet he had not done so. It had been too late. He had made his decision and he would not be swayed. He had lied. Lied to safeguard his son. Selfishly.

He leant back in his soft leather winged chair. He would carry the case to New York. It was too late to do otherwise. Once he knew Edward was safe, he'd tell the Federal Police everything. They could protect his wife and son and the rest was immaterial. His career was now quite irrelevant. It had ceased to exist the second the woman had left his house that Monday and, fearing for the life of his son, he had not that instant reached for the phone. And now he had dealt with his blackmailers. Providing Edward lived, there was no 'terrible retribution' they could hand out that would be worse than the life that lay ahead for him now. Public disgrace. Could he live with it? He thought not.

He rose and lifted the case an inch off the desk to feel the weight, then placed it behind his desk. As he did so he noticed initials embossed on the side; his own initials – like the inscription on a cemetery headstone.

TWENTY

The interior of Victor and Ivan Gross's London offices was a homage to chrome, mirror, leather, plastic and neon. Having made a name – and a fortune – for themselves producing schlock adventure films in the early '70s, they'd later ventured into soft-core porn for the European market with equal success. Then in the late '80s their appetite for hard cash had been replaced by a thirst for critical recognition. They yearned to be taken seriously by their peers, so they searched for, and eventually found, a book that had won a major literary prize, and bought the rights. But by the time they'd hacked it into the form of a screenplay, the writing was on the wall. The author of the book publicly distanced himself from the film and, though Ivan later secured the services of three top-ranking studio stars from Paramount, the film died a terrible death at the box office.

One would have thought that the brothers would have learnt their lesson from the whole episode, but not so. Convinced that the critics had maligned them unfairly, they persevered, and the following year and each year thereafter they tortured a flagship novel into a film. They now considered themselves artists rather than cinematographic prostitutes. They stood alone in this belief.

Guy stared at the pile of identical green-faced scripts on the glass and chrome hexagonal table that stood in the centre of the room. He'd read the shooting script for the first time on the flight from Sydney to Paris and had forced himself to give it a second chance in the Meurice. But if anything, it read worse the second time.

He'd read the original novel while filming in Vancouver. It had been widely tipped for a Pulitzer but had narrowly missed out. For the first time in his life Guy had been tempted to take out a film option, only to find he'd been beaten to it – the Gross brothers had singled it out as their flagship for the year. Then six months later he'd been approached as the actor with sufficient credibility to hold the piece together and win the brothers their first Oscar nomination. Five times he'd knocked them back and five times they'd returned with more substantial offers, both financially and artistically. As the figure reached six million US, Westerman himself had flown to Sydney to beg Guy to name his terms. 'My choice of writer. My choice of director. My choice of co-star and seven million,' he'd said at last.

The brothers had agreed to everything. What did the money matter? They felt sure that with Guy's experience he'd suggest a screenwriter acceptable to all concerned. As for the co-star, as long as she was 'fuckable' – their word – that was okay with them too. So a deal was made. Now here he was in the usual quagmire of horseshit. Alistair Turner had been so enraged by the brothers' constant 'artistic' interference that he'd resigned as writer. And despite Guy's participation as the male lead, each and every serious actress he'd wanted had turned down the co-lead. Integrity obviously still meant something to some people, and Guy had, for a brief moment, felt ashamed of his avarice.

André Picheot, Guy's choice of director, sat opposite Guy with his head in his hands. Guy hadn't had a chance to speak to him since Paris, when André had only agreed after two hours' pleading to stay with the project until Guy had had a chance to have it out with the brothers Gross. Victor stood by the chrome-veneered mantelpiece, under the burgundy plastic-framed mirror, while Ivan sat on a chrome chair by the window.

'You both look so Goddamn gloomy. For Christ's sake, it's a dazzler. A dazzler,' Victor said, as if repetition would help convince them. 'Alistair did a fine job, but let's face it, his track record has never been mainstream.' This was indeed true. Alistair Turner's films had never grossed more than fifty million. Yet the Gross brothers would have given half their wealth for two per cent of the international awards he'd accumulated.

Guy put down his Evian water and took a deep breath. 'Alistair must come back and do a complete rewrite. That's the bottom line. Otherwise I'm off this picture and I would judge that so is André.' Picheot gripped the hair at the side of his head but said nothing.

'André walks off this picture now and André won't work again. Not in this country, not in France, not in the States – not anywhere! Nowhere in *his* contract is there any mention of *his* artistic say-so!' Victor shrieked, then paused for breath, forcing himself to calm down.

'Sorry to have to put it quite as bluntly as that,' he said, placing a hand on Picheot's shoulder, 'but we just can't bear to lose you. You're the best – I really mean that. Okay amigo?'

'Alistair comes back,' Guy persevered. 'You ask him back. You plead with him to come back. That's the bottom line, Victor. Else I walk. And when he comes back, he writes the final draft, not you and Ivan.'

'Okay, *you* get him back!' Victor shouted, losing his cool completely. 'He told me to shove it up my arse last time I saw him – and I don't take that kind of shit from anyone, least of all a fuckin' deadshit writer! Hell, I buy and sell those air-heads every day. And who turns their shit into films that people wanna pay money and see? Me and Ivan – that's who!'

The chrome light-fitting curving down over the chrome table bobbed up and down – such was the fury of Victor's invective. A terrible silence ensued for almost a minute. It was André who broke it.

'I could not give a *seau de merde* if *your* people see the film. It is for *my* people I make pictures,' he said barely above a whisper, now gripping his ears with his hands.

Victor looked down at him in disbelief, then across at Guy. 'What the hell's he saying?'

Guy heaved a sigh. 'He says he doesn't give a bucket of shit about the grosses, he cares about the artistic integrity of the picture. And so should you. Don't you want one Goddamn award-winning movie in your life?'

'Artistic integrity is another way of describing the kind of picture that has the general movie public running for the hills! Hell, of course I want a good picture! It was a great book. But this is Hollywood, not Pulitzer-prizeville. We all gotta make some compromises!' Victor shouted, throwing his arms wide.

'*You* make them, Victor. I told you where I come from. You speak with your lawyers, you'll see I can walk away right now. As for André, you gain nothing by nailing him to a cross.'

Victor was about to begin a fresh tirade when Ivan stood and held up a hand to his brother. He invariably knew when his brother was about to go beyond the limit of what was recoverable.

'Let's go have a drink. We're all a little over-excited and I know it's just because we care too much about the project,' he said, throwing a brotherly arm round his twin. 'Look, it's no big deal to get Alistair back. I'll ask him. He works on the script, gives it a tweak here and there, and we're all happy. Hey? Come on, guys,' he added, turning to Guy and André, 'we got a fine thing going here. Waddaya say?'

Victor thrust his hands in his pockets and breathed hard. André let go his ears for a second and looked across at Guy. Guy looked up at the two brothers. Behind them on the wall hung the large neon sign proclaiming 'Gross Pictures Inc.'.

'*Si on se couche avec des chiens – on se reveille avec des puces,*' André mumbled to himself as he rose.

'What was that, ol' buddy?' Victor asked ingenuously.

'He said he's thirsty, Victor,' Guy lied, choosing to ignore André's reference to sleeping with dogs and waking with fleas. 'Okay. Let's go for drinks,' Guy said wearily. It was the last thing he wanted. He was too concerned with the events of the last few days, too concerned for Gosia and Edward to want to deal with these idiots. Besides, he knew drinks would bring fresh nightmares.

TWENTY-ONE

His back ached and he felt as though his knees had seized entirely. The chain securing him to the wall-ring bit into his flesh just above the ankle, the rest of his body was unfettered. The man had, with only one exception, only bothered with the tape over Edward's mouth when he'd left him alone to fetch the food – and who would have heard him, anyway?

His captor stood a few metres away, leaning against a steel girder near the edge of the building, looking down at the river. It had been five days now – five days of overwhelming fear, days that Edward had spent trying to establish a relationship with his kidnapper. The man liked to talk and Edward had listened, but he knew he was getting nowhere.

'Excuse me. Could you tell me what time it is?' Edward asked.

The man looked round, bored. 'Seven,' he stated flatly.

'My legs are becoming numb. Would you let me stand? Just for a short time? Please?'

Van Rouen continued to look down at the river, ignoring Edward. A tug was pulling four doubled barges downstream – they looked very small from his vantage-point on the thirteenth floor.

'Maybe when I come back from getting food.'

The building was perfect. Not yet half finished, it had been closed down by the unions and blacked. It suited Van Rouen wonderfully. The floor he'd chosen was completely open.

He didn't like shit jobs babysitting, but he charged according to how attracted he was to a particular task, so this one was costing Garcia plenty. If he had to sit around all day it might as well be somewhere with a view – no way was he going to be stuck in some airless basement. The transfer had been fun but little more. No action. Now he was waiting on word from Garcia. Either way the boy was dead. An execution if Garcia decided he should die, an accident if he decided otherwise. Screw Garcia! No way was the boy going to run around answering a lot of questions for the police. He was going freelance after this one anyway. No more taking orders from spics!

The sun was now slipping down behind some '50s council blocks in the distance, glowing blood red. It reminded him of the spectacular sunsets of Mozambique and Angola. Those were the good years. He was his own man. He made the decisions and his group of fourteen white mercenaries and fifty-odd blacks took orders only from him. He'd moulded them into a tight, well-knit fighting team. Shit! What the hell was he doing here with this boy? He longed to be back in action, not knowing or caring whether he would see the sun set at the end of each day. The adrenalin rush of a firefight – that was worth everything.

'How much longer will you keep me here?'

The young man's words brought Van Rouen's mind back from a vision of blood and destruction.

'Not too much longer.'

'Will you let me go?'

'Of course I'll let you go. Your father does as he's told, you're free.' He shrugged his shoulders. How stupid and naïve young people could be, he thought. It beggared belief. 'What shall we have to eat tonight, eh?' he asked, letting up a little. Well, it could be the boy's last dinner, so why not let him choose.

Food was the furthest thing from Edward's mind. He was gripped again by an abject fear. Five days and still no sign of a special operations team. This man would kill him, there was no question. No blindfold.

'Do you want to crap?' the man asked as he walked to the fire stairs.

'Yes.'

'Okay,' he said, walking over to the bed and pulling the key to the padlock from his trouser pocket.

Edward massaged the bruises round his ankles as the chain was pulled free.

'Go on then, have a walk around. Get some blood into your legs.'

Edward rose unsteadily from the mattress the man had brought him on the third day, picked up the roll of toilet paper and walked to the far side of the floor away from the mattress. His brain was on fire. He couldn't just wait to die! But what chance did he have against a man so massive? He looked as though he was quite capable of taking on at least five people his size.

His eyes carefully scanned the entire expanse of the concrete floor, but there was nothing that might serve as a weapon – just a litter of paper cups and food containers.

He squatted behind a girder and took down his pants. His legs were shaking, the knees knocking against each other, as he tried to maintain his balance.

The shrill noise of the man's cellular phone sounded and Edward craned his head round. Each evening around this time the man received a call. It usually lasted only a minute or so. Yesterday it had been even less. The man seemed to just receive orders and instructions, since he said little, just the odd affirmation.

Edward could see the man look over towards him for a moment, then he seemed to mouth something into the receiver, flipping it shut as he finished.

'Done yet?' he shouted.

'Yes, coming right back,' Edward replied. He pulled up his trousers and walked back over to the man. A terrible spontaneous panic gripped his chest. Oh please, don't let me die, his mind screamed.

As he stood by the mattress, his heart pounding, he looked into the eyes of his captor, trying to interpret his thoughts.

'Chinese? Curry? You name it, you got it,' the man said as he strolled back to the spot where he'd been watching the river. He stood with his back to Edward, looking down. With the red glow of the sun waning fast, he appeared to Edward a ghostly silhouette against the evening sky.

'I don't mind. Anything,' Edward replied.

'What d'ya know. As I live and breathe I swear that's the HMS *Cormorant*,' said the man, ignoring him.

Edward could hear his own heartbeat; his eyes were glued to the big man's back. Something was wrong.

'Spent a night on the *Cormorant* once. Won a heap of money.'

What was it? Something in the tone of his voice?

'Come on over here. Take a look. She's a fine ship.' The man eased his weight off the girder and stood right at the edge, the toecaps of his shoes over the lip. He beckoned Edward with the fingers of his right hand, his head still facing front.

'Hell, you may as well enjoy your freedom for a while, I'll soon have to lock you up again.'

The phonecall. He'd been told to kill him now. He was going to throw him out into the darkness!

Edward couldn't breathe. The muscles controlling his lungs weren't functioning. His legs felt as if they'd been turned to stone.

'She's got fine lines, the *Cormorant*. Come and see for yourself,' the voice droned on softly.

Then it abruptly ceased. The silence rang in Edward's ears. The big man's hand had dropped to his side. For a split second Edward was seized with the idea of rushing headlong forward, but before he could move a muscle the man turned slowly to face him. 'Something wrong, buddy?' There was a definite edge to his tone.

'No . . .'

'Well, come on over here then. What the hell's the matter with you?'

A sudden buzzing started in Edward's ears. He moved forward slowly, his mind racing. There was no backing away now – no escape.

As he reached the man, he'd made up his mind. He knew what he'd do.

The strong man put an arm round his shoulder as he arrived beside him, in a gesture a father might afford his son.

'How do you feel, Eddie?'

'Scared.'

'No need to be, big fella,' the man said amiably.

Edward tried to brace the toe of his right foot against a lip of steel that protruded from the concrete. He spread the fingers of his left hand.

'So what'll it be, Eddie? Chinese like last night, or something different? You name it, you got it.' Edward felt the man's fingers tighten on his shoulder.

Edward felt as though his head would explode.

'Chinese would be . . .' But Edward didn't get the chance to finish the sentence. In one fluid movement, the man swept his left foot from under him, while his right hand, which a split second before had been resting on Edward's shoulder balled into a fist and punched him between the shoulder blades out into the abyss.

The fingers of Edward's left hand shot out in the darkness as his right foot stubbed the steel lip and his body tilted forwards over the edge. As they made contact with the cloth of his captor's jacket they closed like a vice.

The force of the blow to his back sent Edward spiralling sideways over the edge, his sheer momentum pulling his tormentor forwards and over with him.

Their screams mingled in the night as they fell, locked in a hideous embrace.

TWENTY-TWO

Garcia checked the room again. He was meticulous. All the clothes he and Luiza had worn in London would be disposed of. They'd used no hire cars – all had been stolen. When he left the country it would be as though he had never arrived. One passport for entry, another for departure.

He checked his watch. Luiza had been gone over an hour. Garcia was angry – why the fuck didn't Van Rouen respond? He'd known something was wrong, but had decided to wait half an hour – if the mobile was on the blink, this'd give him time to find a payphone. After that he'd sent Luiza. It was risky. If the police had taken Van Rouen, they'd be watching the place closely. But it was a risk he had to take. Costra would need to know the boy was dead.

The key turned in the lock, the door opened and Luiza entered. 'They're both dead,' she said shortly.

Garcia stared at her. 'Both? What the fuck –'

Luiza cut him short. 'An accident. That's the way I see it. I checked the whole perimeter. I was careful. No sign of anyone else.'

'Where'd you find them? What kind of accident?'

'Fell off the building. Found them together by the incinerator. Fell feet first, I'd say. Not much blood. Maybe the kid grabbed him, I don't know.'

Garcia thought quickly. Could someone else possibly have been involved? Then he dismissed the thought. Only he and Luiza knew of the location, and any other scenario seemed pure fantasy.

'Jesus,' Garcia whistled softly, a wry smile playing on his lips. 'The big guy'd be mad as hell. All those years of killing blackfellas in Angola, to be pulled out of a fucking building by a kid!' It was a lesson. Even the best had their off days.

'I got all his gear – wallet, car keys, phone,' she continued, pulling the shattered mobile from her pocket. I've got the rest of the pieces in my pocket.'

'Are the bodies visible from the road?'

'No way. The wall's over ten feet. Unless someone climbs in, no one will find them for days, possibly weeks.'

Garcia mulled over all her information in silence.

'I'll go pack the things. Okay?' she said.

'Sure,' he replied, deep in thought.

Luiza walked through into the bedroom.

Garcia walked to the curtained window. He was worried – deeply worried. Van Rouen was dead, along with the Chasen kid. It *had* to have been an unfortunate accident. But if, against all the odds, there was the hand of a third party somewhere, he'd have to watch his back as well as his employer's. He looked into the bedroom, where Luiza was packing two small bags, and his concern increased. The police now had her face on file somewhere. Costra had been angry. He didn't like mistakes. He'd been right – it should never have happened. Why had surveillance of the Chasen house been ordered and by whom? Costra knew more than he was telling. And Chasen? He'd sworn blind that it wasn't any of his doing, pleading that his only concern was his son.

Garcia looked at his watch. Chasen would be leaving in a matter of hours. Stupid bastard. He thought he'd saved his son.

Luiza appeared in the bedroom doorway, holding up a denim jacket. 'Keeping this?'

'No. Stick it in with the other stuff,' he replied.

'Have you made a decision on the girl?'

'We leave as planned.'

Luiza nodded and returned to the bedroom.

Chasen was a dead man for sure, thought Garcia. Costra hadn't said anything – he didn't need to. It was clear now that Chasen was too fragile – he'd crack under pressure. So they'd use him and throw him away. That's why he'd been told to eliminate the son. Tying up loose ends, that's what they were doing, and Chasen would never know he'd done it all for nothing.

His thoughts flitted back to Luiza again. She worried him. She was now on record, her photograph on file. It was only a matter of time before someone would check into her thoroughly, check Interpol. She'd become a liability – a threat to everyone. He could see her through the bedroom door, undressing. Perhaps the best idea would be to take her out. Business after all was business. He cursed himself for allowing her to get too close. And then he reasoned his way out of things. No, to kill her would only be to complicate matters. In two hours they'd be on separate planes to different countries. And there were the logistics of the body to be considered. He'd have to take her somewhere and kill her where there were no prying eyes. That would take time – he'd rather make the plane. Besides, she'd be curious as to why he'd changed his plans so close to departure.

Luiza poked her head round the door. 'I'm going to take a shower.'

Garcia nodded. He couldn't remember the last time he'd had so many problems. But provided all went smoothly at Kennedy Airport, things would be fine. Luiza would be in Madrid in a matter of hours. It looked likely Costra would take care of Chasen as soon as the case was secured. That left the witness – the one who'd caused all the problems. The one who'd been in the wrong place at the wrong time.

He walked over to the sideboard and tipped two fingers of tequila into a shot glass. Damn the Polish girl, he thought bitterly. Had she not been there he wouldn't be in this shit. But what could she do? Luiza would be back in Spain. Yes, it made more sense to leave. If there was any feedback it would be Luiza's problem. Then he'd have to take her out for sure. But the linkage was there, Goddamn it! She'd ID'd Luiza, and Luiza was a link to him. Jesus Christ! What if Chasen was playing a double game and the cases were intercepted at Kennedy, together with Costra's people? Things would become red hot in Europe within the hour. No, the Polish girl would have to go. But Luiza would have to do it. It was her photo on the file for Christ's sake! She'd have to postpone her flight by one day. Costra had given them a name – Dobra. She was a university student. Oxford. She'd have to do it tomorrow, before the hue and cry over Chasen's death crossed the Atlantic.

He drained his tequila. Costra never ceased to amaze him. His intelligence was all-encompassing. He knew everything before anyone else did. How had he known they had Luiza's photo? Costra kept his sources close to his chest. Garcia had worked three times for Costra now and each time the jobs had had a similar scenario. Blackmail and diplomatic staff – though never before such a high flyer as Chasen. The last mark was the German, Heinrich. He'd come across easily. Full of fear and few morals. But they'd made a big mistake with Chasen, and they were paying for it now.

He put down his glass, undressed in the living room and padded into the bathroom.

Luiza liked the water scalding and the bathroom was so full of steam he could hardly see the shower curtain.

He reached up to the small bathroom window and opened it halfway, allowing a little of the steam to dissipate. Within seconds, the vague outline of her naked body took shape through the plastic and just the silhouette gave him a hard-on. Mother of God, this was some woman. A pity that he'd have to let her go, but he couldn't work with her again. What a waste.

He pulled back the curtain and she swung round to face him, her black hair clinging to her breasts. The scalding water was rushing down her firm body, coursing down her cleavage, over her flat stomach and feeding down to the soft triangle of jet black pubic hair.

'Change of plan, *Corazon*. You'll have to see to the girl.'

She smiled, parted her legs slightly and raised herself onto the tips of her toes. Then she tossed her head back, her hair thrown like a length of whipcord, the water spraying onto the ceiling. She turned away from him, smiling back over her shoulder. He laughed as he stepped into the shower and ran his hands over her tight buttocks, slipping his right hand between her legs and taking her black bush in the palm of his hand. How he loved to fuck this woman – she was a one-off. She loved every minute of sex. It was always a feast, never predictable. He withdrew his hand and pulled her back towards him strongly, at the same time slipping his penis between her legs. She took hold of it from the front and glided her soapy hands over the inches that protruded as she pushed back against him. The water was so hot and strong it took Garcia's breath away. He buried his head in the contours of her shoulder, trying to inhale her smell, drinking it in. She moved her head, forcing his lips ever deeper into the flesh of her shoulder as she pushed back and forced his penis into her. She could hear him groan slightly. She liked to hear him groan.

She liked to hear him cry out with pleasure – not to be in control. She tightened and relaxed the muscles of her vagina with a steady rhythm, gripping him firmly then letting him go as she lifted herself off him for a second, then clamped the muscles tight as she pushed down hard onto him. As she did so she heard him shout aloud.

Suddenly his body went completely limp and she turned her head sharply to the right. Garcia's head was lolling on her shoulder. His eyes were open and a torrent of blood was pouring from his mouth. He was dead.

The weight of his body fell forward onto her.

Her mind was now functioning with the speed of a laser. Jesus Christ! Someone else was in the bathroom! Someone had shot him. Could they see her? The blood in her veins felt like ice, despite the scalding water. Her eyes flashed round the small shower cubicle as she allowed Garcia's dead weight to bring her to her knees, their bodies falling as one. Soap in the soapdish, toothbrushes and paste in the toothmug. Nothing she could use. Slowly she inched her hand up the wall, her fingers closing over the haft of her metal periodontic brush.

Garcia was now on his knees leaning against the side of the shower. She'd have to chance a look back. Nothing had happened in the last few seconds. Would he check the body? Depended on how many shots he'd pumped into Garcia's back. Two or more at close range with a .38, even with a silencer, and she wouldn't have bothered – he'd be dead. She craned her head round to the left. Through the heavy steam she was just able to glimpse a shape the other side of the curtain as it disappeared. Thank Christ, he was leaving! This was going to be the luckiest day of her life. She struggled out from underneath Garcia. The cloying smell of blood was everywhere.

She rose very slowly to her feet. As she stepped over Garcia's body, gripping the edge of the curtain, she looked down at his back. Three entry wounds. The man must have sliced the rounds. That was why the internal damage had been so great and the death so instantaneous. That's why she'd survived.

As she pulled the curtain back she strained for noises in the next room. He was rummaging in the drawers. She gripped the steel dental brush like a vice and moved towards the bathroom door, her feet padding blood across the tiles.

The noises in the living room stopped abruptly, and Luiza pressed her body against the bathroom wall next to the door, holding her breath and bracing herself for attack. Then she heard another drawer being pulled open and the sound of rummaging continued. So slowly that her body movement was scarcely perceptible, she inched her head round the side of the doorframe.

He was standing with his back to her, bending over the desk, looking through the second drawer. Medium build, mid-twenties, five-ten maybe. She could take him, she knew that. The knuckles that gripped the dental tool were as white as snow. She mentally coiled her body for the thrust, then launched herself across the room at the man. The distance was a matter of five feet.

He probably never knew what hit him. Her right arm was round his neck crushing his oesophagus with a violent pull, the other hand pounding the metal rod into the back of his neck, crushing the first vertibra at the base of his skull, driving it down into his spinal column, as her knee smashed into the small of his back. The air in the man's lungs was immediately forced out of his mouth and nose, together with a dark jet of hot blood. She wrenched his head back violently, continuing to crush his windpipe, the muscles standing out on her forearm as she ground the pick down against his spine. The force of the impact had driven it several inches into his neck.

She opened her arms wide, allowing the body to fall to the carpet. The room was strangely quiet. Only the sound of the shower in the next room disturbing the calm.

She inhaled deeply through her nose, wiping some wetness from her forehead. She examined it; it was blood and tissue of some kind. Whether Garcia's or this bastard's, she didn't know. Who was he, anyway? Who'd sent him? It was vital that she find out – her life now depended on it.

She walked back to the bathroom and stood looking into the mirror by the basin. The face that looked back was the face of nightmares. The right-hand side of her hair was matted with congealing blood where Garcia had vomited his life over her. Blood traces were everywhere: in her eyelids, her nostrils, her ear. She turned towards the shower cubicle. The water was still running but there was no steam. Shit, she thought, she'd have to shower before she did anything – couldn't walk around like this. And now the water was fucking cold.

Pulling Garcia from the shower wasn't easy. His heavy body jammed in the doorway and she had to push his head in towards his chest with her foot to pull him out sideways. Finally she dragged him across the room and propped him in a corner, the effort causing her to have to sit down on the toilet seat for a few moments to gather her strength.

As she looked across at Garcia, a sudden surge of regret flooded through her that came as a complete surprise. The past few minutes had been a single-minded fight for survival. Now, as she looked at his crumpled body, her subconscious was telling her how much she'd miss him. Shit, it was true – she'd loved his strength, his resolve, his quirky off-beat humour and his detached cruelty. And the sex had never been less than electric. He was the only man who had been her match mentally, professionally, or in bed. She closed her eyes tight shut, trying to force thoughts of Garcia from her mind and to concentrate on bringing down her pulse rate, but the image of his laughing face was still burnt on her brain. Jesus! She'd actually let a man get to her. It had never happened before – she'd never allowed it. She screwed up her eyes still tighter, trying to control her anger, ashamed at her emotional weakness. Then she opened her eyes wide, and stared long and hard at Garcia. It was just another body. Don't even think about it, she told herself. Now was *not* the time. The man was dead. It was over. This was not the time for sentimentality.

Ten minutes later she'd showered, changed into her jogging suit and finished repacking the small cases. All Garcia's effects were spread across the bed – his watch, a ruby ring, Fendi sunglasses, wallet, and his Newton. In the case to be disposed of were his clothes, her clothes, the phones, the guns, and Van Rouen's wallet and keys. She picked up the Newton, tossing it into her case, then scooped up the remainder of Garcia's valuables and threw them in the one to be discarded. Since she couldn't get rid of the body, there didn't seem much point in cleaning up the bathroom. She sat in the living room and drank a shot of tequila from a coffee mug. The dead man lay where she'd killed him in front of the desk.

Garcia's death changed everything. Whoever had killed him knew where to find him and that ruled out everyone but his current client. And for the first time, he'd let slip the name. When Garcia was on a job only the current client knew where to reach him – that was a rule, and Garcia was a man who played it by the book. But if it was someone sent by Mamasian, whoever he was, why hadn't the killer expected her to be there? Because the stupid bastard had thought she was out!

Next question. What was he looking for? Something in particular or just looking to clean up? If he was looking for something special, he'd missed it. Luiza knew where it was and even Garcia didn't know she'd seen him move it. She reached out and picked up the L–Z telephone directory, flipping it open a third of the way through. Stapled to the centre of the page was a sheet of foolscap. She ripped it from the book and held it up in front of her. Printed on it were lines of sequential numbers – nothing else. So, it was encoded. Shouldn't be too much trouble breaking it, she thought, the key would doubtless be on the Newton.

But that was for later. Another major concern still played on her mind. The girl – the one who'd seen her. It would be foolish to leave the country with her alive. With her dead, no one could tie Luiza to anything. She turned to the bathroom door. 'I hear you speaking, lover,' she said aloud. 'She's gotta go.' Then she folded the white paper, put it in her bag, took a gun and silencer from the to-be-discarded bag and added it to hers, picked up the two cases and opened the front door, turning one last time to look at the body lying beside the desk. She closed the door quietly behind her.

TWENTY-THREE

She took the two-forty from Paddington to Oxford. As the train made its slow progress through the depressingly dreary outskirts of north London, she flipped through a copy of *Hello* magazine. She looked every inch the overseas student: baggy taup cotton pants, open over-sized shirt draped over her sweatshirt, Doc Martens and a well-worn satchel she'd bought for five times its worth from a young German girl in Earls Court Road. Her hair was combed back and held in a single ponytail. She could easily have passed for twenty.

'Going back up to Oxford?'

Luiza looked up from her magazine. Seated across from her was a pudgy middle-aged businessman in a brown suit. His eyes ate her up hungrily. She smiled easily back at him.

'A friend of mine is at Oxford. I am going to visit,' she began, in a deliberately thick Spanish accent. 'You say "up" at Oxford?'

'That's correct. Doesn't have anything to do with the geography though,' he said, delighted that the conversation was now off and running. The man leant forward in his seat, unbuttoning the front of his jacket which strained against his beer gut. 'I mean, you'd still go up to Oxford if you travelled south from John O'Groats.'

'John O'Grost?'

'O'Groats. It's in Scotland. But "up" means you're studying in Oxford. "Down" means you've finished. "Sent down" means you've been kicked out, but that's another matter.' He chuckled. He'd actually been kicked out in his second year after being caught in bed with the

Dean's wife. Now he was a third-rate solicitor with his eye on the main chance.

'I see,' Luiza said, flashing her perfect teeth.

'Which college is your friend at? I read law – many years ago, of course.'

'This I forget. This I must discover.'

'Shouldn't be too hard. I'd try the university offices. They're off Little Clarendon Street. Do you know Oxford at all? Have you been there before?' he asked. 'Perhaps I could show you around.'

'You are most kind,' she replied innocently, 'but I meet a friend, my boyfriend, at the station. He will have map.'

He shifted in his seat, a look of disappointment registering on his face.

'Good,' he replied with a smile, not meaning it at all. Luiza returned to her magazine. It was all proving too easy.

Luiza slipped on a pair of plain glass spectacles as she entered the university offices. Again, she looked markedly different to the young Spanish girl the lecherous solicitor had chanced upon on the train. Her make-up was much lighter. She'd highlighted her cheekbones and nose and shaded her cheeks and temples. She looked five kilos lighter and her face had a more angular structure.

She waited her turn in a queue of young students amongst whom she blended easily. Little Clarendon Street hadn't been difficult to find.

'Next, please.' A woman with a kind face and grey-flecked hair beckoned Luiza forward. 'Can I help you?' she asked.

'Yes please. I'm here to see a friend,' she began with a slight French lilt to her voice. 'She wrote to me in Paris, but I can't remember which college. Do you have a list of some kind?' She gave the woman one of her most innocent and beguiling looks. She would have preferred to look at a list than mention the name Dobra – that way she could have been searching for anyone.

'Yes we do have lists. But I'm afraid I'm not in a position to give out addresses. I'm sorry.'

Luiza gave her a nonplussed look.

'Yes, I can appreciate that you might think it a little odd,' the woman said, 'and I'm quite sure you are not a murderess, but many students do not wish us to give out their addresses, so our policy is not to do so. Again, I'm sorry. Perhaps you'd like to leave a message which I could forward to your friend?'

'It's okay, thank you. I'm sure I'll find her soon.' She hoped she would. Gosia Dobra. Five-eight, very pretty, Slavic, soft blonde curly hair.

She walked up the street and turned right towards Somerville College, removing her reading glasses, replacing them with dark sunglasses, and pulling a crumpled cotton broad-brimmed hat from her bag.

Inside the Porter's Lodge she poked her head through the window behind which sat a man dressed in blue.

'Excuse me, have you seen Gosia Dobra today?'

The porter looked up from his newspaper. All he could see was a floppy broad-brimmed hat and sunglasses.

'Who?' he replied.

'Gosia Dobra,' she repeated.

'Not here. You must have got the wrong college. Never heard of her,' the porter replied, then returned to the pages of his tabloid.

'Thanks,' Luiza said brightly, and disappeared. One down and twenty-eight to go, she thought as she flipped through the *Oxford Handbook* she'd bought in the university offices.

She walked down Woodstock Road and popped in at St Cross College to be informed curtly that it was an all-postgraduate college. 'Sorry,' she said politely and wandered down to St John's, where she struck out again.

Next was Balliol, then through the carefully manicured gardens of Trinity to the magnificent edifice of the college itself. No luck again. It had taken her well over an hour and there were twenty-four damn colleges to go.

She cut left down Catte Street, glancing left at the Bridge of Sighs which linked the two parts of Hertford College.

Inside the college gates she stopped at the porter's window.

She couldn't see anyone so she called out. 'Excuse me? Is there anyone there?' A few seconds later a woman of around forty appeared.

'Yes, can I help you?'

'Sorry to trouble you. Seen Gosia Dobra around?'

'Not since this morning. May be in her rooms, don't know,' the woman replied lightly.

'Thanks, I'll take a look,' Luiza said, smiling, and walked through. She turned left as she entered the main quadrangle so as to appear to be definitely going somewhere in case the woman behind her was looking. She hoped she'd made the right choice.

She paused at the base of the stone staircase, pretending to read the multitude of notices on the boards lining the walls as she debated her next move. To enquire further would be to arouse unnecessary suspicion. She didn't want a whole bunch of the girl's buddies telling her someone had been looking for her. The conversation with the porter had been so casual it was not likely she'd think to pass it on to the girl. Besides, to kill the girl in her room might present problems. First of all there was the question of ascertaining which one it was, then the difficulty of gaining entry without arousing suspicion. And what if she wasn't actually in her room at the time, or was with others, or came later while Luiza was inside, and came again with company. No, she had to confront the girl alone. She'd have to sight her, make a positive identification, pick a crowded place where she herself had many avenues of escape – somewhere she could melt into the crowd. She preferred to do her work in the open – inside a building, one was easily trapped.

As she passed back out through the doors of Hertford she noticed a door the other side of Catte Street, cut into the great doors of the entrance to the Bodleian Library quadrangle. If she stood inside the square, she thought, she could look straight through the door towards the entrance to Hertford. It was a good observation point, but it looked as though it was a gate that might soon be closed. She looked at her watch: it was getting late.

She stayed for an hour, walking to and fro, appearing to read a tourist book, glancing every few seconds through the gate towards Hertford. But there was no sign of Gosia. Then an elderly man crossed from the Bodleian Library and pushed the door shut, locking it with an outsized key. Damn, she thought, she'd have to observe from elsewhere.

She missed Gosia by less than ten seconds as she crossed Broad Street to take up a position looking back along Catte Street towards the entrance to Hertford. Her attention was diverted by the sight of Guy Cooper approaching her along Broad Street. She'd seen a few of his films and liked them. Behind her, Gosia entered the

King's Head, unaware that her would-be assassin was a matter of feet away, the other side of the road, her back turned to her.

Gosia sat at a corner table so she could watch the door. Within a minute Guy was standing in the doorway looking around.

'Over here!' she called out to him.

'What'll you have?' he asked after giving her a hug, but Gosia was on her feet already.

'No, I'll get it. My treat. I'll get you a surprise. You'll like it.'

Gosia disappeared to the bar, searching in her old satchel for her purse. Guy watched her standing at the bar, hoping she wouldn't come back with a pint of warm, flat real ale. After twelve years of crisp ice-cold lagers in Sydney it was a drink he couldn't stomach any more. Within a minute she was back holding a pint of dark brown ale and a glass of white wine.

'Old Speckled Hen. Pint thereof,' she said, smiling broadly as she handed him the glass. 'It's the best I've ever tasted.'

'Looks terrific. But if it's so damned good, how come you've bought yourself a glass of wine?'

'I said it was the best I ever tasted. I didn't say I liked it.' She grinned, then her expression changed to one of disappointment. 'Don't you like real ale?'

'Love it,' Guy replied, taking the glass from her.

'Cheers,' she said, holding up her glass.

'*Salut*,' Guy replied, taking down a good third of the stuff. Might as well get it down as quickly as possible, he thought.

'I don't suppose you've turned up anything or you would have called me,' he said, the aftertaste of the beer causing his face to twitch slightly.

'No. Nothing. I've had the most frustrating day of my life, wandering around asking if anyone's seen Edward, not being able to tell them why. No one's seen him since Saturday. I was most probably the last. I thought maybe I'd get lucky and find someone who had seen him being bundled into a car by strangers and made a mental note of the numberplate. Yes I know,' she added, holding up her hand, seeing that Guy was about to interrupt, 'I've been watching too many movies.'

She sipped her white wine. 'Anything your end? Did your friend Critchley come up with anything?'

'They've been running the photograph of the woman past Interpol. As yet there's no response. Usually means they don't have anything on her – they get back pretty quickly if they do. But it could be that she's changed her appearance. If she has, it'll take longer. They'll use computers and form possible composites.'

Gosia's shoulders drooped. 'Oh God. Everything takes so much time and that's what we ain't got.'

'You've been picking up the local patois I see,' Guy observed, trying to lighten the atmosphere.

'How can that bastard leave for the States when his son is still a hostage? I just can't come to terms with that,' she continued in anguished tones. Then she looked back at Guy.

'What does Critchley think is running through Leston's mind? Surely Critchley'd know how much Chasen told Leston, and whether Leston wants to keep it from us?'

Guy stared at Gosia, not knowing what to say. How could he put it without sending her into a fit of rage? 'Look. I'm going to be very frank with you and I want you to listen calmly to what I have to say. As a favour to me. Then we can continue to do our best for Edward in our own way and with whatever means available.'

Her face suddenly took on a desolate look. 'He's told them nothing, has he?' she said softly. 'The bastard's told them nothing. I knew it. And they believe him, don't they? They think *I'm* the crackpot, not him. Jesus Christ.'

'That's what Critchley thinks. Of course they might be keeping it from him as well,' Guy continued, but he didn't think he sounded very convincing.

'Yeah, yeah, yeah,' she muttered. 'So what do we do now, tough guy?' she continued after taking a deep breath.

Guy stared at her for some time. Tough guy. No one had called him that for seven years.

'What's the matter, Guy?' she said, smiling. 'I'll get you a lager. What do you call it – a frostie?'

'No, it's not that. Not that at all. It's just that the last person to call me "tough guy" was Marysia. It took me by surprise. Like going back in a time capsule.'

Gosia looked a trifle awkward, then her face brightened and she stood. 'A frostie it is! Then we plan our next move.'

While she was at the bar Guy tried to think of any positive steps he'd overlooked. Chasen had left for New York and Critchley had told him all had gone smoothly. What was he up to? Discounting that Leston was indeed keeping the true facts from Critchley, it appeared that Chasen was going along with the kidnappers. What did they want from him? Was it something that would take a matter of days or something that would take weeks? Should he go to New York himself – what would be the point? He was beginning to share some of Gosia's frustration. Was Chasen taking something to New York for them? If so, there was every reason to believe, as Chasen surely would, that they would release Edward when he arrived in New York, or shortly afterwards when they took delivery. That would certainly explain Chasen's leaving for the States while Edward was still a hostage. The more he thought about it, the more he liked that idea. It was about the only positive thought he'd had all day. But it was still possible they wanted Chasen to do something for them in New York, possibly something political, using the power of his post at the UN. That also fitted with Chasen's persistence in travelling despite the situation here.

'Fosters!' Gosia said loudly, breaking his concentration. She plonked the pint down in front of him. 'Decided I'd have one too.'

As they drank their beer, Guy outlined his new train of thought to her, preferring to lean towards the courier angle.

'That means we have to sit around again and wait for something to happen, right?'

He had to admire her strength. She was obviously so worried, yet she held it together like a trooper. 'Can't see any alternative. Sorry,' he said.

'Christ, don't apologise. You've been bloody marvellous. It's hardly your fault you haven't cracked the case yet.' Up went the hand again. 'I know, I know, too many movies!' But there was a new-found lightness in her voice, as if she'd decided Guy deserved support and her attitude needed changing.

Guy took a long draught of Fosters. Though perhaps twenty degrees too warm, it was as refreshing a drink as he'd find.

'This place used to be far nicer before they did it up,' Gosia said, trying to introduce a lighter subject. 'Lovely old dirty brown chipped paintwork, brown pews and comfy brown velvet cushions. A dear old man used to sit over there,' she said, pointing to the corner by the door. 'He was a poet. Dead now.'

But Guy's mind was elsewhere. 'You remember you said in Paris you might ask your mother if she had an address for Marysia?'

'Yes?' Gosia sipped her beer.

He paused, then continued. 'I just wondered if you'd asked her yet.'

'Yes, I did,' she said. 'Posted the letter a couple of days ago.'

'Thank you. I just thought you might have spoken to her on the phone, that's all.'

'It's very difficult calling Poland. Takes forever. Would you like me to try? I will if you want.'

'Maybe tomorrow. There's no real hurry. I've waited this long. What's another few days, eh?'

'True,' she replied, then changed the subject. 'Where are you staying? The Randolph?'

'Yes,' Guy replied amiably. 'Shall we have a bite to eat?'

'I'm not that hungry.'

'Gosia,' Guy said sharply. 'You have to eat. Fasting solves nothing. If you're going to help at all, you've got to keep your strength up.'

Her expression changed immediately from melancholy to annoyance. 'Please don't treat me like a child, Guy.' They locked eyes briefly, then Gosia smiled.

'That's better,' said Guy. 'Now you're mad as hell and we may eventually get somewhere. So . . . Browns?'

'I'd rather not go there. It was the last place I saw Edward and it would feel a bit strange.'

'I understand. Where do you suggest?'

'Do you like West Indian food?'

'Love it,' Guy replied.

'Right, then it's the Hi-Lo Jamaican Eating House. It's very unconventional. They ignore you if they don't like the look of you – takes forever to get served. But the food's great. Hot and spicy and the portions are huge. You'll either love it or hate it.'

From the entrance to a bookshop across the road, Luiza took a good look at Gosia as she left the King's Head. Definitely a possible, she thought to herself, but she was walking away from Hertford rather than towards it. Then she noticed the girl was arm in arm with the film actor and changed her mind. Probably not. This one was most likely some girlfriend he'd picked up in London. She watched them walk up Broad Street, then crossed the street and walked by Hertford again. It was going to be a long night.

The dinner was a great success. The head waiter took one look at Guy and sat them at the best table. The reggae music was turned up full blast and the entire restaurant immediately went into party mode. To give the chef his due, the food was remarkable. The dishes kept coming and Gosia just kept eating, surprising both of them with her sudden appetite. Guy hadn't seen a girl eat that much since he'd watched Marysia devour meal after meal as they flew through Europe all those years ago. It all helped to divert Gosia's mind from Edward – albeit temporarily – and her face was alive with smiles.

As they walked back towards the centre of town just over an hour later, Gosia turned to Guy. 'Do you have to get back to London?'

'No. As far as I know, I don't begin principal photography for two weeks – that's if I do so at all.'

'Is there a problem?'

'A script problem. There's still a lot wrong with it. Meantime I'll stay here and see what we can do.'

Gosia stopped by a tree and leant against it. 'Guy?'

'Yes.'

'Do you think Edward is still alive?' she said very quietly. 'I know you've been trying to take my mind off him for the past hour or so, and I thank you for it, but he's always there whenever I shut my eyes. I can see his face, and it's so terrible being powerless to help.'

She turned her face away from Guy, but he could see she was now crying. He put an arm round her shoulder and hugged her to him.

'He's alive. We'll help him somehow. How about we meet tomorrow morning. How does that sound?'

'You're a lovely man, Mr Cooper,' she replied after a few seconds. 'Okay, outside the Bodleian in Old Schools Quad at eleven? By the statue of Pembroke? It's through that door,' she said, pointing across the street to the entrance to the Bodleian.

'See you then.'

She stood on tip-toe and kissed him on the cheek. 'Thanks for everything. You're one of the best.'

Guy didn't know what to say. It was like saying good-night to his daughter. He waved as she unlocked the Hertford door and disappeared inside.

Fifty feet down Catte Street, Luiza stood leaning against the stone wall, her body masked by a car. '*Mañana*,' she whispered softly to herself as she saw Gosia step through the door into Hertford.

TWENTY-FOUR

Chasen glanced up at the locker where the senior flight stewardess had placed the case. It was the first time it had been out of his hand since he'd left Lyall Mews. His Embassy chauffeur in London had tried to put it in the boot, his junior minister had offered to carry it for him on the way to the VIP lounge, and a British Airways staffer had volunteered to take it aboard flight BA 179 to Kennedy Airport for him as he secured a label reading 'security checked' to the handle. Each time Chasen had politely refused. For the past four hours he'd sweated. It was always possible that there was some explosive device in it. He'd discounted this likelihood in London, but now that he was thirty thousand feet in the air he felt very vulnerable, and sweated for the safety of Lily and all the innocent men, women and children on the flight.

Lily slept the sleep of the innocent beside him.

As he'd left Lyall Mews he'd wondered what might eventuate at the airport. His personal effects had the same privileges afforded the diplomatic bag, but he wasn't so sure about his personal hand luggage. He needn't have worried. Peter Haines, his assistant, had whisked them through passport control with the minimum of fuss. His luggage, together with the diplomatic pouch – an off-white sackcloth pouch secured by brass ringlets through which were threaded the eyes that held it securely together, had disappeared in another direction as the Chasen party made its way to the VIP lounge. The thought of placing the case on the conveyor belt at security, for some nameless guard to view the contents on his X-ray monitor, was too horrifying to even contemplate.

He shifted in his wide first-class seat, various unconnected thoughts flying through his mind: of Edward and his captors, of the UN building where his offices would be, and the residence he'd take over from his predecessor. Where and when would they take possession of the case? And the phone? It was in the inside left-hand pocket of his suit jacket. Haines had briefed him on security – that was now a matter for the Americans, who were usually highly efficient. Not too efficient, he hoped. Somehow he had to make sure the case got into the right hands or Edward would not be released.

He switched on his reading light and looked at the time. In an hour or so they'd be touching down at Kennedy and the nightmare would hopefully end.

A steward leant across and asked if he cared for any refreshments. Did he wish to waken his wife? Perhaps she might like to freshen up before the descent which was in forty-five minutes? He shook his head at the steward – he'd wake her later. He closed his eyes once more and the disturbing images returned.

They were met in the airport tunnel by a high-ranking airport security official, an airport staffer, his Minister Richard Hammond from the UK mission, and the Deputy Permanent Minister, Anthony Bryan.

'Richard Hammond, from the mission, Sir Ivor.' Chasen's number two shook Lily's outstretched hand. 'Lady Chasen,' he continued politely, 'welcome to the United States.' He then turned back to Chasen. 'Let me relieve you of that, Sir,' he said, reaching for the case.

'That's alright, I'll hang on to it,' Chasen replied, striding purposefully towards passport control.

'I've arranged to get us through passport control as quickly as possible. The Embassy car's directly outside,' Hammond said.

He was true to his word. While the queues were fifty feet long elsewhere, the Chasen entourage was escorted to a booth to one side. A quick glimpse of the diplomatic passports was all that was needed, then they walked through the customs hall to the exit designated for those with nothing to declare. Chasen's heart was thundering like a pile-driver as he walked past the customs officers, the case gripped like a vice in his right hand.

As he stepped into the main concourse of the airport, several flashes of light startled him. Hammond was immediately at his side, quickly explaining.

'Frightfully sorry, Sir. It's the press. They must have got wind you were arriving. They don't miss much, do they?' he said, then added awkwardly, 'They weren't here an hour ago. Do you feel you might stop for a second, Sir, so they can get some shots?'

'One minute, Hammond, that's all,' Chasen replied, gathering his composure. 'But I'm not giving a bloody press conference, I've only just arrived.'

'Right you are, Sir. Quite understand,' Hammond said, then held up his hands in front of the many reporters and photographers milling in front of them.

'Sir Ivor Chasen has just flown from London, as I'm sure you are aware, and I know you'll also appreciate that he and Lady Chasen are very tired. If you'd like to take the opportunity to take some pictures now, please do so. However, he will not be answering questions. Please bear with us on that point. Thank you.'

The crowd pressed forward, cameras ready.

Lily leant towards Chasen, putting her hand in his. 'I'll take that, Ivor. You're Her Majesty's Permanent Representative to the United Nations – you look like a tourist holding on to that damned bag.'

He looked sharply round to her, momentarily panicked. What choice did he have? It would only be a matter of seconds. He let go. The cameras flashed for a few moments, then Hammond held up a hand.

'Thank you, ladies and gentlemen, I think that should be adequate. Thank you.' With that the press began to disperse. Chasen turned to Lily. Her hands were empty. He felt as though the bottom had fallen out of his stomach.

'The bag,' he croaked. 'Where is the bag?'

'Whatever's the matter, darling? I gave it to one of your people. He said he'd take it directly to the car. What on earth was in it, darling – it weighed a tonne.'

'The man. What did he look like?' he replied sharply.

'Youngish, slim, short fair hair. Why? Whatever's the matter, darling? Don't make such a fuss.'

'Did he give you his name?'

'Yes, he said his name was Turnbull.'

Just then Hammond turned from the retreating press.

'Something amiss?' he enquired solicitously.

'No, nothing,' Chasen murmured, then took his wife's arm and made his way to the exit. His heart skipped a beat. The phone! What about the mobile? Surely they wouldn't let him keep that?

Hammond held open the door of the long wheelbase Infiniti and both Lily and Chasen climbed inside.

'We'll follow in the the Explorer, Sir,' Hammond said and closed the door.

Walt Citron drove with a purpose. He was on a promise. He'd pursued his secretary relentlessly for over six months and she'd caved in at last. He'd told his wife he was leaving earlier than expected. 'Big order to fill down in DC,' he'd said, and she'd believed him. She loved Walt with a lack of guile he'd found endearing for the first few years of his marriage, but disappointingly dull for the last ten. Rita was another thing altogether. Five foot-two, with a mane of wildly luxuriant auburn hair, she made up for her height handsomely with her perfect figure. He smacked his lips just at the thought of her. A couple more minutes he'd be over the Queensboro Bridge across the East River and into Queens. What the hell, he thought, if she turned all cutesy he'd spend the night in town and take off for DC in the morning.

He turned up the radio as he sped past the UN building, travelling north on First Avenue. The station was playing some thumping music, the African-American lyrics of which referred to the vocalist's need for animal sex. He grinned. He sure was looking forward to some himself.

As he made a left on Fifty-Seventh he turned up the music still further and reached for a Coors, snapping it open with his right hand and chuggalugging the beer as he rocked in the seat in time to the pounding rhythm. Then he made a right onto the slip road that led up to the lower level of the bridge, vaguely aware of the thunder of traffic above him on the upper level.

The traffic was remarkably light for that time of night. Walt drummed the wheel of the Volvo as he sped across the bridge.

He glanced across the empty lanes to his right. He could pick out the Roosevelt Memorial at the tip of Roosevelt Island. Then there was a blinding flash of light ahead of him, followed by a deafening explosion that shook him to the core. He swung his head back to the front. A long black car up ahead the other side of the three-foot jersey barriers had erupted in a ball of fire, showering debris in all directions. As if shot from a cannon, it rose into the air, clearing the jersey barrier as it somersaulted forwards, smashing down again into the west-bound lane two hundred yards ahead of him at well over fifty miles an hour.

Walt slammed his left foot down hard, the brakes of the ancient Volvo immediately locking, sending the car sliding at once into a four-wheel drift across the slow lanes. It impacted violently sideways into the right-hand steel barrier of the bridge, the windscreen exploding inwards, then bounced back into the roadway.

It all happened in a split second but to Walt it seemed like minutes. He wrenched at the wheel as the car bounced off the steel supports, his head pulled violently to one side, his body straining against the seatbelt as the car ricocheted back across two lanes. His face felt as though he'd been whipped by broken glass, and cold air poured through the shattered windscreen. He could see the dash and instrument panel spotted with his own blood.

He looked through the remains of the windscreen in horror as the fireball kept coming towards him, now just a chassis careering down the fast lane on its roof, engulfed in flames. The Volvo continued to revolve as it's momentum carried it towards the inferno, despite the brakes – the tyres screaming. Now he was facing a red Mustang which seconds before had been behind approaching at speed. He could see the terror-stricken face of a woman fighting with the wheel as she attempted to control her vehicle. A second later it crashed into the front of his, adding twenty miles and hour to the Volvo's speed as it slid backwards towards the fireball. It felt like an explosion. Walt's rear-view mirror shone like a beacon of orange flame. The shriek of grinding and twisting metal mixed with the tortured sound of shredding rubber on the blacktop as the Volvo and the Mustang locked fenders and strained to wrench in different directions. As one, the two locked cars crashed back into the bridge supports, then were thrown out again towards the centre, Walt's head once more violently thrashed forward. With an excruciatingly intense lance of pain at the base of his skull, he heard a sound like a pistol shot and knew his neck was broken. He struggled to raise it from his chest, but couldn't. His eyes swivelled upwards: the wall of flame was now only twenty feet away and still bearing down relentlessly. He glanced down. His lap looked as though it was covered with diamonds and rubies – the shards of glass mixed with his blood. He stared in disbelief at the locked seatbelt, attempting to move his fingers, but there was no feeling in his body. He opened his mouth in a terrible scream as the Volvo continued its carousel. Then the fireball hit him head-on.

'Shit! What the fuck was that mother?' the driver of a blue pick-up shouted a hundred yards behind. Two cars had screamed past him the other side of the jersey barrier travelling west. He could see the flames and devastation up ahead.

He jammed his foot down and accelerated forwards, then stood on the brakes fifteen feet behind the wreckage and leapt out. The heat was intense. The flames had already engulfed both what remained of the Infiniti and the Volvo, and were licking at the front of the red sports car. Petrol was pouring from the hood of the Mustang. A woman was beating at the driver's window, her face a sheet of blood, her eyes stark with terror.

He raced back to his pick-up and snatched at a tyre lever, running back to the Mustang and driving it hard into the doorframe. The door was shaking violently as the woman pounded from inside. The hairs on the man's arms were beginning to singe. Then the metal gave way and the woman fell onto the road. He just had time to grab her arm and drag her to safety before the

Mustang went up, sending another sheet of flame into the night. Behind him cars backed up all the way to First Avenue. Drivers ran forwards to help, screaming and shouting. On the other side of the carnage three men stood in front of an Explorer, shielding their faces from the intense heat. There was nothing they could have done anyway, no one could have survived in the inferno.

The bridge shuddered as the Volvo's tank blew. As the pick-up driver wrapped a blanket round the woman at the side of his car, he heard the horns of the firetrucks wailing in the distance.

TWENTY-FIVE

Oxford in the summer is a nightmare of coaches and tourists. Sightseers from every corner of the globe converge on the small city, cameras poised, maps in hand. They crush into the souvenir shops to buy the ubiquitous Oxford sweatshirts, and pack out the low oak-beamed taverns. They squeeze into the libraries, speaking loudly in a variety of languages, and are led in herds of twenty or more through the colleges themselves. Saturday mornings in an Oxford summer resemble a canvas by Hieronymus Bosch. Little wonder that students and academic staff make themselves scarce.

Guy breakfasted early at the Randolph, then called Critchley at the Elizabeth. But Critchley had checked out and Guy was redirected to the Shelbourne Hotel in Dublin. He decided to call him later in the afternoon in Ireland. With time to spare before meeting Gosia, Guy occupied himself with the third draft of the notes Alistair had couriered him from London. Evidently Ivan had succeeded in persuading him to rejoin the project.

The sun was shining in through the big picture windows of the reading room, so he decided to take a leisurely walk around the town. One step outside and he realised it mightn't be as leisurely as he'd hoped. A line of tourist coaches disgorging their occupants had virtually blocked St Giles, a line of cars vainly attempting to squeeze past.

He walked past the Wren's Shedonian Theatre, built in 1664 for the great ceremonies of the university, and through the archway into the Old Schools Quad, where he could see the statue of the Earl of Pembroke, the

Chancellor of the university at the time the quad was built, standing at the entrance to the Bodleian Library.

Guy peered across the quad to the gate in the vast door the other side of the square, where he knew Gosia would be approaching from Hertford, but a sea of foreigners weaved in and out before him. He stood on the base of the statue of Pembroke, raising himself a few inches higher. Immediately he caught sight of her, smiling broadly and waving at him. Then she was lost for an instant in the milling crowds. He caught sight of her again – she was making a funny face at him as if exasperated with the crowds. Then she looked around sharply and vanished in the throng once more.

A minute had passed and Guy was wondering where she'd got to, when he heard a man shouting very loudly and several women screaming. He pushed strongly towards the centre, a terrible foreboding in his chest.

'My God, a girl's been shot!' he heard as he ran.

At once, everyone was elbowing and shoving. Children were being grasped by anxious parents, thrust out of reach of an unknown assassin. Guy battled his way through the confusion.

Lying spreadeagled on the cobbles was the small figure of Gosia. A young man was cradling her head in his hands and shouting at the crowd to back off. Guy knelt down beside them, his heart pounding.

'I'm her friend,' he shouted to the young man over the clamour of the hysterical crowd.

Her eyes were still just open and she was breathing in short shallow bursts. A stain of blood had formed on the white summer frock she was wearing. It was half-way down her left side.

'Someone call an ambulance!' Guy yelled, then bent down close to Gosia's face. 'It's me. Guy. I'm here and you're safe. We'll soon have you comfortable,' he said as calmly as possible, a broad smile on his face. If shock set in before they could get her to intensive care, she stood no chance.

Finally Guy heard the sirens of the ambulance approaching and shouts to clear the area. Not long after, the ambulance men broke through, a policeman with them. An oxygen mask was placed on Gosia's face and she was given a shot of something.

As Guy looked down at her face he thought he saw her lips move as if she was attempting to say something, but only a thin trickle of blood ran down her chin. The medic applied a wide square pressure bandage to her side to staunch the flow of blood.

Seconds later she was lifted gently onto a stretcher and sped back to the ambulance in Catte Street. The back doors were opened and in moments Gosia was inside and the medic was attaching a drip.

'You related?' the policeman behind him asked urgently.

'Yes,' Guy replied to save time.

'Jump in, then. I'll take to you to the hospital.'

Guy leapt in and the ambulance screamed off, its siren sounding.

Guy stroked Gosia's hair as they raced through the streets of Oxford, reassuring her all the while. Her eyes were now shut tight and her breathing had almost stopped. The medic shot Guy a look of comfort. Then, after what seemed like an age, the ambulance slowed and stopped, the doors were thrown open and two porters, a doctor and a nurse took charge, hurrying her into the hospital and down the corridor, Guy right behind them.

The stretcher disappeared through swinging double perspex doors and Guy was about to push through when a middle-aged sister held his arm firmly.

'She's been taken directly into surgery. I'm afraid you can't go in there,' she said kindly. 'Would you like to wait here? I'll bring you a cup of tea. How about that?'

Guy looked at the compassionate face but couldn't reply. He opened his mouth but his tongue wouldn't function, his brain overwhelmed with horror, fear for Gosia, dread that she might die, and an all-encompassing despair. The nursing sister put an arm round his shoulders, guiding him to a bench a few feet down the corridor from the theatre, and sat him down. She stayed with him for a while, then went to get him some tea.

Guy felt the touch of a hand on his shoulder and looked up sharply.

'Excuse me, you're Guy Cooper aren't you? I'm Betty Landers from the university office.'

He stared at her blankly.

'Thank you for calling us. Has there been any word yet about her condition?' the woman continued.

Guy shook his head. 'No, she's still in surgery,' he replied, his voice thick with emotion.

'There are some detectives in the waiting room down the hall. I asked them to leave you in peace for the moment but I think they'd like to talk to you as soon as possible.'

Guy just stared at the double perspex doors where they'd taken Gosia.

'Are you Gosia's father?' Mrs Landers continued softly.

'No, just a friend.'

'I see,' she replied, then opened her briefcase and withdrew a sheaf of papers. 'I have all her registration details here. She's Polish, you know.'

'Yes, I know that.'

'Do you know how we can get in contact with her mother?' said the woman.

'I'm afraid not. Don't you have a number for her there?' Guy replied, indicating the papers.

'Well, naturally we rang the number given as soon as we received word of what happened. But we were assured that the number doesn't exist.' She looked up at the ceiling. 'The mother, Marysia Knoll, just can't be reached.'

'Miss Knoll is not her mother.'

Mrs Landers stared at Guy for a few seconds, puzzled. 'I'm afraid you must be mistaken, Mr Cooper. She rang us a few months ago on some other matter and I spoke to her myself.'

Guy continued to look at the page. Under the heading 'Next of Kin' was written: *1. Marysia Knoll. 23 Zielna Warsaw. Tel (48) 405 654. Mother.*

'Oh dear,' the woman said softly to herself. 'I've no idea at all what I should do.' She paused for a second then continued, wringing her hands. 'You say you are not related to her in any way?'

'I have only known her for a few days. She told me she was a friend of a close friend of mine. It now appears that my friend and her mother are one and the same. I've no idea why she chose to tell me otherwise.'

'Do you have her mother's number?' Mrs Landers asked hopefully.

'I'm afraid I don't,' he replied, and the look of depression clouded her face again.

'She's on a Webber scholarship, you know.'

'Yes, I know that, Mrs Landers. I am a trustee of the foundation. That's another reason I came over from France to see her.'

There was a spark of comprehension in her eyes. 'Of course you are, Mr Cooper. I'm afraid I tend to think of you as a film actor rather than a philanthropist.'

'I may be able to help you contact her mother.'

'Yes?' she said, brightening.

'If you are sufficiently sure that she is the mother.'

'I'm sure,' she said. 'Look, I can see you'd sooner be on your own. I've asked the hospital to let us know immediately if there are any further developments. If you can reach Ms Knoll, can you call us immediately,' she pleaded, taking the paper from Guy and replacing it in her briefcase.

'Of course,' he replied.

She placed a comforting hand on Guy's shoulder, then walked back down the hall to the hospital exit.

Guy sat in stunned silence. How was that possible? Marysia had never mentioned a child seven years ago. Where had Gosia been when he and Marysia had been in Europe? Who had been looking after her? How would he possibly get hold of Marysia? He looked again at the perspex door. Please, please let Gosia be alright.

He stood up and began pacing up and down the corridor.

Why had Gosia lied to him? What was she hiding? Was the shooting completely divorced from the Chasen case, but instead connected to Marysia's activities? Ehud had made it clear that Marysia was in deep cover, in hiding from the Hizballah. Could this have any bearing on the shooting?

He stopped pacing for a second then sat. Now he was faced with the prospect of an interview with the police. Should he tell them everything? Because everything included Marysia's possible involvement, and what he'd been told by Ehud would seriously compromise her safety. No, he'd keep that to himself and leave it for Ehud to explore. There didn't seem any point in appraising the Oxford Constabulary of the fact that Gosia's mother had been a Mossad agent. That might come later, but not now.

The perspex doors eventually swung open and a doctor approached him. Guy stood at once.

'Mr Cooper, I think I can tell you she's past the crisis. Still very serious indeed, but we have managed to stabilise her condition a little. She'll be in surgery for another hour or so and then we'll take her directly to intensive care. I just thought I'd step out and tell you how things were progressing.'

'She was shot?'

'Yes, she was shot. At close range with a handgun. I'm not an expert with weapons, I'm afraid, just a surgeon, so I can't be more specific than that. We removed the bullet, which was a feat in itself. Her ribcage slowed it down and it had embedded itself behind the kidneys. A centimetre further and it would have torn them to shreds. In that respect alone she's a lucky girl.'

'Thank you very much for letting me know.'

'That's alright, Mr Cooper, Dr Gold is closing her right now – sewing her up, so to speak. But I don't think there's much point in you hanging around here for the time being – no one will be allowed in for some time.'

'I see,' Guy replied.

'Give your address and a number where you can be reached to sister and we'll call you if there's any change in her condition. I promise.'

'Thank you again.'

They shook hands and the doctor disappeared down the hall. Guy stared into space, his mind in overdrive.

The detective sat on a wooden chair in a small anteroom off the doctors' coffee room. He looked up as Guy entered from the corridor.

'Mr Cooper. Detective Sergeant Bruno Marks, Oxford Constabulary. Good of you to see me. I'm told your friend's condition is no longer critical.'

'Still serious, but she's over the crisis, whatever that may mean,' Guy replied, his mind still full of the image of Gosia lying on the cobbles.

Marks looked round the bare room. 'I'll grab you a chair from next door.' He stepped into the coffee room and brought one back. Guy sat. Marks then took out a notebook.

'I may as well get directly to the point. I gather you were not with the young lady when she was shot. Correct?'

'Correct.'

'So you wouldn't have been in a position to see the assailant.'

'Correct.'

'Have you any reason to believe you know who was responsible?'

Guy looked at Marks for a second. 'It's possible I do, yes.'

Marks leant forward – he hadn't expected this reply. 'Please go on.'

Guy sketched the events that had led up to the shooting, beginning from Gosia's visit to Chasen's home. He told Marks of Edward's disappearance and Gosia's concern for his safety. He included his meetings with Eugene Critchley and Ambrose Leston, but excluded his meeting with Shapiro and any references to Marysia being anything other than Gosia's mother. Marks listened intently, never taking his eyes off Guy for a second. The notebook and pen lay idle in his lap. At length Guy finished talking. Marks leant back in his chair, tipping it on its two rear legs.

'I see,' he said very deliberately. He stood and walked to the open door, then turned. 'I take it you have not read this morning's paper.'

'No, I haven't as yet. Why?'

'Sir Ivor Chasen and his wife were killed in an explosion last night in New York. It appears that a bomb had been placed under the rear suspension of their car. I don't know any more details.'

Their eyes locked.

'Christ Almighty,' Guy managed after a long pause, then took a deep breath and stood. 'Christ Almighty,' he murmured. Then his mind was racing again. 'Edward! You must find Edward Chasen!' he shouted.

'We'll do all we can, Mr Cooper,' Marks said quietly in an attempt to calm Guy. 'I'll have to call London at once, tell them about the boy. His disappearance was not officially reported to the police?'

'No.'

'But the Security Service was notified of his disappearance three days ago?' Marks asked, incredulous.

'Yes.'

Marks shook his head. 'Right. Then that's paramount. I'll get on to it right away. I'd be very grateful if you could come to the station, Mr Cooper. As soon as I get the ball rolling on Edward Chasen we can go through all of what you've just told me again – in detail. Miss Dobra's assailant could still be in the immediate vicinity of Oxford. From what you've told me it appears likely that one of the people responsible for Sir Ivor Chasen's death and the possible kidnapping of his son may have tried to kill the girl because she was a witness. You say that the Security Service are in possession of a photograph of one of those believed to be responsible. Is that so?'

'That's right,' Guy replied.

'They should be moving already on Edward Chasen.' Marks stood. 'I think we'd better leave right this second. If Miss Dobra's condition worsens, we'll be notified immediately.'

Guy made quick mental notes about what he should do. He'd call Ehud at once and tell him what had happened, then drive back to London to see him. He'd also need to call Critchley in Dublin.

'Let's go,' Guy said. 'We'll have to be quick. I have to leave for London – Gosia's mother will have to be told immediately and I'm it. Okay? Half an hour?'

'Should be fine,' Marks replied. 'Let's get on with it.'

As they stepped into the corridor, Guy looked towards the operating theatre. Sitting where he had been fifteen minutes before was a young girl.

'Excuse me just a minute, Sergeant. I'll be right with you,' he said, leaving Marks standing by the exit.

She looked about eighteen, quite pretty but more than several pounds overweight. She was eating a chocolate bar, staring into space. She looked as though she'd been crying – the tears had dried on her cheeks and her eye make-up had run. 'Hello,' he said, reaching her. 'My name is Guy Cooper. Are you a friend of Gosia's?'

'Yes,' she said in a hoarse whisper, then cleared her throat. 'I'm Linda Colles. I heard she was here. Do you know how she is? Has anyone told you?'

'Yes, she's over the worst – or so they think in surgery. She's going to be fine,' Guy said. There was no point in worrying the girl unnecessarily.

'Thank goodness!' Linda replied.

'Listen, I have to give a statement to the police and then try to contact Gosia's mother. But there's something very important you could do, and it needs doing this afternoon.'

'Just tell me. I'll do what I can.'

'Okay. Do you have access to a computer?'

'Yes,' she replied.

'Good, because it's occurred to me that there were literally hundreds of tourists in the square at the time of the shooting, all with cameras. It's just possible someone took the gunman's photo either minutes before or actually at the time of the shooting. Can you write a notice saying I've offered a ten-thousand-pound reward for the right photo. Have it copied. Make a few hundred of them. Then pin them up all over town. Could you organise that with a few friends?'

'Sure. I'll put a message on the Internet too.'

'Great. And something else. Take a leaflet to each of the tour operators in town.'

'I'll get to it right away. Trust me.'

'I will. I'll suggest the same idea to the police – offering a reward.' He took a card from his wallet. 'This is my agent's number in London. I may be away for a couple of days and he'll know where I am. I've got to go now. In the meantime, here's some cash for expenses. Do your best.' He handed her a few twenty-pound notes.

They walked back down the corridor towards where Marks was waiting.

The Israeli Embassy was the second house down Palace Gardens. An armed policeman stood opposite, watching Guy closely as he approached.

No cars were parked in the street. That had been the rule for many years but it hadn't prevented the explosion in '94. Israeli security had seen the car approach in the Embassy monitors, and though the woman had parked some metres down the street and was not strictly within their area, they'd become twitchy within seconds. She'd actually been approached and questioned for some minutes before she abruptly walked away. Within seconds the five pounds of HE in her car had gone up. Fortunately the damage had been relatively slight due to the armour-plated glass windows of the Embassy, but part of the side building had been demolished and the ceilings of several of the rooms had been severely damaged.

Guy paused by the gate. A brass plate read 'Please press the bell and wait for the buzzer'. Guy did so and a couple of seconds later he heard a voice through the entry-phone.

'Good morning. Can I help you?' No mention was made that it was the Israeli Embassy.

'My name is Guy Cooper. I have an appointment.'

'With whom, Mr Cooper?'

'Mr Ehud Shapiro.'

'Thank you. Please wait until the buzzer sounds, then walk through.'

The entry-phone went dead. Guy stood by the door for what must have been two full minutes. The policeman watching him from the far side of the road pulled out a walkie-talkie and spoke quietly into it.

Finally the buzzer sounded and Guy pushed the heavy gate inwards. He walked down a curved path, stopping at the front door of the building where there was another buzzer and entry-phone. He pressed the buzzer.

The entry-phone crackled.

'Mr Cooper?'

'Yes.'

Another buzzer sounded and he pushed the front door open. Inside was a small room which reminded Guy of a vacuum-sealed space chamber, measuring about ten feet by twenty, free of all furniture. Ahead was another oak door, and running the length of the right wall was an armoured glass window set two feet from the floor to the ceiling, behind which sat two uniformed security guards, a bank of video screens before them. The armour-plated front door closed behind Guy with a heavy clunk. One of the guards spoke into a microphone and a metallic voice rang out.

'Would you place identification in the opening provided in the glass please, Mr Cooper.'

Guy pulled his driving licence from his wallet and pushed it through. The guard pulled it out, examined the photo, looked at Guy, then pushed it back to him.

'Thank you, Mr Cooper. Mr Shapiro is coming down to meet you. Please push the door when the buzzer sounds.' He did not smile.

Guy stood in the centre of the empty chamber, the guards staring at him from behind the glass. There was silence for several minutes then the door ahead buzzed and he stepped forward and pushed it inwards. It seemed uncommonly heavy – presumably more armour plating.

On the other side of the door, Shapiro was waiting. Just how a man of his bulk managed to get through the door was a mystery to Guy. He held out a hand.

'Good morning, Guy. Sorry to have kept you waiting but our security measures are paramount and immutable. Everyone else gets the same treatment – even Elizabeth Taylor. Come up to my office.' He gestured up the hall.

Shapiro stopped at a door and opened it to reveal a small office.

'Please sit down. Make yourself comfortable,' he said, pointing to a less than luxurious armchair with wooden arms. 'I am so sorry that events have taken the turn they have. I'm afraid these things never cease to shock me, though I have seen my fair share of terrorist incidents.'

'You believe this is one?' Guy asked.

'I didn't mean to imply that. Not yet anyway. Won't you sit down?' Shapiro replied, as he sat behind the desk. His shoes protruded several feet from the desk at the front – a remarkably scruffy pair of well-worn sneakers, said by the cognoscenti of service agents to be the one give-away that separated the diplomats from Mossad personnel.

'We had no idea that Miss Knoll had a daughter.'

'You mean to say there's something your organisation was unaware of? It seems scarcely credible.' Guy had not meant it to sound flippant, especially in view of the purpose of his visit, and he immediately regretted having spoken.

'When Miss Knoll joined us as a young woman she neglected to tell us she had a child. I think she felt it might influence our decision to employ her. She was highly motivated at the time, I am reliably informed. And she was right, we would not have dreamt of taking on a young woman with a baby. However, it appears from our initial investigations that she indeed left a child in Poland – but we were not to know that at the time. So you see your call came as somewhat of a surprise to us.'

'Have you been able to contact her?'

'Unfortunately as yet we have been unsuccessful. Apparently she's on a field trip associated with her work – somewhere half a day's drive from where she lives. She has a phone, but it is at present either switched off or malfunctioning.'

'If you were in a position to inform me of her address in South Africa I would very much like to fly out at once and break the news to her. I'm sure it would be less of a shock coming from a friend than hearing the news over the telephone or reading it bare-faced in a fax. How does the idea strike you, Ehud?'

'At present we've left instructions that as soon as she is located or telephones her base, she is to call me here in London. They do not know the nature of the news we have for her. We are anxious that she won't contemplate returning to England unless it proves absolutely necessary. It's quite possible that the attack on her daughter was engineered to lure her to England.'

'But the facts would militate against that reasoning,' Guy argued.

'The Chasen connection Eugene Critchley mentioned to me? Yes, I agree with you. Nevertheless . . .'

'So are you in a position to tell me her whereabouts?' Guy asked.

Shapiro paused for a few seconds. 'I had a word with my superiors in Tel Aviv earlier, and they have cleared it with me to tell you, yes. They agree with you that the news would be better delivered by a friend, and we know of no others. Also, you have a high security rating with us thanks to the events of '89 in Poland.'

'I'm on file?'

Shapiro smiled. 'Of course you are on file, Guy. We are very thorough.'

'Then as soon as you let me know where I may find her I'll leave.'

Shapiro took an envelope from his inside jacket pocket and passed it across the desk to Guy. 'The address is inside. I'd be grateful if you could commit it to memory now. In the meantime we will make sure that Miss Dobra is given every possible medical care and her security will be our first concern. Believe me when I tell you that should the person who attacked her return to finish the job, they will get no closer than fifty feet.'

Guy opened the envelope and looked at the address printed on a sheet of foolscap.

'This is her name now? Natasha Sabra?'

'That's correct.'

Guy committed the address to memory, refolded the paper, placed it again in the envelope and handed it back to Shapiro.

'I'll do what I can to reassure her, though when I knew her she had a tendency to take no one's advice, least of all mine.' Guy stood, holding his hand out to

Shapiro. 'I must leave. If Marysia calls you before I arrive, can you think of some white lie?'

'I'll come up with something. It's for the best, isn't it?'

'My thanks again for all your help. I'll be in touch with you on my return.'

'Please. By that time I may be able to share with you the result of any enquiries we will have made.'

As Guy reached the door he turned to Shapiro. 'Is it as difficult and time-consuming to get out of this building as it was to come in?'

Shapiro merely smiled.

TWENTY-SIX

It came as a shock to see her photograph on the front page of the *Daily Mail* at Paddington Station. She handed in her ticket, retrieved her bag from the left-luggage counter and immediately made for the ladies room. In the toilet she changed her clothes, tucked her hair under a blonde wig, put on reading glasses, and altered her make-up once more, this time giving her face a fuller look. She put the passport matching the new look into her bag, then stuffed the clothes she'd been wearing in Oxford, plus the hat and sunglasses, into a plastic supermarket bag.

Rather than buy a copy of the paper, she walked round the busy station until she found a discarded *Mirror* and sat on the seat near it. 'Massacre!' shrieked the front-page headline. Beneath it was a photograph of the carnage on Queensboro Bridge. Lower down was another, smaller photo – of herself, and the words 'Female Jackal?'. The main copy referred to Chasen's death. It also stated that the police were searching for the mystery woman. It was time to move fast.

Heathrow was now out of the question, as was Gatwick. That left the ports, the only one of which she was familiar with was Holyhead in Wales, the route to Ireland via Dun Laoghaire. This in itself presented problems because of the continuous police presence there – Special Branch plain clothes on the lookout for the IRA. She considered her options. She'd have to chance the ferry trip and hope to lose herself in the hundreds of students and backpackers on the British Rail ferry to Ireland, then pick up a flight from Dublin. If she got lucky at both ports, no one would be looking for her there. And Dublin Airport was a breeze compared to London. Besides, with the IRA truce, security had been stepped down. It seemed the logical choice – the one with the least risk.

There was also the question of the gun – where to lose it. There was no time to do the job properly. She decided to clean it thoroughly, disassemble it, and place it piece by piece in various litter bins around the station, wrapped in whatever garbage was available. Even if one piece was discovered, it would still take time to search the whole station and put the entire weapon together. And even if they did so, it didn't matter – she had made a clean kill at Oxford. No one had seen her, no one had looked at her as she'd briefly stepped to the girl's left side and fired point-blank into the side of her stomach, the Browning concealed in her handbag. A gut wound seldom failed to deliver. The woman screaming had helped her enormously – there was nothing like panic to mask a quick escape. She'd pretended to panic herself, pushing and thrusting away from the melée, shouting that there was a gunman loose. Within half a minute she'd been outside the square, walking down Brasenose Lane towards the station.

Yes, by the time they had pieced together the Browning and the silencer, she'd be long gone. Besides, the gun was clean. There was nothing to link it with her. Garcia had arranged the purchase and Garcia was dead.

The train slowed as it approached Holyhead. Luiza looked around her in the carriage. The couple opposite were still asleep. They were curled up together like Rodin's *The Kiss*, and had been since the train left London. This had been a blessing – no idle chatter from that quarter. Next to her was an elderly woman who'd spent the entire journey filling in crosswords in a book exclusively devoted to puzzles.

There was a shudder as the train finally stopped, waking the couple opposite. The woman to Luiza's left packed her puzzle book away in a string bag, and the aisle immediately filled with passengers reaching for baggage. A voice on the tannoy on the platform announced they had arrived at Holyhead, and advised passengers for the British Rail ferry to walk to the left-hand end of the platform.

Her ticket was checked in a hall adjacent to the Isle of Innisfree ferry. A man in a grey suit was standing to one side, watching the passengers as they stepped forward, but he seemed tired and his heart wasn't really in his job – he'd probably had this tedious task for weeks without incident. Luiza kept her head down and to the left as though she were still half asleep. The ticket inspector returned her ticket and she boarded the ferry.

She made her way back to the stern of the boat where there were rows of comfortable seats in lines and sat in one by the window so that she could look along the companionway outside at those boarding. If they'd ID'd her she stood little chance – she was trapped.

As her eyes scanned the cabin, her thoughts drifted back to the newspaper article. So they'd decided to kill Chasen. Probably a sensible move, she thought. Sooner or later he'd break and name names. His death was a bonus. Now there was no one alive, barring Bruton, who could present testimony about her, and there was no way he could admit to involvement and stay alive – he knew that. Her story would be simple – she'd chanced upon Aubrey Bruton in a Mayfair club and he'd invited her to a party at a friend's house in the country. Nothing wrong with that. Then Chasen had driven her home. The question of Garcia's killer was something else

– something that bothered her greatly. Those who had killed Chasen had clearly meant to kill Garcia because he was the sole person who knew of their identity. That was where they were so wrong, she thought with relish. They had made a grave error – one for which they would pay dearly. It wasn't a matter of revenge, it was one of principle.

Half an hour later, she saw the gangway drawn from the side of the ferry, and soon after the ship slid gently away from the dock and made its way out towards the sea.

TWENTY-SEVEN

The rotors of the Jet Ranger kicked up the dust of the veld as it swooped low searching for the helipad. Guy looked out of the window at the cluster of thatched huts inside the high brush fence that surrounded the central *boma*. A group of eland looked lazily upwards from the shelter of some thorn trees. Away to his left two adult giraffe and their baby continued their loping canter away from the whirlwind.

A big man in khaki shorts and shirt waved up at them, directing the pilot to an area that had been cut into the veld grass atop a small *kopje* a hundred yards or so from the main buildings.

The flight from Jan Smuts had taken less than an hour. To Guy it had seemed endless. Sala Sala was around a hundred and ninety kilometres from Jo'burg in the Northern Transvaal.

Guy had been too preoccupied with his thoughts to take in the magnificent panorama below him. Would Marysia guess that he'd come with terrible news? Had she changed so much that he'd be looking at a different person? And what if she insisted on returning to England, regardless of the personal risk? But the continuing thread throughout the sleepless night from London had been how he might best break the news so as to spare her as much shock and pain as possible. He hoped he'd find the right words when the time came.

'Remain strapped in till I've cut the engines and the rotors have stopped,' the pilot shouted at him over the roar of the chopper. Guy raised his thumbs and watched the man in khaki walk towards them.

As the blades swung their last lazy arch and dipped, Guy opened the door and turned to the pilot. 'What time must we leave this evening?'

'Seven latest. I'll arrange facilities at Smuts. I'll be here sixish in case you wish to leave earlier.'

'Have dinner on me. Okay?'

'Thanks Mr Cooper. I will,' he replied with a grin. 'It's going to be hot today – Africa hot!' he added as Guy stepped from the Bell.

'Mr Cooper! Welcome to Sala Sala!' the man in khaki roared as Guy walked towards him. Built like a bare-knuckle prizefighter, he stood over six-two and the skin on his face looked as though he'd walked a thousand miles through a dust storm. 'We received your fax late last night. As you asked, we have kept your arrival a surprise. You are lucky we had space available. My name is Jan Koos. Sala Sala belongs to me.'

'Sadly I won't be able to stay the night,' Guy replied quietly as they walked back to the buildings. 'Ben's coming back to pick us up at six.'

'Pity,' he said, slapping Guy on the shoulder. 'Maybe next time, hey? So, you are a friend of Natasha's? She's become like one of our family over the time she's been with us. The boys worship the ground she walks on, as do the animals. We used to have problems rounding up the baby elephants – since she arrived the problem no longer exists. Now we have a fresh problem: they wish to occupy her *rondavel*!' He chuckled – it was as if someone had kick-started a tractor. The sound jarred on Guy. His body ached, and his mind was consumed with worry and apprehension.

As they entered the inner river-reed and *gwarri* bush fence Guy's heart started to race. After seven years he was seconds away from seeing her again. His eyes scanned the inner area.

'Natasha is out with Carlsburg right now bringing in the wildebeest. She shouldn't be too long,' Koos said.

The immediate tension went out of Guy, and his shoulders dropped. 'Can we call her? Does she or Carlsburg have a walkie-talkie?'

That laughter again. 'Natasha, yes. Carlsburg no – he's a donkey,' he said as his entire frame shook with mirth. 'You see, all the animals will follow Carlsburg. Mind you, most follow Natasha, but between the two of them even the bull elephants obey. If you like we can call her from the office. Would you like to speak to her?'

'I would prefer it if you called. I'd rather she didn't know I'd arrived. Perhaps you could think of some reason to ask her to return as soon as possible – I think the news I have for her is best given face to face.'

'Not bad I hope?'

Guy pretended not to hear, looking towards the horizon.

'I'll make up some excuse, don't worry,' Jan replied, looking a bit confused.

The main reception area was wide and open at either end, an early morning cool breeze sweeping through it. Massive beams of raw *sickelbos* trees supported the thatched roof.

As they reached the desk a woman of around thirty-five walked towards them from the bar area, dressed in a white short-sleeved shirt, jodhpurs and white gumboots.

'Lena, this is Mr Cooper. He's a friend of Natasha's.'

'Delighted to meet you, Mr Cooper. Has anyone arranged a room for you yet?'

'No, we only stepped in this minute. I was just telling your husband that I have to return to London on this evening's flight, but if you have a room for the day I would be very grateful.'

'That's no problem.'

'I'll leave the arrangements to you, Lena,' Koos said. 'I must make a call on Mr Cooper's behalf.'

Lena picked up a key. 'If you'd like to come with me, I'll show you to your *rondavel.* It's the best we have – a friend of Natasha's deserves the best. We love her dearly. You're not taking her away with you, are you?'

'I'll do my level best not to,' Guy replied. He meant it.

'It wouldn't be the same without her, hey?' she said in her thick Afrikaans accent.

Guy's rondavel was set away from the others. A veranda ran round it and the thatched roof, which extended almost to the ground on all sides, provided shade. Guy stood at the doorway as the woman fussed around, mentally willing her to leave and give him time to think.

'Through here is the bathroom,' she said, opening the door to the left of the bed. It was simple yet functional.

'Out the back is an African shower. Cold water only. Most of our guests prefer it – they think it's more authentic and actually it is. I always shower outside in the morning and take a bath in the evening. The cold water at four tends to wake me up and get rid of the cobwebs. Do you want to take a look?'

'Don't worry, I'm sure I'll find it,' Guy said with great control. If the woman didn't leave him in peace soon, he felt his brain would explode. 'I think I'll take a quick shower now before Natasha returns. It was a long flight. How far away is she?'

'Probably less than a mile from the feed-pen. We have a film crew here tomorrow to shoot a commercial so we have to have the wildebeest on hand. Look, I'll leave you to your shower. When you're finished come back to reception and I'll show you the direction she'll be heading back, so you can walk out to meet her if you want.'

Guy sat on the end of the bed pressing the palms of his hands into his eyes. 'I really must lie down for a second . . . If you'll excuse me, Lena,' he said quietly.

At last she got the message. 'Of course, Mr Cooper.'

Fifteen minutes later Guy was back on the steps of the main boma compound and Jan was pointing towards a group of wooden buildings about half a mile from the helipad. Koos held a beer in one hand and a few sticks of biltong in the other.

'Can I tempt you with a beer?'

'No thanks, Jan.'

'*Droë wors*?' he said, holding out the dried meat. 'It's red hartebeest – very tasty.'

'Maybe later,' Guy replied politely.

'She'll be coming from that direction – from the stream. If you like, you can walk down. By the time you get there, she'll most probably be in sight.'

'She doesn't know I'm here?'

'No, I told her that one of the kudus was not well, and she'd better come and check.'

Guy thanked him and walked down the few steps and out of the inner compound towards the second fence, relieved beyond measure to be alone and able to collect his thoughts.

The area had been planted with small *Protea rompelliae*, their deep pink flowers oblivious to the heat. There was an abundance of acacia and thorn trees under which sheltered the fawn grey kudu, the white transverse stripes on their backs and flanks catching the light.

Guy searched the ground the far side of the buildings to which he'd been directed by Jan, but there was no sign of Marysia, the donkey and their herd of wildebeest. A group of bushbuck glanced in his direction, then ambled off through the thorn trees.

As Guy reached the pens, an elderly coloured man in a navy blue earth-caked overall looked up at him from his plastic bucket of pellets and grinned through broken teeth, waving an arm at him. '*Sau bona, menheer!*' he called happily.

'Hello,' Guy replied, forcing a smile. 'How are you today?'

'Sharp, baba!' the old man shouted back and laughed as he disappeared towards one of the pens.

Guy looked out into the distance. A small cloud of dust was beginning to swirl on the horizon. His pulse quickened and he began to walk in that direction.

Little by little Guy began to make out vague shapes within the cloud of dust. A small figure, carrying a bucket similar to the one the old man had held, was walking down a *kopje* towards him. To one side ambled an animal roughly the size of a small pony. It had to be Marysia and Carlsburg. Behind her and on either side were around fifty blue wildebeest. They walked at a snail's pace, the horns rocking backwards and forwards with their easy gait. Guy halted.

She drew closer. Her features were still indistinct – a mixture of dust and the heat-haze causing them to appear to wave from side to side. When she was fifty feet away, she abruptly stopped dead in her tracks. The donkey carried on a few feet then also stopped and swung its head back to her.

'Guy?' she called out to him.

He walked forward, stopping ten feet from her.

Her expression was one of blank shock. Then she opened her fingers and the bucket fell to the ground.

'Oh God, Guy . . . please tell me she's alive.'

'She's alive, Marysia. I promise she'll be fine. There's been an accident, but she's fine,' Guy called out urgently, walking over to where she stood in the dust.

'What's happened?' she breathed.

'Gosia's in hospital. She's no longer critical.'

'Tell me! What happened!' she shouted. 'Tell me!'

'She was attacked in Oxford. Shot. But she's not going to die, she's going to be fine.'

Guy stepped forward in an attempt to comfort her, when she held up a hand, closed her eyes and fell to her knees. 'Wait . . . Give me some time,' she whispered, then placed her hands on her thighs and started to breathe deeply, inhaling and exhaling in a slow rhythm.

Guy stood before her, feeling a terrible sense of inadequacy, yet knowing she had her own way of dealing with her feelings. The wildebeest began to graze on the few blades of greenish veld grass available, and Carlsburg, rather than steal the pellets from where they had fallen, was instead nuzzling the back of Marysia's neck as if sensing her despair.

Fully five minutes later she raised her head and opened her eyes.

'I must get back to her at once,' she said simply, her face ashen.

'We leave at sixish. Ben's coming back with the Jet Ranger. I have reservations on this evening's flight.' He could see she'd made up her mind.

As they walked on towards the pen, the queue of wildebeest at their rear, Guy told her every detail of the past few days. Marysia listened in silence, occasionally running her hand through her short chestnut hair, her face set grimly.

'You're right – she will be fine. She'll survive. I know that. I know that.' Her voice had a strange staccato quality, as if she was convincing herself. Then she stopped and again drew a deep breath. 'I know that as well as I know you are my dearest friend,' she said. Her eyes were filled with tears, yet she smiled at him. 'I have missed you so very much – you have no idea. I thank God you are here with me now,' she added, placing a hand on the nape of Guy's neck.

'I tried to reach you many times, but it was impossible. You wouldn't let me.'

'I know.'

Guy watched her. She looked in shock. As he reached out towards her, her arm fell to her side and she stared up at the sky as if in a trance. Her eyes began flitting wildly in all directions; then she opened her mouth and began to scream. Guy immediately grabbed hold of her, wrapping her in his arms, as her body shook violently with her tears.

Guy waited in Marysia's small living area for her to return from Jan's office. He'd given her the hospital telephone number as soon as they'd got back. He hoped to God Gosia had suffered no relapse since he'd left London.

He paced round the small room as he tried to kill the time. The decoration was entirely functional. A photograph, almost bent double by the heat, was pinned to the wall. That was the extent of the decoration. Guy uncurled the edges to reveal a snapshot of a very small Zulu girl in a pair of outsized shorts – presumably Marysia's – standing next to an equally small baby elephant. A table along the wall was cluttered with bottles and tablets. As he heard footsteps out the front, he felt the impact of a blow to the wall behind him. He was about to investigate its source when Marysia stepped through the door in front of him. She looked white and drawn.

'She's still in a serious condition but they're all very optimistic,' she said quietly as she walked to the kitchen. She filled a badly beaten tin kettle. Guy watched her as she walked to the kitchen. She looked as though she was barely in control. He'd need to stay close to her.

'Would you like some coffee?' she called from the kitchen doorway.

'A coffee would be fine,' he called back.

As she brought the cups out into the living room there was another hard crack on the wall behind her. She didn't seem to pay much attention.

'Have you got visitors?' Guy asked after a few seconds.

'Oh, that's Smiley,' she replied abstractedly, 'the boldest of the babies – elephants, that is. They see me coming for miles and head straight for home thinking I'll break out the oranges.' Her speech was again fast and stilted.

'And you don't?' Guy replied, trying to inject a light touch.

'Usually, yes. Though you have to draw the line somewhere – too much citric acid's not so good.'

'Do they all have names?'

'No, we don't give them names. Jan insists on that. He likes us to care for the animals rather than treat them as pets. Wild animals are supposed to be wild, even the babies. This is supposed to be a game park not a zoo. Rules is rules.'

'So where does "Smiley" fit into all this,' Guy probed. The more he could take her mind off Gosia the better.

'*They* don't have names. *I* have the names for all of them.'

'But do they *know* their names?'

'That's up to them – I don't pry,' she replied, then quite suddenly she brought her hands up to cover her face. 'Oh God,' she moaned softly. 'What can I do?'

Guy crouched next to her and put an arm round her. 'You have to hang on for a few more hours. Then we fly back. Just hang on to me. Gosia will be fine, we both know that.'

'Yes, we do,' she said, barely audibly. 'It's just so hard – the waiting. I can't bear it!'

There was another thud on the rear wall. Marysia looked up, wiped her eyes on her forearm, squeezed Guy's arm and stood.

'You're right, of course.' Then she cleared her throat, wiping her face with her hand, and walked back into the kitchen. 'Come with me,' she added as she picked up a bag of oranges.

The second she opened the back door, the frame was filled with the head and trunk of a baby elephant that must have stood five feet high. Behind it, jockeying for position, were another five.

'Hi there, Smiley. You come for breakfast, hey?' she said as she held an orange under its bottom lip. The strong trunk swept it back into its mouth. Then she stepped between the elephants, handing out the fruit, making sure each one had their share, including Bashful who seemed the most timid and hung back. The tears were still flowing but she was smiling through them.

'I know they look cute, but always remember their strength. Only Smiley and Bashful were hand-reared by me – the others came from Kruger.'

'They send them to you?' Guy replied, watching her with the animals. She was showing a lot of strength.

'They do now. Every now and then they have a culling programme and the orphans have nowhere to go. I know it's sad to kill any of them, but the land can only support so many, so some have to be sacrificed. Jan gets as mad as hell when they arrive. 'No more elephant', he keeps telling me, but how could you turn away these little critters?'

Guy was about to ask her another question to keep her mind occupied when the young girl he'd seen in the snapshot on her wall rushed past him towards Marysia shouting something he couldn't understand – she seemed quite upset.

'*Mama Tash, mama Tash! U ya hamba?*'

'Calm down Otilia *ungane*. Yes, I am leaving for a while. *Yebo mange* – very soon,' Marysia replied as the little coloured girl clung to her legs. Then she turned to Guy. 'Now we're all in tears, eh?' she said laughing as she wiped her cheeks.

'*U ya boya?*' the tiny figure cried desperately.

'She asks if I'm coming back,' Marysia said. '*Ngia themba ngalo* – I hope so,' she said to the girl.

'Otilia, this is my friend Guy Cooper.' The girl tried to hide her face in Marysia's shorts. 'Come on Otilia, you remember the English I taught you, don't you?'

Otilia ran a hand across her face as she stared up at Guy, leaving a smudge across her cheek.

'Very pleased to meeting you,' she said as she held out a hand. Guy shook it gently and Otilia began to giggle, one hand again clutching Marysia's legs. Then she ducked her head round the back of Marysia's knees and whispered. '*E ndoda ya k'ho?*'

'*Ai! U mgani*,' Marysia replied with mock horror.

'She asked me if you were my husband and I told her we were just good friends,' Marysia said, ruffling Otilia's hair. 'Now go and learn more English. My friend and I must have time to speak. We are old friends.'

As Marysia watched Otilia run down to the pens, Guy surreptitiously reached for an orange and passed it to Smiley, who'd had his trunk under Guy's armpit for several minutes. As it disappeared down the elephant's throat Marysia turned. 'You don't think you got away with that, do you?' she said sternly, then looked Smiley directly in the eye as she pulled affectionately at his ear. 'And you get no more treats. Ever! Well, not till this evening anyway.'

As they walked back into the living area, the front door was nosed open and the most pregnant warthog imaginable tiptoed into the living room. Its grey back was covered with a crest of long black erectile hair and its slender legs and tiny cloved feet looked quite inadequate to support its weight.

'That's Beauty. She moved in about six weeks ago. Don't let the tusks scare you, she's a real softy, providing she gets what she wants and you give her space. Someone killed her mate so now she's a warty without a sounder – that's the name for a group of warthogs.'

Beauty teetered across the room as if on points, brushing past Guy as she headed towards the kitchen and her dish of milk.

'That's the ultimate in romance – sharing your life with a wild pig. She's due to pop within a few days, then she'll be really grouchy. I must remember to tell Lena to look after her.' Then the smile abruptly vanished from her face, replaced by the desolate look of a child.

'Would you like some time to yourself?'

'No,' she replied, taking his hand. 'I'd rather be with you. I can't be alone now.' Guy could see she was trembling.

Marysia looked out across the veld towards the sunset. She'd said all her goodbyes. Now they waited for the helicopter.

'I should have been there,' she said quietly.

'This had nothing to do with you and your work,' Guy replied.

'We don't know that yet. I should have been there. When I find the person who did this to Gosia, I shall tear their heart out,' she said stonily.

'Why did you never tell me of Gosia?' Guy asked, aware that she was drifting into dangerous emotional territory. Marysia's expression softened as she looked up into his face. He could see the blood-red sun briefly reflected in the corners of her eyes. It seemed to dance like a ruby next to the emeralds.

'It sometimes seems a lifetime ago, and at others so close I could almost touch it. Actually, when I look at Gosia I can see it was, but in reality it was only twenty years ago.

'It would be too easy to say that I was only a child. I was fifteen, but times of struggle make one grow up very quickly. Janusz was eighteen. He was really quite spectacular. Apart from being the most beautiful man I have ever seen, he had a burning integrity. Just to be near him was like being infused with a passion for life. He was a man of absolutes – there were no half measures for him, no compromises.'

She turned to face Guy and smiled briefly. 'Do I make him sound dull and predictable – the young radical? If I do, then I've failed. He was filled with such happiness, hope and love – every minute of the day was a gift to him, and a large part of it was always filled with laughter.

'In the '70s Poland wasn't a place of deprivation but quite an easy place to live for most of us. Sure, it was a communist society, but we didn't suffer the deprivations and lack of freedom the way the Czechs, Russians and Hungarians did. Nor was there the atmosphere of fear that existed in the Soviet Union and East Germany. We had most of the necessities of life – to the Czechs we must have appeared like Parisians. It was only those that chose to buck the system that put their lives at risk – those like Janusz, who felt they were living a lie and that change was imperative.'

She held out a hand to Guy without looking at him. 'Shall we walk? I need to move.' They began to stroll down the hill. 'You remember the Wierzynek restaurant on the corner of Saint Mary's square in Kraków?'

'I haven't forgotten the smallest detail.'

As they walked, the call of a hyena howled through the stillness. When Marysia continued speaking it was in softer tones, tinged with sadness.

'It was in one of the university coffee shops behind the Wierzynek that I met Janusz for the first time. It was in a lane near the Kurza Stopka. I can see him this minute, surrounded by his friends, roaring with laughter. He was very slim, with short soft golden hair and eyes that seemed on fire, threatening to burn a hole right through me if I didn't look away, and lips I knew I had to kiss at once.'

'Did you?'

'Yes,' she replied, with a short laugh. 'I don't know what gave me the courage, but I kissed him on the lips then and there. He just stared at me. It was the last thing he'd expected. My friends were shocked – they thought me very brash. But he was very sweet to me. He laughed, and from that moment on I was part of his group and not much later, a part of his life.'

She looked up at a hornbill as it dropped like a stone from a branch just ahead, then flew with surprising grace away from them.

'Of course, at first he thought of me as no more than a child – his *myszka*. He was always very busy, both with his studies – he was a medical student – and politics. He had joined the KOR at sixteen and passionately believed in the movement.'

'The KOR?'

'It was the major underground dissident movement in Poland in the early '70s. It was the forerunner to the Committee for Workers' Protection and, subsequently, Solidarity. It goes without saying that membership of

KOR brought with it its dangers. Though life for most people was generally without fear of the police authorities the way the Russians feared the KGB, the KOR was the constant target of our secret police, the *Sluzba Bezpieczenstwa*, or SB. It was only a matter of time before Janusz was targetted.

'He realised the danger he was in but chose to ignore it. In some respects I think he viewed his work with KOR as a kind of game – you know, "catch me if you can – and even if you do, what can you do to me?". He believed with all his heart and soul in what he was doing, but all the same it excited him to be one step ahead of the SB – they'd never catch him. But things took a different turn when his closest friend, the secretary of the Krakovian branch of KOR, disappeared one night.

'Everyone knew Petr had been arrested by the SB, but there'd been nothing anyone could do. If you didn't have connections in the Communist Party, even asking the whereabouts of a person arrested for a political reason would be as good as evidence of guilt by association. We never heard from Petr again – no one did. He just vanished off the face of the earth.'

The sun had almost set and the last rays lit up the tops of the thorn trees above their heads like a halo. In the distance, a small herd of eland shuffled slowly across the plain towards the waterhole.

'We'd better make our way back – it will be getting dark soon and we're tempting fate out here,' she said. 'Some fine animal may think it's dinnertime.'

As they turned towards the *boma*, Guy put an arm round Marysia's shoulder.

'I pleaded with Janusz to be more careful, but he would laugh and tell me I exaggerated, that he was not so very important, that the SB had people more important than himself to occupy themselves with.

'Three months passed without incident. Janusz spent most nights with me at my mother's home. I was seven months pregnant at this stage. Then one day in late March they came for him.'

Marysia stopped and wrapped her arms tightly around herself, at the same time looking up at the sky and closing her eyes.

'He was reading me a passage from *As You Like it*. You probably know the piece. "Hereafter in a better world than this, I shall desire more love and knowledge of you." We heard old Mr Baran shouting loudly from downstairs. He knew who they were and who they had come for and was doing what he could to warn us. But there was nothing we could do.

'Janusz just looked at me and smiled, then took me in his arms and held me tightly. The noise from downstairs grew. My mother shouted at them, but was told to be quiet. Janusz knelt down and placed his head against my stomach, listened, then kissed it. Then he told me to hide behind the curtain and not to question him at all, there wasn't time. I could see he meant it. We had to think of our unborn child, and in forty-eight hours he'd be back. I did as I was told.

'They came straight to our door. I could hear Mama shouting – she'd followed them up the stairs and was demanding to know what they wanted at such a late hour. I heard more muffled voices and then a hammering on my bedroom door. Through the curtain I saw Janusz look up, cross himself, then stand and walk forward.

'When he opened the door, three men stepped through. They all wore the shabby grey raincoats that were the trademarks of the SB in those days. Two stood on either side of Janusz while an older man with steel glasses faced him, standing very close in a deliberately threatening stance. The man demanded his *dowod*, his identity card. Janusz told them he'd mislaid it – he could perhaps come to the police headquarters the next day when he'd had time to search for it. The man with the glasses did not reply, he merely gestured to the other two, and Janusz was marched through the door and down the stairs. I could hear Mama crying as she shuffled after them, demanding to be told where they were taking him, and old Mr Baran trying to comfort her. Then there was the crash of our heavy front door and a terrible silence, broken only by Mama's weeping. I stood transfixed behind the heavy curtains. I don't think I'd breathed for several minutes. I didn't know what to do. Then Mama came into my bedroom and I parted the curtains and stepped towards her. I shall never forget the look in her eyes. She knew we would never see Janusz alive again. She was right – we never did.'

They'd reached the thatched slatted walls of the *boma*. Marysia was about to open the gate when she stopped and turned – the last rays of the sunset lighting her face with a translucent rose tinge.

'He was found a week later. He'd drowned in the river, they said. They had the forms to prove he'd been released.' She paused momentarily.

'You must forgive me – I haven't talked of Janusz for many years. He is constantly with me in my heart – as is Sam.' She was fighting her emotions.

'I cried for many days. But I knew I owed the baby and Janusz my strength.

'Even before Gosia was born I had decided to leave for Israel. I had a personal mission. I was so young, and I needed something to believe in to take my mind off my crushing loss. I was determined to do something positive, and that led me to Israel.'

'And Gosia?' Guy asked quietly.

'I left her with my mother. It was the hardest decision I ever made. Now I couldn't even consider making the same decision, but when you are little more than a child you think differently. I had a vision, a purpose. I would return for my child – Janusz's child. But I knew she'd be in safer hands with my mother than with me. I never told them of Gosia's existence when I arrived in Israel – they would never have taken me had they known.'

She looked at Guy. 'You may think that I had no instinct as a mother, but it was not so. I missed her terribly – she was my one link to Janusz. I returned to Poland as often as I could over the years. When she was old enough to comprehend what I had to tell her, I did so. Contrary to what you might believe, we had become very close. She told me she understood – she was a very intuitive little girl. She knew when I had to leave and she never pleaded with me to stay. So now you see that my place must be at her side.'

TWENTY-EIGHT

'There's got to have been a leak at the Service. That was Marysia's initial reaction, and mine,' Guy said. He was seated opposite Shapiro in his office at the Embassy.

'Who else knew of Gosia – that she'd overheard the conversation?' Shapiro asked. He had a large sheet of paper on his desk covered with notes. Several names and dates were highlighted and lines connected the circles drawn round them. In the centre was Gosia's name.

'As far as I'm aware, going strictly by what Gosia told me, the only people who knew were myself, Eugene Critchley, Ambrose Leston, Neville Cunningham and yourself,' Guy paused, 'and of course Chasen.'

'She may have told other people but omitted to tell you,' Shapiro observed.

'Unlikely, but if she did it would have been people quite unconnected with the whole affair, people like her tutor, friends at college and such-like. Hardly people who would try to kill her.'

'I appreciate that, Guy, but we must be thorough. We have to be certain we've thought of everyone who knew, and then discount them.' He looked up from his notes.

'Let's start from basics again. As far as I can see, there are two plausible scenarios. One – that Gosia was attacked to flush Marysia from cover. And two, that Gosia was shot so she could no longer testify that she witnessed the threatening conversation with Chasen. I am more inclined to believe the latter. To my mind, the former seems to fly in the face of all logic because we'd have to believe that the entire affair was organised for the sole purpose of bringing Marysia out into the open –

something that could have been achieved far more easily by simply shooting Gosia. They could have left Chasen completely out of it. I think it's more than likely their purpose was to persuade Chasen to take something to New York with him. Remember, they killed him within an hour of his arrival in the States, so they could hardly have wanted him to perform some task associated with his official duties, either at the Embassy or the UN. What makes me choose to prefer the 'courier' scenario is that I'm in touch with Tel Aviv daily and our Intelligence people have told us they are unaware of any movements between the Middle East and London.'

'You mean they have a list of people?'

'Suppose I just say we keep an eye on the comings and goings in the UK.'

'There's still the question of Edward,' Guy reminded Shapiro. 'Has there been any word of his whereabouts?'

'None. I've asked the police to let us know the moment they have any further information.'

'So we come back to the leak. At the moment it's more likely that it occurred after the meeting with Ambrose Leston and Neville Cunningham. Either one of them could have leaked the information. Of course, Eugene Critchley could also have done so – but I find that almost inconceivable.'

Shapiro smiled wryly. 'I'm glad you said that, Guy, as any nefarious dealings on Eugene's part would call my position into question wouldn't it – bearing in mind he introduced you to me?'

Guy was about to justify his statement when Shapiro held up a hand. 'Don't worry, Guy. I understand you're attempting to cover all bases. So am I. But let's get back to the leak. It doesn't necessarily have to be either Leston or Cunningham – it could have been anyone working at Thames House. Remember, the photograph was passed through several hands before it reached Leston's desk.'

'But no one else would have known its significance. Only Leston and Cunningham did.'

'Not true. Those that took the photograph would have known that the girl was connected to Chasen – it was taken at Chasen's London house. Subsequently Gosia is asked in for an interview concerning Chasen – the significance would be clear to anyone.'

'But again, only those two would have known that Gosia was in a position to identify the woman. And I'm sure it was the woman in the photograph who shot Gosia,' Guy interrupted.

'Let's not jump to any conclusions. It could have been her, but it's unlikely that she would have been operating alone,' Shapiro replied. 'And they would have had to be tipped off by someone who knew that Gosia had overheard the conversation with Chasen – knew what she looked like, and where they could find her.'

There was a pause in the discussion.

'Good point,' Guy stated. 'Even if they knew Gosia had to be silenced, and given that both Leston or Cunningham knew her name and that she was an Oxford undergraduate, how would the assassin be able to positively identify her without taking a photograph?'

'It's possible they did do just that.'

'Very unlikely. We stepped into a taxi within minutes of leaving the meeting with Leston and Cunningham and she took the train to Oxford half an hour later.'

'Hold on a minute, Guy.' Shapiro held up a hand. 'Firstly, every person who enters the MOD is automatically videoed. Secondly, what did Critchley tell Leston initially? Let's get that straight.'

'I don't know exactly, but probably that she'd overheard the conversation and seen the woman.'

'In that case Leston might have been prudent to have had someone standing by to take a photograph of her as she left – that is, if he's our leak.' Shapiro was silent for a while, thinking, then he patted the dossiers to his right. 'I asked our people to give me the files on both Leston and Cunningham. I've been through them both. Leston's file is thick, Cunningham's isn't. From what's down in Ambrose Leston's file, I find it hard to believe he'd stoop to dealing with criminals for financial gain. It's just not in his make-up. He might betray his country for philosophical motives, but otherwise, I really doubt it.'

'So you're more inclined to believe that the leak is Cunningham? I can't believe it's Critchley.'

Shapiro toyed with the diagram on his desk. 'With good reason. Think for a moment. When Gosia came to you initially, you contacted Eugene Critchley, correct?' he asked.

'Correct.'

'If he were part of the conspiracy, that would be a very strong coincidence wouldn't it? Remember it was you that contacted him, asking for help, not the reverse.'

'Which leaves us with Cunningham.'

'I wish it were as simple as that, but it seldom is. It could be Cunningham or anyone in his section.'

Silence filled the room as they thought.

'Do you happen to know whether the woman's photograph has been circulated to all UK exit points?' Guy asked.

'Yes, but she's likely to be a professional, with all that that entails – disguises, passports, contacts in the travel industry. Special Branch are pretty good when it comes to entry and exit points, but there are limits.'

'Would there have been cooperation between the New York Police Department and the British?'

'Yes, of course. We've also been in touch with the States. We share a great deal of information – it's a two-way highway that benefits us both. But all they've been able to give us up till now is that a quantity of semtex was used. As far as they can see, nothing out of the ordinary happened between the time Chasen left the plane and the time the car exploded on the Queensboro Bridge, so they have little to go on.' He paused. 'The thing that puzzles me, is why they should have killed Chasen if he was still doing as he was told. He'd only just arrived in New York, and wouldn't have had time to do anything.'

'Like what?' Guy interjected.

'Like delivering whatever they wanted him to deliver. It's the most probable reason I can think of for the blackmail.'

'It's possible that he did, but that no one saw it happening. Apparently there was a pretty big crush at the airport.'

'It's possible, I suppose.'

'If we go with this theory, then when was whatever it was delivered to Chasen? And by whom – the girl?'

'As far as we know, she was the only person, apart from the usual staffers, who saw him during the time between her first meeting with him and when she was photographed leaving Lyall Mews two days later,' Shapiro replied, adding, 'And on the second occasion she was carrying nothing.'

'We know that for a fact?'

'Well, judging from the photographs Critchley passed on to me it would have been difficult for her to have concealed anything – certainly anything bulky.'

He searched under some papers and brought out several eight by ten photographs, passing them across the desk. Guy studied the topmost snapshot – a blown-up head and shoulders of the woman – and his face hardened. Then he leafed through the remainder, pausing at a full-length shot of her walking down Lyall Mews.

'You see? She is wearing a reasonably tight-fitting dress. Small handbag, no coat. She was wearing the same going in,' Shapiro stated.

'It could have been a microchip or something similar,' Guy offered as he studied the photo.

'I think we're all thinking along the lines that these people are criminals rather than spies. We may be wrong, but I don't think so,' Shapiro replied.

Guy leant forward in his chair. 'Well, if Chasen's purpose was to transport something from London to New York, he must have been passed it by someone else – probably after the second visit of the girl. And it was subsequently taken off him by someone the other end, but no one was aware of it at the time.'

'Sorry to be the devil's advocate, but it's also possible that was their initial plan, but when things became complicated by Gosia, they decided to bail out and cover their tracks. That would have meant killing both Chasen and Gosia,' Shapiro said.

'And Edward,' Guy added. 'He's still missing. If you're right, it doesn't sound too hopeful as far as he's concerned.'

'I want to talk to Critchley. He's still in Dublin?'

'As far as I know.'

'I'd like to ask him if he's heard anything more from Leston or Cunningham and if so, what they've come up with.'

'Leston is in Brussels, I think.'

'No way, Guy,' Shapiro stated bluntly. 'You can bet your life he's in the deepest possible shit. He's on record as having been appraised of all the facts a week ago, yet he chose to do practically nothing. Now Chasen and his wife are dead. No, he won't be in Brussels. More likely he's meeting with the Director-General or Deputy Director-General Operations as we speak. His pension's on the line, I'd say.'

Just then the telephone rang. Shapiro answered it.

'Shapiro.'

He listened for a while, then put down the phone.

'They've found Edward Chasen. He's dead. Leston wants to meet.'

Silence filled the room as they took in the news. Then Guy spoke.

'He wants to see you alone, or are we both included?'

'Just me. He has some new photos he wishes to show me. He didn't sound too happy.'

TWENTY-NINE

Marysia drove directly from Heathrow to the John Radcliffe Hospital in Oxford, assuring Guy that she was under control emotionally and that he was better served meeting with Shapiro.

Gosia was still listed as serious when Marysia arrived and had not regained consciousness. During a ten-minute meeting with the surgeon who had operated and the physician who was looking after Gosia, she was told that her daughter would soon be out of danger and that no major damage had been done to any vital organs. The length of time before regaining consciousness varied from patient to patient, depending on the extent of the injury, the length of surgery and the constitution and age of the patient.

Marysia sat beside Gosia's bed and held her hand. A central line had been inserted in the vein under her ribs to give her fluids. In her mouth was an endo-tracheal tube. Marysia willed her to open her eyes.

She'd been sitting with Gosia for some time, when there was a light tap on the door. 'There's a friend downstairs at reception asking for you,' a nurse whispered. Marysia nodded, kissed her daughter lightly on the cheek, then left the room.

Guy stood by the reception desk.

'How is she?' he asked.

'Still the same. She hasn't regained consciousness yet. They assure me she will.'

'What would you like to do now? Do you want to stay here for a while?'

'Yes. I'll stay as long as she's in danger. My place is here.'

'Can I get you a tea or coffee?'

'A tea would be good,' she replied, sitting down.

Guy stole a glance at her as he helped himself to two cups of tea from the machine in the corner. She looked tired, gaunt and broken – he'd never seen her like this before.

'How was the meeting with Ehud?' she asked when Guy returned with the plastic cups.

Guy sat beside her. 'They've found Edward's body,' he said quietly.

Marysia looked up at the ceiling, then closed her eyes.

'He fell from a building,' Guy continued, filling the silence. 'Another body was found beside him. Marks told me.'

'Don't tell me anything more. It can wait.'

THIRTY

'My thanks for coming to see me, Mr Shapiro,' Leston said as he eased himself into his chair.

Shapiro sat down opposite and waited for him to begin.

'It seems we may possibly have a common purpose here, though I think we both agree it's unlikely Sir Ivor Chasen's death is in any way linked to Miss Knoll.'

Leston sat perched on the lip of his chair, his expression of calm failing to mask his tension. He was patently deeply rattled. Shapiro had been right – Leston had probably been given a thorough carpetting. Shapiro remained silent, seeing if he could fluster Leston.

'I am disturbed to hear that you think there's a leak in my department,' Leston continued smoothly.

'Neither of us is in the business of pointing fingers prematurely,' Shapiro replied, 'least of all at members of your department. However, both Miss Knoll and I are anxious to eliminate the possibility that Miss Dobra's identity was leaked somehow to her assailant.' Shapiro was being as delicate as he could given the circumstances. Leston's expression gave nothing away. He was quite aware that the most obvious link to the shooting lay through his people, but this door he would do his best to close at once.

'The problem,' Leston said, 'is that it has not been firmly established that Miss Dobra was not sighted the night she overheard Chasen's conversation with the woman. If she was, then they knew her identity from that moment.'

'If so, why did they take so long to act?'

This was a more difficult question for Leston to answer. He took his time. 'It's always difficult to get within the minds of these people, as you know, but again I follow what you're intimating.' Leston tapped the balls of his fingers together in a nervous gesture. 'The matter you raised concerning my deputy, Cunningham, is more difficult. I find your suggestion that he leaked the girl's name to others hard to countenance. He has the highest security rating.'

'So did Philby,' Shapiro interjected, without his usual delicacy. Leston looked up sharply, then continued as if Shapiro had said nothing.

'As I say, Cunningham has the highest security rating and has been my number two for several years. If he had criminal proclivities, I would have spotted them before now. However, the point is this: I can hardly preclude him from any further meetings, should we have any, without furnishing him with a good reason. I do owe him that courtesy – merely informing him that Mossad, together with the girl's mother and a film actor, view his hand in the matter with suspicion will not be sufficient.'

'I quite understand your situation, Sir Ambrose. I asked for a private meeting today to bring my views concerning Mr Cunningham's possible involvement to your attention. How you choose to approach the matter from here on in is up to you.'

'It is indeed, Mr Shapiro,' Leston said quietly. 'Now, in the spirit of our usual cooperation, I think you might like to view these photographs.' He opened a desk drawer and handed a bundle of photographs across to Shapiro.

'They were taken on Thursday afternoon by our people. The top-most is of a car at the entrance to the mews near Sir Ivor Chasen's London residence. You can see the figure of a man leaving the car. The rest of the pictures are in sequence.'

Shapiro slowly leafed through them. In the second photo, a man was walking away from the car. The shots then became ever closer on the man, who was carrying a medium-sized black case. Unfortunately there was no clear view of his face, he was walking away from the camera. Eventually the camera had swung back to the car, and had caught the front portion from the wing mirror to the edge of the driver's door. The driver could be seen through the window. A woman around thirty, slightly overweight, with curly blonde hair. The last shot was blurred, as if the car had suddenly taken off. Then there was a succession of shots of the man again, this time leaving the door of Chasen's house. He no longer carried the case.

'Have you been able to identify them?' Shapiro asked, committing both faces to memory.

'The man, yes. The woman, as yet, no. We've sent her photographs for analysis and enhancement. Our initial view is that she was attempting to alter her appearance. She could well be the woman who met with Chasen.'

'So you now believe that the conversation Miss Dobra overheard actually took place.'

Leston shifted in his seat, loath to admit he had made such a fundamental error of judgment. 'We do,' he replied in little more than a whisper.

'The man?' Shapiro continued.

'He spent, or should I say misspent, his life as a mercenary. In the late '70s and early '80s he fought in Angola with Mason's people. Made a nuisance of himself.'

'Have you passed this information on to the police?'

'We have. However, the man is dead. He was found with the body of Edward Chasen near a derelict block of flats in South London.'

Shapiro said nothing. He hadn't been told of any second body.

'It appears that both fell from one of the upper floors. We believe that Edward had been held there for several days and that their deaths were the result of a struggle. No identifying personal effects were found on either body.'

'I presume Cunningham knows of these photographs?'

Leston's expression turned dark. 'This matter is Neville Cunningham's brief. I assigned it to him. I will not take it from him till I have reason to believe he cannot be trusted. As yet I have no such reasons,' he replied tartly, adding, 'it was his idea to send them for computer enhancement.'

Shapiro returned to the photos. 'The case?' he began.

'Yes indeed. The case,' Leston jumped in, 'It does suggest that the purpose of the hostage situation was to put pressure on Sir Ivor to take something with him to New York – free from the prying eyes of customs officers at Kennedy Airport.'

Shapiro could hardly believe what he was hearing. Suddenly it was Leston's hypothesis that Chasen had been blackmailed to smuggle something into America. Five days ago the idea had been fanciful.

'So the switch must have taken place at Kennedy?' he said finally.

'That would appear to be the situation. In the photos taken by the press corps at Kennedy, Sir Ivor's hands are empty.'

'It would be too much to hope that any of the photographers captured the courier on film accidentally?'

'Yes, it would, I'm afraid,' Leston snapped. He himself had asked the very same question of Cunningham only hours before.

'So how do you intend continuing from here?' Shapiro asked, eyeing Leston closely.

'From this moment on, our position in this matter will be solely an advisory one. The police have set up a special task force headed by Chief Superintendent Rawlings. Our ambit is strictly limited to matters that threaten national security and matters threatening the economic wellbeing of the United Kingdom. As Stella Rimmington so succinctly stated in her HMSO "brochure",' he said, emphasising the word with distaste, 'in which she introduced the public to the Security Service, "We have no plans to become involved in the investigation of, for example, the misuse of illegal drugs, or organised crime".' Leston was patently one of the old school who had no time for the new spirit of 'openness' stemming from the Security Service Act of 1989, preferring the veil of secrecy, the dark corridors, which allowed him to do as he pleased beyond the prying eyes of the Home Secretary.

A flash of anger crossed Shapiro's face. How this man could simply wash his hands of the matter was quite amazing. Had Leston done his job properly in the first place, Chasen and his wife would most probably still be alive. As would Edward. Now he was about to pass the buck to the police. It was still more annoying that the entire affair would probably end up being just an embarrassment to Leston, for though his superiors would be blue with fury, there was little they could do to him – he was a top civil servant on the verge of retirement. To take disciplinary action would require a thorough investigation ending with the blame firmly laid at his door, and despite their new-found 'spirit of openness', this was something the Service was ever keen to avoid, preferring the course of action that involved a brush and lifting the carpet.

'May I have copies of these photographs?' Shapiro ventured, knowing full well the answer.

'Classified,' Leston snapped.

'Will you be sharing them with Rawlings?'

'Should he ask for them, yes.'

'I feel sure he will. They could prove critical to the investigation,' Shapiro said, rising. 'My thanks again for sharing this information with me. Would you like me to keep in contact on this matter, Sir Ambrose?'

'It would be more useful for you to liaise with Rawlings. I'm sure he'll give you every cooperation.'

THIRTY-ONE

'I'm not going back in that damned building till they fix the aircon, it's like walking into a fuckin' igloo. For Christ's sake, we live in a temperate climate, the sun shines al' day, and we blow a blast of ice right through the building the whole twenty-four hours!' Mamasian paced beside his Bel Air pool. He hadn't enjoyed Costra's briefing.

Harry Costra sat on the edge of a chaise longue, sweating, his head under the shade of the umbrella, the sun pounding down on his body.

'The problem's with the management of the building. They say the lease stipulates between sixty-five and sixty-eight degrees. Any higher, the other lessees complain,' Costra explained.

'Well, let them go fuck themselves. Anyway, enough. What does Whitehall say?'

'He says they know Chasen was carrying, but they don't know what.'

'They'll never know.'

'That's right, they'll never know.'

'But the point is, Harry, we really stirred them up and that's a bad thing. Now Chasen's dead we got to think of a replacement and they're going to be watching their guys like hawks. Major breakdown in the system. We either change the route, cut out London and do it all through Amsterdam, or we have to wait a while and try again.' He looked up into the sun and ground his teeth. 'Shit, there was never a fuckin' problem with Adrian Bouvier! Good as gold for years, then the arsehole dies, and I end up picking a mother like Chasen. End result, we got no one! And that's damned inconvenient.' He paused for breath, then launched off again. 'So why all the bodies? I said to clean up, not start a fuckin' war! Freakin' bodies all over the place; two fell outta buildings, two blown away in an apartment, and the witness gunned down in front of half the Japanese tourist population of Oxford!' he screamed.

Costra stared at him. Though he tolerated Howard's outbursts, there were limits. He eyed Mamasian coldly. 'Let's get this straight, Howard. I'm not the hired help round here, I'm a partner, so don't fuckin' scream at me, okay?'

Mamasian looked into Costra's eyes. He could see he'd overstepped the mark.

'Okay, okay. Whatever . . . Just tell me what's going down, Harry. We're partners – we know that.' It was the closest he'd ever get to an apology. Costra eased his attitude.

'Right. You want to know, I'll tell you. We agreed to take out Chasen, soon as he'd delivered. Right?'

'Right.'

'We agreed the kid should go, right?'

'Yeah, yeah, just get on with it, eh?' Mamasian said, waving a hand.

'And Garcia? He was too risky. And your buddy Bruton, you said to leave alone. No problem there,' Costra continued.

'I'm talkin' about *our* guy!' Mamasian interrupted. 'The one you sent in, for Christ's sake. What happened there?'

'He screwed up.'

'I'd say so,' Mamasian muttered. 'Big time.' He stood and began to pace by the pool. 'It's been too messy, Harry. Promise me it'll never happen again. What really burns me up is the way it all fell apart the London end. What the fuck was Garcia up to?'

'We've used him in Europe before. Never been a problem. Always clean as a whistle. Maybe he was just due a bad break.'

'He's dead, right?'

'Right.'

'Then he earned it, I'd say. The major deal is, who killed *our* man?'

'Must have been someone else in the room with Garcia, or arrived as our man was leaving. If it was one of Garcia's team – let's say the girl – then there'll be no feedback to us.'

Mamasian held up a hand. 'We have to be sure that no one else was involved.'

'We don't have to worry about Whitehall – not his style. And the fact the delivery was clean would rule out another player from this end. They'd have nothing to gain by killing the man I sent after Garcia unless they planned to help themselves to a piece of the action over here, and they didn't.'

'What about competition that end?'

'No way. They'd have to have known what was going down and no one did 'cept the Paki, and he turned the goods over and delivery was clean.'

'Anyone see the change-over?'

'No. Clockwork in New York. The merchandise is in Cleveland as we speak. So competition it ain't. Wouldn't make sense.'

'What about the guy that flew out the building with the Chasen kid?'

'Doesn't matter. He's dead and there's no link to us. Maybe he got careless, who cares? Why the hell should anyone want to push him out with the kid? If the police had found them and they'd got killed in a screwed-up rescue attempt we'd know all about it by now. They'd have to release a statement.'

'So it was Garcia's woman?'

'Had to be.'

A small Mexican woman arrived with a tray – a pot of tea for Mamasian, an iced one for Costra.

'Thanks, Maria,' Mamasian said, passing the cool drink to Costra, who was beginning to pant, he was so hot. If he'd been a dog, the NSPCA would have had Mamasian up on charges.

'Look, we've got a good team over here,' Costra continued after taking a great gulp of his iced tea. 'I'd vouch for all of them. No one this end is playing for the pot. So I'd say that our man in London just plain fucked up – took out Garcia without having the smarts to make sure he was alone. Simple as that.'

'I hope you're right,' Mamasian said, pouring himself some scalding tea.

'What about Chasen? Any feedback there?'

'They'll know it was connected to the London end, but they'll have nothing to go on. That's where they run into walls. Trust me there. By the way, Brooks wants to discuss the figures with you. He thinks we should spread the accounts wider. Makes sense.'

Mamasian sipped his tea. 'Yeah, maybe. Course, a bigger spread means we have to keep an eye on more things, Harry.'

'I don't think that's true nowadays, Howard – new wave technology an' all,' Costra explained. 'Anyway, he needs to talk.'

'Brooks is never happy unless he's changing things. He's smart, I grant you that, but why change a winning formula?'

'Got to move with the times, Howard.'

'Isn't that the truth,' Mamasian replied, his eyes drifting to his vivarium. 'Want to see my latest beauty? African giant red velvet mite. It's not, strictly speaking, a spider – more of a relative. Large body, small legs. Pinkish. Beautiful velvety textured hairy body.'

'Sounds peachy,' Costra said with obvious sarcasm.

'It is, believe me. Beautiful yet without venom. I sometimes like them that way.'

THIRTY-TWO

Guy sat in his suite at the Randolph making notes. Marysia had called from the hospital to tell him Gosia had regained consciousness. She was still on a central line but was being moved from intensive care to a private room down the hall. The prognosis was good, but she would need rest and careful attention to prevent any possible complications setting in.

Guy picked up the phone and dialled the Israeli Embassy.

'Ehud Shapiro, please.'

'Who is speaking?'

'Guy Cooper.'

'One moment, please.' The operator put him on hold – they never admitted the existence of anyone until the caller's identity was confirmed. A few seconds elapsed.

'I'm afraid he's not available at present. Would you like to leave a message, Sir?'

'Please ask him to call me as soon as is convenient.' Guy left his mobile number, then hung up. The next call was to Critchley in Dublin.

'Guy. Good to hear your voice. I see you've opened quite a Pandora's box. I'm so glad to hear Miss Dobra's on the mend.'

'Well, it was very much touch and go. Are they running the woman's photo there?'

'Indeed they are. "Have you seen this woman?", the usual tabloid copy. Don't usually find it in the *Irish Times*, but there you are.'

'I suppose now that you're back in Dublin you're out of touch with how things are shaping up at Thames House,' Guy ventured.

'Well, I couldn't resist calling Ambrose,' Critchley replied with the merest hint of amusement.

'How did he sound?'

'Sanguine. Yes, I'd judge that would be the most apposite word, though I think I was the last person barring the Director-General he felt like talking to.'

'Did you ask how he viewed his future role in this?'

'In a roundabout way, yes. It appears he's handed the whole thing over to Rawlings at the special task force. Says it's not his agenda any more. Of course he'll still keep the file open and keep adding to it – at least Cunningham will.'

'What do you make of Cunningham?' Guy asked.

'Do you want a gut response?' said Critchley rhetorically. 'My intuition tells me he's a bit of a smug bastard, too clever by half. Fiercely ambitious too.'

'Is there anything else you can tell me?' asked Guy.

'Nothing I don't think you already know. Have you spoken to Rawlings?'

'Yes, I spoke to him briefly yesterday. They know the identity of the man found with Edward's body. They've also found two more bodies in a flat in Earls Court. They think there's a connection.'

'They must have some good evidence,' said Critchley.

'Well, if you come up with anything further, let me know.' Guy said. 'You have my mobile number?'

'Yes, they gave me your first message. I'll see what kind of a profile I can get on Cunningham from my various sources and let you know what I come up with.'

'Thanks. Goodbye.' Guy replaced the phone. It was time to get to the hospital.

Guy stopped at the sister's office on the third floor and tapped lightly on the glass door. It was a different woman to the one he'd met earlier, but she'd obviously been briefed to expect him. She looked up from her papers and smiled, then stood and opened the door.

'Good morning, Mr Cooper,' she said warmly. 'Mrs Dobra told me to expect you.'

'Can I see Gosia today?

'I think so. Not too long, though. She's asked after you many times. Got in quite a panic when she first regained consciousness – exactly the last thing we needed. Wanted to know if you were alright. The fact that she was lying in a hospital bed with a hole in her side didn't seem to worry her in the least.'

'I'm sorry,' said Guy.

'No need to be. Do you want to go in now?'

'If that's alright, yes. Her mother's in with her?'

'Yes. Five minutes or so, maximum.'

She led the way down the corridor past the lift, multiple occupation wards on either side, then turned right. Guy followed. The adjoining corridor had no wards but closed doors every fifteen feet or so. Guy presumed they were the single occupancy rooms. At the head of the corridor stood a tall man with a crewcut, wearing jeans, an anorak and sneakers. Their eyes met and the man smiled.

'Who's that?' Guy whispered to the sister.

'I don't know his name, but he has been cleared by the Constabulary. Some sort of extra security I think,' she replied.

Fifty feet on, a policeman was sitting in a chair by a door. As they arrived he stood.

'Guy Cooper. I'm a friend of Miss Dobra,' Guy said. The sister stood to one side, saying nothing.

'Mr Cooper. Yes. I do have your name down. You can go in if it's okay with sister.'

She nodded affirmatively, knocked lightly on the door and opened it a foot or so. Guy waited to one side.

'Gosia. I've got a visitor for you. It's Guy Cooper. Do you feel up to seeing him?' she asked softly.

The room was filled with flowers. Gosia lay completely flat on her back with a low pillow on a simple hospital bed, her head turned slightly to the door, her face creased with a big grin. The tracheal tube was gone but the central line was still present. Over the centre of her body was a raised cat's cradle that held the weight of the bedclothes from her body.

As Guy closed the door behind him, she opened her mouth to say something, but it seemed to cause her some pain and she winced. Marysia placed a hand on her forehead.

As he drew up a chair, Guy saw that Marysia looked deeply concerned. He sat close to the bed on the opposite side to Marysia.

'It's good to see you,' he said, smiling broadly at Gosia. She returned his smile, mouthing the words, 'Me too.'

'I bet you were surprised to see your mother, eh?' Guy said.

Gosia nodded then mouthed the words, 'I'm sorry I lied.'

'No need to be. I know why you couldn't tell me. You know that old English nursery rhyme, the one about "James James, Morrison Morrison, Weatherby George Dupree"?' Guy asked. She shook her head, still grinning.

'Well it goes on: "He took great care of his mother, though he was only three." Something to that effect, anyway. You were just doing a good job yourself. I understand. But so was I, so I found her because I knew she'd want to be with you.'

Her eyes left his and focused on Marysia.

'Well, I'm not going to stay long,' Guy continued. 'I'll leave you with your mother.'

Gosia looked back sharply at Guy and her expression changed. She mouthed a word. 'Edward?'

Marysia interceded quickly. 'He's fine, little one. They released him and he's in America with his father. He sent his love and said he'll be in to see you as soon as he returns.'

Gosia closed her eyes, the relief flooding her face, though she looked very pale and drawn.

'You must sleep now,' Marysia said softly. 'I have left our number with the sister. If you need me any time of the day or night, tell her and I'll be straight here.'

She leant over and kissed her daughter on both cheeks. Though she was smiling, her eyes filled with tears.

They drove in silence towards Hertford College. Guy judged Marysia needed some time to gather herself emotionally, so he said nothing. When he stopped and parked at St Giles, Marysia didn't move. She continued to stare out the window.

'She's going to be fine,' Guy said gently.

'I know. But when do we tell her about Edward?' she replied. 'I've never lied to her before.'

'You did what you had to. She couldn't have handled the news just now. We'll tell her the truth when she's more able to deal with it. By the way, who was the man in the corridor, with the crewcut and sneakers?' Guy asked.

'Aharon. One of our people. Security. Ehud sent him. Says he's good. I believe him. By the way, Cunningham called me at the hospital asking after Gosia. I'm sure he meant well, but empty gestures are the last thing I need right now.' Marysia looked down at her lap, closing her eyes for a second, then looked back at Guy. 'Okay. Let's go.'

Outside, Marysia threaded an arm through Guy's.

'How much does she know of what happened to her?' he asked.

'She knows she was shot, that's all. She's still in shock. I'm not about to pump her with questions.'

They walked on in silence for a while, then she turned her head again to Guy.

'What are Ehud's thoughts?'

'He's sure Gosia was targetted because of the Chasen connection, rather than to bring you out into the open.'

'What about Cunningham?'

'Well, Ehud tends to rule out Leston as the possible leak. But as he rightly points out, that doesn't leave Cunningham alone as the source – the whole of his section knew of the photograph of the woman and Gosia's connection to Chasen. He agrees with our hypothesis that Chasen fulfilled his task of delivering something at Kennedy, and that they took him out to cover their tracks.'

They crossed Catte Street and turned into the entrance to Hertford. Marysia stopped at the notice-boards and scanned them. Linda's reward notice took centre stage. The others had been rearranged to give room. She walked on through into the quad, turning left towards the stairwell that led to Gosia's rooms on the top floor.

As they approached Gosia's room, a cleaner looked up from the rubbish bin she was emptying. As Marysia unlocked Gosia's room, she walked forward.

'Excuse me, are you Gosia's mother?' she asked.

'Yes, I am.'

'I'm so sorry. I'm Mrs Beamish, her scout – I look after her room for her. Is she going to be alright?'

'Yes, she's over the worst now, thank you,' Marysia replied.

'I'm so glad. Everyone has been asking after her. I've left some messages in her room. It's a terrible thing about Mr Edward. I looked after him too. Such a nice boy.'

'Yes, it's terrible.'

'Well, please remember me to Gosia when you next see her.'

'I will,' Marysia replied.

The room was a decent size with a ceiling gabled at either end, a small bed along one side and a washbasin near the door. A photo of Marysia stood framed next to the bed.

On the bed was a small pile of messages. Marysia picked them up and glanced through them.

'Just messages from friends wishing her well,' she said, putting them in her bag.

'I spoke to Critchley after you phoned this morning,' Guy said after a few moments.

'Did he have anything useful to say?'

'Not a great deal. He's going to see what he can find on Cunningham.'

Before Marysia could say anything, Guy's phone chirped in his pocket and he flipped it open.

'Cooper.'

'I'm sorry, I missed that. Is that you, Guy?' a voice asked.

'It's me, yes.'

'It's Linda, Gosia's friend. How is she?'

Guy told her the latest news. When he'd finished, Linda said, 'We've been snowed under with photographs, mostly from the tour operators. We've sorted out all those that were taken on Saturday in the immediate vicinity of the quad and those inside. Shall I bring them over to your hotel? Where are you, London or Oxford?' she asked.

'I'm right here in Hertford,' he replied. Guy jotted down her room number and said they'd be over within five minutes, then flipped the phone shut. 'They've got photographs taken the day Gosia was shot.'

They locked Gosia's room, walked to Linda's room and knocked. The door opened immediately.

Inside was a hive of activity. Three students sat on the floor sorting through photographs. A bin in the centre was filled with discarded shots and envelopes.

'I'm Linda. You must be Gosia's mother,' Linda said, shaking Marysia's hand. 'I'm relieved she's out of danger. Now,' she continued, walking over to the three piles of photographs. 'The pile on the left contains those taken outside the quad. We think most were actually taken in the morning. The middle pile contains shots taken inside the quad. The last pile is the one we think could be the most useful. There's actually one that includes Gosia,' she said, finding the photo and showing it to them. 'That's the only one, unfortunately, but from that photo we worked out who was actually in the quad at the same time. That was how we could discard the snaps taken before. So far there are none taken at the exact time Gosia was shot. But there are some we haven't looked at yet – we're still sorting.'

'Great work, Linda. We may as well look at the third pile first.'

'Sure, sit over by the window for the best light. I've got a magnifying glass.'

Guy and Marysia sat themselves down. Linda handed Guy the magnifying glass and Marysia pulled out the photograph of the woman published in the paper, laying it between them.

'Look for a woman carrying a newspaper, magazine or holdall,' she said to Guy as they began.

'Why a newspaper?'

'No one heard a shot, so she must have used a silencer. She would have had to have concealed it in something – they're pretty long.'

Guy picked up a pile, passing each photo to Marysia after he'd studied it. Most were pretty amateurish.

'Is this the one?' he asked, turning it towards Linda.

'That's it. You can see Gosia at the back. She's just stepped through the gate and she's waving.'

Marysia leant over Guy's shoulder as he studied every inch of the photograph with the magnifying glass. He then handed it to Marysia and she did the same.

Together they pored over the photographs for more than an hour, Marysia examining the best ones at least five times with the magnifying glass. Finally she turned to Guy.

'I haven't picked anyone, have you?'

'No,' Guy admitted.

'She's got to be there somewhere.'

They began again, going through the three piles once more, occasionally being passed a fresh one by the students. Eventually, exhausted and frustrated, they decided to call it a day.

'Don't be discouraged,' Guy said to a disappointed Linda. 'You've all done a great job. I'm sure the woman we're looking for is here somewhere, we just haven't seen her yet. Keep sorting if you can. We'd better get moving. If you come up with anything fresh, give me a call.'

'Okay. Give all our love to Gosia. And please let me know when it's okay to visit,' she said to Marysia.

'I will. Thank you for being so wonderful,' she replied. 'Thank you all.'

As they walked through the Porter's Lodge, Marysia stopped abruptly and grabbed Guy's arm.

Guy stared up to where she was pointing. It was a small video camera.

Marysia ran up the four steps into the porter's alcove. A desk ran the length of the room, at the end of which was a closed-circuit television monitor. The screen was split into four, each with a different viewpoint. On the other side of the reception desk, a woman stood placing mail in pigeonholes.

'Excuse me!' Marysia called, 'I'm Gosia Dobra's mother. That television over there. It's a security monitor, am I correct?'

The woman looked a little nonplussed. 'Yes, it is,' she replied slowly, confused. 'We monitor the comings and goings from in here.'

'Do you record them on tape?'

'Yes we do.'

'How long do you keep the tapes? Please tell me you don't change them daily,' Marysia said, anxious.

'We keep them for seven days, then re-use them,' the woman replied.

'Hold on a second,' Marysia said, swinging round to Guy and speaking quickly in an undertone. 'We don't know precisely when Gosia's identity was leaked, right?'

'No, it could have been any time after the meeting Gosia and I had with Ambrose at the MOD.'

'When was that?'

'Thursday.'

'So if anyone had come looking for Gosia, hoping she'd be at Hertford, they could have come any time since Thursday?' She didn't wait for an answer. She turned abruptly back to the woman. 'What day do you change tapes?'

'Friday morning,' she replied.

'Shit!' Marysia shouted. 'If she came up before Friday, we missed her. Damn!' She leant across the desk. 'May I see the tape that includes all of Friday, please? Can you run it on the screen? It's important.'

Guy could see from the woman's expression that she wasn't exactly enjoying Marysia's abrasive tone, so he cut in. 'We think it may be possible that the person who shot Gosia outside the Bodleian on Saturday morning may have visited the college sometime during the days before. If this is the case, she will have been picked up by the cameras. Unfortunately it would seem you have scrubbed all but Friday. Could we take the tape with us?'

'I see,' the woman replied slowly, taking in the information. 'I'm afraid I'm not in a position to just hand over the tapes to you. I don't have the authority. However, if you could get the police to ask for them officially, I'm sure it would be possible to view them.'

Marysia turned to Guy. 'Come on,' she said, turning to leave.

'Hold on a second!' Guy called after her. He then turned back to the woman.

'There's something you might be able to help us with,' he began politely. 'End of last week. Can you remember anyone asking after Gosia – someone who you weren't familiar with?'

'I've already told the detective. As you can imagine, hundreds of people come through here every hour, and a fair proportion of them pop in here asking after friends, asking questions, collecting mail, so it's hard to remember exactly. But I do seem to remember a girl asking after Gosia. I can't remember a thing about her, just that she popped her head in and asked if she was in her room. Said she was a friend.'

'What day?' Marysia cut in.

'Again, I'm not exactly sure. Thursday, maybe Friday,' she replied.

'What time of day Thursday or Friday?'

The woman thought for a while, casting her mind back. 'I'm pretty sure it was late afternoon. That's the time I leave, and she arrived as I was collecting my things.'

'You can't remember anything about her appearance?' Marysia cut in.

The woman thought again, then shook her head. 'I'm sorry. People are firing questions at me all day – if I recognise the voice, I often hardly look up,' she replied.

'Doesn't matter. If she came in here she'd be on the tape. Am I right?'

'That's right,' the woman replied.

'Could you please identify for the police which tape contains all Friday's comings and goings for us?' asked Guy. 'We're going directly to the police station and I know they'll want to see it.'

'I'll keep it safe for them,' she replied.

'Thank you very much for your help.'

Guy turned to leave. Marysia was already at the door.

'Why on earth wouldn't the people at Hertford have turned the tapes over to the police?' Marysia said, as Guy caught up with her in Catte Street.

'Gosia was shot outside the college. Why would they think an in-house surveillance tape would be relevant? Anyway, it probably just didn't enter their heads.'

'Fair enough, but I can't believe the police didn't think of the security camera in Hertford. Surely they'd have noticed it when they made their initial enquiries?'

'They must have missed it – they're just the local constabulary, not Mossad,' Guy replied.

'More's the pity,' Marysia said crisply as she quickened her pace.

They sat in Marks' office at the police station in St Aldate's, staring at the screen.

'Let's concentrate on the bottom left quarter – the one which has the Catte Street entrance. If we try to look at all four we'll miss something. When we've done this one we'll rewind and look at the others,' Marks said. Guy and Marysia nodded, their eyes fixed on the television monitor. The digital read-out at the bottom displayed the time and date. Five-thirty p.m. Friday.

'I know you think we might be looking for a woman, but let's keep an open mind. The woman who asked after Gosia might very well be precisely who she said she was – a friend. Agreed?' He looked at Marysia and Guy. They both nodded. Marks pressed a button on the remote control.

They sat in silence watching the screen. Every few minutes Marks would press the freeze frame as someone entered. Then he'd press the frame-by-frame button until the closest shot appeared. They'd all study the picture, then if it wasn't likely, they'd carry on.

After an hour, Marks stopped the video briefly and called out to someone in the next room. 'Hey, Charlie! Can you bring us in some coffee?' A young man in the next room nodded through the glass partition and rose.

An hour, two coffees and maybe eighty pauses later, Marks froze the tape again. 'Do you want to relax your eyes for a moment?' he asked.

'No. Please continue,' Marysia replied, not taking her eyes off the screen. Marks rolled the video. It now read five-fifty.

As Marks pressed the button routinely for the hundredth or so time, the figure of a woman entered the frame.

'There!' Marysia pointed to the screen. The woman looked up to her right at the porter's window. 'Freeze the frame!'

The woman had angular features, wore sunglasses and a broad-brimmed hat.

'Got you.' Marysia's voice was scarcely audible.

Both Marks and Guy shot her a quick look, then studied the monitor.

'It's her,' Marysia said. Marks advanced the frames, but the woman was now angled to the side as she looked right into the porter's open window.

'Go back a few frames,' said Marysia. Marks complied. They studied it closely, then compared it with the photograph of the woman from task force headquarters in London.

'The make-up makes her look slimmer,' said Marysia, 'but I'm sure. If she'd only take off those damned glasses you'd be sure too.'

'What do you think, Mr Cooper?' said Marks.

'I don't know. Let's go on and see if there's a better angle,' Guy replied. Marks hit the button.

The woman looked up through the porter's window and appeared to say something, then turned back, facing the camera. Marks stopped the tape again and they all studied the face. He then advanced it until she walked out of sight under the camera and into the quad.

'Hold it right there, Sergeant,' Guy said. 'Look at the upper right quarter.' The woman appeared on the top-right screen. She was further away from the camera positioned at the right-hand end of the quad, so it wasn't as close a shot. She paused as she entered the stairwell, then disappeared. Ten seconds later she re-appeared.

'Hold it!' Guy shouted.

Marks hit the pause button. 'Why hold it there?'

'Look,' Guy explained. 'If this was the woman who asked after Gosia, why didn't she go up to her room to see if she was in? She doesn't have time – we can see that! She just enters the stairwell, then ten seconds later she's out again! If she was a friend of Gosia's, as she said, she'd at least have gone up to her room to see if she was in. But she doesn't. We see her in and out in ten seconds!'

'Good point. Let's go on.' Marks advanced the frames again.

The woman walked back through the quad and into the porter's lodge area, where she was again picked up by the first camera. Without stopping, she walked back out the entrance to Hertford, paused briefly at the road for the traffic to pass, then crossed to the other side of Catte Street.

As she reached the wall of the Bodleian, she paused again, stepped through the gate, then turned to face the entrance to Hertford, taking off her glasses.

'Bingo!' Marks said as he froze the frame.

'She's a hell of a long way away,' Guy observed. Looking at the quarter of the video in question, she was perhaps only an inch high.

'We'll see what the tech people can do. But I'd wager you're right, Mrs Dobra.'

'I know I'm right,' Marysia said coldly.

Marks pressed the stop button and ejected the video.

'Charlie, come in here!' he shouted. A few seconds later the man who'd brought them coffee entered. 'Can you make a clean copy of this at once?' he asked, handing Charlie the video. 'Then get a car and take the original to Rawlings at task force headquarters. I'll tell him it's on the way.'

'Right you are,' Charlie replied, disappearing with the video.

'And shift yourself! It's important,' he shouted after the departing figure. Marks picked up the phone. 'Get me Rawlings at task force London will you Jen?'

Marysia picked up the photo of the woman and studied it again.

'Yes, Marks here, Sir. I think we may have identified the assailant. We may have her on video. I'm sending someone down with it right now. I've stopped the tape on the subject. See what your lab people can do to scrub up the picture. Miss Dobra's mother is convinced it's the same woman as the one pictured leaving Chasen's house. I tend to agree with her.' There was a short pause. 'If you could send back a hard copy of whatever your guys can come up with I'd be most grateful. Thank you, Sir.' Marks replaced the phone.

'He'll get his tech crew on to it. Then we'll see.'

'Do you mind if I make a quick call?' Guy asked.

'Help yourself,' Marks replied.

Guy dialled. 'Linda? It's Guy Cooper. Can you bring the three piles over to the police station at St Aldate's as soon as possible? It's important. Great. Bye.'

'Were any of the witnesses from the square at all helpful, Mr Marks?' Marysia asked at length.

'Well, we interviewed all those that stayed. Bear in mind that by the time we arrived some had disappeared. We took statements from over two hundred people. None saw anything.'

'What about the young man who was with her when I arrived?' Guy asked. 'He was holding Gosia's head. He must have been very close when it happened.'

'Yes, we have his statement. He said he was a few feet behind her. He didn't notice her till someone screamed and pulled sharply to the right.'

'Someone pulled to the right, away from her?'

'That wasn't our target, sadly. It was a Japanese lady who was directly behind Miss Dobra. We tried to find her but she must have panicked and run. We've asked all the tour operators without success.'

'No one heard a shot?' Guy asked.

'No one.'

They sat in silence drinking coffee until there was a rap on the glass partition. A policewoman gestured to someone out of sight behind her. Marks made a beckoning gesture.

Seconds later Linda walked through the door, clutching a plastic supermarket bag.

'Linda, this is Detective Sergeant Marks who's heading this end of the investigation,' said Guy.

'Hello,' she said nervously. 'I've got them all here.' She pulled out the stacks of photos and placed them on the table. Pieces of torn paper had been slipped under rubber bands identifying which pile was which. Guy pulled the band from the one marked '3'.

'This is the most likely batch. The top-most is the one that actually contains Gosia waving at me. The ones with it have been sorted after identifying the people's clothes in the top one.' He laid them out on Marks' desk. Marysia, Linda, Guy and Marks then huddled round the desk, poring over them.

Marks was about to gather them up and move on to the second pile when Marysia shouted. 'Here! Look at this! You can only see the hat but it's the same one as in the video!' She thrust it at Marks, pointing with her finger at a spot on the photo. 'She's moving forward towards the centre of the quad from the Catte Street gate!'

'Hold on. We can't see Gosia. If she's moving forward, Gosia should be in front of her,' Guy interjected.

'Maybe she is – we just can't see her! She's in the middle somewhere.'

'Give me back the shot of Gosia waving,' Marks said sharply. Linda shuffled through the pack, pulling it out. 'Here!' she said.

Marks looked at it through the glass. 'Here she is, waving. She's about five feet inside the quad. Right, now let's see who's around her, see what they're wearing. If she moves forward at about the same speed as the crush around her we can more or less pinpoint her position.' He made some mental notes.

'Look there,' he said after a few seconds, pointing out something to Guy. 'The woman with the blue shirt. In this one, she's about three feet away from Gosia, and in this one here – the one you picked out with the woman in the hat, she's moved forward about fifteen feet. She's about twenty feet from where Gosia was shot. We can't see Gosia because of the crowd but she must be in there somewhere because the woman in blue is near her.'

'And the woman with the hat would be about fifteen feet behind her moving forward. That's enough for me,' Marysia said calmly, but her words had a chilling edge.

'It may be enough for you, but it's far from being enough to convince me, Mrs Dobra. Let's see if there are any other pictures with either the woman in blue or our subject.'

They studied the shots for another hour without success. But Marysia was convinced. She kept the two photographs aside. At length Marks looked up.

'I think we're wasting our time looking again and again at these shots. It's another task for our technical people. You'd be surprised what they can come up with, believe me.'

'I believe you,' Marysia replied. It had been her stock in trade with Mossad for over fifteen years.

THIRTY-THREE

There was a knock on the suite door. In the bathroom Guy wiped the remains of shaving cream from his neck and walked into the living room. The knock was repeated.

'Come in,' he shouted, thinking it was the maid.

'It's locked,' Marysia called from outside.

Guy opened the door.

'I'm going down to the hospital,' said Marysia, entering. 'Anything further from Rawlings or Marks?'

'Quite a bit. Critchley rang this morning. He's been milking Rawlings for fresh information almost hour by hour. Must be payback time for services rendered long ago. Someone's obviously told Rawlings to be helpful. Anyway, the man who died with Edward was the same man photographed at Chasen's home.'

'When was this? Do my people know?'

'Yes. It was Ehud who told me that. Leston told him. The photos taken at Chasen's London home the day before he left for New York show the man quite clearly carrying a medium-sized case. When he left Chasen's he wasn't. So it all points clearly to the premise that Chasen was carrying something to the States for someone.'

'Which was picked up at Kennedy before the car blew.'

'Must have been.'

'Have they ID'd the man?'

'Yes, a South African ex-mercenary called Van Rouen. He was either in their files or Interpol's.'

'What about the pick-up? Any leads there?'

'No, but they're still interviewing the journalists who were at the airport briefing.'

'The FBI will be worried as hell. No one knows what was in the case. Could have been anything. Bomb components, cannisters of nerve gas similar to the one they used in Tokyo – anything.'

'Rawlings now thinks along the lines that the people running the operation made a decision to destroy any links, and that meant killing the team here.'

Marysia pondered this new information and Guy went on.

'Rawlings has a lot more details of the bodies at the Earl's Court apartment. One man was found naked in the bathroom, another fully clothed in the living room. Neither had any ID. The forensic people have established that the naked man had sex only minutes before he died. Semen traces in the shower.'

'So where's the woman, right?'

'Exactly. But first of all, it's vital we try to reconstruct what happened in that apartment based on what we know. Maybe Rawlings is right, that someone who wasn't a London team member was sent in to clean up – to kill them all. If so, he didn't succeed, the woman survived.'

'Could *she* have killed both men?' Marysia posed. 'The man who died with clothes on could be another member of the team rather than an outsider.'

'If he was, why would they be killing each other? Doesn't make any sense.'

'Argument over the girl? Maybe they disagreed over the division of the money they were paid? Could be a lot of things,' Marysia replied. 'If the man *was* an outsider, could the men have killed each other in a struggle?' she said, thinking along fresh lines.

'No. The naked man was shot at close range in the back with a .45. The other man was stabbed in the back of the neck with a metal orthodontic brush. If the woman killed them both, why would she have changed weapons? She shoots one, then throws the gun away and stabs the other? Don't think so.'

'Maybe the gun was knocked from her hand?'

'Possible, I suppose. The gun that killed the man in the bathroom was found next to the second man's body in the lounge.'

Marysia was now thinking hard. 'I'll just think out loud. Stop me if you think I go wrong, okay?' she said.

'Fire ahead.'

'It's the semen traces that I'm thinking about. The dead man in the shower was presumably screwing someone when or just before he died. He could have been masturbating, of course, then again it could have been a man rather than a woman in the shower with him – '

'No. Forensic have found strands of long black hair in the shower. They say they're a woman's.'

'Good. Then we have the guy who was shot in the back, possibly in the shower with a woman when he died.'

'Check.'

'If the other victim shot the naked man, he should have shot whoever subsequently killed him while he had the chance. But he didn't. Why?'

'Because he never meant to?'

'Back to the argument over the woman scenario?' She could see that Guy had his doubts. 'You can't discount it,' she said. 'Give me another reason.'

'Because he didn't see the man had company. Lots of steam maybe. Maybe his body masked whoever was in the shower with him.'

'Okay, let's think along those lines. He thinks he's done the business on one of them, then waits for the others to get home. If, as Rawlings thinks, he's been sent to take out the London team, that leaves the woman and the South African, who he either knows is already dead, is next on his list, or is on someone else's list.'

'There could have been a lot more in the team – those three are the only people we know of.'

'That's true, but let's just follow my line for a moment. The dead man in the lounge was killed from behind – the rod entered the back of his neck.'

'Okay.'

'He'd be watching the door like a hawk, and would surely have heard anyone entering, wouldn't he? I mean, the man would be a professional.'

'Yes,' Guy conceded.

'So it follows he didn't think there was anyone else in the room.' She looked at Guy. 'The gunman thinks he's made a clean kill. Except he hasn't. The woman in the bathroom waits for him to turn his back, takes the toothbrush or whatever it was, because it's the only thing to hand, and buries it in the back of the gunman's skull. That explains both bodies.'

'And Van Rouen? Rawlings thinks Edward dragged him out of the building with him,' said Guy.

'Pushed out of the building by another of the clean-up squad, would be my guess. Which would mean there's still one of the London team running around. Which brings me to my main point.' Marysia was now pacing like a tiger, warming to her train of thought. 'If this is at all close to what happened, think about the woman – let's get into her head. As far as she is concerned, she's done her job. Chasen left with the case. So there she is in the shower, and the bullets start flying. The killer doesn't spot her. She kills him, then she's got to think, "Shit, if I hadn't been screwing lover boy, I'd be dead!" It won't take her long to reason the organisation now considers her a liability because of the photo, and Gosia being a witness.'

'Sure, she's been photographed, but that's not the end of the world. Besides, that's her problem, not theirs,' Guy argued.

'Not if she can name names. If I were those guys, I'd have made sure only the link-man knew, but it's possible she also knew, and that would make her dangerous as hell,' Marysia countered. 'Christ, she was sleeping with one of them. He may have been the leader – who knows what he might have confided in her? Now she's going to wonder about the South African. Maybe it was an accident, maybe the guy screwed up. But now she's going to think really hard about it, isn't she?'

'So what's her next step? Run?'

'Well, all of this is pure speculation. But we have to use the facts available to us. That's all we have to go on. She'd know that to kill Gosia, if she could do it cleanly, would mean the end of her one living witness,' Marysia continued.

'But if she thinks there's still another man out there somewhere, and that he killed Van Rouen –' Guy began, but Marysia cut in.

'You've got it! She's going to be faced with a choice. Kill the witness, or try to get to the people who ordered her assassination before they can get to her,' she said.

'If she knew who they were.'

'Of course. If she knew. Also remember, they killed the man she was sleeping with. Maybe she didn't give a damn about him, but if she did, it'd give her even more incentive.'

'Of course our major problem is we have no idea who's behind the whole thing. The case went to the States, but they could be based in Guatemala or Zurich for all we know.'

'We also have to remember that by now she must know from the papers that Gosia is still alive.'

'There's no way she'd even consider trying again. Besides, Gosia's safe – no one would get past Aharon.'

Just then the telephone rang. It was Critchley.

'I have some interesting news for you, my friend,' the old man said. Guy hoped he'd get to the point soon.

'The woman was spotted in Madrid on Sunday night.'

'Sunday night!' Guy exploded. 'It's Tuesday, for Christ's sake!'

'No one knew till this morning. Rawlings is as mad as hell, I can tell you.'

'But why –' Guy began.

'Stop interrupting and I'll tell you everything. Calm down.'

Marysia picked up the other telephone.

'An English businessman called the British Embassy in Madrid Sunday evening. Said he recognised the woman the police were looking for – picked her from the snapshot in the paper. He suspected she'd tried to alter her appearance – a wig and so on.'

'Where had she arrived from – London?'

'No. Dublin.'

'Dublin? Why wasn't she picked up leaving London, entering Ireland and again leaving Dublin?'

'I've no excuses to offer, I'm afraid. Suffice it to say they missed her. But here's the most salient point. The message was logged by the night staff on Sunday night, but wasn't passed through to London till Monday first thing. There it was sat upon till this afternoon. Guess who did the sitting?'

'Cunningham.'

'A veritable mindreader you are, Mr Cooper. Cunningham himself.'

'What excuse did he offer for the delay?'

'Said he'd passed the information down the line and it was mislaid. Ambrose is looking into that aspect with renewed interest, I can tell you.'

'Why wasn't the information passed immediately to Scotland Yard? This is a police matter, not a diplomatic one.'

'Guy, you're just not familiar with the vagaries of Embassy protocol. Any information of this nature would be assessed and dealt with by an Embassy staffer – '

'A member of the Service?' Guy interrupted with annoyance.

'Exactly. It would be his job to alert London. And that would mean the Service there, not the police.'

'Wonderful! Bloody marvellous,' Guy muttered in disbelief. 'Hell, she could be anywhere in the world by now!'

'True. However, Rawlings is on to Interpol as we speak. He's sending a man to Spain to check.' Critchley paused for reaction. As there was none, he continued. 'So there you are, my friend. That's my news in toto. I'll continue to give you updates in the unfolding drama of Cunningham. Judging from Ambrose's demeanour when I spoke to him, the young man's in a deal of trouble.'

'Thanks for calling, Eugene,' Guy said finally.

'Tell Miss Knoll I thought it was payback time,' Critchley said, and hung up.

'I have to go,' she said simply.

'To the hospital?'

'To Madrid.'

Guy stared at her. She meant it.

'What do you mean? Your place is here with Gosia.'

'My place is in Spain. And regardless of what you might say to try to convince me otherwise, I am going to Spain. This woman tried to kill Gosia.'

'Marysia, this is an international police matter. What do you have in mind – you're going to find her and kill her? Is that what you're saying? How will you be any different to this woman if you do that? Tell me that!'

'What makes you think I'm going to kill her?' she shouted. 'What gives you the right to say that? And don't presume to judge me, Guy Cooper. Remember Kraków? You were forced to kill in anger then!'

Guy sat down slowly, his head in his hands. He'd seen this side of her nature before – her face was set.

'And what of Gosia while you fly on your trip of personal retribution?'

'Gosia will be fine. She's in no danger now.'

'She is your daughter. I am an old friend. I merely offer advice because I care for you deeply and fear for you.'

'I've left her many times when I've had to. She knows that when I leave it's because I *have* to leave. She never questions my decisions as you do.'

'You don't have to leave at all! You choose to! Think of all the years you were away from Gosia. All the times she maybe wished you'd stayed. Now it's her turn, for God's sake! Can't you see that? Now is the time to realise she needs you with her – desperately. She's lying in a hospital with a gunshot wound, and your nature just won't allow you to make the obvious moral choice.'

'Don't lecture me on moral behaviour!' Marysia shouted loudly.

She stared long and hard at Guy, then her expression softened and she crouched down on the carpet next to him, crossing her arms over his knees.

'I'm sorry,' she said. 'My anger's not directed at you. You know that. You've been wonderful to both Gosia and myself. But I have to go. It's like a schedule that's been forced upon me.'

She leant forward and kissed him gently on the lips. Guy looked into her pale emerald eyes and was taken back to their first meeting seven years before in London. She had lost none of her beauty.

'Can I join you?' he said at length.

'If you wish,' she replied. 'First we go to the hospital. Then we make plans.'

Guy and Marysia sat by Gosia's bed and explained their plans.

'I understand, Mama. Don't worry about me, I'm really feeling so much better.'

'If you need me, I'll be here within hours. You know that.'

'Yes.'

Marysia moved over and lay next to her daughter on the slim bed, an arm round Gosia. They lay cheek to cheek for several minutes. Then Marysia turned her head to one side and kissed Gosia on the forehead.

'We must go. Ehud will look after you while I'm gone. Just call him. He can always get in contact with me.'

'Don't worry, Mama. I will see you when I see you. Take care.'

THIRTY-FOUR

Marysia paid scant regard to either speed limits or the radar cameras which flashed as they passed them every ten minutes or so. Guy sat strapped into his seat hoping for the best as they sped along the A40 from Oxford at well over a hundred miles per hour.

'Can we get one thing straight?' Guy asked, after they'd been on the road for twenty minutes.

'Anything,' Marysia replied.

'Your name. I'm confused by all the Sabras, Dobras and Knolls. Which is it?'

'Dobra by birth, Knoll when I arrived in Israel, and Sabra in South Africa.'

'And Marysia?'

'Marysia from birth till South Africa, when I had to change it.'

'That's a relief,' Guy said with a wry smile, but Marysia didn't seem to notice.

They turned onto the M4 and began picking up the signs to London Airport.

'You have a very loyal daughter.'

'She's special. I'm very lucky. But she'll be fine. If I thought otherwise, I would never leave. But three innocent people are dead, and Gosia was very nearly the fourth. I have to do something.'

They drove on in silence again. 'I've always told her that should she need me, she can reach me. She's always known where I am – I made very sure of that. But after the Hizballah operation, I couldn't come and go as I pleased in Europe, so I told her that she could also call you and you'd be there for her. I knew you'd be happy to help her for me.'

'You think you are in danger now?'

'Maybe,' she replied lightly. 'Our people will be looking for the unexpected. And I shall be as well. But our direction must be to find the woman who shot Gosia, then work our way back to identify those behind the killings.'

They turned left off the M4 towards the airport. Guy pulled his phone from his pocket and dialled.

'May I speak to Ehud Shapiro please. Tell him it's Guy Cooper.'

'One moment please, Mr Cooper.'

A few moments later Shapiro was on the line.

'Guy. Are you at Heathrow?'

'Approaching. Do you have any contacts in Madrid?'

'I have one name. He is not associated with us directly, but he is the man to speak to – if you can find him. His name is Zvonko Grlic. He's a fiercely proud Croat. He comes from Zagreb, but has lived in Madrid for thirty years. If there's anything to be known in Madrid, Zvonko will know it. But everyone knows that, so he keeps a low profile. Marysia may know how to get in touch – they were close.' He paused for a second. 'I have little new to tell you. Good luck. Keep in touch.'

'I will,' Guy replied. 'Thank you for all your help.'

'It is nothing. We take care of our own,' Shapiro said, then hung up.

Guy put down the phone and began to make a note of the name. Marysia leant over to look. He'd got as far as the christian name when Marysia spoke.

'Grlic. I know. He's a wonderful man. Dangerous, egotistical, exotic, but possessed of a great heart and a fine sense of the bizarre.'

'Ehud says he's hard to find.'

'He is. But unless his habits have changed, I think I know where he'll be.'

She stood on the brakes and swung left off the motorway towards the airport. Then the phone rang. Guy flipped it open.

'Rawlings here. Many thanks for the tape and the photographs you gave to Marks. Just got the stuff back from our technical people. Scrubbed up pretty well. There's no doubt that the woman standing outside Hertford College on the tape is the same as the woman in the photograph taken at Chasen's. As far as the tourist snap goes, it would be hard to introduce as evidence in court, but I'm satisfied it's the same woman again.'

'I hear you're sending a man to Madrid following the sighting.'

'Correct. Could be a wild goose chase – we've had over a hundred sightings since the photo was published in the dailies. But since Gosia told you originally that the woman had a Latin accent, it may be she's going to ground. I'll keep in touch.'

'Thank you, Chief Superintendent, I'd be grateful,' Guy replied, unwilling to share his plans with Rawlings.

Guy flipped the phone shut. 'Rawlings. Both the tape and the photo are positive. It's her.'

'Then let's get moving,' Marysia replied as she pulled into the Heathrow long-term carpark.

Luiza turned the small computer over in her hand. On a sheet of creased foolscap she'd printed a succession of random numbers. Between the two, they provided the key. The screen of the Apple Newton shone brightly, a small box in the centre of the screen requiring her to enter the password.

During the two days she'd been back in Madrid in the security of her small but luxurious apartment in the heart of the fashionable Salamanca district, she'd achieved a great deal. She already had the name – Mamasian.

Garcia had let that slip. Also the fact that his employers were American – 'fucking yanks' was a phrase he'd used more than once. So that was the direction she'd chosen. But she had to get into the files to confirm, there was little point in heading off to the States with just a name. But she needed to be ready, so she'd had her usual man supply a suitable passport, together with a tourist visa complete with photograph of herself as a timid schoolteacher. The reservations had been made and she was due to leave in two days. She needed one day at home preparing, so the heat was on to crack the password. It was now five hours since she'd begun to concentrate and she was getting nowhere. She'd typed over a hundred words to no avail, and without it the screen remained motionless.

As the night wore on her frustration grew. Her name, his parents' names, their previous codenames, his city of birth, his favourite writers – none unlocked the computer. She racked her brains for any phrases he used, anything that would have come to his mind when he locked the word in. But the screen just glowed back at her.

She put down the Newton and walked to the bathroom, throwing her towelling dressing-gown over the lip of the basin.

As the hot water beat down on her body she was reminded of the terrible look in Garcia's eyes as he died, and a wave of emptiness surged through her chest. She reached out and turned off the tap, wiping the water from her eyes, staring at the ceiling, realising that her heart was racing. She walked to the bed and sat wet and naked on the edge, covering her face with her hands.

She'd loved him – she knew that now. There was no way she could deny it any more. The grief, the terrible loss she felt, the emptiness. Never expose your emotions to the pain of loss. That's what her father had told her when her mother had died. He'd suffered terribly. And it had been the same for the day her father had picked up his revolver and turned it on himself. Life without him had seemed inconceivable, but she'd survived. She'd promised herself never to open her heart again. But now it was pounding and her eyes were filled with tears.

She stood, punching her fists in the air, and cried out with frustration. Was it possible that she'd come to love a man for the first and only time, only to have him taken from her in such a cruel fashion? She closed her eyes and clenched her teeth. Then she froze. Her heart . . . *Corazon*!

She jumped from the bed and ran to the living room, snatching up the small computer, her fingers keying in the letters with fierce stabs. *Corazon*. A second later the screen dissolved and she was in.

THIRTY-FIVE

The night was warm and the air filled with tempting smells of wood fires, of roast suckling pig and baby lamb as Marysia and Guy walked from the hotel down to the Plaza de Isabel II and across Madrid's Calle Mayor into the heart of the historic area of Madrid known as the 'Madrid of the Austrias'.

It was past eleven and the narrow streets were nose to tail with cars and motor scooters, the magnificently decorated baroque bars and restaurants heaving with Madrilenians.

'Zvonko's one of the most charming and likeable men you'll ever meet. It's easy to lose sight of the fact that he was once one of the most powerful men in the Madrid underworld. He was tough as nails when the need arose, but I always found him to be a man of his word. He left centre stage many years ago, but he's still very influential and not much happens without his knowledge. He loves life and lives every second to the full. He calls himself *Corbata*.'

'What does that mean?' Guy asked.

'*Corbata* means necktie or cravat. In the seventeenth century the Croatian soldiers were widely acknowledged as the bravest, most savage fighting men serving in the Austrian Imperial Army. In the war against the Turkish Empire, the Turks fought on horseback with sabres, targetting the necks of their opponents. As a gesture of arrogant defiance, the Croatians tied bands of red silk round their necks as if to say: "Here is your target. Come get me if you can!" Hence the word "cravat".'

As they walked further into the square, past the crowded *tapas* bars, Marysia pointed to the façade of the

Casa de la Panaderia, built in 1619, with its magnificent carved stone window arches and murals. 'Under Philip III, this part of the city was the nerve centre of society. I love it – the style is so gloriously baroque.' She guided Guy through the Arch of Cuchilleros and ducked down a narrow side street.

'Here we are,' she said, stopping outside the wooden door of the Meson de Carducho. 'Just a quick word before we go in. I'd like to play this my way. I know the man well, so trust me. He's a tricky man, likes to do things at his own pace. You can't just go in gangbusters and ask for his help. We'll have to flatter his ego, take some time. I know we're in a hurry, and the last thing on my mind is idle chat over a bottle of wine, but that's the way it may have to be, so expect a little frustration.' She then stepped inside.

The restaurant was packed. The interior was sturdy oak tables and chairs, stone floors and a low ceiling stained dark brown with a century of wood and cigarette smoke.

'Nothing's changed,' she shouted above the hubbub into Guy's ear. 'He'll be in his private room. That's through there,' she said, pointing to a door marked '*privado*' to the left of the beaten-metal-topped bar. Then she elbowed her way towards an elderly woman who looked up from preparing a dish of *rationes* – the Spanish hors d'oeuvres. Recognising Marysia, the woman threw an arm upwards and called out to her. Guy stood by the door and waited. A minute passed while Marysia and the woman embraced and chatted animatedly, then Marysia fought her way back to Guy, the woman disappearing through the door behind her.

'Her name's Angelina. She's been in love with Zvonko for forty years. This is her restaurant. She makes the greatest *tapas* in Madrid, as you'll no doubt discover.'

The woman reappeared and waved them across. Marysia took Guy's hand and they struggled over through the drinkers.

Angelina guided them down a short corridor and tapped on another wooden door. There was a muffled roar from within and she turned the handle and pushed.

Inside, a great bear of a man sat at a dining table, filling up a carved mahogany armchair. He looked close to twenty stone. His head sat, without any evidence of a neck, on broad shoulders. His bare arms were as thick as an average man's thighs, and his eyes were the merest slits set within rolls and creases of fat. A short thick white beard covered his cheeks, upper lip and chin.

Marysia walked into the light of a hanging chandelier and he threw his arms wide and clapped his hands excitedly.

'*Pajarilla*! It has been too long! You have neglected me all these years. Come share my food and wine.'

As Angelina left the room, he rose from his chair and clasped Marysia to him in a bear-hug.

'This is my friend Guy Cooper, *Corbata*,' Marysia said when he finally let her go.

'Welcome, Mr Movieman. Come. Sit,' he said, wedging himself back into his chair. 'Please taste the *Pulpo a la Gallega*,' he continued, lifting a baby octopus from its bed of olive oil and red peppers.

Three glasses stood on the table, together with a selection of *tapas*.

'When Angelina told me you were here, I called for all your favourites,' he said, squeezing Marysia's cheek. 'This one here is my *Pajarilla*'s favourite,' he said, pointing to a blood-red dish. '*Sangre con tomate*. Literally blood with tomatoes. But in Angelina's kitchen it becomes a little miracle.' He speared a cube that floated in the sauce and offered it to Marysia.

Guy shot Marysia a quick look, hoping she could speed matters up a little. She didn't return his glance.

'And to celebrate, we drink *Viña Tondonia* '82,' Zvonko added, filling the glasses. 'To the old days!'

'To the old days!' Marysia echoed as their glasses met across the table.

'You come to me for information,' Zvonko said as he fingered a sliver of *Boquerones* into his mouth, the oil and vinegar dribbling into his white beard. 'There was a time when such beauty would come to me for love. But now they come to pick my brains. It is I that must go to them for love. Such is life.' He roared with laughter at his own humour.

'I come to you as a friend.'

'Of course you do, *Pajarilla*,' he replied, chuckling. 'Show,' he said, his eyes creased with amusement.

Marysia reached into her coat pocket and withdrew the photograph of the woman which Ehud had given her. Zvonko held it at arm's length.

'My eyes,' he said with a resigned happy shrug. 'I do not care for spectacles – I am too proud.' He then studied the photo as a poker player would his hand of cards – there was not the faintest change of expression. He then laid it down carefully away from the food, tore a piece of bread from the loaf and began dipping it in the *Huevas con mayonesa*.

Guy stared at the Croatian, then at Marysia, as they ate and drank in silence. Marysia did not press Zvonko for a response to her obvious question and none seemed forthcoming. The man was playing his games, and Marysia was playing along. She was a fine actress, but it was taking an interminable time. Finally Zvonko refilled their glasses and made a toast.

'*Por nosotros*!' he shouted, lifting his glass, and they all drank.

At length Guy could stand it no longer. 'Do you know the woman in the photograph?' he asked. Marysia shot him a sidelong disapproving glance.

'Don't worry, little sparrow,' said Zvonko. 'I can see he is a man in a hurry. He does not know my rules.' His eyes swivelled to Guy. 'In Madrid we always eat and drink first, and it is only then that we like to do business.' He mopped up the remains of the rich blood and tomato sauce from one of the *tapas* dishes, wiping his mouth with a beautifully decorated lace napkin and placing it next to his empty plate. Then he smiled at Marysia. 'Yes, I know the woman. *Ojos de la oscuridad* – in English, the one with the eyes of darkness.'

There was another silence, and this time Guy knew better than to break it. A minute passed as the Croatian beamed at Marysia.

'Is she in Madrid?' she said at last.

'No, she is not.'

'Do you know where she is?'

'Yes, I know where she can be found.'

'Do you wish to tell me?'

'Has Mr Movieman got deep pockets and long arms?'

'They will be my pockets, *Corbata*,' Marysia replied.

'One thousand US dollars is my special price for you, *Pajarilla*.'

'Agreed,' Marysia replied without hesitation. Zvonko held up a hand.

'I have a better idea. We play. You win – the information is free. I win – I get a kiss from my *fiera*,' he said as he pulled a dog-eared deck of strange-looking cards from his pocket.

'Agreed. But tonight you will lose,' Marysia replied, a twinkle in her eye.

'You play *mus*, Mr Movieman?'

Guy shook his head.

'Our Spanish card game. It is played with four persons, but my *Pajarilla* and I invent a game for two. We call it *mus* for lovers – *para amantes*. In its proper form it is a very old Spanish game – many hundreds of years. You may think it is like your poker. Maybe like your bridge. You see?' he said, fanning the cards towards Guy. 'There are four *palos* or suits, like with your poker or bridge: *copas* – the cups, *oros* – the gold coins, *bastos* – the clubs, and *espados* – the daggers. That is the origin of your spades and clubs,' he explained, showing the last two suits to Guy. One looked like a primitive caveman's club and the other a dagger. 'The clubs and the *espados* – spades. You see? It is interesting, eh?'

Guy nodded, sneaking a look at his watch as the Croatian picked up the pack. This was taking forever, and with the passing of each minute the woman could be further away.

Zvonko dealt four cards to Marysia and four to himself. They both studied their hands. Then Zvonko and Marysia stared intently at each other. Guy studied them both – no flicker of an expression from either – it could have been a scene from *The Cincinatti Kid*. A minute passed before Marysia swivelled her eyes to Guy, raising her eyebrows twice. Zvonko's expression didn't alter. Another twenty seconds, then it was Zvonko's turn to shoot Guy a glance. He flicked his tongue out the right-hand side of his mouth, sucked in his bottom lip and closed his eyes tight shut for a fraction of a second. Another twenty seconds, then Marysia deliberately picked two olives from a *tapas* dish and placed them in front of her. Zvonko abruptly threw down his cards and roared with laughter and the whole room shook.

'I lose! I have nothing,' he bellowed.

Marysia slowly laid down her cards. 'Thirty-one!' she said as she leapt up and threw her arms round Zvonko, embracing him. 'You lose, but I kiss you because I love you, *Corbata*!'

'We play this game to make us laugh – that is all. There must be four,' Zvonko told Guy, refilling their glasses. 'The gestures with the eyes and tongue are the signals we give to our partners to tell them what we have. It is like your game bridge – the bidding, if you like. That is why we watch each other. The trick is to give the smallest gesture so only the partner sees. But when we played many years ago, my *Pajarilla* always played with me. The others, they always look at my beauty, never at me, so we win. That is so?' he said, chuckling at Marysia.

'We were a team – the best!' she replied.

'Indeed – the best.' Zvonko picked up her four cards, then laid them down. Then he looked seriously at Marysia. 'The woman. She is in Segovia. She passed through Madrid on Monday.'

'You have an address?'

'I have an address.'

Marysia lifted her glass. '*Forza en el Canut*!'

Zvonko laughed loudly, slapping his giant thigh. 'You have such a memory! But seriously, take care, little sparrow. She has many faces – I know them all. Though she is not in your league, she is nevertheless an adversary to be reckoned with. She killed Pablo Alvares with her bare hands when she was eighteen, or so they say. I knew her father – he put a gun to his head years ago.' He raised his eyebrows to the heavens. 'She is very beautiful. *Que buena esta esa tia* – she is *una verdadera fiera* – a real sexual tigress! Oh for an hour with that one! I think she would kill me with pleasure – but I would be so happy.' He again roared with laughter.

It was well past two o'clock when Zvonko let them go and they stepped into the warm night air of Madrid, the pavements still packed with Madrilenians. Four bottles had been brought to the table and finished. Guy estimated Zvonko had dealt with at least two, while he had consumed less than half. Considering the balance, Marysia was sound as a bell – a quite remarkable feat considering they had finished with two gigantic brandies – *Gran Duque de Alba, Gran Reserva.*

Marysia set a brisk pace as they strode back to the hotel.

'I'm sorry to have put you through all that, but as I told you before, he has the information so he chooses the game. I had to play by his rules.'

'I don't know how you do it,' Guy said as they threaded their way down the narrow street, searching in his pocket for some coins to give an old woman who held her hand out to him.

'Drink so much?' she replied. 'To be *Corbata's* friend, one must drink with him, and that usually means to excess. But if you notice, you don't see much evidence of drunkenness in the streets of Spain. They handle their liquor well. I come from Poland as you know – need I say more?'

The old woman glanced down at her hand and gazed at the coins in shock – she was obviously more used to knock-backs or misers. Marysia merely grinned at Guy as they moved forward.

Then she stopped in her tracks.

'There is something I must ask him – something I had quite forgotten. Please stay here, I won't be long.' With that she placed a hand on Guy's shoulder, turned and was instantly lost in the crowd, leaving Guy standing at the corner of the Plaza de Isabel II, bemused.

Guy stepped back out of the milling throng so that he wouldn't be dragged along with the crush of late-night drinkers. The bars were still a melée of party-goers, the restaurants still packed with diners, all talking at the tops of their voices in typical Spanish fashion.

'Sorry to have kept you waiting, but it was important.' Marysia was back again, gone only two minutes. He put an arm round her as they walked towards the Gran Via.

'What was so important?' he asked casually.

'I needed to know of contacts within the Spanish police. Now I have one.'

Guy inched his fingers into Marysia's handbag, closing them on the short barrel of a gun. Marysia swivelled and cracked the palm of her hand down sharply on the back of his hand. Guy let out a cry of pain.

'My God. Was that you?' said Marysia. 'I thought I was being pick-pocketed. What on earth were you doing?' She stopped, taking his hand.

'I think you know what I was doing. You went back for what you knew Zvonko would provide you with.'

Marysia backed him up against a wall and whispered, 'Guy Cooper. You have a lot to learn about life. You carry insurance should you lose the things you value most. When you travel on a plane you are reassured that the security precautions preclude terrorists from taking explosives aboard. In Australia you sleep soundly at night, secure in the knowledge that your house has a double lock and alarm. Yet you'd gladly track down a killer who even Zvonko deems to be dangerous without so much as a penknife to protect youself. You have no right to pass moral judgments on me should I wish to protect *myself*.'

Guy stared deep into her angry face. The silence lasted for several seconds, their faces only inches from each other. Then he kissed her.

The seventh and last chime of the great bell of the Cathedral of Segovia hung in the air for several seconds, then melted into the silence of the town.

Luiza walked slowly down the main hall of the house, carrying flowers. Her bags were packed and waiting at the front door. Since she'd arrived, the thought had been with her that maybe she would never visit the house again – never again look on the powerful face of her father.

She was dressed formally in an ankle-length cream lace dress, secured at the neck and ankles with small pearl buttons. Her hair was tied back behind her head and secured by three ornate tortoiseshell combs. Across one shoulder she wore a richly woven antique *chal* – the traditional Spanish shawl. It was a ritual. Each time she visited the family home, she dressed in these clothes out of respect for her dead parents. As she reached the main living room she hesitated, then turned the handle of the door and walked inside.

The air was thick and musty, the stench of rotting vegetation overpowering. A thin layer of dust covered the surface of the inlaid table that occupied the centre of the room, flanked by several period chairs. On the table stood a beautiful eighteenth century Venetian vase, filled with dead flowers.

Luiza eased shut the door behind her, moved to the table, then looked up at the wall ahead. The strong features of her father gazed down at her from the portrait on the wall – the head tilted upwards, the eyebrows arched arrogantly. To the right hung a matching portrait of her mother, her face marked by self-doubt, timidity and reserve. It was not a beautiful face, but one which called for compassion. A mother she had never known.

She crossed herself, dropped her eyes and moved to the table, placing the flowers next to the vase. Then she prised open the French windows, allowing a cool breeze to drift past her into the room.

As she turned back to the table, the rays of the sun picked out the swirling particles of dust. She lifted the vase and walked to the door.

A few minutes later she returned and arranged the flowers. The air in the room was now sweet with the scent of roses and irises. The sounds from the narrow street leading down from the Cathedral were muted – a dog barked and the excited voice of a small child responded to it.

Satisfied with the arrangement, Luiza sat on the sofa that stood across from the portrait of her father, her face devoid of the smallest trace of make-up. She stared at the stern features, the face of another man still in her mind. Minutes passed while she remained motionless. Then she got up, walked to the windows and shut them with finality. Looking at the portrait one last time, she crossed herself, then left the room, shutting the door softly behind her.

THIRTY-SIX

Guy looked down at the sleeping face of Marysia, her body curled tightly into his. He'd always known he loved her and possibly that she loved him. But he'd loved Coco and had been committed to her. Now he was alone and Sam a memory. Their time had come.

The sun flooded in through the double windows of his bedroom, the muffled sound of horns of the infuriated taxi drivers blaring down in the rush-hour traffic outside the Palace Hotel.

He moved his head slightly and Marysia murmured, then snuggled deeper into his shoulder.

What would the next few days hold in store for them? Now that they'd found each other again, would their happiness be destroyed by a relentless quest to bring the woman to justice? Would Marysia put their happiness and that of Gosia's at risk to that end? He knew how single-minded she could be, and he knew the life she had lived. She'd been right the night before, he did live in a different world to her. In his, justice was the province of the authorities, the police, the courts, the judges, the prisons. To her, justice was personally administered. An eye for an eye. She had stared pain and death in the face. She had seen so many die. To her, the decisions were simple.

He looked down at her face again. It was so unsullied by the ravages of cynicism and pain that it was scarcely believable that she had lived the life she had.

As he gently threaded his fingers though her short soft hair, brushing the strands from her forehead, the jarring sound of the telephone rang through the room. He reached out as her eyes blinked open.

'Cooper,' he said.

'Señor Cooper. It is eight o'clock. Your car is available when you wish it,' the voice said.

'Thank you,' Guy replied. 'Could we have breakfast for two right away?'

'Of course, Señor Cooper.'

Marysia rolled onto her side to face him and raised a leg, draping it over his midriff. 'Good morning *coheña*,' she whispered.

'Is that Spanish for "dirty old man"?' Guy replied, smiling.

'No, that's Polish for "my love".' She rolled on top of him and kissed him with a fierce intensity.

They sat in the adjoining room eating their breakfast fifteen minutes later. The coffee had the consistency of mud and the bacon was thick as a slice of toast.

'We have to talk about what you plan to do if and when we catch up with the woman in the photograph. My role in all of this at present seems to be that of observer – someone along for the ride. It can't be like this. I must know and I must be allowed a voice.'

Marysia placed her knife and fork on the plate and leant forward, taking Guy's hand in hers. 'Of course you must. So, I will tell you exactly. I mean to find her, and I mean to turn her over to the authorities. That is all.'

Guy looked at her steadily. 'Marysia, is that what you truly mean? I must know, and I must be convinced before we go a step further.'

'You mean, do I intend to mete out a very particular personal form of capital punishment to someone who has killed many and tried to kill the one I love – my blood?'

'That's exactly what I mean.'

Marysia looked across at the window as if searching her mind for her true feelings. Then she turned to Guy. 'Had I never met you, I would be seeking her out with a gun and either she or I would be dead. But my love for you has complicated matters.'

'But even if I weren't here, there would be Gosia to think of. How could you have considered placing her happiness in the balance?'

She thought for a while. 'It's true what you say. I'm afraid I get carried away with emotion. It is a consequence of the life I've lived since I was a child, I suppose. When I saw my child in the hospital and felt she might die, a terrible wave of hatred entered my body – one that threatened to consume my entire being. Even when I knew she would live I felt the same fire. But you've made me feel I owe too much to Gosia to throw it all away in an act of revenge. And now we have each other. So you must trust me. What more can I say?'

'I just want to get one thing clear. We're going to Segovia to turn this woman over to the authorities?'

'That's correct.'

'And the gun?'

'If she threatens either of us she is dead.'

'Then let's get this over with.'

The traffic gave no sign of easing as they reached the outskirts of Madrid and joined the main north-western artery towards Segovia.

The Spanish drivers as usual played out their personal games of rally-sport, forever inching their way forwards at the expense of their fellow drivers, in many cases four or more cars abreast occupying the three lanes of the motorway. Ahead some forty kilometres Guy could see the outline of the Sierra de Guadarrama, the mountains that lay between them and Segovia.

The driver of a small truck passed them at speed, and braked heavily as he tried to swerve in ahead of them, sounding his horn. Marysia's response was to accelerate hard. The man stood on his brakes and swore, wrenching the wheel of his truck back into his own lane, his tyres screaming.

'Zvonko said he couldn't guarantee that she was still there,' she said casually as the traffic halted, oblivious to the angry calls of the truckie. 'So we just have to hope for the best.'

'And if we establish that she's there?'

'I make a call to the police contact Zvonko gave me and we stay to make sure she's picked up. Does that sound too violent for you, tough guy?' she replied teasingly.

'That sounds just fine. What about Rawlings' man? He said he was sending someone. Surely he should be told.'

'I like to do things my way. I'm sure word will filter through. Trust me.'

A look of resignation crossed Guy's face, one that was not lost on Marysia.

They passed through the two-kilometre tunnel and emerged the other side of the Guadarrama mountains, but the countryside didn't change. As far as the eye could see was a barren parched landscape dotted with an occasional neglected olive tree. The airconditioning inside the small Fiat was not up to the task of dealing with the temperature, so they drove with all the windows down, the wind rushing in and beating their faces.

'In many ways I miss my previous lifestyle,' Marysia said, running a hand through the hair at the nape of Guy's head. 'The first few months in Africa were a welcome relief, then I felt as though I had moved from Formula One racing to taxi driving.'

'That's understandable enough. It happens to soldiers at the end of every war. They're accustomed to living life on the edge, then they're suddenly put out to grass and their mind and body find it hard to adjust.'

'It's easy to justify violence to oneself – orders, *bueno publico* – the national interest. The things I did were for the good of my people, they had a legitimacy. Yet there were times when I knew I was actually enjoying the danger – the adrenalin rush of living life minute by minute, aware that it could end at any second. Does that sound bad?'

'No. Maybe you were simply subconsciously adjusting to your lifestyle, to make the danger bearable. But do you think you can make the further adjustment back to a normal life – a dull one occupied by myself,' Guy asked, smiling across at her.

'We shall have to see, won't we? Your life doesn't sound so very dull to me,' she replied, then added in a teasing undertone, 'I must be getting old.'

It was close to eleven a.m. when they dipped down the Avenida del Padre Claret into Segovia with its massive Roman aqueduct, around fifty thousand feet in length, supported by one hundred and sixty-six arches towering more than a hundred feet in the air.

Marysia eventually stopped the car behind a tour bus and consulted her map. 'The Calle de los Desamparados. It's in the heart of the old town, very near the Cathedral. We'll leave the car down here and walk up.'

'We just walk up to her door and see if she answers?'

'Sure. We ask her very nicely to come with us. I'm sure she'll oblige – Zvonko says she's a real *mensch*.'

'So what do you suggest, smart-arse? You tell me.'

'We set up base camp in the Plaza Mayor, and then I go check out the place.'

'Sure. You drop me like a bag of groceries in a café then pull out your Smith & Wesson and start blasting. I just get to listen to the gunfire.'

'Look, I thought we'd been through all of this,' Marysia said calmly. 'I explained I had no intention of putting a bullet in her, much as I'd like to. I initially check out her house alone because it's possible she's either seen you with Gosia or she'll recognise you anyway. Unless it escaped your attention your face was plastered across every tabloid in England less than a week ago.'

Guy decided to keep his mouth shut. As usual she had a point.

'And it's a Beretta, more's the pity, not a Smith & Wesson. Last time I used an automatic the fucking thing jammed on me after three shots.'

'I expect three were enough?'

'As it happens they were, but it made me think,' she replied.

'I'm impressed,' he said archly, then opened the door. 'Let's go, eh?'

'Sure. Keep your hat and sunglasses on – the last thing we need is the attention of your adoring public.'

They passed under the central arch of the aqueduct and made their way through the crowds up into the heart of the old town. The streets were packed with the locals and a horde of Japanese and German tourists, who saw every step as a magnificent photo opportunity.

'Why is everywhere we go called the Plaza Mayor – it's a bit lacking in originality, isn't it?' said Guy.

'In a way, yes, in a way, no. Remember, most Spanish towns have their origins as medieval fortified walled cities. The central core of each town was initially called the Plaza Mayor or main square. They chose not to chop and change – unlike the Americans, who rename places at the drop of a hat to accommodate their assassinated presidents.'

'True. I must say I always preferred Idlewild to JFK.'

'See what I mean?'

The square was not as large as Guy had expected. A road ran round the sides, and in the centre there were newspaper stalls and a bandstand. Under the arches of the buildings surrounding the square were myriad small and large cafés with tables and chairs set on the pavement. Marysia made for one on the corner facing the Cathedral.

'Order me a tea and keep those sunnies on. I'll be back as soon as I can,' she said and walked off towards the Calle Escuderos.

'See if you can keep your hand out of your handbag!' Guy called to her.

Marysia's cold tea stared at him from the far side of the table. He was on his fourth coffee and it tasted bitter. Marysia had been away for over fifty minutes and he was beginning to feel nervous. The café was filling, and a furious game of *mus* was in full swing under the arches behind him, four voluble geriatric Spaniards chiding their partners and boasting of their great hands as the betting began. A waiter placed a small complimentary dish of boiled green peppers drenched in olive oil at his side as an incentive to continue to order. Guy glanced up and returned his smile. Quite why the man thought marinated capsicum was a suitable complement to espresso eluded Guy – he'd ordered a coffee and a tea, not drinks. He'd never understand the Spanish, and the feeling seemed to be mutual.

The sun disappeared behind a very threatening dark thunder cloud just as he felt a hand on his shoulder. He whipped his head round, startled. It was Marysia.

'Sorry. Shouldn't have crept up from behind – didn't mean to make you jump.'

She sat opposite and after a cursory glance at her tea, waved to the attentive waiter. '*Café solo, por favor.*'

'Coffee? Since when?'

'I'm full of surprises,' she replied.

'So, what's the scoop?' Guy asked, leaning forward.

'There's no sign of life at the house. The windows are shuttered and the gate's padlocked. It doesn't look promising. We've no means of finding out if there's anyone inside, short of knocking on the door or breaking in.'

'What do you suggest?'

'I suggest we stake out the house till it gets dark – see if there's any movement.'

'If there is, it could be anyone.'

'Sure. Then we'll check it out.'

'And in the meantime, if she's been and gone, she gets a head start wherever she's off to next.'

'We'll have to cross that bridge later.'

The waiter arrived with Marysia's coffee, placing a single miniature blood sausage swimming in an inch of oil next to it.

'Looks irresistible, doesn't it?' Marysia said, popping it into her mouth and wiping a dribble of olive oil from her chin with a paper napkin.

'Look. I want to get something clear,' Guy said, attempting to take his mind off Marysia's *bon bouche*. 'I have no intention of following this woman round the world, always one step behind. I have better things to do – as, I'm sure, do you. If she's here, then fine. If she's already been and gone, then I'm afraid I vote we leave it to the professionals.'

'I *am* a professional,' Marysia interceded, her jaws now mercifully still.

'Were. You retired.'

'They retired me.'

'Whatever. You're out of it, one way or another. And we should remember Gosia.' He paused for a second. 'By the way, we should phone her – see how she is.'

'I just did so. That's what made me even later.'

'How is she?'

'Fine. Sends her love. Wants to get out of hospital right now. I had to call the specialist and insist they keep her there for a couple of days. I'll have to be the one to tell her about Edward.'

'She still doesn't know – I'd forgotten. Won't someone let it slip? Her friends must be visiting her. What about the newspapers?'

'I asked the sister to have a word with the staff and any visitors before they went in. I couldn't do much more. But to get back to your point, I'll agree to this. If she's gone and the trail leads nowhere I'll leave it to Rawlings and Interpol. But if we find anything that leads us further, something immediate, then I carry on. Whether or not you join me is up to you. I don't mean that callously – I'm just saying that I would like to follow it through.'

Guy thought for a moment. 'And what about Gosia? Don't you owe her something? You said you'd be back in a couple of days. What about your word? And what's she supposed to do while you act as the arbiter of international justice?'

'She's a big girl now and she's on the mend. I love her dearly and if I can't clear this mess up in a very short time I'll call a halt. Can't say fairer than that.'

'And what's our move if night falls and there's still no sign of life at the house?'

'We take a look inside.'

'Oh yes? Is that Marysia Knoll-speak for burglary?'

Marysia finished her coffee, signalled to the waiter then turned to Guy. 'Not stealing anything,' she whispered innocently, as if breaking and entering was not of the slightest significance.

'And I come too?'

'If you want to.'

'I don't *want* to. I'd just feel happier if I were there, in case you need help.'

Her face broke into a radiant smile as she rose from the table, walked round to Guy and folded her arms round his neck, giving him a sloppy kiss on the cheek. 'You know, that's the nicest thing you've ever said to me, tough guy.'

Before Guy could reply she backed away towards the café. 'Got to pee. Won't be a moment.'

The afternoon wore on, Marysia leaving the table every fifteen minutes or so to check on activity at the house while Guy read the *European* and the *New York Herald Tribune*, both more than four days out of date. The waiter turned from solicitous to unctuous as the bill rose.

Around him, Japanese tourists fought politely to take the perfect snapshot of each other, while the Germans organised their Nikon automatic timers so they could be photographed together. The British drank noisily as they forked through their paper bags of cheap souvenirs and marvelled at each plastic replica of the Aqueduct.

At one o'clock Marysia returned dejectedly from yet another trip down the Calle de los Desamparados and sat heavily opposite Guy, who was by this time reduced to revisiting the fashion pages of the *Tribune* for some vestige of information that had escaped his attention the first three times he'd read them.

'You are a treasure,' Marysia replied excitedly.

'That I know. But now the not-so-good news.'

'Tell me, *Corbata*.'

'Her plane left for Los Angeles fifteen minutes ago.'

'That's unlucky. Thank you for all you've done for me. I'll see you soon, I hope.'

'I hope so too,' Zvonko replied then hung up.

Marysia stood in the booth for a few seconds, trying to collect her thoughts. If she told Guy the news of the woman's departure to Los Angeles, he'd insist they told the authorities. Marysia had other plans for her – more personal ones.

She looked across at Guy, fiddling with the notepad. She was in two minds whether to share the information with him and allow the law to take its course. But the police screwed up the simplest task. If they were to fuck up in LA, the woman might well disappear from view forever and the trail would be lost, as would the identity of the American connection – those behind the case. Taking a deep breath, she walked over to Guy.

'Bad news. We've missed her.'

'How do you know?'

'Zvonko made a few calls. She had a fresh passport made two days ago. She left last night for Los Angeles,' she lied.

'Shit! We were so close.'

'But now we have a connection – a number. We must follow it up.'

'First we tell Rawlings.'

'Of course we tell Rawlings. But right now we get back to Madrid and hitch the first plane out of here to LA, then find out who this number belongs to. You can call Rawlings from the airport.'

'What name is she using?'

'Trabat,' she replied evenly.

Guy looked at her and slumped in his seat. 'Marysia,' he began slowly, 'is this ever going to end?'

She reached out and took his hand. 'Give me two days. Three at the most. I must go. Come with me if you like, but either way I must go. I want to be there at the end.'

He smiled wearily as he squeezed her hand. 'I'd better come and hold your hand.'

'That's what I like to hear, tough guy,' she replied.

THIRTY-SEVEN

Brooks sat looking up at the bank of television screens hanging angled towards him from a steel bar, his face bathed in a steady bluish light. On only two did the figures move – the Tokyo exchange, and the Hong Kong Hang Seng. The screens to the left were static: the London FTSE, the Frankfurt DAX, the SMI in Zurich, the Paris CAC 40 and New York had closed for the day. It was 8.15 p.m. On the desk in front of him was another bank of computer hardware which duplicated exactly the equipment at the Wilshire office. Often he'd sit till the early hours of the morning waiting for the Asian markets to close, and it was certainly more convenient to do so at home.

He stared at the screens for a full minute, closed his eyes, then blinked them open – he'd found the answer to the financial conundrum that had plagued him all day. The enquiry into American stockbroking practices in the fall of '95 had made the transferral and laundering of cash flow considerably more complicated. Korea was the key – he'd buy Omada stock using the Geneva funds, sell to Hamada in Seoul, who in turn would sell through the New York brokers as soon as the exchange opened in the morning. Hamada would take the profits from his last investment off the top, ostensibly as commission, leaving him with the cash flow for the Thai deal – it would be more than enough.

Brooks reached down, opened a drawer and lifted out an ice-cold Evian water. He began to tap the computer keys with a sudden urgency – time was of the essence. The tranfer request took just seconds. He studied the screen for confirmation. It took less than a minute. A thin smile of triumph crossed his face as he watched the Omada stock gain ground – insider information was his stock in trade. It looked as though Bass had come up trumps again.

He drained the Evian, and his fingers danced on the keys. This was Brooks' adrenalin rush. What the track and the craps tables were to gambling junkies, the stock market was to Brooks. He lived for it. He didn't smoke, he didn't drink, and as for women, they provided welcome physical relief as and when he felt like it.

Ten minutes later Brooks shut down the system and looked at his watch. It was past eight-thirty. Time for a break – a quick plate of Jumbalaya at the Lincoln.

He pulled the heavy steel meshed reinforced door closed behind him and locked it. The time-controlled bolts slid home into their housing in the wall. He then crossed to the small wall safe that was recessed into the living room wall above the wet bar and placed the key inside, closing it and spinning the dial. As he did so, he heard the entry-phone buzz in the hall.

Brooks looked up from the safe. Not that stupid bitch Susan again? He swore. He thought he'd made it clear as day – he'd call her when he felt like it. He walked through into the hall, snatching his coat off the stand.

He had the door half-opened when he stopped and looked up at the video monitor above and to the left of the door. A woman in a short black dress was standing outside the building looking up at the camera. He watched as she pressed the button again, holding her finger down. The buzzer rang relentlessly in Brooks' ear. He closed the apartment door again and pressed a key on the console.

'Scott? Is that you, Scott?' a female voice asked.

'Lady, you must have the wrong number. There's no Scott here.'

The woman let her hand drop and the buzzing ceased. Brooks could see her lean towards the intercom. She looked stunning. Shoulder-length black hair, short black evening dress, heels and small black clutch-bag. A red silk scarf was wrapped casually once round her neck, the ends reaching to her slim waist.

'This the Whitcroft building?' she asked.

'That's right,' Brooks replied.

'Apartment five?'

'Right again. But there's no Scott here. You must have the wrong address.'

'No way. Scott said the Whitcroft building on Ocean and Lincoln – Apartment five.'

'Take it from me, this is my home. No Scott.'

She stepped back a pace from the camera and looked directly up at it, crossing her arms and smiling coquettishly as she spoke. Brooks couldn't pinpoint the accent – Puerto Rican maybe?

'And just who the hell are you, when you're at home?' she asked.

'I'm not Scott.'

'You got a name? Or just "not Scott"?' she continued, pulling the long red silk scarf slowly from around her neck and running it through her shapely fingers.

'My name's Brooks. I'm telling you you've got the wrong address. Can you handle that, lady?'

He could see her expression change from sensuality to annoyance as she pulled a mobile phone from her small black handbag – her piercingly dark eyes fixed on the camera.

'Sure, I can handle that, arsehole. Thanks for the help.' She looked away and began to punch some numbers on the phone, then held her head to one side, the mobile disappearing under her thick mane of gleaming black hair.

Brooks studied the woman with interest. He liked the feisty kind.

'Shit!' the girl screamed into the phone. 'Fuck you too!'

Brooks watched in disbelief as she then smashed the phone repeatedly against the wall of the building, shards of black plastic flying from the telephone.

Brooks pressed the entry-phone button. 'Hey, lady! Will you quit that! If you feel like destroying your phone, go ahead, but take it easy on the building – I live here.'

'I'm happy for you, arsehole,' the woman replied, then threw the phone down and walked out of vision.

Brooks chuckled as he reached for the door. Then the phone rang. Shit, at this rate he'd never eat. He snatched up the phone in the hall.

'Brooks here.'

'Hi Alan. It's me. Susan,' the voice said uncertainly.

'Oh yeah? Well, I'm busy.' A tide of anger welled up in him. The woman was becoming a menace. 'Let's get this straight, Susan. *I* ring *you*, right? And while we're at it – I want the key back pronto, got that?'

As he slammed down the receiver the buzzer sounded again in the hall. Jesus Christ, what now, he thought with another wave of annoyance. Then he smiled. Maybe it was the crazy lady. He hoped so – she looked sexy as hell. He looked up at the monitor as the buzzer continued to sound. Her finger was pressed to the entry-phone button and she was leaning on it, her face turned up to the video camera. Brooks pressed the button.

'Still looking for Scott?'

'Hey, arsehole,' she began, taking her finger off the buzzer and smiling broadly. 'How would you like to say you're sorry for acting like a shit?'

Brooks chuckled. This woman was something else. 'Just what do you have in mind?'

'Well,' she replied languidly, 'you see, I kind of have a little problem now.'

'Oh yeah? And what might that be?' Brooks would play her game. Who knew, it might be fun.

'Well, it's like this. I need to make a call and I got a little carried away with this little mother.' She smiled into the camera as she held up what remained of her phone. 'You think I could use yours?'

'Don't see why not. Come on up. Fifth floor.'

'What number?'

'It's all mine.' He was about to press the door release button when he paused. 'And take it easy on the furnishings in the hall, okay?'

'You got it, arsehole,' she replied, winking.

Brooks pressed the button and the buzzer sounded below.

As he walked back into the living room, the buzzer sounded again. Brooks returned to the hall.

'Hey, arsehole. The fuckin' door's stuck. Won't open.'

'Hold on a second,' Brooks replied as he pressed the release once more. The buzzer sounded below. He could see her press forward then look up at the camera.

'Shit! It's stuck.'

'Stay right there – I'll come down.'

'I ain't going nowhere,' she replied as she gave him a promising look.

As Brooks exited the lift on the ground floor and walked down the hall, he could see her through the glass panels of the door. She was leaning against the wall, her arms crossed. He opened the door.

'So . . .' she cooed. 'Hi there, arsehole. Hadn't pictured you this way. You're kinda cute.'

Brooks' eyes devoured her body – this was pure fantasy time. He couldn't believe his luck.

'Why don't you come on up,' he said.

She brushed past him, giving him a teasing sidelong glance as she did so. Brooks followed her to the elevator. This was getting better by the second.

As they waited for the lift doors to open she turned to face him, taking a small step forwards and pressing the full length of her body against his.

'Maybe you're not so much of an arsehole after all,' she whispered.

Brooks drank in the smell of the woman. He couldn't pick the aroma – it was part perfume, part newborn baby. Either way, it was pure sex.

As the lift doors opened she pressed her hips forwards into Brooks', pulling the silk scarf from her neck and slowly looping it round his. Brooks could feel his erection growing.

The lift doors began to close so Brooks held out an arm and they slid back again.

'Shall we go on up?' she murmured into his ear.

'Sure,' Brooks croaked and stepped into the elevator. Luiza was one step behind. The doors began to close. He pressed the button for floor five. It was the last directive his brain gave his body.

THIRTY-EIGHT

Marysia ran her finger down the list, stopping midway. 'Mamasian, Costra & Brooks, Financial Consultants', it read. She turned to Guy. 'Okay? We go on up?'

'Sure, why not. At least this time I do the talking.'

'Just leave the action to me.'

'Don't even joke about it – I'm keyed up enough as it is. Just what are we going to find up there? A bunch of Italians or Puerto Ricans lounging around cleaning their guns and weighing the white stuff?'

Marysia smiled as she hit the elevator button. 'Too many movies,' she said.

The main reception area was 'nouvelle chic tasteful'. Facing the lift was a long thin reception desk completely barren save for three telephones and a computer screen. Behind it sat an exquisite African-American girl, who looked no more than a child, but who could easily have walked the haute couture catwalks of Paris. As Guy and Marysia walked towards her she looked up. Her mouth smiled, her eyes didn't.

'Good morning, can I help you?'

'Yes, I'd like to speak to someone about a financial matter.'

'Of course. Do you have an appointment?'

'I'm afraid not – I've just got in from Europe.'

'Would you take a seat for a moment. I'll see who's available, Mr Cooper,' she said, appraising Guy – she knew her movie stars. 'Can I organise a coffee for you both? Perrier? Citron pressé?'

'A tea and a coffee would be fine. Thank you.'

'Please . . .' she said, directing them to a suite of Italian minimalist furniture.

'It's not what I expected,' Guy said quietly as they sat.

'I know,' Marysia replied, her eyes taking in the girl at the desk.

Two minutes later a young man dressed in a charcoal Cerruti suit walked towards them carrying a tray on which was a silver plunger of delicious-smelling coffee, a silver teapot, cream jug, sugar bowl and two cups. He placed them on the polished onyx coffee table next to the copies of *Variety* and the *Wall Street Journal* – a selection which in Los Angeles covered most things.

'Miss Rednapp will be with you in a couple of minutes,' the young man said, adjusting his perfect cuffs. 'I hope you don't mind waiting, Mr Cooper.'

'Not at all,' Guy replied. The young turk smiled his Hollywood smile, then turned and walked soundlessly back behind the reception desk.

They'd scarcely had time to begin their drinks when a door to the right of the reception desk opened and a woman of around fifty walked towards them. Short jagged hair counterpointed her crisp cream designer suit, highlighted at the neck by a simple black silk scarf.

She held out a hand – her face wore the same ersatz welcome. 'How do you do, Mr Cooper. I'm Sappho Rednapp. I'm sorry to have kept you waiting. Things are a bit hectic,' she said, gently shaking Guy's hand. Her eyes switched from Guy to Marysia. She held out a hand again.

'Marysia Knoll. Pleased to meet you,' Marysia said warmly.

'Perhaps we could discuss matters in my office. I'll get the coffee sent in.'

Ms Rednapp's office was a stark contrast to the area they had just left. Her large desk groaned under the weight of stacks of documents rising two feet on either end. The furniture was heavy and old-fashioned Hollywood – lots of thick studded burgundy leather.

'Please take a seat,' she said, closing the door behind her. 'I believe you'd like to discuss some financial planning?'

'That's correct.'

'May I just say how much I enjoyed *An Affair with Death*, Mr Cooper.' She ran a hand through her jagged hair. It made absolutely no difference to her appearance. She then looked enquiringly at Guy. 'Exactly how can we be of help to you, Mr Cooper?' she prompted.

'I'm here in the States to do three films back to back. One contract will cover them all. Sol Westerman at ICM is doing the deal and my lawyers will be handling all the usual details.'

'Who are they, Mr Cooper?'

'Newman and Steadman.'

'I know Fred well. Please carry on.'

'As you may or may not know, I live in Sydney now. I have several off-shore accounts, and up till now my affairs have been dealt with out of London. However, I was curious as to what other avenues might be available, looking at the long-term – should I wish to marry, for instance.' Guy glanced towards Marysia.

Ms Rednapp steepled her fingers and for the first time the easy smile was absent. 'This area of our work was until recently taken care of by one of our partners. I'm afraid he's not with us any longer. However . . .' her voiced trailed off for a second then she cleared her throat and continued. 'How long will you be in Los Angeles, Mr Cooper?'

'It looks like for the best part of eighteen months.'

'I see.' She was about to continue when Guy interrupted her.

'That wouldn't have been David Helbron by any chance?' he said, plucking a name out of the air.

'No, Alan Brooks.'

'Has he set up shop himself?' Guy asked lightly.

'No, I'm afraid not. There was an incident at his home – I'm afraid he's dead.' Her face remained motionless.

Neither Guy nor Marysia let their faces mirror their thoughts.

'I'm so sorry, Ms Rednapp. I had no idea,' said Guy.

'Presumably the other two partners are Mr Mamasian and Mr Costra,' Marysia interjected.

'That's correct. Mr Mamasian is our CEO and Chairman, Mr Costra his co-founder. Alan Brooks joined the company only recently.'

Marysia opened her mouth to speak.

'I'm a senior associate,' Ms Rednapp added, pre-empting her.

'When did this tragedy occur, Ms Rednapp?'

'Just yesterday, Mr Cooper.' She looked down at her desk and wiped at a speck of dust. 'I'm afraid it's still too distressing to discuss Alan's death. You'll have to excuse me.'

'Of course.'

They sat in silence for a few moments, Guy searching for a way to end the interview with the woman. Her eyes were beginning to fill. There was little else to say and certainly little more information unconnected with finance was in the offing. 'Look. Perhaps I could make an appointment and call back tomorrow sometime when you're feeling better. Is there any chance that a meeting with Mr Costra or Mr Mamasian could be arranged?'

Ms Rednapp was briefly taken aback, as though her professional capabilities were in question, but recovered quickly. 'I will have Mr Costra's secretary look at his appointments for tomorrow – Mr Mamasian seldom joins us here in the office – but at this stage I can almost guarantee it.'

'Is Mr Costra in the building today, by any chance?' It was Marysia who spoke.

'I'm afraid not. He's managing the funeral arrangements for Mr Brooks – he had no wife, no family.'

'I see,' said Guy, pushing his chair back and holding out a hand. 'Thank you so much for seeing me. I hope we'll meet again – perhaps with Mr Costra?'

'I'll call you as soon as I've spoken to his secretary, then I'll get back to you to discuss a window of opportunity for the meeting that suits you. Where are you staying?'

'The Chateau Marmont.'

'Of course. Well, it's been a pleasure meeting you Mr Cooper, and you Miss Knoll. We'll be in touch to arrange a time tomorrow.'

'Thank you very much, Ms Rednapp.'

She walked them to the lift. The beauty at reception was as immobile yet lovely as she'd been when they arrived – a task as difficult as a street mime performer's. Two minutes later they were back on the street.

THIRTY-NINE

Costra was tired but not fearful. There had been times like this before, times when he knew there was someone out there. Brooks' death was more than a random killing. Call it experience, call it instinct – he knew. But he'd been there before. Whoever was making a move would have to be damned good. But now was the time for analysis. Who had killed Brooks?

He'd been lucky. Brooks' ex had dropped by and found him. Thank Christ she'd got it into her head to call the office. If she hadn't, they'd have been in serious shit – the cops nosing around before he'd had time to send round a team to clear out the safe. Thank God for small mercies. The body had still been warm when she'd stepped into the lift. Brooks was slumped in a corner, a red scarf wrapped round his neck. It was only when the cops had tried to shift him into a bodybag that they realised his neck had practically been severed by the wire sewn into the fabric. Maybe they got their jollies calling to tell him the details. Scum! Better men than they had tried to get under his skin. Fuck them.

His thoughts drifted back to Brooks. He'd never cared much for the sonofabitch but it wasn't a good way to die.

The Cadillac Fleetwood sped down San Vicente and across Bundy. Costra looked out the window at the high trees of the Brentwood Country Club as he picked an ice cube from his Scotch and popped it into his mouth.

Brooks had been stupid. Why live in such a high-risk area as Santa Monica? It was madness. With his money, security was fundamental. He clenched his fat hand and swore silently – the last thing they needed was unwarranted media attention. And the Feds weren't fools. Though they'd never got close to nailing Howard or himself in fifteen years, they'd be lapping it up, relishing the prospect of nosing round the office and Brooks' home. They'd find nothing – the apartment had been sanitised of any incriminating financial data within a half hour of Susan's hysterical phonecall, and the master disks were now well away from their prying eyes.

Christina was now on her way to New England just in case. The kids had refused to budge, so he'd offered them a trip to Europe. Now they and their useless lovers were sitting in their first-class seats bound for Paris. And Howard? He'd retreated into the vault-like security of his Bel Air home like one of his spiders in full defensive mode, convinced there was a move by a rival organisation afoot. Kaspar would look after him – that was, if whoever had taken out Brooks was determined on taking it further up the chain of command.

Costra leant forward and refilled his drink. Who'd killed Brooks? He'd had his finger on the pulse of the US drug scene for so long now that he'd have known if some new player was attempting to muscle in. The South Americans left them alone – his major diplomatic coup of the last ten years had been to convince them there was plenty of room for them both without squabbling. No, Howard was paranoid, the threat did not lie in that direction. Still, as long as Howard kept his head in for a few days Costra would have time to identify and remove the fly in the ointment. All would be well. His people had hit the streets less than an hour after he'd received the shocking news, but the fact that no one knew a thing pointed to a single player. But why Brooks? Another major question. He was the figures guy rather than the man that pointed the finger. Why Brooks? There'd been no attempt to break into the safe, nothing had been taken. Who had he upset?

The Caddy slowed as it reached the Pacific Coast Highway, turned right and shot past Gladstone's Restaurant towards the Malibu Colony. Costra picked another ice cube from his glass and rolled it round the back of his neck. It had to be personal. The alternative was that it was a warning to the entire firm. That was a sobering thought, but he'd handled himself quite adequately for all these years and was unafraid. If someone came for him, he'd be ready. The more he thought about it, the more he welcomed a swift outcome of the situation. He'd find a replacement for Brooks this week.

He pulled open the compartment next to the drinks cabinet and lifted out his Heckler & Koch with its customised grip delicately tooled to accommodate his small fat fingers. The cool black metal felt good in his sweating palm. He checked the clip – it was full. He placed it next to him on the seat and leant back, resting his head and closing his eyes. Come and get me, he thought.

Pete nosed the long limo slowly towards the cream gates. The driver's window slid down, and he held his left arm out towards the video camera and made the long-standing prearranged signal that the car was secure. The heavy gates slid silently into the wall on either side and they drove through and up the short drive.

As Costra stepped from the car, the front door opened and Eli walked towards him.

'Mr Mamasian just called. Wants you to ring him back soon as you get in.'

'Shit!' Costra swore as he walked up the steps to the door. 'What the hell does he want now – I just left him.'

Eli glanced down at Costra's right hand, noticing the Heckler & Koch. It wasn't often he saw his boss carry a gun. He usually left that to him.

As they walked through the front double doors, Eli glanced back. The gates had slid to and the Fleetwood was moving down under the house into the garage. He closed the doors, then returned to the small room to the left of the entrance and sat by the video monitors.

Costra walked across the Sienna marble towards the living room. 'Tell Guido I'd like lunch at two,' he called out loudly. 'Tell him to bring it up to the bedroom. And no calls, okay?' His feet clicked over the marble.

'Sure, Mr Costra. Two and no calls,' Eli shouted back.

Costra swung the living-room door shut, strode to the coffee table, put down his gun, picked up the phone and dialled Howard's mobile. As he looked out across the Pacific, he took some gulps of the cold air, picking the sweat-drenched shirt from his chest. The room was like an icebox, the temperature set to fifty degrees.

The phone cheeped. Costra swore, and redialled.

'Mr Mamasian's residence.'

'Harry Costra here, Maria. Where's Kaspar? Howard's not answering his phone.'

'He's down with the spiders, Mr Costra. Mr Kaspar's with him.'

'Well, he's not answering his phone. When Kaspar gets back, tell him I returned Mr Mamasian's call. And tell him I'm taking a shower. I'll call him in an hour.'

'Okay Mr Costra,' the cook said.

He flipped the phone shut and walked to the door, taking off his jacket and draping it over his shoulder.

As he entered the gigantic master bedroom he reset the airconditioning to manual and pressed the fan switch, standing beneath the vent. A stream of cold air shot downwards as he threw the jacket onto the bed and peeled off his shirt. The saving grace of being without the lovely Christina was that he could turn the temperature down to zero if he wanted.

What the hell did Howard want now, he mused, stepping out of his trousers and boxers and walking to the bathroom.

The white tiles felt cold and soothing under his bare feet. He reached for the faucet, turning the cold on full as he stepped inside the shower recess, then closed his eyes and turned his face up into the stream of icy water as it gunned down over his head.

He stood facing the taps for a good minute. The freezing water felt great. Then he turned, reaching for the soap as he wiped the water from his eyes. It was then that he saw her and his blood froze.

She was crouched in the left-hand corner of the bathroom. The door must have masked her when he'd entered. She slowly raised herself off her haunches as their eyes met. She was grinning. In her hand was a gun, a black matt silencer attached to the short barrel. Costra instinctively held up a hand and opened his mouth, but her gun arm immediately stiffened.

'Make a sound and you're a dead man,' she hissed.

Costra stood transfixed, feeling as if he might shit himself any second. It had to be the one that had killed Brooks, just had to be! But why? Who the fuck was she? Holy Christ, what the hell could he do? She was going to kill him for sure – he could see her forefinger had taken up the first pressure on the trigger. If he shouted or made a sound he'd be dead before they ever heard him – where the fuck *were* Pete and Eli!

The water continued to pound down on his head as she slowly walked towards him.

'You look pretty scared, fat man,' she said, smiling thinly.

Costra was beginning to shake. The freezing water was now no longer a blessing but a torture.

'You going to kill me?' he whispered, chancing she wouldn't pull the trigger unless he called for help. He had to keep her talking! Couldn't just wait for the bullet.

'Maybe. Maybe not.' She lowered the gun a few inches, it was now aimed at his genitals.

Costra's mind was racing. No way could he scream out to Pete. How had the bitch got past Eli, past the cameras? Had she made her move during the two minutes or so when he'd arrived and Eli had come out to meet him? Could he bargain with the woman? Was he sure it was the bitch who'd killed Brooks? Why, why, why, his mind screamed. Then it suddenly became clear. Jesus Christ, it was Garcia's fuckin' broad! It just wasn't possible. Had the bitch come halfway across the world because he'd whacked a piece of shit like Garcia? Was this payback for killing the fuckin' spic?

'You know who I am, don't you, fat man?'

Costra's limbs were beginning to shake uncontrollably. Did she know she was also on the hit-list he'd sent with their man to London? Maybe he should bluster? Just keep her talking. 'You want to kill me, you'd better do it. I'm not afraid to die. But you can walk away from here one rich lady. You just think for a second. This ain't a smart thing.'

They locked eyes.

'Oh yes? You'd let me walk with a bundle of your money?'

'We could work something out.'

Costra's mind was again a mass of blurred thoughts. Could he rush her? Could he survive one bullet hit? Maybe she was getting a buzz out of his fear.

'Maybe,' she said slowly, as if deliberating. 'What do you figure you're worth?'

'I got close to half a million c-c-cash inside,' he stammered – the shakes were now affecting his speech.

'You ain't worth a whole heap, are you, fat man? I'll think about it. Turn around and face the taps,' she whispered.

'I turn around, you'll k-kill me,' Costra managed. His limbs felt numb, he could hardly breathe.

'Doesn't make much difference, if that's what I have in mind. Let's just figure this – you don't turn, you're dead meat right now.' She raised the gun, her arm rigid, pointing the barrel at his head. Costra turned. A second later she brought the gun down hard on the back of his head. He slumped down the side of the recess.

Luiza reached up and turned off the water, quickly pulled a spool of tape from her pocket and wrapped a length round his ankles, binding them tightly together. Then she pulled his arms round his back, taping them together. She tore a length of tape and taped his mouth, then stepped from the shower.

She walked to the bathroom door, pressing her ear to it. There was no sound. Then she walked back to the shower. Costra's eyes were beginning to flutter as he regained consciousness. Luiza crouched again before him.

'You *do* know who I am, don't you, fat man?' she teased. Costra's pupils danced wildly in response. 'Sure you do. I'm the one you tried to take out in London. That's right. That's me. And you know something? That was a big-time error. Major bad move.' She laughed softly. 'You know, there aren't many in life who have the privilege of knowing the exact moment of their deaths. You're one of the lucky few.'

She stood. The stench of faeces was overwhelming as Costra lost control of his bowels.

'Got to go, fat man,' she said, raising the gun and directing it at Costra's pulsing stomach. Costra fought to part his lips but the tape held fast – his short scream was no more than the faintest internal roar.

FORTY

'She's started already. Brooks is dead, the others are on the list. She's working her way up to the top man – he'll be last. She's off and running,' Marysia said as they sped back in the cab to the hotel.

'We don't know that for a fact,' Guy replied, ever the pragmatist. '"There was an incident at Brooks' home", that's what Rednapp said. He could have drowned in the pool, for heaven's sake.'

'What's wrong with you, Guy? You really want to believe something like that? We know she's here, she has their number on her notepad, he's one of the three partners – the most junior – and he dies the day we arrive. She killed him – simple as that.'

'She'd have had to have been damned quick, we only missed her by hours in Madrid! She only had a telephone number. How's she going to work out who she's after, where they live, what kind of security they've got, then get in there and kill them?'

'She's a pro. Believe me, it's easy.'

'Jesus Christ,' Guy murmured. 'Killing people is so damned easy, eh? Okay, that's your stock in trade. But let's check first. Look at the back editions of the newspapers, do a bit of homework.'

Marysia looked at him in disbelief. 'I make a call. If you recall, I worked for what's known as an Intelligence organisation. They'll tell me in five minutes.'

'Then we tell the police. They have to know, as do Costra and Mamasian before she catches up with them.'

'The police *know*, for Christ's sake – you phoned Rawlings!'

'He wasn't there, I had to leave a message.'

'Then he knows. What do you think, they'd forget to tell him? Come on, they know the name she's using! You think they're stupid?'

'They don't know who she's after!'

'So we're going to tell them?'

'Too right we are!'

'We do no such thing!' said Marysia sharply.

Their eyes locked and they stared at each other for several seconds.

'You will condone her executions?' Guy said slowly and deliberately.

'I will condone them and I will relish them. Let them kill each other. They are the people behind the deaths of Chasen, his wife and son, and the attempt on Gosia's life! Let the dogs go eat each other!'

'If you think along those lines, then you're not the woman I thought you were,' Guy interrupted. 'I will not do so. I will do what I think is morally responsible, and that doesn't include sitting back while a psychopath takes a knife or a gun and kills other human beings.'

Marysia shifted in the back seat of the cab. 'If you had been bound and gagged and had been made to watch Gosia and myself pack-raped then stabbed to death, would you intervene if some right-minded citizen pulled a gun on them?'

'We're talking about a professional killer here, not right-minded people!' Guy countered, then stared out the window – Marysia always seemed to cut to the heart of the matter and come up with some hypothetical scenario which was quite unanswerable.

'We live in a civilised society. That society has developed a system of justice by which we live. We have to allow it to take its course or we drift into anarchy,' Guy said after a few moments.

'Civilised society? Shit! Look out of the window,' she said, pointing to the window. '*This* is anarchy – well, pretty close to it and getting closer by the minute. Hundreds of people die on the streets of America every day. People like Brooks, Costra and Mamasian don't give a Goddamn about your members of civilised society, and it's these people who peddle the drugs that've got society in the shape it's in today. They peddle them to *children*, for heaven's sake! And if anyone gets in their way, they arrange for them to die. Now, correct me if I'm wrong, but you seem to think that it's preferable for these people to be given the opportunity to either do a runner to South America, or arrange for a highly paid lawyer to argue points of law so that they can walk away scot-free or plea-bargain themselves down to a few years in a penitentiary. If that's your idea of justice, please tell me. These men arranged for a woman to put a bullet into Gosia! Well, now it's that same woman who's bent on putting them to death, so let her get on with it, I say!'

'We don't *know* that!' Guy shouted angrily. 'We don't know that,' he repeated in the silence that followed. 'We think that's the case. All logic tells us that is the case, but even a person with a smoking gun should be allowed his day in court. Surely you can't be telling me that a person is not innocent till proven guilty? Do you want to do away with the criminal justice system altogether? Is it going to be up to people like you to decide if people are guilty, then put them to death?'

The cab swung hard right off Sunset and up the driveway to the Chateau Marmont. They sat in silence as it came to a halt. Guy paid off the driver and they walked up the steps to the hotel.

As they entered the suite, Marysia made for the telephone in the master bedroom while Guy stood by the window, trying to calm down. There was no way he could allow events to take their course – he had to do something, tell someone. Behind him he could just make out Marysia's voice in the bedroom, then the receiver was slammed down and she strode into the room.

'Brooks was murdered yesterday in the elevator of his building. Strangled and practically beheaded with a steel wire sewn into a woman's scarf. I think we can safely attribute that to our friend. The police have both Costra and Mamasian's residences under surveillance in case the matter is drug-related. They're not fools; they know what these people do for a living.'

Guy said nothing. He continued to stare out of the window.

'So what do you want to do now, Mr Morality? Someone you want to ring? Some public-spirited act you'd like to do? If you consider me such a monster, and I'm not the person you once thought me to be, I suggest you fly back to your movieworld and wash your hands of the whole matter – don't stick around here for my sake.'

Guy was about to reply when the telephone rang. He snatched it up as they stared at each other.

'Cooper.'

'Hey, Guy! I've been trying to track you down for days. Why the hell didn't you tell me you were in La La land!' It was Victor Gross.

'I can't talk now,' Guy replied with all the control he could muster. But before he could hang up Victor screamed down the line at him.

'I've done every fucking thing you asked and you get the shits with me? Hell, what kind of behaviour is that? We let that literary arsehole walk all over us, and you've got the fuckin' script you wanted, so just ease up will you? If you'd had the courtesy to call me over the last few days I wouldn't be interrupting you and your girlfriend –'

Guy slammed the phone down.

'Who was that?' Marysia asked.

'One half of the Gross brothers. Pick either – they're both as evil as each other.'

'I'm going to take a bath,' Marysia said as she made for the bedroom. 'You do as you think fit. Maybe you should give thc guys at Mamasian, Costra & Brooks a call and give them a bit of advice – hell, they could be in danger.'

Guy sat down by the phone, wishing he'd never involved himself in Marysia's schemes.

FORTY-ONE

Mamasian put down the phone, his eyes glazed. 'They killed Harry,' he said in the faintest whisper.

Kaspar stood behind him, cracking his knuckles, waiting to see how to react.

'They killed Harry,' Mamasian repeated, almost to himself. 'Harry's dead.' Again there was silence. Mamasian stood like a statue, arms by his side.

'I'll make some calls,' said Kaspar. 'Don't concern yourself with your security – that's my job. No one gets near you, I guarantee it. I'll have six men here in twenty minutes.'

'Someone killed Harry,' Mamasian continued, as if in a dream. 'All these years . . . Harry was indestructible, untouchable . . . Who the fuck's doing this? . . . Who?'

'I've got to make some calls, Mr Mamasian,' said Kaspar. 'Please stay within the house.' He went out, closing the door behind him.

Mamasian closed his eyes. First Brooks, now Harry. It had to be business. The answer's got to be there, he thought. It's there plain as day, you just can't see it.

Then it slowly came to him. He'd made a mistake. Just one, in all these years, and it had pulled down the whole house of cards. Chasen had been the catalyst. Garcia had been taken out, but one had escaped. The woman. It was her – the woman. Garcia must have told her. When Garcia had died, she must have thought she was next and planned to attack rather than run. So much for Garcia's reputation for 'no linkage'. He'd talked. She knew. Still, he was dead, Mamasian thought with some satisfaction. The woman was on the loose. She'd killed Brooks and Harry, now she'd come for him, before he got to her. Yes, that was it, clear as day. Suddenly he felt very afraid. Sure, Kaspar was one of the best, he'd make sure that the house was secure, but Harry would have had the same security system and Harry was dead. The woman was good, no mistake. He could hear Kaspar through the door on the phone. He'd soon have an army on its way. If the woman showed up, she'd be history, he thought, willing himself to calm down. Then a thought occurred to him. He picked up his digital phone and dialled. It rang for some time, then was picked up the other end.

'Whitehall?'

'Yes,' came the drowsy reply.

'It's Mamasian. Costra's dead. I need some quick answers.'

'Give me a moment to think – it's the middle of the night here.'

Mamasian abruptly looked at the windows, startled, as the powerful spotlights were switched on, bathing the twenty feet of barren gravel that ran round the perimeter of the house in white light. 'Costra's dead. It's got to be Garcia's woman. I need some quick answers. Do they know about us in London, or just about the woman? Is there any hard evidence linking us? I must know that right now. If she comes looking for me and we take her out I've got to be able to deny everything.'

'As far as I know it's all supposition as of now. They know Chasen was used as a courier. Nothing else.'

'You sure of that?' Mamasian barked. 'What about the woman?'

'They know she was part of the team, but they don't know who she worked for.'

Mamasian swore. 'And now the bitch is leading them right to us! Do they know she's here in LA?'

'I don't know.'

'Well find out!' Mamasian shouted. 'It's what I fuckin' pay you for! I need to know! Right now. You hear what I'm saying?'

'It's three in the morning, for heaven's sake. What the hell can I do now?'

'You're so damned clever, you work it out. Let's be very clear about something: I go down, sure as hell I'll point the finger at you. You follow me, Pinstripe?'

'I follow you,' the man said, and hung up.

FORTY-TWO

She'd been right as usual. What the hell could he do? Sure as hell Costra and Mamasian would be watching their backs, and what was it to him anyway? Why the hell should he run around after an assassin bent on their murder. If Marysia felt it her mission to personally apply the cuffs to the woman, that was her business, but he'd had enough.

Marysia walked through from the bedroom. 'I'm going to order up something to eat. Want anything?'

Guy was about to answer when the phone rang. 'Jesus Christ, if that's Victor Gross again he can find another actor,' he snapped.

'I'll get it,' Marysia said and leant over to pick up the receiver. She listened for a second then passed it to Guy, placing a hand over the mouthpiece.

'Critchley,' she said, handing the phone to Guy and walking back into the bedroom.

'Guy? It's me. Got your contact number. Glad I caught you. I've some interesting news for you both,' Critchley said.

'What's up?'

'This is all unofficial. A friend of mine at Kennedy. Your woman is right there in LA. Came in using the name Andreu.'

'Andreu? Can't be her. Your source must be wrong.'

'Oh, it was her alright. Believe me.'

'There must be some mistake. She was travelling under the name Trabat.' Guy's mind was a blur of confusion. What the hell was going on? Andreu? Trabat? Had Zvonko made a mistake? Had the woman had several passports? If the police had been expecting her, why had they not picked her up – why had it been an 'unofficial' source of Critchley's who had spotted her? Had Rawlings received his message? Guy was vaguely aware of a distant voice in his ear.

'Guy? Are you still on the line?'

'Yes . . . yes,' he replied in a daze, then snapped out of his reverie. 'Did Rawlings get my message? I left a message for him. Told him she was on a plane to LA. Gave him a name!'

'Look, I can't help you there. Last time I spoke to Rawlings was some time ago – he never mentioned it.'

'Get on to him! Right now. Tell him.'

'I'll see if I can rouse him – it's the wee small hours over here.'

'Make sure you do,' Guy snapped. 'Look, I'm sorry, Eugene, I didn't mean to yell at you. I know you're just trying to help, but at the moment I'm hard pressed to keep Marysia from finishing the job with her bare hands. If she knew where the woman was this instant, she'd be out the door.'

There was a blip on the line. 'Could you hold on a second, someone's trying to get through.' Guy pressed the call-waiting button.

'Miss Knoll, please. It's very urgent.'

'One moment,' Guy said and pressed the button again.

'Got to go, Eugene. I'll call you back. Dublin?'

'No, London. You know the number?'

'I do.' He cupped the phone. 'Marysia! Call for you. Urgent. Pick it up in the bedroom.' He listened till he heard her voice then put down the phone. Within two seconds she shouted.

'Turn on the television! Right now!'

Guy quickly scanned the room for the remote, snatched it up from the coffee table and pressed the on-switch. A cartoon character filled the screen.

'Which channel?' he shouted.

'I don't know – flick through! Eyewitness News!'

Guy began to flick. On the fifteenth or so press he stopped. A helicopter was buzzing over a section of coastline, then a large house came into frame as a reporter's voice cut in.

'– are still in the area. It's possible the assailant is still in the vicinity. All roads leading back to the Pacific Coast Highway have been sealed. The dead man, Harold Costra, was sixty-two, married with two children.'

The camera zoomed in on an ambulance in the driveway amongst at least five black and whites. Several medics were rolling a stretcher towards it. On top was a zipped black bodybag.

'If there's any further news, I'll get right back to you, Ted. This is Sue Anna Rizac in the Airnews chopper.' The anchorman appeared. 'After the station break, Arnold Scheer will be back with the sports round-up.'

Guy flicked the off-switch as Marysia strode into the room.

'The police did a fine job protecting Costra,' he stated coldly.

'What can I say? They're the people you rely on. That's why you choose not to carry a gun,' Marysia said bluntly.

'You told me they had the house under surveillance. Was that the truth?'

She said nothing.

'And Rawlings never got my message. Or he did, but you gave me the wrong name.' They locked eyes for a few seconds then Marysia looked away.

'Look, Guy. I haven't got time to argue with you now. She's out there as we argue the toss, and she's thinking of Mamasian. I'm going to find her. It's not too difficult to figure her next move and she's going to have to be very quick to get to Mamasian before the police do.'

'So let *them* do it, for Christ's sake! Why do you need to be in at the kill? What's the matter with you! I'm calling the LAPD right now!'

Marysia ignored him, stormed out the door and slammed it behind her.

Guy raced to the door after her. As he reached the front reception he heard her cab pull away. It took him two seconds to run through the revolving door and shout after it. The cab braked and Guy climbed in the back, his face a mask of controlled fury.

'You know where you're going?'

'Sure I do.'

FORTY-THREE

Kaspar replaced the phone. Rosario and his team were on their way – their task to stay on the gate and keep the cops and the newshounds outside. Kaspar sat in his control room looking at the six screens. The lights were coming up to speed, two minutes before they reached their optimum brightness. His eye flicked from monitor to monitor. He cursed silently to himself – it was practically impossible to check all screens simultaneously. He'd told Mamasian that six months ago, but the old fool had ignored him. He needed two men to make the system work. In Moscow he'd had one man per camera – that way no mistakes were possible.

His eyes flicked to the left. Had he seen a movement? No. He darted his eyes from screen to screen. Shit, he should have insisted on dogs. Stupid.

Maria stood in the kitchen counting the soft shell crabs. Ten would be enough, she determined, then she stood on tip-toe, pulling down a large copper pan.

There was a sudden flash of white outside the kitchen window and she glanced round. It must be Mont Blanc, she thought – he usually showed up around preparation time and he usually got lucky. She walked back to the fridge, opened the door and pulled out a small plateful of scraps of beef from the night before.

She walked to the back door and pulled the top bolt to the left, then did the same with the lower bolt and pulled the door open. She stepped out into the small enclosed yard looking round at ankle height for the cat. There was a sudden movement behind her and she whipped her head round. A pure white figure stood before her, the face a mask of white body paint, the body squeezed into snow-white latex. She opened her mouth in shock as the lead pipe came down in a sweeping movement towards her temple.

Mamasian walked to the bedroom window looking down at the white lights, looking for shadows. He was sweating with fear, he noticed with alarm. If she was coming, she'd come soon. She could be in the grounds right now. Maybe even already somewhere in the house! Maybe Kaspar had missed her.

He crossed to his bedside chest of drawers. His gun: where had he left the Beretta? He pulled out the drawers, throwing the contents onto the bed. Shit! Where had he left the gun? Downstairs – it had to be in the study. For a second he contemplated retrieving it, then decided against it – who knew, she might be down there waiting.

He returned to the window, his mind a jumble of disjointed thoughts. Only Kaspar stood between the woman and himself. Kaspar was good. But Pete and Eli were good, and it hadn't helped Harry any. If the Russian failed him, he was trapped. He was dead. He couldn't just sit and wait, he'd go mad.

He looked out towards the vivarium and a thought flashed through his head. He strode to the door and unlocked it, poking his head out into the corridor.

'Kaspar!'

'Yes, Sir,' the Russian called from the monitor room.

'How long before Rosario and the team get here?'

'Any minute now, Mr Mamasian!'

'Good!' Mamasian pursed his thin lips then stepped back into his bedroom and relocked the door.

Luiza held the weight of the Puerto Rican cook off the ground for more than thirty seconds, listening hard for any movement inside the door. There was none. She eased the woman to the flagstones and crouched behind her. Then she looked into the kitchen. She'd got some blood on her. She'd need to clean the suit before she left the house – the stains might show on the screen as she left. She'd have to be quick. She didn't know how many there'd be inside. She didn't much care – so long as she got to Mamasian first. She crouched again and unwound the white tape from the gun and silencer. She didn't notice the white cat as it padded soundlessly behind her into the kitchen.

Kaspar blinked again. He was concentrating hard so as to miss nothing on the screens. Where the hell was Rosario? He'd estimated they'd take around fifteen minutes if they drove hard and got lucky. It had been twenty already, and every moment was vital. He knew he couldn't leave the screens, but his place was upstairs with Mamasian.

'Maria!' he shouted over his shoulder towards the kitchen. There was no response. He cursed. 'Stupid spic . . . Maria!' he shouted with added vehemence, but there was still no reply. He pushed off with his right foot, keeping his eyes riveted to the screens as the chair rolled towards the door.

'Maria! Answer me, for fuck's sake!' He turned around, angry now. The stupid bitch had opened the kitchen door! 'Maria, shut the fuckin' door! And bolt it, for Christ's sake!' he screamed down the corridor, then swivelled back to the screens. The monitors glowed before him – motionless. Still there was no sign of Maria. Kaspar began to sweat. There was something terribly wrong. Why hadn't Maria answered? The seconds ticked by. He had to make a move. Someone was already inside.

Kaspar closed his hand over the Uzzi and checked the clip. Then he stood and stepped out into the hall.

The first bullet caught him in the right eye. As his muscles spasmed, his finger hit the trigger and a burst of more than five shots raked the hallway. The second shot hit him in the throat and by the time the third splintered the apex of his rib cage he was dead.

Mamasian was already at the window, fighting with the stubborn latch as the shots rang out as loudly as artillery shells. He swallowed hard, his mind racing. It had begun. In seconds either Kaspar would be at the door or he'd be face to face with his executioner. These seconds were vital. He had to somehow survive till Rosario arrived. Maybe five minutes, that was all. If Kaspar was dead, she'd already be on her way up. But she'd have to find him, and she wouldn't know who else was in the house. He had maybe half a minute.

As he pulled the catch towards him and pushed the sash window upwards, he could just make out the footfalls on the stairs.

Marysia reached forward, her hand full of ten-dollar bills. 'Driver. Stop here, please.' The cab began to slow. 'I said stop! Right here. Now!' she screamed. The driver was so surprised he stood hard on the brakes and both Marysia and Guy were almost launched head first into the partition in front of them. The cab pulled over to the right.

Marysia scanned for footholes in the wall. Guy raced after her in the darkness, pulling her down and spinning her round. 'Why stop here? What the hell's wrong with the driveway!'

'If she's there, I don't feel like walking into a bullet. If *you* do, the drive's fifty feet ahead.' Her tone softened.

'Trust me, Guy. I know what I'm doing, and I'm just trying to look after us both.' She walked to the stone wall and began to climb. Guy had little option but to follow.

Mamasian loped down the path towards the pool and the glasshouse, his chest heaving with the effort. He had to reach the vivarium and hide. It would be a sanctuary of sorts – maybe he could hold out there till help arrived. She'd think twice about following him inside. But how long before she'd come looking for him by the pool? Where the fuck were Rosario and his people? He just had to hang on for a few precious minutes.

He reached the bottom of the path and turned sharply right into the vivarium, closing the door behind him.

Luiza waited till the body was still, then lowered the gun a couple of inches. She'd been lucky – the burst of the Uzzi had sprayed bullets both sides of her and into the floor in front of her, but none had hit her. She'd sighted him just as she was about to mount the stairs and had swung round in time to squeeze off three quick shots.

She raised the gun again and braced her arms as she moved down the hallway to check out all the rooms. It would be just too lucky if this man had been Mamasian's only minder. Too lucky but just possible. She checked the ground floor soundlessly and moved up the stairway, pausing at the top. Three doors left, four right. She braced herself slightly to one side then kicked hard with the heel of her foot at the first handle. The door flew inwards. A split second later Luiza was inside, her eyes scanning the room, the trigger under half pressure. No one. Too bad. Time to move on. She was out in the hall in moments, crashing open the second door. Again, no one. She was in the third room in an instant. Then it was the right-hand side of the landing. As the first door cracked under the impact of her heel she saw the window dead ahead – it was still open an inch or too. She sniffed the air and smelled recent human presence. Two strides and she was at the window looking down. A figure was limping down the oleander-fringed path. Between the trees she could make out a swimming pool, the aquamarine water illuminated by underwater lights. The figure reached the bottom then ducked into a glass-house by the pool. It had to be her man. She raised the window and stepped out onto the roof.

'Give me a leg up,' Marysia whispered as they reached the high wall of the Mamasian estate. She placed her foot on the platform Guy made and leapt up onto the wall, swinging her body under the razor wire that fringed the top – there were barely two inches of clearance.

She lay flat along the top and looked towards the house. The lights were intensely bright. A movement caught her eye to the right, some distance below. She could just make out a pool and what looked like a large greenhouse. A figure in white was running easily towards it. As it reached the pool, the lights of the greenhouse dimmed by degrees then went out altogether. The figure abruptly disappeared.

'See anything?'

'Just the house,' Marysia lied. 'No sign of movement. Here, take my hand and I'll pull you up. Keep very low at the top – there's razor wire. Duck like hell when you get up here, then drop down the other side.'

As Guy dropped down the far side, Marysia grasped his arm and pointed towards the house. 'I think it's better we split up. You check out the house. Don't go in, just look for signs of life.'

'Or death,' said Guy. 'I think we should stick together.'

'I want to skirt the perimeter. I'll meet you out front in ten minutes. Remember, don't enter the house till I get there.' She squeezed his arm tightly. 'Trust me, I do this for a living.'

'Did. You're retired now.'

'Whatever. I know what I'm doing. I'd trust your judgment on a film set – trust mine now.'

'Okay. Ten minutes.'

'Ten. Now go, we don't have time to argue.'

Guy watched her run into the shadows, then he set off towards the house.

Mamasian closed the glass door behind him, gasping for air. His leg hurt from the short drop to the ground from the bedroom window. He leant back against the doorframe to catch his breath. A quick glance at his watch. Rosario would be here by now for sure – he just had to hang on for another couple of minutes. He looked desperately round for his snake stick with the forked tip. He caught sight of it, half hidden by a hanging plant. Picking it up with his right hand, he staggered down the centre aisle of the glass-house, swinging the tip at the lights. The bulbs exploded every four strides as the steel tip made contact. As he limped forward he flipped open the cages to his left and right, cooing to his darlings as he went. By the time he'd reached the end and made his way back to the door the vivarium was a glow of eerie pink – only four globes remained in the centre transepts, together with the infra-red heat units. He watched with satisfaction as the snakes, scorpions and arachnids probed their open doors with interest and dropped to the floor or crawled upwards towards the roof. Now he was in his element amongst his friends.

Mamasian stood at the far end of the vivarium and breathed hard. Whoever tried to come for him had an obstacle course to be reckoned with. A smile creased his face. He felt at home with his babies – they'd never harm him; he knew their moods. But one wrong move from the woman and they'd be on her. This was a moment to savour. The fear that had been with him for the past hour or so was evaporating fast, replaced by the frisson of expectancy. He reached behind him and his fingers closed on the doorlatch of his favourite – his *Atrax robustus*. He then crouched in the shadows and waited.

Luiza stood back from the doors of the vivarium, in the darkness, watching the old man through the glass as he swung his stick at the lights. It amused her to study the old man's panic. It was so useless. He'd be dead in a couple of short minutes. If she'd wanted to, she could have shot him where he stood, but she had other plans. She craved the satisfaction of watching him beg.

She glanced back towards the house and was suddenly aware of her latex suit – the white now made her a target. She pulled back the hood, allowing her jet hair to fall free, then unzipped the front down to her navel, pulled it off her shoulders and stepped out of the catsuit entirely. A small gust of cool breeze blew across the pool and she shuddered. She ran her hands over her naked body. Then she walked forward, pushed the door inwards and stepped inside.

Mamasian strained his eyes as the door opened. A woman naked except for the smallest of briefs stepped through, her luxuriant jet hair falling either side of her white-painted face. She had, he mused, the most perfect body he had ever seen. She looked like a wonderfully deviant Pierrot clown. He couldn't help a smile, despite the circumstances. In the dim light, she was obviously unaware of the movement only inches from her feet.

As she closed the door behind her and took one small step forward, a pool of ultraviolet light bathed her body in a rose glow which appeared to make her flesh shimmer. Mamasian glanced down at her feet. She'd been lucky, but he could see a scorpion inching its way down the side of a cage, as if sensing the warmth of her calf centimetres from its head. He concentrated on relaxing the muscles of his body, knowing the slightest movement might alarm the spiders that surrounded him. She held the gun by her side and he could just make out her expression – it was one of confidence and quiet triumph.

'So you are Mamasian,' she said languidly, pointing the gun at his position in the shadows.

'That is I,' Mamasian replied archly. They eyed each other for a few seconds then he continued. 'I gather I have upset you.' He looked down at her handgun, searching for a silencer. 'You mean to kill me,' he said, his eyes flicking to the windows, willing Rosario to appear.

'I mean to watch you die.'

They could have been discussing the futures market.

'Because you lost a lover?' he said, searching desperately for any words that would give him time. The scorpion had stopped by the woman's calf; he could see its tail twitching nervously. He willed it to strike. 'You wager your life because a man who has killed and tortured many others finally receives his just desserts?' Mamasian shot another quick look at the floor by the woman's feet – there was movement everywhere. Move, you bitch, his mind raced! 'You disappoint me. You are a professional and events have proved you are good –

very good. We are one and the same – we prey on others. Yet you come here to kill me, you put your life in the balance, because I ordered the death of one worthless man.'

'We are all worthless. If I knew I were to die this minute it would be of little significance to me.'

Mamasian knew he was running out of time. The woman hadn't moved a muscle in a minute – she could pull the trigger any second. He had to make his move. 'If that is so then allow me the pleasure of my few remaining days. In contrast to you, I wish to live. Life is of some major significance to me.' As he spoke, his fingers released the catch on the cage to his right and he rested the back of his hand on the soft sand within. The funnel-web – the one spider with which he was least familiar. It was a chance he'd have to take.

'But that is my pleasure, don't you see, old man? To know how much you wish to live, then cut you down.'

She opened her mouth, sucking in the stiflingly humid air of the room, then brought up the gun and fired.

The bullet ripped into the soft flesh of Mamasian's upper thigh. The old man screamed and sank to the ground. But somehow he found the strength to keep his right hand steady at the door to the cage on his right. As he stared at his tormentor, he felt the soft palps of the funnel web probe the side of his palm. Then he felt it move towards the centre and he thrilled with pleasure.

'Both black and female. Black as night. Black as death. And equally unpredictable. But both quite beautiful,' he murmured to himself.

Luiza watched the old man as his face twisted with pain. She could see the blood flowing from the wound in his thigh. She brought up the gun a second time and pointed it at Mamasian's forehead, but as she did so his right arm shot towards her. She felt an acute shaft of pain in the soft flesh at the side of her ankle as she fired at Mamasian's head. He catapulted backwards into the cages behind him.

Luiza tried to move forward, but the pain in her leg was so intense she dropped to one knee. Inches from her face the funnel-web reared once more on its back legs. Then it darted forwards, the twin chelicerae held high in front, stabbing the fangs once more into her foot. This time she cried out – the pain was so fierce. She dropped the Browning, balling her hand and bringing it crushing down on the black spider which seemed glued to her flesh.

She closed her eyes tight shut, pressing the spot where the funnel-web had bitten her twice. When she opened them a few seconds later she saw the movement around her on the floor. The entire area was seething with arachnids of every size and description. Holding her breath, she raised herself very slowly from the floor. Her foot felt numb. Stepping very carefully, she moved back towards the door. The doorframe came into sight and she reached behind her for the handle. It was then she felt an arm whip round her throat. She felt a crack at the base of her skull and lost consciousness.

Guy crouched on the lawn just outside the glare of the spotlights and listened. Minutes had elapsed and he was unsure what to do.

He looked back to the pool area where he had last seen Marysia. She was probably making her way round the far perimeter.

He looked back at the house – every window shone light but there was not a sound. It didn't feel right.

After one more quick look behind him for Marysia, he stood and walked slowly into the gravelled area in front of him, into the harsh white spotlights, raising his right hand. Still silence. No movement at either the door or any of the windows.

He walked slowly towards the window. The body of the Russian was clearly visible through the pane, lying in a pool of blood. Guy ducked down and took stock of his situation. Christ, they'd arrived too late. The bloodbath had already taken place.

He inched his way to the door. It was bolted. The back door – maybe the back door was open? He crept round to the right of the building, keeping his head down.

At the rear of the building he came to a small yard. A white cat was sitting near the open door cleaning itself. Guy inched round the door. The body of a middle-aged woman lay by the open kitchen door, beside her a broken plate and a bloodied length of pipe. Very slowly Guy reached down, checked the woman's pulse – there was none – picked up the lead pipe, then entered.

Marysia dragged the unconscious woman through the door and out of the vivarium towards the pool, flicking a black spider away.

She pulled the shirt up from under the waistband of her trousers and ripped a length of the material, wrapping it round Luiza's legs and securing them tightly. Then she rolled her over and ripped a second piece, tying her wrists together behind her back. She knew she'd have to be quick – the woman would soon regain consciousness. Luiza moaned and tried to turn her head. Marysia snatched the hair at the nape of her neck, pulled her head back and wrapped the material round her head so the thickest part of the gag crossed her mouth. Then she opened the door of the vivarium, swept the floor by the opening with her shoe, stepped over Luiza and pulled her back inside. As soon as the legs were clear of the door she stepped lightly back over the naked form of the woman and walked outside again, closing the door behind her. It was only then that she realised she'd been holding her breath for what seemed like several minutes, but was probably less than two.

She looked back through the windowpane. Even in the dim rose glow she could see the spiders, ticks and scorpions circling the naked woman. A tarantula was lifting its legs onto her thigh, probing her flesh with its palps. Several feet further inside she could see the body of Mamasian. She crossed herself.

As her eyes drifted back to Luiza she noticed the mobile phone by the door. It began to cheep – she could just hear it through the glass.

Marysia looked back up towards the house, then back at the phone. Was there time? She opened the door, bent down and snatched it up from the floor, shaking a red insect from the broken casing, then re-closing the door. Curiosity had got the better of her. She pressed the 'send' button.

'Mr Mamasian?' the voice said. Marysia remained silent. 'Mr Mamasian? Can you hear me?' the voice asked calmly.

Marysia said nothing.

'Mr Mamasian? Is that you. Please say something –'

Marysia opened the door and dropped the phone to the floor. The woman was now lying prone, her head lolling to one side. Her chest was heaving as if she were short of breath. Marysia shuddered then jogged through the oleanders up to the house.

Guy was crouched beside the body of the Russian when he saw Marysia's face at the window. She gestured frantically at him to leave, pointing behind her in the direction of the driveway.

Guy stood and ran back through the kitchen to the rear of the house. As he flew through the kitchen door he heard the police sirens.

'Let's get out of here fast. The whole world's arriving,' Marysia shouted at him. 'Back the way we came!'

'Did you find anything down there? Where's Mamasian!'

'No idea. No sign of him. Who's the dead man inside?' she countered.

'Must be one of his minders. There's a dead woman in the kitchen.' He caught his breath then continued. 'Marysia, we've got to stay.'

'What the hell do you mean, stay?' she yelled at him. 'This is not our business! What are we going to do, for heaven's sake – we saw nothing!'

Guy looked down the drive – the headlights of several cars were sweeping up the hill towards the house.

'I don't want my people compromised! Guy, do you hear me,' she cried out. 'Don't do this to me. Please leave now!'

As the cars rounded the final bend she ran back through the trees. Guy stood for a second then ran after her into the darkness.

FORTY-FOUR

A two-mile length of Sunset was choked with camera vehicles by two-thirty a.m. and the Bel Air killings were headline news on all the major networks by five.

It took Guy and Marysia over an hour to get back to the Chateau Marmont. They'd had to walk several miles into Brentwood to call for a cab.

Back at the hotel Marysia spent another hour on the telephone to her sources in London and Los Angeles. At three a.m. a senior member of the LAPD released a short statement. Two men and two women had been killed in the early hours of the morning at the residence of Howard Mamasian in Bel Air. The elderly financier had been one of the victims. No details of how they'd died would be available to the news services until the coroner had finished his report.

They caught the eight-thirty flight to London and arrived at Heathrow just before three in the afternoon the following day. Guy was surprised but relieved by Marysia's sudden decision to leave – after all, there was no reason to take it for granted that the woman was one of the victims. But Marysia said she'd promised Gosia to return within four days and she'd be true to her word. Guy didn't argue.

The massacre in Bel Air made the front pages of all the English papers. The names of all the victims were released but still not the mode of death. On page three were printed two file photographs, one of the Spanish woman and one of Gosia – it made for sensational copy.

Guy folded his copy of the *Express* and added it to the wad of papers under his arm. He could see Marysia in the bank of telephone booths close to the luggage claim exit.

So the Spanish woman was dead – found near the pool in a greenhouse. Yet Marysia had said she'd seen nothing. She'd told him the police had Mamasian's estate under surveillance, yet there'd been no evidence of that when they'd arrived. Then the name – Andreu, rather than Trabat. Had that really been Zvonko's error? And she'd been content to leave the country within hours of fleeing the Mamasian estate, before the names of those who had died in Bel Air had been released. Marysia had had her own agenda – to believe otherwise was rank naïvety. Guy felt an all-prevailing sense of sadness and emptiness.

At five-fifteen they reached the outskirts of Oxford. It was only then that Guy broke the silence.

'We have to tell Gosia everything,' he said.

'I know. Perhaps it's better if we're both there. I know she loves you dearly – you're fast becoming a father figure.'

'I think I'll give you some time alone. Half an hour, maybe. I'll take a walk, then join you.'

'Perhaps you're right,' Marysia said as she turned the car into the drive of the Radcliffe Hospital.

As the elevator door opened, Guy kissed her softly. 'I'll be back soon.'

Marysia smiled back at him, stepped into the lift and the doors closed.

The sun was beginning to dip through the elms that flanked Banbury Road. Guy walked slowly, reflecting on the past few days. There was no easy way to ignore the cold logic of Marysia's actions, yet despite his entreaties she'd remained silent, refusing to discuss the matter. It was as if she'd closed a door on the subject, and by doing so had driven an immutable wedge between them.

As he turned and began to walk back towards the hospital gates, a succession of vivid images of Gosia flashed through his mind. Gosia in Paris, her expression one minute a mirror of concern, the next a picture of youthful wonder as she gazed at all the beauty that surrounded her. Gosia in Oxford the night they'd eaten at the Hi-Lo, her slim face wreathed in smiles. And the pitiful white face that had lain on the cobbles. If Marysia was right that Gosia viewed him as a father figure, then the feeling was mutual – Gosia could easily be the daughter he'd never had. He looked at his watch. It had only been twenty minutes, but he couldn't wait another minute to see her.

As he opened the door to her room, Gosia looked round. She and Marysia were sitting together on the bed, locked in each other's arms.

'Guy! How wonderful to see you,' she cried out, holding her arms out to him. 'I've missed you so much, I can't tell you.' She buried her face in his shoulder, then stood back, holding Guy at arm's length and beaming. Her face was still wet with tears.

'I'm so sorry about Edward –' Guy began, but Gosia squeezed his hands.

'I knew I'd never see him again. I shall miss him terribly,' she said, and her eyes brimmed again. Then she forced a smile and beckoned towards her mother. 'Come over here and hug us.'

The three of them stood for several minutes, wrapped in each other's arms.

'I must go and make some arrangements at the Portobello,' Guy said eventually, 'or we'll all have nowhere to stay.'

'Are we all going to be together for a while?' Gosia asked.

‘I think you need a few days with your mother. I’ll have to go to Paris, I’m afraid.’

‘I think I need a few days with you both,’ Gosia said pointedly, looking from Guy to Marysia and back.

Guy smiled. ‘Whatever. I’m not leaving just yet.’

FORTY-FIVE

The clothes were laid out on Guy's bed, the suitcase nearly filled. There was a soft knock at Guy's door. He stopped packing and opened it. It was Gosia.

'Am I disturbing you?'

'Of course not, find a space and sit down. I won't be much longer, then we can relax and have a drink.'

'What time's your flight?'

'Four this afternoon,' he replied, squeezing a sweater into the case.

'We're going to miss you more than you'll ever know.'

'I'll miss you too. Sometimes I feel as though I've known you a lifetime.'

Gosia smiled. 'You *have* known my mother a lifetime, well practically,' she replied. Guy stopped packing.

'What have you come to say, Gosia?' he asked with a wry grin.

'Okay, you've found me out. How shall I put it? The last two days have been wonderful, yet so strange. I know you both love each other – you've loved each other for years. Yet, now you're so far apart and it's very sad to watch. You're going back to Paris, to your work. Marysia's going back to Africa. All those years apart, longing for each other, and yet you walk away when you have your one chance of happiness.'

Guy sat on the edge of the bed and put an arm round Gosia. 'My thoughts have been filled with little else but you and Marysia since we returned from America. But she –'

'She's the most strong-willed person in the world,' Gosia cut in. 'That's her nature. That's what makes her what she is. But that's a wonderful strength. That's the one reason she's survived all these years. She's been an inspiration to me. I'm certain that leaving me behind when she left for Israel was the most terrible choice a mother could ever make – to leave her child. But I never for one second doubted she loved me, and you must never doubt she loves you. Whatever she did or said while you were after those people, I know she would have felt it was for the best. You must never think of her actions as a betrayal.'

'A betrayal? Why should you say that?' Guy asked.

'I can see it in your eyes each time you look at her.'

She studied him in silence. Then she took his hand. 'I beg you, Guy. Never doubt it. Please don't just walk away.' Then she stood. 'By the way, I have a message,' she continued in a sudden cheerful tone. 'She'd like to see you before you leave.'

'Well, I was hardly thinking of leaving without saying goodbye,' Guy said, laughing.

'Well, she asked me to tell you that she's gone for a walk and perhaps you'd like to join her.'

'A walk? Where is she?'

'Holland Park. She says you know where.'

As he approached the Orangerie along the pathway from Holland Park Road, Guy saw her. She was sitting in the centre of a park bench, her hands thrust into her jacket pockets, swinging her legs to and fro like a child as she watched him walk towards her. She looked enchanting.

He stood in front of her, then held out his hands, which she took in hers.

'You remembered!' she said, her emerald eyes sparkling. 'All those years ago. The first day I met you, we walked to this very spot through the rhododendrons and sat under the cherry tree.'

'Of course I remembered. And Eugene Critchley spied on us from the other end of the bench, with that fat old dog.'

They both laughed. Then Marysia looked up at the cherry tree behind her and stood. Guy watched, captivated, as she spun round in circles like a child before a Christmas tree. After a few moments she stopped. Her mood was suddenly serious. 'I lied to you,' she said at last.

'You did.'

'You've lost your faith in me, haven't you. You no longer trust me.' She looked up into his eyes beseechingly. 'If I hadn't kept some facts from you, everything might well have turned out very differently.'

'It wasn't your decision to make, Marysia,' said Guy. 'I suppose we share common ideals, we just differ as to the best way to achieve them.' He paused, debating whether to ask the question. 'I have to ask this. The Spanish woman –'

'Did I kill her?' she cut in. 'No. It's your choice whether you believe me.' She walked a few feet from the park bench and stood with her back to him. Guy willed her to turn, but she didn't.

'I talked to Critchley last night,' said Guy after a few moments. 'Leston now appreciates there has to be a mole somewhere in the Service, but he won't admit it – doesn't want anyone digging in his patch. Afraid of what they may turn up. He's thinking of retirement.'

Guy studied her back. She didn't move, nor did she speak. She hadn't bitten. She didn't seem to care. A great weight lifted from his shoulders.

She turned. 'Will you come and visit me?' she said suddenly, furrowing her brow.

'In Africa? Of course.'

'Will you promise always to be my friend?'

'I will always be your friend. I promise.'

The emerald eyes twinkled. 'And will you sometimes be my lover?'

Guy couldn't help himself, he laughed out loud. She cocked her head to one side and made a funny face at him.

'If you like,' he replied.

'You can have other lovers while I'm not with you.'

'I can?' Guy asked with amusement. She could be adorable when she wanted, and right now she was working hard.

'Actually, no you can't,' she said in mock anger, then laughed. 'Come here, tough guy,' she said, holding out her arms and hugging Guy to her.

'Can you ever change?' Guy said after a few moments, looking deep into her eyes.

'My nature? Perhaps not, but maybe I could win back your trust. Why don't you try changing me?' she said coquettishly.

'That could take a lifetime,' Guy replied, smiling.

'Sounds pretty good to me,' she said.

Guy lifted her chin and kissed her softly on the lips.

'When shall I see you?' she said, barely audible.

'In Africa, soon,' Guy replied.

FORTY-SIX

Neville Cunningham closed the door of his bijou country cottage and strolled down the lane towards the pub. It was a weekend to celebrate. Information had filtered through from above that the pressure put on Ambrose Leston had borne fruit; the old fool had agreed to an early retirement and Cunningham was the obvious successor – the youngest man to head up the department in its long history.

He hummed a passage of Verdi's Luisa Miller as he passed the small pond halfway down the narrow leafy lane, slowing his stride to accommodate the easy rhythm of the aria. God was in his heaven – well quite possibly he wasn't, but all was very definitely right with the world.

He glanced idly round as a car turned into the lane at the top of the hill behind him, then moved slightly right to allow it room to pass.

Even in full cry he could hear the car accelerate behind him as it sped down the hill. Ignorant bastard, he thought idly. Probably the Preston lad who clipped his hedges – he always drove too fast.

Neville Cunningham's final aria was abruptly cut short as the car hit him full in the back, catapulting him forwards into the flint wall that lined the laneway. He stood no chance. 'Whitehall' died instantly.

The car braked heavily fifty feet down the lane and a woman looked back briefly. The only sounds were of pheasants calling to each other. Then the car drove on.

Author's note

The Chasen Catalyst is in many ways a sequel to my first novel, *The Webber Agenda*, though it can be read as a separate entity. The background of what is referred to in *The Chasen Catalyst* as 'The Microsat Conspiracy' is the subject of *The Webber Agenda*.

Acknowledgments

I would like to take this opportunity to thank my editor Louise Thurtell for her tireless and invaluable work. Also my sincere thanks to Fiona Daniels, for her incisive comments and editorial assistance.

My thanks also to the following people for their great help with my research:

Dr Mike Gray of the Australian Museum
Conrad Sandler of Spycatcher: Personal Protection & Surveillance Systems
Jane & Alex Postan
Beverly Baxter
Andrew Strokon
Anthony O'Brien
Jeffrey Bloom
Scott Citron
Nick and Sheelagh Hippisley-Coxe
Gosia Dobrowolska
Janusz Dobrawolski
Natasha Rollason
Rosalind Briant

My thanks also to Bill Rees and Donald Hartono at Choice Connections for their continued invaluable technical computer support.

And in memory of Adza Vincent. A splendidly eccentric and wonderful theatrical agent, and the best friend one could wish for.